FORGED IN ASH

Also by Trish McCallan

Red-Hot SEALs Novels

Forged in Fire

Praise for Trish McCallan

2013 RITA® Finalist, Best First Books
2013 RITA® Finalist, Best Romantic Suspense

"With so many stories about Navy SEALs out there, you might think there couldn't be anything new to add to the subgenre, but McCallan will prove you wrong. Full of suspense with some paranormal elements too, her first entry in the Forged series is a pulse-pounding adventure."

—4 stars, RT Book Reviews on *Forged in Fire*

FORGED IN ASH

A Red-Hot SEALs Novel

Trish McCallan

The characters and events portrayed in this book are fictitious. Any similarity to real persons, living or dead, is coincidental and not intended by the author.

Published by Montlake Romance, Seattle

www.apub.com

ISBN-13: 9781612185347
ISBN-10: 1612185347

Cover design by Laura Jochum

Library of Congress Control Number: 2013915035

Printed in the United States of America

This book is dedicated to my family:

To Iris Rose Hahn—my grandmother, a beautiful woman inside and out.
To Ray Monsey—the best father a woman could ask for.
To Keith and Ann Monsey—I can't tell you how cool it is to have other writers in the family!
To Val Morrow—my sister, who I don't get to see nearly enough.
To Kevin Monsey—my baby brother, who's all grown up now with kids (and it won't be long before it's grandkids) of his own.
Thanks to each and every one of you for your constant support!

I love you all!

Prologue

April

JILLIAN MICHAELS AWOKE TO AGONY.

To every cell in her body screaming. In unison.

She pitched forward, her head slamming into something rigid. Through ringing ears came the unmistakable explosion of shattering glass, the shriek of shearing metal.

For what could have been forever she slumped there, the pain mushrooming up and out, consuming her, dragging her into a gray lethargy. Until something cold and wet plopped on the top of her head and trickled down the back of her neck, rousing her.

Something stirred in her mind, a vague urgency; she needed to remember something.

Something important.

She forced blurry eyes open. A dashboard took shape. A steering wheel. The fuzzy dangle of quilted dice attached to a key ring. She recognized the swinging dice, the jangle of keys, the small oval clock embedded in the dashboard—she was in her minivan. Had she been in an accident? Was that why every inch of her hurt? Panic flared, flashing through her like lightning.

She tried to straighten, but the agony grew fangs and claws—tore into her head, ripped through her chest, seared down her legs and arms. She wanted so badly to sink back into that blessed void, but she needed to remember something.

Something essential.

Her arms weighed a thousand pounds apiece as she lifted them to scrub the blur from her eyes. Her fingers came away smeared with blood.

She was bleeding.

The panic swelled again, pushing against the lethargy and her aching chest burned hot and cold.

Remember. Remember. Remember.

Her gaze, which was blurring again, locked on the swinging dice. And that shrill internal alarm went silent. The dice were mesmerizing. She focused on them, the soothing back and forth sway, while an image took shape in her mind.

Small hands handing over a messy square of tissue paper decorated with a trio of misshapen bows. "Happy birthday, Mommy. I made it all myself. Do you like it?"

Her brain snapped into crystal clear focus.

The kids? Were her babies in the van too?

"Bree? Wes?" Her voice emerged breathless, laced with a disturbing rattle.

She tried to turn and look into the back of the van, but the seat belt bound her in place. When she tried to move her head, the world went dark and dizzy.

"Wes! Bree? Lizzie. Answer Mommy," she cried.

The silence that greeted her plea was terrifying. She scrabbled for the seat belt buckle, terror skittering through her veins as she tried to reach into that gray void and release the memory of what had happened.

Maybe the kids weren't even in the van. They could be home,

with Russ. Her brother was good like that, willing to watch the kids for a couple of hours. Yes. Yes. That made sense. The kids were probably home with her brother.

Please, please, let them be home.

Shaking fingers found the seat belt buckle and with a quick tug the two plates separated. The tension binding her shoulders vanished. When more icy wetness plopped on the top of her head, she glanced up. The moonroof was open. Was it raining?

Rubbing her eyes clear, she glanced at the windshield, and choked back a cry of horror. Water lapped at the top of the glass, and as she watched, the last sliver of glass disappeared beneath the waves. The car was sinking.

Her heart crashed inside her chest, then tried to climb her throat as she thrashed toward the space between the bucket seats. If her babies were back there, she had to get them out now. She would wake Bree and Wes; they could help her get the little ones to safety.

She caught a fuzzy glimpse of Wes's blond head and limp body as she threw herself between the bucket seats. Oh God, he wasn't moving. Neither was Bree, who was hanging forward against her seat belt beside her brother, her bronze hair shadowing her face. Jillian swiped the haze from her eyes, only to freeze as her vision cleared and the back of the van came into view.

The black fuzz blanketing her mind dissipated like thinning smoke and the memories flooded in.

A shrill, keening scream broke from her. And then another and another. And another . . .

"No. No. No."

The cough of guns. Her babies crumpling. Blood. So much blood. A river of blood.

"No. No. No."

A blow to her head. Another to her heart. Agony. Falling into a tunnel of black.

"No. No. No."

Somewhere in the distance a woman screamed—broken shrieks of grief, of horror, of unimaginable loss.

Why? Why had they done this?

The very heart of her shattered, broken into a billion irretrievable pieces.

Why?

Amid the ruins of her soul, vengeance stirred, forged her existence into deadly purpose—a raw, pressurized force that sought only revenge.

The screams snapped off in mid shriek. Methodically, she backed through the space between the bucket seats and used the neck rest to pull herself up. Balancing on the driver's seat, she reached for the edges of the moonroof. Her babies were dead. They'd been dead long before those bastards had strapped them into the van and sent them to this watery grave. If she remained in the van much longer, she'd join them.

Except . . . she couldn't join them. Not yet.

She had to get out of the van. She had to survive.

And then she'd find them. Every last one of them. She'd find them. And one by one she'd make them pay.

Chapter One

July

LIEUTENANT MARCUS "COSKY" SIMCOSKY HELD BACK A GRIMACE as his mother straightened the trio of medals decorating the left breast of his naval dress whites.

"Relax, Mom," he said calmly as he shifted his weight over his crutches. "It's just a hearing, nothing to worry about."

Marion Simcosky patted his chest and stepped back. But worry still clouded her gray eyes. "That's what you and the boys keep telling me, dear." She sent him a shrewd smile. "So why is half the fleet parked on the courthouse steps in their dress whites?"

It was hardly half the fleet. More like all 124 of his brothers from SEAL Team 7, and another hundred or so from his sister teams—the SEALs who weren't out on rotation. They'd started arriving on the steps of the Seattle federal courthouse an hour before he, Rawls, and Zane had arrived.

That immediate and unconditional support was team life. Your brothers always had your back, even against the United States government.

Marion shot the closed grand jury doors an anxious look, her silver hair almost glowing in the cloistered light of the courthouse hall. "I wish you boys had taken Amy's advice and hired an attorney."

They'd considered hiring an attorney—for advice anyway, since legal counsel wasn't allowed during grand jury testimony. But hell, in the end it wouldn't have made a difference. They weren't going to plead the Fifth. They hadn't done anything wrong.

Lieutenant Seth Rawlings, who looked too damn pretty with his dress whites playing up his blue eyes, touched Marion's elbow. "All they did was ask a fair amount of questions," he said in his most soothing Southern drawl. "Nothing to get all worried about."

Rawls had testified before the grand jury first and judging by his tousled blond hair, the experience hadn't gone as slick as he claimed. His whitewashing was fine with Cosky though. Mom had been worrying about him nonstop since she'd arrived at Sacred Heart's emergency room three months earlier to find him half-dead.

Hell, truth be told, she'd been worrying about him since he'd joined the teams, although she'd never admit it to him.

Just as she'd never admitted her fear all those years his dad had patrolled the streets of Federal Way.

A hard knock of guilt rocked him. He knew she was hoping the injury to his knee and thigh would sever his ties to the teams, that he'd retire and choose a safer profession.

But Christ, just the thought of sitting at some damn desk for the rest of his life made him want to blow something up. He'd been completely focused on becoming a special operator since Billy Pruett, his best friend since grade school, had introduced him to his grandfather, Commander Handel, SEAL Team 3, way back in junior high.

That day had defined his life, his mother's as well. No doubt she cursed the day he'd met Billy on the playground.

Billy had rung out of BUD/s—twice—and they'd lost touch years ago. But Cosky made a habit of visiting Handel, that old bullfrog, anytime he was in town.

The hallway in front of the grand jury room was almost empty. Security had stopped the reporters and curiosity seekers at the courthouse doors—thank Christ—so when he caught movement out of the corner of his eye he shuffled around on his crutches to get a better look.

Beth, his LC's fiancée, was headed their way after a trip to the restroom. She seemed to spend half her time in the can these days. Apparently the baby was sitting directly on her bladder.

"Is he still in there?" Beth asked as she neared them, shooting a worried glance toward the jury room doors.

Their LC, Lieutenant Commander Zane Winters, was on the hot seat at the moment. Cosky's turn was next.

"It's not these questions that worry me," his mom said, a slight quaver to her voice. Worry lines bracketed her mouth. "It's where their questions will lead."

Beth reached out to rub his mother's arm. "I'm sure this hearing is just a formality, Marion. They have the support of the public, the passengers from flight 2077, and Amy Chastain. There's no way the grand jury will actually indict."

When the double doors opened, Cosky straightened too fast and winced at the grinding pain that ripped through his knee. It was already swelling. He could feel the pressure against the compression sleeve.

Zane's calm green eyes locked on Beth as he exited the room and he offered her a reassuring smile. Cosky knew how much the smile cost his CO. Zane hadn't wanted Beth anywhere near the courthouse, just as Cosky hadn't wanted his mother here. With their names and faces splashed across every damn paper and television in the county, he, Zane, Rawls, and Mac were walking, talking bull's-eyes. Every terrorist cell they'd spent the past fourteen revolutions hounding would be swarming after them like hornets to honey, which put the people they loved at risk.

When reporters had tracked his mother down, Cosky had moved her out of his childhood home and into a rental under an assumed name.

Not that he and Zane had any luck keeping the women home. They'd been determined to support their men.

The double doors opened.

"Lieutenant Simcosky?" The jury forewoman asked, a polite smile on her middle-age-softened face. "We're ready for your testimony now."

She held the double doors open for him and followed him into the wood-paneled room. A collection of men and women sat in an elevated jury box to his right. Facing them was the witness stand. Cosky swung his way over to it and seated himself. The forewoman waited until he'd stowed his crutches, before she stepped up to administer the oath—*to tell the whole truth and nothing but the truth.*

Which they'd been doing from day one—not that it had done them a damn bit of good. They'd still ended up in this box, in front of the grand jury.

The federal prosecutor rose from the table across from him and approached him with a casual, pseudo-friendly air. "You understand that these proceedings are merely a fact-checking investigation into the events of March twenty-ninth and thirtieth?"

Cosky simply nodded.

What the bastard wasn't mentioning, according to Amy Chastain—who should know considering she'd been a highly decorated FBI agent prior to her marriage and had testified in plenty of grand jury rooms—was that his *fact-checking investigation* could easily turn into a criminal investigation and from there into an indictment.

"State your name for the record, please." The prosecutor slowly ambled into the center of the room.

"Lieutenant Marcus Simcosky, Officer in Charge, Squad 1, Alpha Platoon, SEAL Team 7."

"Thank you Mr. Sim—"

Cosky calmly continued listing his credentials. "Fifteen years of active duty with Naval Special Warfare Group 1. Fourteen deployments in Afghanistan, Iraq, Paki—"

"Mr. Simcosky." Raising his voice, the prosecutor cut Cosky's recital off. "This proceeding acknowledges your service to our great country."

"It's Lieutenant Simcosky," Cosky responded flatly. "If this court acknowledges my service to this country, then it must also recognize the service of Commander Mackenzie, Lieutenant Commander Winters, and Lieutenant Rawlings. In which case, it no doubt recognizes that it's our combined sixty-plus years of covert ops experience in tracking, assessing, and handling terroristic threats to the United States of America that made us particularly capable of assessing and reacting to the events in question."

"Lieutenant Simcosky," the grand jury forewoman broke in, her voice quiet, but firm as she nudged the hearing back on track. "You were booked on flight 2077. Is this correct?"

Cosky gave a tight nod. "Yes, we were on leave. Flying to Hawaii for a buddy's wedding."

"Could you please take us through what happened that day?"

"While waiting to board the bird, we were notified that flight 2077 had been targeted by hijackers. Intel indicated the guns were already on board and that the group intent on jacking the flight had already taken two birds in Argentina and slaughtered the passengers."

"And where did this information come from?" the prosecutor asked.

"Through fresh intel off a covert op, the details of which are classified," Cosky said.

The grand jury sure as hell didn't need to know the *fresh intel* had come courtesy of one of Zane's handy-dandy premonitions.

"Commander Mackenzie notified John Chastain, special agent in charge of the Seattle field office's counterterrorism division. Our orders were to stand down, keep an eye on the Tangos, and let the feds sweep things up."

The jury forewoman nodded her understanding. "At what point did you realize the Seattle field office was compromised?"

"As soon as Mac made the call to Chastain. Within minutes the hijackers tried to depart the gate."

"Isn't it true you broke protocol and stepped in to detain the suspects, regardless of your stand-down orders?" the prosecutor pounced.

Cosky raised his brows and stared him squarely in the eye. "We believed it was advisable to hold the suspects until the feds arrived. Would you have preferred that we'd let the suspects go so they could target another bird?"

"When did you suspect Agent Chastain was compromised himself?" The jury forewoman sent the prosecutor a quelling glance.

"We *knew* that Agent Chastain had been compromised the next morning. He approached us in secrecy and admitted he'd been tapped. He told us his wife and sons had been kidnapped to force his compliance. He requested our assistance in locating and freeing his family."

"And you didn't consider contacting local law enforcement so they could handle the rescue of Agent Chastain's family?" The prosecutor's tone was accusing.

"Agent Chastain was certain his office and DHS were compromised. He was also certain contacting the local PD would filter back to his field office and from there to the kidnappers, and his family would be executed. After reviewing his evidence, we agreed with his assessment. There were additional concerns that the hostages were in grave danger given the hijacking had been aborted. We didn't feel we could wait to take action, so we contacted Admiral McKay who agreed with our evaluation and gave us the green light."

"Isn't it convenient that Agent Chastain and Admiral McKay are no longer available to confirm your account of that day?" the prosecutor said dryly.

No longer available?

Cosky gritted his teeth, swallowing a tide of rage. Chastain and McKay deserved better than this farce.

"They are *no longer available* because they were murdered." Try as he might, Cosky couldn't quite mask the contempt boiling within him. "You call that convenient? Perhaps you should run that description by their wives and children."

The prosecutor's round face flooded with red. An unhealthy red. "You're well aware I used that term in conjunction with you and your teammates' vigilante behavior and the fact neither Agent Chastain nor Admiral McKay are alive to testify to their involvement in the events you describe."

"Chastain's and Admiral McKay's murders are linked to the events of March twenty-ninth and thirtieth." Cosky's voice turned arctic. "Chastain was killed immediately following the release of his wife and children. McKay was bombed within hours of giving us the go-ahead. Their deaths are not a coincidence."

"Their murders are under investigation," the prosecutor said tightly, the flush slowly fading from his face. He sent a stiff smile toward the jury box. "But their murders, tragic as they are, are not the focus of this proceeding. Your vigilante behavior is the focus of this hearing, and the fact you and your buddies left a string of fatalities behind you."

Cosky crossed his arms. "The fatalities took place during the insertion to release Amy Chastain and her children from their captivity." He paused, trying to wrestle back the sarcasm. "The kidnappers were reluctant to release their prizes."

"Isn't it true that you were shot multiple times, in fact—near fatally wounded during this assault?"

With a frown, Cosky settled back against his chair. Where the hell was the bastard going with this line of questioning? "That's correct."

"So you were unconscious during most of this battle and thus unable to verify that lethal force was necessary."

Was he fucking kidding? What a Pollyanna asshole.

"Are you aware of the firing capacity of a single MP5?" Cosky shot back.

When the prosecutor frowned and opened his mouth, Cosky turned to face the jury. Hell, nothing he said was going to convince this clueless bastard. His best bet was to hope that some of the jury members had a kernel of common sense.

"A single MP5 can rattle off hundreds of rounds per minute. The men holding Amy Chastain and her children had four of these weapons on the premises, along with assorted handguns and rifles. From the Argentine example, there was little doubt the hijackers were willing to slaughter women and children. So to answer your question—yes, fatal force was absolutely necessary in order to free the hostages."

Soon after, the jury forewoman released him from the witness box. Cosky didn't budge. It was time the prosecutor answered some of his questions.

"Has anyone looked into the first-class passengers and tried to identify the seven people the hijackers were after?" he asked the prosecutor and caught the momentary freezing of the attorney's tall frame.

"There's no evidence to suggest there was a list of names."

The fact the guy had responded to the question was a surprise—his answer wasn't.

Cosky's gaze narrowed. "Agent Chastain was given a list of first-class passengers. He was told to make these passengers available if he wanted to see his family again."

"So you and your teammates claim," the prosecutor said in a bored voice. He walked over to the table across from the witness stand and stacked his papers together. "Yet no evidence of this purported list has shown up in any of Agent Chastain's personal effects."

Cosky's mouth tightened. Christ, save him from idiots in high places.

"Considering his laptop and cell phone went missing following his death, the lack of concrete evidence is understandable. Perhaps you don't understand the ramifications of this list? Every person booked into first class on that flight was a scientist and several of these scientists are working on projects with military applications."

"Yes, yes." The prosecutor waved him off. "The passengers will be looked into."

Bullshit.

Cosky swore beneath his breath. The lack of interest in the passengers totally stymied them. Didn't those assholes realize how important those seven names were? Someone had tried to hijack a plane to get their hands on them.

His frustration was at a high boil as the jury forewoman escorted him out of the room.

Zane took one look at his face and barked out a tight laugh. "I see you warmed up to that bastard as much as I did."

That earned a slight smile. But the smile quickly faded.

Zane slung an arm over Beth's shoulder as they headed down the hall, matching their paces to Cosky's crutch-enabled hobbling.

Cosky shook his head in disgust. Apparently, the poor sucker couldn't walk, talk, or sit without touching her. Then again, Zane had almost lost Beth to Russ Branson—or whoever the hell the guy had been, so he should give him a little slack.

The thought of Branson brought another surge of frustration. You'd think it would be easy to track down the identity of the mastermind who'd orchestrated the hijacking and kidnappings, but the bastard had turned out to be a ghost. Too bad Zane hadn't managed to ask him one damn question before killing him.

"My brother's offered up his apartment when he deploys, until Beth and I can buy a place," Zane said as the group started walking again. "So we need to start looking for someone to take over my share of the condo."

Cosky simply nodded. It had been only a matter of time before Zane moved out. Beth hadn't complained about sharing the condo with them when she flew down to visit. But hell, the lovebirds undoubtedly wanted their privacy—particularly with a baby on the way.

"Aiden's looking for a place," Rawls said as he rejoined them.

Fucking hell.

No way.

Cosky jerked hard and his crutches skidded on the marble floor. Off balance, he pitched forward.

"Are you okay, dear?" His mother caught his elbow and steadied him.

Warmth heated his face. How humiliating, nothing like having your mother save your ass. He took a deep breath, let it out slowly. But the tension didn't ease.

"Aiden needs to stick it out where he's at, and work through whatever his problem is with Tag," he said harshly.

Which was true. But not the reason he was eighty-sixing the idea of Squad 2's sniper moving into the condo.

Rawls shot him a surprised look and shrugged. "That falling out is between him and Tag, not our fence to mend. Besides, with Aiden about, we'll see more of Kait. My mouth's still watering from that chili she brought to the barbeque last year."

Every muscle in Cosky's body tightened.

The last thing he needed was Kait underfoot. He'd barely weaned himself from those damn dreams as it was.

Hunger stirred at the memory of ghostly fingers skating up and down his spine, and a waterfall of golden hair caressing his sweaty skin.

Shit, this was exactly why Aiden wasn't going to move in with them. The last thing he needed was a constant fucking reminder of Kait.

"Who's Kait?" his mom asked in a slow, thoughtful voice.

The interested sidelong glance she sent him had Cosky swearing beneath his breath. Mom had been getting increasingly vocal about "*her grandchildren*" since Zane had met Beth. Since he was her only child there was little doubt where the nonexistent rug rats were supposed to spring from.

"Aiden's angel of a sister," Rawls said. "The prettiest girl you've ever seen and a mean cook to boot."

"Really?" his mom said. "Cosky's never mentioned her."

Great. She sounded suspicious now.

"Because she's nobody," Cosky snapped.

Which was the truth. He'd spent the past five years making sure she remained nobody to him.

No way in hell was he abandoning that strategy now. Even if it meant cutting Aiden off.

August

By the time Cosky pulled out of the clinic's parking lot and merged into San Diego's traffic, numbness buffered the shock. Still—the orthopedic surgeon's words echoed through his head.

"The good news is the plate and screws are in good position, and the tibial fragments remained aligned. But the translucency and widening lines between the bone grafts indicate non-healing."

The knifing pain that pierced his knee as he shifted his foot from gas pedal to brake, while merging his truck onto the San Diego freeway, reinforced the surgeon's diagnosis.

The leg had been giving him hell since he'd weaned himself from the pain meds, but he'd shrugged the pain off, blaming it on the aggressive physical therapy regime. The surgeon had made it clear from day one that the percentages were against him. It would take a hell of a lot of luck and hard work to rejoin SEAL Team 7.

He wasn't afraid of hard work, or the pain that came with it. Plus, it had seemed like luck was on his side. The reconstructive surgery had gone well, the leg had been weight bearing at three months—exactly as the doctor expected. Everything had been on course . . . or so he'd thought.

Until today.

Cosky swore as the car in front of him suddenly stopped, and he wrenched his foot from gas to brake. Agony ripped through his knee. Slowly, the pain settled into a deep, throbbing ache.

He'd suspected the knifing pains weren't normal when he'd casually mentioned them at his checkup, and the doc had sent him down for X-rays.

". . . without additional surgery and bone grafting, the plate will eventually break . . ."

The shocked numbness had given way to simmering frustration by the time he reached his condo's parking lot. The emotion was heightened by the low-slung Mustang parked in what had been Zane's space before he'd moved out.

Cosky parked beside the vintage Mustang without feeling even a hint of his normal envy. He'd tried like hell to keep Aiden out of the condo, but when his vehement stonewalling started to raise questions, he'd backed down. He didn't need Zane and Rawls—and sure as hell not Aiden—realizing exactly why he was so reluctant to bunk with the man.

He'd never live it down.

He eyed the cherry-red sports car morosely as he shoved open his door. Just because Aiden had arrived didn't mean he'd brought Kait. From the boxes and garbage bags towering in the passenger and backseats, there wasn't room for anyone else. He did a quick recon of the parking lot and relaxed when he recognized all the cars.

As he eased out of his truck, he tried to convince himself that it didn't matter if she did show up. It had been years . . . his reaction wouldn't be as overpowering. He was a different man. She was a different woman. The sparks might not even be there.

Yeah, like hell.

If the attraction wasn't still simmering, he wouldn't have thrown up every objection he could think of when Rawls suggested Aiden as Zane's replacement.

He'd just locked his truck, when the front door to the condo opened and Aiden jogged down the steps.

"Hey," Cosky said, nodding at the half wave his new roommate shot him.

"Hey." Aiden reached his Mustang and yanked open the passenger door, grabbing all four boxes on the seat. "Looks like we're going wheels up, figured I'd move my stuff while I had the chance."

Cosky scowled; if not for his leg and the medical leave they'd put him on, he'd be prepping for deployment too.

Well . . . if he hadn't been booked on that plane to Hawaii, and hadn't tried to save the day, and hadn't been thoroughly fucked for his efforts.

For Christ's sake, they'd done everything by the book, but apparently that didn't make a Goddamn difference these days—rather than kudos, everyone had been reassigned to paper pushing pending the investigations. Once his medical leave was up, he'd be joining them, training the new plebes would have been more welcome.

"You need another pair of hands?" Cosky asked as Aiden closed the passenger door with his hip.

Aiden adjusted the load in his arms, his black hair gleaming beneath the sun. Sharp eyes raked Cosky's frame, lingering on the right knee. But he just shrugged. "Knock yourself out."

His new roommate had disappeared inside the condo by the time Cosky reached the Mustang. After opening the driver's door, he dragged a pair of garbage sacks out, slung them over his shoulder and started for the Condo. A half a dozen steps later, pure agony seared his knee. An icy sweat soaked the back of his T-shirt.

His leg went numb beneath him.

Which was new.

And unwelcome.

Son of a bitch. He stumbled to a standstill and dropped the bags, then bent over, digging rigid fingers into the joint.

"You okay?" Aiden asked from somewhere above him.

Oh, hell yeah, just peachy keen.

Cosky gritted his teeth and kept massaging. "Overdid it at PT."

"Ice will help," Aiden said, and Cosky couldn't tell whether he'd bought the lie or not. "You need a hand?"

"Nah, I'm good."

Aiden grunted and shrugged, then loped over to grab the two garbage bags at Cosky's feet. With another surge of frustration, Cosky watched him vanish into the condo.

Well, he couldn't stand here forever. After a few seconds of kneading and praying, he straightened and took a careful step. His knee let loose with a burst of tingling, but it accepted his weight.

Slowly, babying the hell out of his leg, he hobbled up the sidewalk and took the stairs in a one-two shuffle. The numbness settled deeper, electrified by periodic bursts of tingling.

Something told him this new symptom was a bad sign.

A black cloud settled over him as he opened the freezer and grabbed two bags of peas. He smacked the plastic bags against the fridge door, before limping back to the living room. Sitting down on the couch he took off his shoes, shoved his sweats down over his athletic shorts, and dragged them off one leg at a time. In the old days he would have kicked them off, but with the way his luck was running, the simple act of kicking would probably snap his leg off and send it flying across the room.

He'd arranged the bags of frozen peas over the compression sleeve by the time Aiden appeared.

Cosky glanced up. "You all set?"

"Yeah."

Aiden settled into the leather recliner to the left of the couch and studied Cosky's pea-shrouded knee. "How's it healing?"

Cosky started to lie, but the words stuck in his throat.

". . . unlikely to completely heal . . . additional surgery . . . more scarring, disability to the joint . . . no possibility it will withstand the rigors of your profession . . ."

No possibility.

Fourteen years of deployments, of dodging bullets, bombs, and flash grenades on foreign soil, only to fall in an attack on US soil, by US citizens.

Fate had a nasty sense of humor.

God only knew what Aiden saw on his face, because he frowned and leaned forward. "That bad, huh?"

Cosky's shrug was too tight. "It's not healing."

"Damn." Aiden pinched the bridge of his nose. He opened his mouth, only to close it again. Suddenly he lurched up and paced to the window.

The guy was antsy as shit. Maybe Cosky's situation was hitting too close to home. Aiden had spent weeks in the hospital himself after they'd dragged him up to that rooftop in Baghdad and from there into the evac chopper. Nobody had expected him to walk again, let alone reclaim his seat in the Zodiac.

Aiden abruptly spun around. "You know my dad was Native American?"

"No," Cosky said.

What did Aiden's ethnicity have to do with anything? Beyond looks of course, since Aiden did look like his dad. Commander Winchester had had the same broad shoulders and long, lean frame. They'd shared the same high cheekbones, black hair, and dark eyes too.

Kait on the other hand . . . His mind flashed to a long, thick golden braid. She took after their mother. You'd never know Aiden and Kait were siblings, not by their coloring anyway.

A whisper of ancient cravings brushed his mind . . . sleek, cool skin sliding against his naked, sweaty body. Alarmed, he buried the image. Those damn dreams had haunted him for years, the last thing he needed was resurgences of those sweaty, sleepless nights.

"Dad was full Arapaho. He disowned it, but it was still in him. He had certain . . ." Aidan paused to swipe a hand over his head. "Hell, I rarely mention this. Most people . . ." He trailed off and shook his head. "But you and Zane are close. You accept his . . . gifts . . ."

What the hell?

Cosky leaned against the sofa's armrest. "What are you talking about?"

"The flashes, the ones Zane has. You trust them."

With an impatient shake of his head, Cosky rescued a sliding bag of peas and rearranged the bundle across his knee. "What the hell do they have to do with anything?"

"Remember when you pulled me out of Baghdad?"

Cosky tensed. He'd thought they were past all those damn thank-yous.

Aiden gave a sharp bark of laughter. "Relax; I'm not going to smother you with my gratitude. That mortar shell blew a chunk off my spine. Docs said I would never walk again. Sure as hell never run."

Cosky's face tightened. "I'm aware they aren't always right."

He glared down at the bags covering his knee. Of course he knew the docs weren't always right . . . but, the knifing pains, the numbness, the tingling. Yeah, his instincts whispered they were right this time.

The bone wasn't healing. He could sense it. Hell, he could feel it.

"Yeah, that's the thing though . . ." Aiden walked over and stood in front of the couch, staring down into Cosky's face. "They were right."

Cosky frowned. "Come again?"

"The docs were right. I saw the X-rays. Hell, Rawls saw the X-rays, he'll tell you. My spine was toast. I shouldn't be on my feet."

Cosky straightened. "But you are," he pointed out. Except . . . Rawls's voice suddenly echoed in his mind.

"I'm tellin' ya, Cos. It ain't natural. He was missing a chunk of his spine. Far as I know, that shit don't grow back."

"Rawls mentioned it," Cosky admitted slowly. "He thought you'd been in some secret experiment."

Aiden barked out another laugh. "No shit?" The amusement faded. "No experiment. I'm walking because of Kait. Because she has a gift—like Zane. Only Kait's gift is in her hands. It comes from our father, passed from generation to generation. Sometimes . . . not always . . . but sometimes, she can heal. Sometimes she can do amazing things. Like regenerate a chunk of spine." His gaze dropped to Cosky's leg. "Or generate bone in a knee that isn't healing."

Chapter Two

"You what?" Kait Winchester froze in front of her front room's window, pulled the phone away from her ear, and stared at it.

Maybe this was a joke. Her brother had a twisted sense of humor. He was probably pranking her. Except . . . he had no idea that she had feelings for the man he'd apparently volunteered her . . . gifts . . . to help. Or, at least, that she used to have feelings for the man. Strong feelings. The kind of feelings that sparked tingling in certain parts of her body

The kind of feelings she didn't want to revisit.

A blast of static exploded through the ear set, followed by the low rumble of Aiden's voice.

Kait leaned her head against the cool glass of the window and pressed the phone back against her ear. "Back up. You did what?"

"I told Cos you might be able to help his knee." This time the horrifying news came through crystal clear. Her stomach tightened and started a series of agitated flips.

"Why in the world did you tell him that?" Kait asked, her fingers almost crushing the plastic casing of her cell.

"Because he's desperate. His knee isn't healing. He's looking at additional surgery, disability to the joint. He won't be able to requalify for the team."

She snorted. Yeah, like that was the end of the world.

But after a moment, Kait sighed. To some of them, being forced off the teams would be the end of their world. Her brother, for example, would mourn that loss to his dying breath. Her father had missed the adrenaline ride so much he'd taken a foolish risk, on a mission he hadn't been needed for, and ended up paying with his life.

Of course, special operators couldn't ride the lifestyle forever. At some point they had to retire—the human body, no matter how well honed, couldn't handle the punishing training and deployments forever.

But in general, the warriors in the SEAL community handled the transition easier if retirement was their choice.

Cosky's lean, powerful frame flitted through her mind. He was one of the hottest, most impressive examples of masculinity she'd ever laid eyes on—which explained the tingles and the sweaty palms she'd experienced in his proximity.

While his square face and gray eyes were majorly distracting, he wasn't exactly handsome. His nose had been broken too many times for that. So his sexiness lay in his lean strength, and his fluid, graceful stride.

Her heart ached to think of him losing that gracefulness, to think of him facing a life of disability and pain because of some lowlife's selfishness and greed.

If she could make a difference . . .

Not that there was any guarantee she could help him. While her track record wasn't disastrous, it wasn't exactly impressive either.

"You know as well as I do there's only a thirty percent chance of it helping," she finally said, hating the tightness in her voice.

Wolf, her newly discovered half brother, counseled her to focus on the thirty percent she had helped, like Aiden and Demi. But somehow Kait's memories always veered back to those she hadn't been able to help. Like Aunt Issa.

Her throat tightened beneath an echo of grief.

The thirty percent of people she'd helped through her lifetime would never make up for the seventy percent she'd failed.

What if Cosky became one of the seventy?

"It's not like you're gonna hurt anything," Aiden coaxed. "He's facing surgery anyway. If your healing doesn't take, he's got the surgery to fall back on, so what's the harm? You can't make it worse . . . and if the healing takes . . ."

What's the harm?

She swallowed a sarcastic laugh. How about the intimacy such healings required? How about the fact he'd be all but naked and she'd be rubbing her hands all over that mouthwatering body? How about the fact it had taken her ages to push the man out of her head and her dreams, and that was without exchanging even one freaking word with him?

How about the fact that he'd made it obvious that while he'd been attracted to her, she hadn't been worth his time?

Talk about ego crushers.

But then Aiden didn't know any of that. He'd been half out of his head because of pain and pills. He hadn't picked up on her reaction to Cosky or his reaction to her when they'd brushed past each other in Aiden's hospital room.

"You did tell him most of the time the healings don't work?"

"Of course." Aiden's voice sharpened. "I gave him the percentages." His voice lightened. "Interestingly, thirty is the percentage the doc gave him before surgery. You think that's good luck, or bad?"

"And he's agreed to this?" Kait asked, rolling her hot forehead against the icy window. The man had been avoiding her for years. He must be desperate if he'd agreed to Aiden's suggestion.

"He said he'd think about it. But he took your phone number."

Wow. Kait's lips twisted. He'd finally asked for her phone number . . . five years too late and for all the wrong reasons.

"You'll do it, right? If he calls?" Aiden asked.

Kait sighed, stepped back from the window, and straightened her shoulders. As if she could say no. "Sure."

"Good. Good."

There was no relief in his voice, but then, he'd never doubted she'd agree. He knew her too well; if there was even a fraction of a chance she could help one of his wounded teammates . . . they both knew that chance had to be explored.

"He's going to keep this quiet, right?" She turned from the living room window, heading for the freezer and the emergency stash of Ben and Jerry's she kept for just this kind of occasion.

"He won't say anything," Aiden assured her.

No doubt he was right. The last thing Cosky would want was his teammates knowing he'd visited a spiritual healer.

"So you all moved in?" she asked.

The fact Aiden was moving in with Rawls and Cosky had given her pause—her brother's change of address would pull Marcus Simcosky in the peripheral of her life again—until she realized how rarely she visited Aiden anyway. When he wasn't on deployment, or out training, he visited her. "I still don't get it; why not just buy your own place?"

Lord knows he had the money. Their parents' estate had left them well-off. They could live on the interest from the inheritance for their rest of their lives, without touching the principle. Not that she could convince Wolf of that—or that, as their father's eldest son, a third of the estate should go to him.

Aiden had inherited the same wealth she had, but he'd inherited even more from their lineage. He'd manifested the same gift their father had honed through the years—a gift that had turned John Winchester into a very wealthy man, and provided the money his children now enjoyed.

Her brother rarely mentioned the investments he made based on his inherited sense of *knowing*. He was well aware that acquiring more money was of no interest to her. Aiden though—it was a challenge to him, a game.

"I like having roommates." Aiden's voice cooled.

"Then why didn't you stay where you were?" He'd seemed to get along great with Tag and Trammel.

"Just felt like a change," he said, his voice even cooler, which meant he didn't want to talk about it.

Sure enough, he changed the subject.

"Word came down today. Wheels up in forty-eight."

Kait's chest tightened and her heart picked up speed. It didn't matter how many times they went through this. The fear never loosened its hold. She'd accepted that years ago. Learned to live with it.

"Try to make it home in one piece," she offered their ritualistic farewell.

He laughed, also part of their ritual. But the sudden hesitation after the laugh wasn't.

She cocked her head and waited.

"Wolf called this . . ."

"Oh, no!" Kait groaned. The last time Aiden had deployed, Wolf had all but moved in with her, as though she were incapable of surviving on her own even though she'd been living alone for years.

"I didn't call him," Aiden protested, his voice rising. "He just knew. I don't know what pipeline he's tapped into, but he's tied in good."

Or, Wolf had simply *known* Aiden was deploying. It made sense. Her father had possessed such a sense of *knowing*, as did Aiden. It was obviously tied to the male chromosome in their bloodline. And Wolf shared those genes.

"For God's sake, tell me you stressed that I don't need a babysitter. I've managed to survive on my own for twenty-nine years."

"He's your brother, *hookecouhu hiteseiw*. He wants to protect you."

Perfect, Wolf had Aiden giving her Arapaho pet names now too.

Kait huffed out a breath. "Do you even know what that means? And he's *our* brother. But I don't see him following you around like a hopped-up rottweiler."

Aiden's dead silence froze Kait's fingers on the refrigerator handle. "What?"

His breathing sounded strangled. He coughed. "I'm pretty sure he's babysitting me too."

Something told Kait Aiden wasn't talking about while he was walking around Coronado. "What happened?"

"We ran into a snag on our last insertion. Got stuck between floors. Wolf and some badasses swept in and unstuck us."

Kait's mouth opened in shock. She'd known that last assignment had gone south. Two of Aiden's teammates had flown home in body bags. It hadn't occurred to her that Wolf had prevented Aiden from the same fate.

"I don't know why I'm surprised he's on some kind of covert team. He told us he had enemies who would use us against him. That's why he wanted to keep our relationship secret. What team was it?"

"Not any branch I've seen. They were Arapaho. Or at least they were speaking Arapaho." He paused, the silence just hanging there. "Like I said, he's piped in."

So Wolf was serving his country. It didn't surprise her. Wolf was their father's son, just as Aiden was. It made sense he'd have the same sense of duty, honor, and warrior capabilities as the rest of the men in her life.

Sadness swept through her. If only Wolf had reached out earlier, before their father's death. It hurt to think of how much her father had lost by cutting himself off from his heritage. He'd lost the chance to connect with his eldest son, a son he would have loved as much as he'd loved her and Aiden.

She shook the regret aside. "Who do you think he works for?"

Tucking the phone between her shoulder and ear, she opened the freezer and grabbed the tub of ice cream. She pried off the top and peered inside. Not much consolation in there.

"No idea. But he called the shots and, damn, his team kicked ass."

His Arapaho team.

Kait's gaze narrowed in thought. Before the Northern Arapaho had been forced onto the Wind River reservation, they'd been a high plains tribe with a strong warrior society. Many of the modern Arapaho people still possessed those warrior inclinations.

Like her father and brothers.

"I'm thinking of visiting Wind River," Kait said tentatively. She already knew how her brother would react. He'd picked up their father's bias years ago.

"The reservation?" Aiden's voice rose in surprise. "Why the hell would you want to go there?"

"Because they're our people. Because it's our Arapaho blood that carries our gifts. We have relatives there. Aren't you even curious?"

She'd been curious for years, particularly after her healing ability had manifested itself. But her father had reacted with such anger when she'd asked about his family or the reservation, she'd pushed the questions aside. And then his death had numbed her. It had taken Wolf's arrival to stir the curiosity again.

"They aren't our people. Dad didn't want anything to do with the res. The teams were his family—not a bunch of child abusers who drowned their gifts beneath drugs and booze." Aiden's voice flattened.

"Wolf's not a drunk, or a drug user," Kait said quietly.

"Yeah, and Wolf doesn't live on the reservation either. He bugged out early, just like Dad. We're better off sticking with the teams." There was dismissal in her brother's voice.

Well, the teams might be his family, just as they'd been their father's, but while the SEAL community was supportive, she'd never felt as entrenched in the culture as her father and brother. And then there was Wolf—she'd learned more from Wolf in the past year about her Arapaho healing abilities than she'd ever learned from her dad.

Maybe her grandfather and grandmother had been monsters, but regardless of her father's warped childhood perspective, not all Arapaho were drunken, drug-dealing sociopaths. What if she could find answers on the reservation, learn how to boost her healing?

"Anyway," Aiden's voice turned brisk. "Don't be surprised if Cos calls. Things look pretty grim for him."

After a final round of stay-safes, Aiden broke the connection.

Kait tossed the ice cream's lid onto the kitchen counter, grabbed a spoon from the dish drain, and dropped it inside the carton. Phone in one hand, solace in the other, she padded back to the living room and settled cross-legged on the couch.

She didn't have a massage table, so Cosky would have to lie on the couch or the floor. Assuming he called, because his knee would have to be pretty bad for Marcus Simcosky to call her.

She wasn't an idiot, nor did she have any illusion about her looks. She was attractive and men noticed. She'd been picking up on their nonverbal cues since puberty.

So she knew he'd reacted to her as they'd brushed past each other in Aiden's hospital room. She'd recognized the catch in his stride, the intensity and heat in his eyes. She'd watched sensuality flush his face and soften his hard mouth.

He'd wanted her.

One look, one electrifying brush of bare skin on bare skin as their arms touched, and he'd wanted her.

Just as she'd wanted him.

Sure it had been pure animal attraction, primal lust. But it had been stronger than anything she'd felt before . . . or since.

She'd been so sure he'd turn around, follow her back into Aiden's room, strike up a conversation, and ask her out. When he hadn't, she thought he'd decided on a more private approach. She'd expected him to call. She'd waited three days for that call before the realization set in.

Marcus Simcosky was a confident man. The kind of man who went after what he wanted. Ergo, if he'd wanted her, really wanted her, he would have come after her by now. He would have tracked her down. He would have asked her out.

He wasn't dating anyone, so there was nothing holding him back. She'd known that from the conversations she'd listened in on between Aiden, Rawls, and Zane, while sitting at her brother's bedside. And those conversations had brought another revelation. He was avoiding Aiden's hospital room. Unlike Zane and Rawls, who had visited almost every day prior to their next deployment, Cosky hadn't visited her brother again. It had been such an obvious abandonment, even Rawls and Aiden had commented on it, although no one seemed to know why.

Kait knew—it was because of her.

If he'd been a less confident man, she would have approached him, explored that instant, overwhelming hunger. But he didn't lack confidence. If he'd wanted to pursue the attraction between them, he would have. And damn if she was going to pursue him and try to convince him she was worth his time and attention.

No matter how many nights she'd dreamed about him.

Or how many mornings she'd woken aching in places better off not dwelled on.

Cosky glanced in the review mirror and punched the accelerator, bracing his elbow against the door handle as his pickup shot forward. From behind him, a car backfired. The explosive sound echoed in the air, as staccato as a gunshot. A rusted two-door sedan, the same one that had been riding his ass for the last mile, took the corner on a greasy plume of exhaust and settled in behind his bumper, tailing him so closely he could clearly see the driver—a thin, jaundiced woman with ratty brown hair.

There was no question. He'd picked up a tail.

She was of European descent, which didn't mean shit these days with domestic terrorists giving the foreign ones some serious competition for murder and mayhem. Although he doubted she was a Tango. Terrorists trained their cell members better. The woman was a complete amateur. Or an idiot. Or both. Only a moron would tail him so closely he could see her face.He glanced in the review mirror as the sedan backfired again. Black exhaust slicked the street behind him. At the very least a professional would choose a less conspicuous ride.

"Unbelievable."

He'd noticed her the moment she'd pulled onto Silver Strand Boulevard behind him. She'd been impossible to miss. If the backfiring hadn't caught his attention, the jet-engine muffler would have. The damn thing was noisier than a Black Hawk on liftoff, which was why he hadn't realized at first that she was following him. Sure she'd mirrored him turn for turn, but coincidences happened. By the fourth turn he'd started to wonder, so he'd tested her by taking sudden random corners, by speeding up and slowing down, by sailing through yellow lights and stopping at green. She'd matched every maneuver.

Yep, he was being tailed—by an idiot.

It would have been laughable if his knee weren't howling and his life clinging to the edge of an abyss.

She was probably a reporter, another vulture eager to pick over the carcass of his naval career. He scowled, that familiar python of frustration wrapping around his chest and squeezing the air from his lungs.

Damn it!

The media shitfest was finally settling down. They were able to step off base without being mobbed by the press. Yeah, this hiatus would disappear if the DOJ decided to launch a criminal investigation, but for the moment they'd been given some breathing room. The last thing they needed was another opinionated piece hitting the papers, or airing across the networks.

A molten ice pick stabbed through his knee and he exhaled a tight curse, shifting to take the pressure off his leg. When the pain didn't lessen, he dug his fingers into the protesting joint. He should have eased back on the bike, but he'd wanted to work his body to the point of exhaustion.

His mind shifted to Kait Winchester, to long aristocratic fingers and a waterfall of sleek, pale hair. With luck his body wouldn't have the energy to react to the hour of torture he'd signed it up for.

Grimacing, he groaned. Christ, this visit was a bad idea. There was a reason he'd avoided Kait for the past five years. But he didn't turn the truck around. Apparently his need for a miracle overrode his sense of self-preservation.

The last thing he wanted, though, was to bring the press down on Kait's door, so when he arrived at her apartment complex he drove past. He'd dump his tail and circle back to keep his appointment. Of course, his tail would just attach herself to him again, later. Or maybe she'd fixate on Rawls, or Zane, or heaven help them—Beth. Zane would blow a gasket if some whack job started tailing Beth. He might as well put an end to this woman's game and send her on her noisy way.

With that in mind, he pulled into the restaurant parking lot for Coronado Ferry Landing Shopping. His tail had to wait for several cars to pass before she could follow. He cruised around the center parking aisle and picked a space on the far left. The woman pulled into a slot in front of the sidewalk, which ran the length of the restaurant strip. Perfect, she'd have to cross the entire parking lot to reach him, giving him plenty of time to assess her approach.

He hit the latch to the glove box and the compartment fell open, exposing his Glock. After stashing the weapon in the waistband of his jeans, he slid out of the truck, doing his best to ignore the slivers of ice piercing his kneecap. The hot breeze brought a whiff of barbeque and his stomach growled. Too bad all this unwelcome attention had made him late for his appointment, that barbeque smelled damn good.

He doubted the woman was dangerous, but it never paid to trust one's life to assumptions, so he tucked his T-shirt behind the Glock for easier access, and watched her slam the rusted door of the sedan and start toward him.

Marcus Simcosky was better looking in person than he'd been in the newspapers or on the television. There was a cold intensity to the flesh-and-blood man that the digital and print images lacked.

Jillian Michaels shoved her hands into the pockets of the poncho she'd liberated from a clothesline south of Portland, Oregon. Even with the summer sun overhead and the heavy wool shielding her, she couldn't seem to warm up. She'd been freezing for months.

She studied the man she'd come thousands of miles to kill—or at least, one of the men—as she headed across the parking lot. His face was guarded, watchful. It had been a miracle she'd recognized him when his truck passed her stakeout point along Silver Strand Boulevard. She'd been parked along that stretch of road for days, hoping one of the men she'd come to kill would cruise past. Praying she'd recognize them, trying, without success, to think of another way to track them down.

The newspapers hadn't been exactly forthcoming with addresses, and they were unlisted in the yellow pages. Googling their names hadn't produced any results, either.

Her steps slowed as she stared at him. She hadn't expected him to be so tall or tanned or muscular. She hadn't expected the confidence and strength he exuded, or the subtle sense of threat. She hadn't expected him to look so damn . . . capable.

He'd hovered near death for days. Spent weeks in the hospital. But he didn't look sick. Not like she did. But then he'd had the luxury of recovering in the hospital, or in the homes of family and friends. Nor was he on the run, sleeping in stolen cars, scrounging out of trash cans, ransacking empty houses in the hope of finding enough cash to fill his gas tank or enough food to fill his belly.

A horn blared. The squeal of brakes followed. Jillian jumped back, realizing she'd stepped in front of an oncoming car. Not that the car could do any damage. She was already dead. A lifeless husk held together by vengeance and determination. She glanced across the pavement and found her soon-to-be victim watching her with cold detachment. He must have seen the car headed directly for her, but he hadn't bothered to shout a warning.

Bastard.

Had he hoped the car would finish the job, kill her where bullets and icy water had failed? He wasn't one of the men who'd kicked down her door, kidnapped her family, and stolen her life from her; nor one of the men who'd come after her in the hospital, after she'd reported what happened to the police. But he was involved. He was one of the bastards who'd killed her brother, and spread those lies about him.

A flush of rage warmed her. Her fingers curled into claws. She shoved them deeper into the pockets of her poncho. When her hand bumped against the cold steel of the revolver she'd stolen from a house in San Diego, she forced her fingers to unfurl and take hold. The voluptuous folds of the poncho hid the bulge of the gun. She wouldn't have to pull it out; she'd just point and fire through the cotton.

And while he lay there, the parking lot filling with his lying, murderous blood, she'd shoot him again and again. One shot for each of her babies and another for her brother.

He'd be the first to pay for what they'd taken from her, but they were all going to pay. Every last one of them. She was going to make sure of it.

Her muscles tensed in determination and she took another step forward, the gun warming in her tense grip. She'd start with him, this murderous SEAL, and then she'd go after his friends. And before she killed the last of them, she'd force him to tell her how to find the others. Those bastards who'd broken into her house and kidnapped her family and taken her life from her.

The rage swelled with each step, liquefying her frozen chest, warming arms and legs that never shed the chill picked up in that icy lake all those months ago.

As her hand tightened around the gun, a cry rose behind her. A thick, sobbing wail. The sound stopped her in her tracks. Her fingers lost their grip on the gun. The cry came again. So familiar. So beloved.

Time and space warped in and out, surrounding her like ripples on sunbaked asphalt. She turned in slow motion, the sun spinning dizzy and brilliant overhead. She stopped breathing, waiting for that familiar, beloved cry.

A stroller rattled down the sidewalk. Her gaze locked on the fragile blond head that bounced slightly with each rotation of the wheels. On the lift and flop of wheat-gold hair.

Blond curls, a dimpled smile, bluer-than-blue eyes.

Don't cry, baby. Don't cry. Mommy's here. Mommy's coming.

Jillian turned.

Smile for me, sweetie. Smile for Mommy. Let Mommy see those dimples.

She stepped onto the sidewalk and fell in behind the stroller, her vision tunneled on that beacon of a blond head. Her heart stuttered as chubby, denim-clad legs kicked in time to those hiccupping sobs.

Chubby little legs, stocky little body. Round arms giving sticky hugs.

In the distance a woman wept. Broken gasps of grief. Jillian blocked the sound and focused on the stroller.

Don't cry, baby. Don't cry. Mommy's here. Mommy's coming.

What the hell?

Cosky watched the woman who'd been tailing him turn and head in the opposite direction. Maybe she hadn't been following him after all. Coronado Ferry Landing was a popular shopping and eating area; maybe the whole thing had been a weird coincidence. But that many turns, for that long? An unlikely coincidence.

It was more likely she'd thought he was someone else and hadn't realized her mistake until she'd climbed out of her car and gotten a good look at him. Maybe she'd been too embarrassed to approach.

He frowned and shook his head slightly. He could have sworn there'd been recognition on her face, a fixed, frozen expression, as though she knew him—or thought she did.

Relaxing, he watched her head down the sidewalk. She never looked back. When his knee locked up and his thigh started to spasm, he climbed back in the truck and fired the engine.

Before exiting the parking lot, he shot another glance toward his stalker. Some terrorist she'd turned out to be. The whole thing was weird though. And not just the tailing, but the coat she was wearing too. Wool was too heavy for Coronado in the summer. It was in the mid-eighties. She should have been sweltering. He shook the questions aside and headed back the way he'd come.

Ten minutes earlier

Robert Biesel pulled into Coronado Ferry Landing's restaurant parking behind a rusted, sputtering sedan. The exhaust-riddled eye-ear-and-nose sore had been a lifeline since he'd been following Simcosky closer than normal. The weekend traffic was thick, the drivers aggressive and impatient, which upped the chances he'd lose his target. Sure he had a partner to tag team Simcosky with, which cut down on the threat of discovery; but he couldn't tell Phillip where to intercept the SEAL unless he knew what street the bastard was headed down.

And then that crazy-ass sedan had joined the fun. The car's exhaust had shielded him from view and given him a beacon to follow once he realized the frizzy-haired woman behind the wheel was tailing the big bastard too.

He circled the parking lot and found a space twenty feet from Simcosky. His vantage point gave him a clear view of both cars. Shoving his beige and boring Oldsmobile into park, he turned off the engine and slumped down to limit exposure, wishing he could kick back and take a nap.

"It's a one-nighter," Manheim had told him. "You'll be back on surveillance in twenty-four hours, forty-eight tops."

Robert snorted in disgust. There was more work involved in grabbing eight scientists and faking their deaths than Manheim realized. Hell, making the explosion look like a laboratory accident had taken precision and timing. But had the bosses given them a couple of extra days? Hell no—they expected everyone to work around the clock.

The sedan had grabbed a parking space along the sidewalk. Robert eyed the woman behind the wheel and twisted to look behind him. Simcosky was waiting next to his truck with his feet spread and arms crossed. A rendezvous was definitely in the works, but from the cold expression on Simcosky's face and the intimidation in his stance, it didn't look like a friendly one. Maybe he was having girlfriend troubles.

As the woman climbed out of the sedan, he picked up the bottle of Coke from the console beside him. Twisting off the cap, he took a sip, and grimaced as warm fizz flooded his mouth. The woman headed in Simcosky's direction. His gaze traveled up a thick, wooly overcoat—was she fucking insane? It was ninety degrees out there—and settled on a thin, haggard face.

Which he instantly recognized.

He choked, and soda went down the wrong pipe, burning all the way to his lungs. A seizure of coughing gripped him.

Holy freaking shit.

Through streaming eyes, Robert watched the woman he'd shot twice and dumped into the icy depths of Lake Katcheca almost step in front of an oncoming car—and wouldn't that have been sweet? It would have saved him from this sudden, immense headache. Except she caught herself at the last minute and jumped back.

The damn woman had more lives than an alley cat.

What the *hell* was Jillian Michaels doing in Coronado? More importantly, why was she meeting Marcus Simcosky?

The old man was going to freak over this, and guess who'd feel the full force of all that rage?

Robert broke into another rabid round of coughing, his heart pounding so hard he felt it in his head. He'd come close to joining Branson in the grave when Jillian had given them the slip at the hospital. The only thing that had saved his ass was Phillip stepping up to corroborate Robert's insistence that he'd checked the woman's pulse.

Which she hadn't had when he'd buckled her into the van, because she'd been dead. He knew dead when he saw it. She'd been dead. Just like her kids.

He dragged in a couple of breaths and smothered the coughing. By the time he swiped the tears from his eyes, Jillian was walking down the sidewalk, away from Simcosky.

Robert turned to watch her. Had she noticed him and abandoned the meeting? He checked the pickup again. Simcosky was watching her with confusion too.

The fact she was in Coronado and interacting with one of the SEALs the bosses were so obsessed with was going to bring the hornets of fury down on his head.

And running was useless. How the hell was he supposed to hide when his entire body was one gigantic tracking device? Nothing could keep him from joining Russ in the grave this time.

Unless . . . he watched Jillian grow smaller and smaller. If he could grab her before his men caught sight of her, before the bosses were any the wiser . . .

He grabbed his cell phone. For this to work, Phillip needed to stay across town.

"Hey," he said as soon as the call was picked up. "Looks like Simcosky's headed home. Why don't you head over to Orange Avenue and catch him at Tenth?"

"Sure," Phillip said. "Give me a heads-up if he changes course."

"That's what I'm here for," Robert said and ended the call.

Dropping the cell onto the passenger seat, he checked on Simcosky again. His original target was climbing back into his truck.

Swearing, he turned to glare after Jillian. He could hardly grab the woman here. Not with half the city in the parking lot, and a Goddamn SEAL watching.

A few minutes later, Simcosky took off, but in the opposite direction of Jillian.

What the hell was going on?

Jillian was his priority, so he let Simcosky go. Settling back he waited. As soon as the chance presented itself, he'd grab her.

And make sure he used up every one of those lives of hers.

Chapter Three

Cosky doubled back to Kait's apartment complex. The building was surrounded by parks. Across the street from the main entrance was a grassy, tree-studded swath of ground complete with baseball diamond, metal bleachers, and a set of pillared, open buildings with picnic benches and barbeque pits. Nestled against the building's back was another grassy area, this one housing tennis and basketball courts and a bike trail.

The apartment complex itself was huge; it swallowed the entire block, a seven-story tower of steel and glass. It looked expensive as hell, which probably meant it had an elevator. An amenity that wouldn't have concerned him four months ago, but since she lived on the sixth floor that elevator was a major concern at the moment.

He parked in the visitor slot next to the sidewalk. How the hell could she afford a place like this? Coronado apartments were budget breakers. He had to share a three-bedroom condo with Rawls and Zane—now Aiden—just to afford a place off base and that was with their military discount.

And their place didn't have anywhere near the amenities this place boasted, yet Aiden said Kait lived alone. But then he didn't know anything about the woman, regardless of how many times he hammered into her during those damn dreams.

An image took shape in his mind: long legs wrapped around his waist, and a sweet ass in his hands. Tension seized him, the kind of tension his earlier workout was supposed to discourage. He scowled as his cock swelled.

Son of a bitch.

He'd only seen Kait Winchester twice. Or at least, he'd only seen the actual woman two times. A slender, stoic beauty with shaking hands accepting the flag draping her father's casket—and a drawn, white-faced angel at Aiden's bedside.

He'd been dreaming about her since.

Except, in his dreams she hadn't been hurting. Not like she'd been in reality. He'd recognized the pain in her eyes. He'd seen that same pain often enough in his mother's eyes after his father died.

Their second meeting was crystal clear in his mind; they'd brushed past each other in the hall outside Aiden's hospital room. The contact had only lasted a split second, but it had stopped him in his tracks, and set every nerve on fire. His pulse had warped into overdrive. He'd started to turn, to follow her back into the room. That's when alarm bells had kicked in. She was dangerous. If one glance stopped him cold and one touch caused instant arousal, then he needed to steer clear.

Now.

Before he got a taste of her.

Such instant, overwhelming attraction led to things he had no intention of exploring—like obsession and need.

So he'd retreated, and avoided her for the next five years, but even now, five years later, he could still smell that sweet citrusy scent that had clung to her skin.

He glanced at the cane braced against the passenger floor as he climbed out of the truck, but left it there. No way in hell was he gimping his way to her door, cane in hand. It was humiliating enough limping there under his own steam. It was also uncontroversial proof that he'd lost his mind.

What was he thinking?

He'd avoided the woman for five years because of the fire she lit under his skin and now he was going to lie there on her massage table and let those hands, that had been plaguing his dreams for more nights than he cared to remember, roam over his bare skin? One of those bullets must have been a head shot, because he'd sure as hell lost his mind.

A woman with spiky pink hair tending a stainless-steel coffee cart greeted him with a flirty smile when he reached the front doors. He ignored her, concentrating on the gold plate with its rows of numbers and names next to the entrance. He found K. Winchester, apartment number 607 and pressed the button beside the name.

"Yes?" a woman asked immediately.

Cosky stirred uncomfortably beneath the rasp of her voice. They'd made the arrangements through text messages, so he hadn't heard her speak. Nor had he expected her voice to affect him on such a visceral level. Wasn't that just perfect? Now her damn voice could join her hands and hair in an erotic dream trifecta.

"Kait Winchester?"

"Lieutenant Simcosky?" The lilt at the end of that smoky voice turned his name into a question.

"Yeah."

There was a short pause, as though she was surprised he'd shown up. That made two of them.

"I'll buzz you in. There's an elevator at the back of the lobby.

I'm on the sixth floor, apartment 607, end of the hall, on the left," she said in that raspy voice, as though she'd just crawled out of bed.

An image flashed through his mind—golden hair spread across a dark pillow. He swore softly as his body tightened. Shit, he was already twitchy as hell, which didn't bode well for lying there chaste as a priest while her hands roamed over him.

"You're visiting Kaity?" the coffee girl asked. "She's at the end of the hall, sixth floor."

"So I heard," Cosky said tersely, reaching for the door as soon as the buzzer sounded. The image of pale hair sliding across silk sheets followed him into the lobby. This was insane. But he kept walking.

Aiden claimed that there was magic in those slender, aristocratic hands. And his teammate had the miracle to back that claim up.

Cosky wasn't so sure. But nobody had expected Aiden to walk again. They sure as hell hadn't expected him to run. Yet, there he'd been, barely six months after they'd pulled him into the Black Hawk, running a mile and a half in nine minutes.

Nine. Fucking. Minutes.

So Cosky would lie there and let those sexy hands of hers drive him out of his mind, in the hope he'd be blessed with a miracle too. Because without one, his seat in the Zodiac would be handed over to someone else. A gimpy leg had no place on the teams.

A trio of coeds spilled out of the elevator and approached him, their toned arms cradling tennis rackets. He ignored their flirtatious smiles, and lurched along faster, trying to catch the elevator.

It closed two feet before he reached it.

Swearing beneath his breath, he jabbed the up button. Four months ago he would have hauled ass up the stairs without a second thought. But then four months ago he'd given this building a wide berth. He'd have signed up for a battery of psych evaluations, rather than face the threat of her massage table.

Four months ago he'd still possessed a brain, in the upper quadrant of his body.

By the time the elevator reached the sixth floor his leg was shrieking like a Black Hawk shedding its propellers and the last thing on his mind was sex. Thank you Christ.

Not that he'd ever had trouble bringing his body to heel, but at least he wouldn't have to struggle with that particular demon during the next hour. Not when cutting off his leg, without anesthesia, sounded like a viable alternative to its current bitchiness. As he limped his way out of the elevator and toward her apartment, her massage table was sounding better and better. At least he'd get off the damn leg.

He pressed the buzzer beside her door and fought the temptation to lean against the doorjamb while he waited for her to answer. He probably should have brought the cane, although the humiliation of hobbling his way into her apartment, cane in hand, just might beat out the humiliation of crashing face-first at her feet without the cane to stabilize him.

When the door opened, he breathed a sigh of relief. There was no sign of that loose golden hair from his dreams. She must have pinned it to the back of her head. She was also wearing a loose, peach T-shirt and baggy, lightweight cotton sweats, which meant everything of interest was covered.

So far, so good.

Until she opened her mouth.

"Aren't you supposed to be using a cane, Marcus?"

There was something far too intimate in the way her throaty voice caressed his name. Something that made his body flex and fix on her with too much interest.

Besides, only his mother called him Marcus. "I go by Cosky, or Cos."

Intense brown eyes studied his face, and her eyebrows lifted. "I'm not one of your teammates."

He stiffened slightly. What the hell was that supposed to mean? Before he had a chance to ask, her mouth was moving again. The shape of those curvy, pink lips distracted him for a moment. By the time he shook the distraction aside, he'd missed most of her response.

". . . by refusing to use the cane, you're setting your progress back?"

Forcing his weight onto the leg in question, he locked down any sign of pain and stared back. "It's fine."

"Riiiiight." She raised her eyes to the ceiling and shook her head. "Of course it is. That's why you're here."

He studied her heart-shaped face, for the first time recognizing the stubborn tilt to her chin. "We going to do this out here, or can I come in?"

She flushed slightly, but stepped to the side. "Can you make it on your own? Or do you need a shoulder?"

As in her shoulder?

Like hell.

"I'm fine," he snapped, hearing the grit in his voice.

"So you said." She stared right back, without giving an inch, disbelief rounding her eyes and compressing her lips.

Her eyes were dark brown, her eyelashes and eyebrows dark as well. The dark coloring was striking beneath that golden hair. Would a true blonde have eyes so dark? Maybe those golden strands were courtesy of a bottle, rather than nature. Not that it made a damn bit of difference.

"You coming in, or not?"

When he brushed past her he caught a whiff of something sweet and tangy—citrusy, like lemons, or oranges, an echo of the scent that had haunted him for the past five years. He'd never cared for lemons or oranges, so why the *hell* would his skin suddenly tighten and tingle? Or his belly clench with sharp, inexplicable hunger?

To combat the unwelcome reaction he bore down hard on his leg and focused on the shards of glass digging into his knee. Three steps later, and the tension in his muscles had more to do with pain than hunger.

The short hall was lined with photos. Most were of her father, Commander Winchester—whom Cosky had served beneath back in his Minnow days—and her brother Aiden. But there were two women on the walls as well. The one, a golden-haired beauty in yellowing photos, looked enough like Kait to be her twin, or her mother. The other woman was small and round with a short bob of silver hair. Cosky studied the picture as he passed, seeing an echo of Kait in the shape of the face and the stubborn chin.

Kait's monument of pictures was proof of how important family was to her. It reminded him of his mother's entryway. Mom had lined the entire hall with photos too. He couldn't walk through the door without staring himself in the face.

The hall emptied into the living room. He didn't see a massage table. Instead she'd spread a white sheet across the couch, anchoring it in place by tucking the excess fabric beneath the cushions. Next to the sofa, a coffee table bristled with an array of plastic bottles, and a pile of folded towels.

"I'm surprised you came," Kait said from behind him. "I didn't think you'd be open to metaphysical healing."

Metaphysical healing? That's what she called it?

"The jury's still out." He turned to face the mouth of the hall, where she stood watching him. Their eyes locked and he could have sworn the room shrank by half. A current of electricity skittered down his spine.

"I'm not surprised." A shadow touched her eyes. With a slight twist to her lips, she stepped forward. "You're not the type."

"There's a type?" Cosky tilted his head and thought of Zane, of premonition after premonition that had saved their asses more times than not. Some events couldn't be ruled by logic. They had to be accepted on faith.

"Yeah, there is. It involves a degree of openness, which you don't have."

Cosky stomped on a burst of irritation. She'd known him for all of two minutes, hardly enough time to box him into a *type.* "If I were a cynical man, I'd think you were setting up excuses for this experiment's failure."

She shrugged and took another step forward. "Aiden said he told you that most of the time this doesn't work." She frowned at him, frustration flashing across her face to settle dark and brooding in her eyes.

With a slight shimmy of her shoulders, she seemed to cast her frustration aside. Dark brown eyes zeroed in on him again and Cosky felt the room shrink another few feet. A wave of citrusy scent wafted past him.

His skin tightened and started to prickle.

Just. Perfect.

He broke eye contact by turning toward the couch. Anything to avoid that intense gaze; it was doing freaky things to his heart and respiration, which was the last thing he needed under the circumstances.

"How do you want me, on my back or stomach?"

"Your stomach. I'll work on your back first, try to relax you. The more relaxed you are, the better your chances for healing. I told you to wear shorts, remember? I need skin on skin contact."

Skin on skin contact. Every muscle in Cosky's body twitched. The hair on his arms, legs, and the back of his neck lifted.

He almost turned and headed for the door. Almost.

Until Aiden flashed through his mind. Aiden running that nine minute mile. His hands dropped to his waistband instead.

"I'm wearing shorts beneath the sweats."

"The bathroom's to your left if you want privacy," she said, her voice was huskier, closer.

Prickles played up and down Cosky's spine.

Damn it, there was something in her voice he didn't want to hear. Something husky and thick and ravenous. Something too damn close to arousal. He hesitated a moment then gritted his teeth and yanked his T-shirt over his head. With a quick shove his sweats slid down his thighs. He sat on the couch, bent to unlace his boots, and pulled them off. His sweats followed.

Without looking up, he turned and stretched flat on the couch, crossing his arms so they served as his pillow. He turned his head so it faced the back of the couch.

See no evil, want no evil.

He swallowed a curse of derision, far too aware of the tension through his crotch. Too damn late for that.

His skin tightened at the faint whisper of her footsteps on the carpet, but they stopped across the room, and a new age melody swimming with flutes suddenly rippled through the air. The music shielded her approach and he tensed, straining to catch the sound of her footsteps beneath the flutes.

It was her citrusy scent that warned him she'd joined him. Suddenly her body heat warmed him from ass to shoulders and that fragrant cloud enveloped him, bathing him in citrusy sweetness. Every cell in his body locked, fixed on her with growing hunger.

Son of a bitch, he was already in trouble and she hadn't even touched him yet.

"Here," she said, as the back of his neck heated. "You can use one of these as a pillow."

A slender hand placed one of the folded towels in front of his head. He held his breath as her body brushed his, and then unfolded his arms and dragged the towel beneath his cheek.

"I'm going to put one under your ankles too," she said, her body burning a path down his side as she brushed against him. "It will support your lower back." He tensed as she lifted his bare feet and slid the towel beneath them.

To his left came the sucking sound of a plastic bottle being squeezed, followed by the oily *shush-shush-shush* of well-lubricated hands rubbing against each other.

"I'm going to start on your upper back and shoulders," she said, her voice husky.

The warmth radiating along his side migrated up his back as she leaned over him. That sultry, citrus cloud cinched tighter, enveloping him, until he felt encased in a fragrant bubble.

He flinched as her hands touched down and began sliding up and down his back in a series of long, lingering strokes. Suddenly her scent was the last thing on his mind.

In his dreams, her hands had been cool and soft and sinuously smooth, gliding over his skin in a silken skim, leaving his flesh itchy and ravenous in their wake.

In reality, they were hot.

Strong.

Determined.

They dug into his back with strength and confidence, kneading muscles that were growing tenser by the second. Heat flowed from the point of contact, spreading out in fiery waves, setting fire to every muscle, every nerve, every bone, until his entire back felt aflame.

Tingles were the least of his worries.

Spontaneous combustion was a definite concern.

"Does it hurt when I touch you here?" she asked, her breath a cool mist against the nape of his sweaty neck.

Her touch shifted from kneading to caressing and he realized she was massaging the mangled, scarred memento of the two rounds to his back. She leaned closer, her body brushing his waist, her hands sliding gently up and down and around the blistered scar tissue.

Her hands lightened and slowed, taking on a rhythm that was more caress than massage.

Was she *petting* him?

A puff of humid breath washed against the back of his neck again. It sparked an electrical charge, which zipped up his spine and into his brain. He went light-headed and dizzy.

Jesus Christ. "I'm not hurting you, am I?"

"No." The word sounded like he'd gargled with gravel.

Her burning hands inched higher and bore down again, her fingers digging in and squeezing, then settling into that kneading pattern. He tried not to breathe, but it was a losing battle. Each laboring breath drew her scent deeper into his lungs and muddied his brain, until he was drowning in her.

Standing next to the couch, Kait took a deep breath and bent over Cosky. He flinched when she settled her left palm on the ridge of muscle to the right of his spine, and then fell rigidly still.

Bracing her arms, Kait placed her right hand on top of her left and bore down, slowly rotating her arms so her palm crawled up his back in a series of lazy, counterclockwise circles. The muscles beneath her fingers were hard and hot, steel sheathed in silk.

Her belly tightened beneath a wave of heat and her head went light. Kait choked on a shallow breath. Good lord, she'd been so fixated on the feel of him, she'd forgotten to breathe.

It was almost impossible to believe that Marcus Simcosky, the man she'd been drooling over for more years than she cared to admit, was stretched out across her couch wearing nothing but a loose pair of athletic shorts—his muscled, tanned flesh just lying there, awaiting her pleasure.

Of course, he hadn't arrived with the intention of providing her with a buffet of sensual delights, and she fully intended to keep her promise and massage the hell out of that gorgeous, lean body in the hope she might channel some of that magical energy and jump-start the healing of his knee. But good God, she wasn't an idiot. The good lord had provided her with a six-foot-four-inch specimen of mouthwatering masculinity, and nothing was going to stop her from enjoying the unexpected treat.

Particularly since this would be her only chance to experience the joy of his long, lean body beneath her hands.

It was clear from Cosky's flinty expression, clipped replies, and rigid muscles, that he wasn't enjoying this session like she was. If his knee didn't show marked improvement after this healing, he wouldn't be stretching himself across her couch again.

But he was here now, his flesh hard and silky beneath her fingertips. Separating her hands, she widened her thumbs and dug her fingers into his tight back, lifting and kneading the rigid muscles. Rather than loosening, his back tightened even further.

She frowned; maybe she was digging in too deep.

"Am I hurting you?" she asked, easing back slightly.

"No."

Since his voice sounded tense and a ripple shook the flesh beneath her fingers, she eased back even more. He wouldn't admit it if she was hurting him. Men and their silly pride.

As she neared his shoulders and the round, red scars that mottled his sleek skin, her touch gentled. She caressed the raised, rough tissue with the very tips of her fingers, carefully gliding over the puckered flesh.

Bullet wounds.

Although she'd never seen such scars before, she recognized them immediately.

Her chest tightened and her hands slowed, gliding back and forth over the angry, red puckers of flesh. She'd known he'd taken a couple of slugs to the back. But hearing about the damage and having the aftermath beneath her hands were two totally different beasts.

They were so small—barely the size of a quarter—so innocuous for the amount of damage they'd caused.

Nausea climbed her throat as she imagined the bullets plowing into him, puncturing his beautiful back—destroying muscle and bone. She stroked the scars again. This time the flesh beneath her hands twitched.

"You're certain I'm not hurting you?" she forced the question through the sudden constriction in her throat. To think of how close he'd come to dying . . .

"No."

But his voice sounded tight. The scars were red and raw. Maybe they were sensitive. She lightened her touch even more, ghosting over the area with the tips of her fingers. The skin beneath her hands twitched harder, a clear indication he wasn't appreciating the attention. As the muscles of his back visibly tensed, she shifted up his body and bore down again, digging her fingers into his shoulders, kneading and releasing, kneading and releasing.

"Relax," she said, reveling in the feel of him beneath her hands. Lord, he felt so good—hot, hard perfection.

A fire kindled in her belly and slowly spread, heating her from the inside out. Liquefying bone, melting muscle, bubbling through her blood.

She paused, wiping sweat from her forehead and bent over him again. But within seconds perspiration was burning her eyes and trickling down her scalp.

The heat was a good sign. Successful healings always ended with her drenched in sweat and craving a shower.

Except . . .

This heat didn't feel the same. It was thicker, heavier, with a sexual charge.

So how much of this fire was a result of lust? And how much was healing energy? Was she even channeling the healing energy?

The inferno her hands stirred up sank deep, penetrating to his core. The fire infiltrated his blood, bonded with his bones, until the very heart of him loosened and locked on her with primal hunger.

The pressure in his groin exploded, flooded his cock and balls. Christ. He needed to chill out, or things were going to get humiliating fast.

"You need to relax," she said from above him, her hands stilling and lingering on his shoulders. And then she did that flirty little caress again and a bolt of electricity shot straight from her fingers to his cock.

He went rigid beneath her hands.

"Seriously!" Exasperation rounded her vowels. "Relax. You're too tense."

Another of those flirty caresses, as though she were attempting to calm him. He choked back a groan, tingles prickling along his spine, electrifying every cell. Which wasn't very . . . relaxing.

"You're hard as a fricking rock." She didn't sound admiring.

Cosky shoved down the urge to roll and drag her to his mouth. Gritting his teeth, he reached for his formidable control.

Which, for the first time ever, wasn't so formidable. His body ignored the dictates of his mind and slipped its leash entirely.

Every cell, every nerve, every atom within him locked on her. On those hot, strong hands and the burning heat of her body. The urge to roll clawed at him, demanded obedience from his arms. He groaned beneath the onslaught.

She snorted out a laugh. "Well at least I know you're awake," she said, apparently oblivious to the frenzy taking place beneath her hands.

Or maybe she was just used to this ramped-up reaction. Maybe this happened every time she dug her hands into some stranger's flesh. A surge of acid dampened the fire. Could that be what was happening? He'd never reacted with such urgency to a woman's touch before, to the smell of her skin. Could this frenzied reaction be a side effect of her gift? He was thirty-five years old, for Christ's sake. He knew what it felt like to want a woman. This went beyond want. This bordered on something he didn't want to name, or believe in. He was on the thin edge of control, for God's sake, after mere minutes beneath her hands.

This wasn't normal. Something else was at work here. He could almost hear Rawls's laughter at that classic bit of rationalization.

"This isn't working," she finally said and her hands left his body.

Disappointment rolled through him, which was ridiculous. He hadn't had any expectations this supposed healing would work.

Zane's visions were different. They were finite, easy to corroborate. They happened in real time, in real life. But how did you prove something as insubstantial as healing through touch? Hell, for all she or Aiden knew, her supposed successes could have simply healed on their own. Still, it had cost him nothing to give it a try.

And . . . Rawls's voice kept drifting through his mind. *"Far as I know, that shit don't grow back . . ."*

"Since the massage isn't relaxing you, I'm going to just concentrate on your leg." She shifted beside him, her body brushing his and her hands sliding down to the back of his thigh.

She started in with that hot, kneading slide again.

As her hands climbed higher and higher, his heart lurched, and then took off like a jackhammer. It stopped altogether when her fingers brushed the hem of his shorts.

His ass hardened. An urgent command went out to his arms, his hands, his fingers. *Stand down!*

Christ, he needed to get her away from the danger zone.

"The damage was to my knee," he said around a mouth full of grit and prayed she'd move those hands to a safer location.

"Front or the back?"

He swallowed a groan of relief as her hands moved back down his leg. "Front."

He heard the rustle of clothes as she straightened. Her touch vanished. So did her body heat. That citrusy cloud he'd been steeped within eased as well. He would have been relieved, but the damage was already done.

"Why don't you turn over? I'll work on the front for a while."

Cosky swore beneath his breath. Considering the baseball bat that had sprung to life in his shorts, and the way his libido had hijacked his control, turning over was the last thing he should do.

"Yeah," he cleared his throat, "that's not a good idea."

"Do you need help turning over?" Her voice was closer again, and her heat was back, and that damn scented cloud . . .

"That's not the problem."

"Okay." She sounded exasperated again. "You mind telling me what is?"

What the hell. It wasn't like he could hide his condition, not with the Louisville Slugger tenting his shorts. She was bound to notice his avid appreciation.

"Let's just say my body's enjoying your attention," he said, and waited, curious how she'd respond.

A sharp breath sounded behind him. Apparently her initial response had been surprise. Why the hell that should please him so much was something he didn't want to examine too closely.

She recovered from her surprise quickly and laughed. An airy no-big-deal kind of laugh.

Irritation pinched him. Hard.

Was she so used to men getting erections at her touch that she could laugh it off?

"It's simple male physiology, Lieutenant. I can ignore it, if you can."

His teeth snapped together hard enough to hurt.

Could she now?

They'd see about that.

Without giving himself time to think, he grabbed the edge of the sofa and rolled.

Chapter Four

Kait choked back a gasp as Cosky suddenly rolled over, her eyes taking an immediate inventory of how much his body was enjoying her attention—from the visible tenting of his shorts, it was evident he was enjoying her ministrations *dramatically.*

Yeah . . . She cleared her throat, wondering if her face was as lobster red as it felt. Obviously, she wasn't the only one feeling the sexual heat.

Avoiding his gaze, she swiped at the perspiration trickling down her face and turned to her array of massage oils. She made a clumsy grab for the closest bottle, which she promptly knocked over. She grabbed the one next to it and got busy pooling the oily liquid in her hands, spending more time than necessary warming it between her palms. Sidling down the couch, she leaned over his knee and cleared her throat again.

"Let me know if I press too hard," she said, having a devil of a time controlling her eyes, which kept trying to migrate to the right so they could explore that intriguing bulge he was so completely unself-conscious about.

Her throat went dry as she leaned down and rested her hands on his knee, gently spreading the massage oil over the joint. His skin was as hot here as it had been on his back, but it wasn't nearly as sleek. The damage to the knee was extensive, as was the scarring. The main scar started at his kneecap and knifed down at least seven inches like an angry, red artery. She could feel him watching her, feel the weight and heat of his gaze on her face.

"What the hell," he said, and the irritation in his tone brought her gaze up and over to his face. "I smell roses."

His eyes were such a light gray they looked almost silver. A glittery, shimmery stainless steel kind of silver.

"Roses," she repeated absently, her attention captured by that gleaming gaze, and then his complaint sunk in and suddenly she smelled roses too.

With a silent groan, she turned her attention back to his knee and the scented oil she was working into his masculine flesh. The rose-scented oil. She'd mistakenly grabbed the bottle she'd used on Demi. In retrospect, it probably hadn't been the best idea to bring all her scented massage oils out. But at the time she'd been flustered, and trying to keep busy until he arrived. She hadn't even realized she'd emptied her bathroom vanity onto the coffee table. By the time she'd come to her senses and realized she didn't need half a dozen bottles of massage oil, he'd been pounding on her door and it was too late to haul them all back to her bathroom vanity.

Not that she was going to tell him any of this.

"This particular massage oil is made out of rose hips which have natural healing properties," she said in a virtuous voice.

"Hell." He sounded disgusted and disbelieving. "Aiden put you up to that, didn't he?"

"Of course not. I'd never let Aiden dictate what oil to use." She tried for a righteous tone; although it was exactly the kind of thing her brother would try to cajole her into doing. "It's well documented that rose hips have healing properties."

Which wasn't a complete lie. Rose hips did have natural healing properties; she just didn't have any idea whether this particular oil was actually made out of rose hips. All she'd cared about at the time was that it smelled like roses. Demi loved roses.

"In other words, I'm going to smell like a damn rose garden," he grumbled, his tone anything but appreciative of the healing properties of roses.

Her lips twitched. Oh lord, Aiden would rag on him unmercifully once he got a whiff of him. "Yes, you are. You can always take a shower after we're done. The oil will wash off."

Although, in truth the scent was likely to linger even after showering; some of the oil would sink into the skin, which was much harder to wash away. She was smiling as she glanced toward his face. This time, while her gaze avoided his pelvis, it skimmed his broad, tanned torso and stopped dead. A thick red scar ran down the middle of his chest.

The surgeon must have cracked his rib cage open to repair the damage those bullets to his back had done.

Although she didn't know the specifics, or exactly what kind of damage the bullets had done, she had known he'd spent hours in surgery, and that the bleeding had been life threatening. She hadn't known they'd cracked his chest and spread his rib cage. With a hard swallow she turned back to his knee, and her still hands. Apparently her eyes hadn't been the only part of her anatomy to stop in shock. She forced the stark image of that scar out of her mind and started back in with the light circular massaging.

The damage to his leg had been severe and fairly recent. She didn't want to put any undue pressure on the joint and add to the damage.

"I'm fine," he said, his voice surprisingly gentle.

He must have caught her staring at his scar.

"The chest shots healed in no time. It's the round to the knee . . ." His voice tightened with each word, but his face remained flat, unresponsive.

Her strokes lightened to a soothing caress. "I know."

His bark of laughter was as tight as his voice. "Of course you do." He paused, and the tightness in his tone eased slightly. "Can you tell if it's working?"

He meant the healing. Kait frowned, arching her neck as a trickle of sweat ran down her scalp. She was uncertain how to answer the question. She was hotter than hell, something she associated with a successful healing. But she was also far too attracted to her patient, and a good share of the heat was in places she'd never experienced in a healing before—like her nipples and the damp flesh between her thighs.

Pausing, she twisted to grab a towel off the coffee table and wiped the sweat from her face again. "I'm not sure."

"You feel something, though?" he pressed, bracing himself up with his elbows.

Kait shrugged. Ignoring the ache in the small of her back from the awkward position, she leaned back over his knee and started in again with that gliding massage. "Maybe. I don't know yet."

"Does it always get this hot?" he asked, something odd, almost watchful in his voice.

She concentrated hard on her fingers, even though the impulse to check out that massive erection to her right was almost impossible to ignore. "Heat is definitely a factor."

"I see," he said after long pause.

From the dryness in his voice he saw far too much, and knew exactly why she was being so vague. Which didn't surprise her. He would have picked up on her attraction to him as easily as she'd picked up on his to her. Okay, maybe not as easily—female physiology was better at hiding the response than the male body was—but still, the damn man was a SEAL. His life depended on his acute observational skills. He had to know that she was as turned on as he was.

Suddenly she was tired of skirting the issue. She was twenty-nine years old for God's sake. Sexual chemistry was a fact of life and nothing to be embarrassed about. Besides, he felt it every bit as much as she did, so it wasn't like she was alone in this attraction.

Straightening, she reached for the towel again and wiped her face. "There's always heat in a healing. But this chemistry between us makes it difficult to distinguish between the healing heat and sexual heat." She paused, locked her gaze on his face, and raised her eyebrows. "It's rather silly to pretend that there's nothing simmering between us. We both know it's there."

The words came out as a challenge, which she hadn't intended. Still, she awaited his response with curiosity. Something slid across his face, something hard and hungry, but it was gone almost instantly. He lowered his elbows back down to the couch. His shoulders followed, and when he was lying flat again, he draped his right forearm across his eyes.

"Yeah . . ." His voice trailed off. His flat, uninterested voice.

This time she couldn't stop the quick glance to his crotch. His shorts looked like they'd ballooned another inch or so. He may not have responded verbally, but he'd definitely reacted physically to her admission.

So who was skirting the issue now?

Another wave of heat rolled through her, only this time a good dose of irritation threaded through the lust. The irritation escalated as the dampness and swelling between her legs increased.

The tingles skating up and down her spine and into the nape of her neck didn't help.

She wanted him, wanted to feel that hot hard weight of him against her, inside of her. She'd wanted him for years. She wanted him more than she'd ever wanted another man.

And she was tired of him pretending she was the only one feeling this way.

He wanted her too. They both knew it. It was time he admitted it. Out loud, to her face.

And she knew just how to drag that admission out of him.

Cosky closed his eyes, his muscles rigid beneath her touch, trying to banish the memory of the heated glow suffusing her face as she'd admitted to the attraction she felt for him. He shouldn't have pushed her but, damn it, he'd expected the subtle challenge to warn her off, back them both off, set them squarely on the moral high ground.

He sure as hell hadn't expected her to grab hold of his innuendo and lob it directly at him.

As soon as her hands started up again, gliding over his knee with that slow circular sliding rhythm, he raised his arm slightly and stared at her. The folded towel lifted his head just enough to afford him a perfect view of her face. Her rosy, perspiring face.

She caught her bottom lip between her teeth, which drew his attention to her lush mouth. His belly tightened beneath a surge of rampant hunger. There was a hint of a dip in the middle of that ripe bottom lip. His mouth watered. What would it feel like beneath his tongue? What would it taste like?

What did she taste like?

Oranges? Had that citrusy scent permeated her skin?

His balls tightened at the question. And his cock throbbed like an abscessed tooth.

He tried to drag his eyes away, but they refused to budge; which was bad news when she suddenly shot him a flirty little look out of the corner of her eye. It was the kind of look a woman gave a man when she had him squarely in her crosshairs.

Or when she knew she was in his crosshairs.

It was the last look he wanted to see coming from her. Particularly now, while he was lying all but naked and fully aroused beneath her hands.

Jesus, he was in trouble. Big trouble.

A groan tried to escape his throat. He swallowed it and forced his arm back down and across his traitorous eyes. In the darkness that fell as his eyes closed, her hot, strong hands abandoned his knee and began a teasing, erotic glide up his thigh.

Every stroke, every teasing caress, brought them closer to his shorts and the storm taking place beneath them.

There was pure seduction in her hands, in their purposeful climb up his leg.

He wanted to be wrong about that. He was too damn close as it was to dragging her down to his mouth, rolling over, and driving into her like a rabid animal. It was hard enough keeping his own impulses in check, let alone hers.

Her fingers teased the hem of his shorts and hung there, a silent invitation.

He choked on another groan, took a deep breath, and opened his eyes.

She was watching him steadily, her face rosy with heat. A silent invitation in her eyes.

"No," he said, and winced as the denial came out more questioning than determined.

She tilted her head, still watching him, her hands just sitting there, burning against the top of his thigh.

"Why? You want me. I want you. We're both single. Uninvolved. It harms no one." Her words sounded collected, her question sophisticated, but her cheeks were growing rosier by the moment.

"I'm not looking to get involved."

Which would have sounded more convincing if his ass hadn't taken on a life of its own and lifted slightly, encouraging her fingers to slide beneath the hem of his shorts.

"I'm not asking for an involvement," she said, and her fingers did this hot little shimmy and scrape that sent his balls up into his belly.

She was killing him.

"I'm asking for half an hour," she added in a silky voice, her fingernails slipping beneath his shorts and lightly scraping his skin.

He gritted his teeth, a shower of sparks playing a fourth of July fireworks show up and down his spine. Half an hour? If she kept that up it would be more like two seconds, followed by a solid week.

She leaned forward slightly, her fingers exploring deeper beneath his shorts. His cock twitched in anticipation and stretched forward, eager to greet her.

"What's the harm?" she whispered, her fingers going still again.

The harm was that she'd sink into him, bond to his bone and he'd never be able to cut her out. Never feel complete without her.

He didn't need that kind of complication. Not now. Not with his whole damn life lost in complications.

He opened his mouth with the intention of saying no, of shutting the offer down hard, before it took him places he couldn't afford to go. Except, that wasn't what came out of his mouth.

"I don't have any condoms."

Where the hell had that come from? It was hardly a denial.

"I'm on the pill."

The words just hung there, throbbing in the space between them. His gaze locked on her face, on the fullness and faint trembling of her lips. Her eyes held his squarely; her gaze was bright with hunger, but pink was flooding her cheeks. And not the pink of arousal. She wasn't nearly as blasé about this as she wanted him to believe.

He hesitated while every atom in his body screamed yes and every cell in his brain screamed no.

The hesitation went on long enough to crack her confidence. Red flooded her face. Humiliation crested in her eyes. She pulled back, jerking her gaze and hands away at the same time.

He wasn't even aware of moving.

One second he was flat on his back, the next he'd jackknifed up, reached for her, and dragged her down to the sofa, where she lay atop him, draping him from hips to shoulders.

He took her mouth in an urgent, raw kiss. Her lips were soft against his, sweet—but without the citrus tang he'd expected. They tasted like . . . roses . . . which was the oddest thing, because he'd never tasted a rose before. Until her.

As his hands dove into the knot of hair pinned to the back of her head, pins went flying. A thick braid slipped down. He caught the end, stripped the band away, and combed his fingers through the bound pale tresses until a waterfall of gold spilled down, cocooning them within a veil of shimmering gold. A swath slipped over his shoulders in a silky slither, and goose bumps raced over his skull and down the back of his neck.

His heart stopped for one long minute and then leapt into double time.

The feel of her silky, cool hair sliding over his hot, sensitive skin was unbelievably erotic. Even more so than it had been in the dream.

But then, he had the unmistakable feeling that was going to be the theme song of this particular moment . . .

He opened his mouth, urging her lips apart, stopping long enough to trace that sexy dip in the middle of her bottom lip with his tongue—the slight indentation that had been driving him crazy for the past few minutes. She quivered against him and parted her lips, and her tongue darted out, brushing his own. The light erotic slide of tongue against tongue sent a pulse of electricity down his spine and into his balls.

With gentle pressure he bit her bottom lip and drew it into his mouth, suckling it. She jolted against him, and the cool curtain of hair caressed his shoulders again, inciting another shower of sparks.

If her hair felt like liquid sex, and so damn good against his skin, what would her skin feel like against his? Driven to find out, he slid his hands down to the middle of her torso, where he grabbed a fistful of fabric and dragged it up. She pushed herself up so he could strip the shirt over her head and then folded herself over him again, her brown eyes glowing and intense, her hair a tousled shimmer of gold falling along either side of his head.

He groaned as her lips found the side of his neck and latched on, suckling. Christ, each tug of her mouth against his skin sent pulses of fire straight to his cock. Each brush of her sleek, damp skin against his chest tightened his balls.

His hands felt huge and awkward as he slid them up the length of her spine, searching for her bra. He unhooked it, barely paying attention as it slipped down her arms and she lifted herself enough to shake it loose. Aching to feel the cool, sleekness of her against his palms, he trailed his hands up her spine, and around to her chest, cupping her breasts. They fit his palms perfectly—not too big, not too small, simply perfect.

She gasped as he gently squeezed the soft mounds, and shivered when he brushed his thumbs across the turgid nipples. But within seconds his focus changed. How would those delicate mounds feel against his tongue? Inside his mouth? Did she taste like roses or oranges there?

Driven to find out, he slipped his palms back around to her spine, sliding them down and down until they dipped beneath the thin cotton of her sweats to grasp the cool globes of her ass. She arched against him, her breathing quickening, her heart pounding against his until he could hear it in his head—connecting them.

Her mouth swooped down and fastened on his, her tongue plunging between his lips in a parody of lovemaking—the thrust and retreat, thrust and rub. Cosky's lungs seized. His head swam as her tongue fucked his.

And Jesus, an explosion of roses and oranges surrounded him, enveloping him in a scented bubble of pure sensation. When her hips pressed down, grinding against his, the glimmering veil of hair draping them glided over his hot, tight skin. His entire body clenched, and he came close—far too close—to losing it completely right then. Right there.

He needed to get the rest of her clothes off her. Bare skin to bare skin. Muscle to muscle. Sex to sex.

After a slow squeeze of those perfect cheeks, he slid his hand back up to her waist and eased her thin pants, along with her panties, down her hips. Without taking her mouth from his, she lifted her hips, allowing him to push the cloth down her thighs. She did the rest by stretching out across him, breast to chest, thigh to thigh, as she kicked off her pants. When her knee bumped his, something niggled at him, something important, but he lost the thread as her hands tightened around the waistband of his shorts and tugged.

He dragged his mouth from hers and growled softly, "Not yet."

She laughed, her fingers sliding beneath his shorts. Swearing, he captured her hands and dragged them around her back, and pinned them there.

The instant he felt that hot damp clasp around his cock, he'd lose it. The urge to roll and bury himself inside her silky channel was already digging into him, more urgent by the second, and that was with the thin layer of cotton between them. She needed to be ready for him. Ready to let go and fly.

She wasn't there yet.

But she would be. Soon.

She punished him with a nip to the side of his neck, followed by the slow soothing sweep of her tongue.

"Think of where else I could be licking you," she whispered into his ear, just before she took the lobe in her teeth and tugged.

Jesus Christ.

His entire body quaked beneath her as an image of her mouth locked around his cock slammed into his mind. He drove the image away and took her mouth again, while his hands glided over to the cheeks of her ass. He traced the crescent between the twin moons and widened his fingers, squeezing and releasing, squeezing and releasing, matching the rhythm of his hands to the plunges of his tongue. She did another of those sultry shimmies, her pelvis brushing against his, which drained the blood from his brain into his crotch, leaving him light-headed above and throbbing.

And then her legs separated, falling alongside his, until the damp flesh between her thighs was riding the bulge beneath his shorts.

He groaned, his back arching, pressing his cock into her. The movement dragged her breasts up. Her nipples brushed his hot skin, bringing another flush of heat. With one last squeeze, he shifted his grip to her hips and lifted her, dragging her forward until her breasts, with their engorged, dark nipples, were even with his mouth. She froze when he licked the right nipple—stopped breathing as he caught the peaked flesh between his teeth, gently bore down, and tugged. The next tug brought a choked cry.

When he drew her nipple into his mouth and suckled hard, she writhed against him, rubbing herself harder and harder against his crotch.

To ease the need burning between them, he pushed a hand between their hips and worked it between her legs. She was hot and wet and ready for him—her flesh quivering against his fingertips. He parted the damp folds of her sex and stroked her opening, feeling the clench of her around his invading finger. A shiver shook her and ran through him. He went dizzy. Hungrier than he'd ever been before in his life.

Ever.

With anyone.

He penetrated her with just the tip of his fingers and felt the wet, sleek flesh cinch around his fingernail, caressing him, trying to draw his finger deeper inside her. With a keening cry, she threw back her head, and pressed herself hard against his hand, forcing his finger deeper inside the tight, wet clasp of her sheath.

Just the thought of that tight, soaked space clamping around his cock almost sent him into hyperdrive. With a deep breath, he froze, every muscle in his body tense as he battled the urge to roll and drive into her.

His cock swelled to the point of pain and his balls drew tight against the base of his penis. He swore, forcing his body to heel. Once he had his muscles under his control again, he released a slow breath and dragged his finger out of her.

She greeted the withdrawal with a moan of discontent.

He shifted beneath her, forcing his hand deeper between her legs, and worked two fingers inside, while brushing her clit with his thumb.

She screamed, pressing hard against his hand. With each thrust of his finger in her wet, swollen sheath and suckle of his mouth against her wet, swollen breast, he could feel the tension in her tightening. Her hips rocked urgently against his, constantly stroking his swollen, throbbing cock.

A tingle started in the base of his spine, spreading up and out. Jesus, he was out of time. As close to the cliff as it was possible to get without flying.

He scraped her clit with his thumb, thrust both fingers into her as deep as they'd go, and stroked the walls of her twitching sheath. She screamed again, her body arching.

With her cry still ringing in his ears, he rolled, dragging her beneath him. With one quick movement he shoved his shorts out of the way, pushed her legs wider, settled between them, and nudged his cock into her wet, tight opening.

He tried to take care, to ease into her, to give her time to adjust to his girth and hardness. But she didn't let him. Her legs rose, curled around his hips, and squeezed. She arched up, driving his penis deeper and shattering the remnants of his control.

With one savage thrust, he buried himself completely inside her.

She came apart beneath him, her body bowed and shaking. Her face a tight grimace, caught somewhere between ecstasy and pain. Her sheath clamping and releasing, clamping and releasing, stroking his cock from base to head.

Groaning, he pulled back and thrust again, and then again. Driving into her.

Dimly he heard her scream again, her body rigid beneath him as her orgasm rolled through them both, and her wet, tight sheath clamped down hard on his cock, milking his own release.

He bucked above her, his hips hammering. His heart hammering. His blood hammering. Caught in turbulence unlike anything he'd ever known before, he emptied himself into her convulsing depths. Boneless and spent, his lungs grabbing great gusts of air, he collapsed onto her limp body.

For what might have been forever he drifted in and out of consciousness, more at peace than he could ever remember feeling, the feel of her wet, soft body beneath him as natural as breathing.

But as his body stirred and his mind awakened and his cock started to harden inside her, unease crept in, infecting the contentment.

He wanted her again.

He'd barely recovered from that first bout of earthshaking sex and he already craved a second one. Already craved her. And it would only get worse. Instinctively he knew that, knew that every taste of her would increase the craving.

Like any hard-core drug, the more you used, the stronger the craving, and the harder to walk away.

Damn it, he should never have given into the need and taken that first taste.

Boneless and replete, Kait stretched beneath the heavy weight of Cosky's body. He twitched above her, an involuntary spasm that brought a satisfied smile to her lips. She wasn't the only one still recovering from their trip to the stars. Still smiling, she turned her face into the sweaty side of his neck and nuzzled his damp skin.

He was so beautiful like this—his hard, heavy weight pressing her into the couch, his face flushed and sweaty and oddly vacant as though he'd dropped all his shields. Even the hard muscles covering her felt lax and lazy—with the exception of the muscle still lodged inside her. That particular part of him was growing less lazy by the second.

In fact, it was growing darn right *hard.*

The realization he wanted her again so soon widened her smile. The glow of contentment brightened to brilliance.

She'd been dreaming about this, about him, for years, but the reality blew the dreams to smithereens. Nothing had come close to the perfection of this moment. The perfection of him, of her, of the way they'd come together. Of how perfect they fit, like pieces to a puzzle.

What a shame it had taken her so many years to step past her pride and comfort zone and reach for what she wanted.

She sighed and kissed the side of his damp neck, the salty taste of him tangy on her lips, and he hardened to full glory inside her. Her smile melted into a silly grin. He was certainly determined to make up for lost time, which worked perfectly with her plans for the rest of the day, the week—heck, the rest of her life.

He shifted on top of her, and she gasped slightly as his heavy body drove the air from her lungs. For a second he seemed to press himself deeper within her, anchoring her to the couch, but then he froze.

"I'm fine," she assured him, as he suddenly pushed himself up and off her body.

He didn't ease back down as her arms tightened around his shoulders. Instead, he pulled back hard, breaking her hold. Her smile vanished. Unease stirred.

The sense of peace dissipated as he pulled out of her, as though her contentment had depended completely on that connection linking them. As he straightened beside the couch, an icy draft swept over her and she longed for a blanket, or a sheet—anything to guard against the sudden chill.

"What's wrong?" she asked.

"Nothing." He eased back from the couch with slow, careful movements, as though he wasn't sure his knee would accept his weight. "You've had your half hour. So we're even, right? That's what you asked for."

It took a second or two for the words to hit her. But when they did, they hit hard.

"*What?*" Kait sat up, her voice rising. She angled her head to get a look at his face. It was hard. Flat. His gaze was hooded, cold chips of silver staring back at her.

As though she were a terrorist he was interrogating. The enemy.

Or maybe nobody. Nobody to him at all.

"You asked for half an hour, of sex, for the healing," he said patiently, as though he were reminding her.

That icy draft streaming over the couch penetrated her skin, sinking through muscle and bone, settling into the core of her—numbing her from the inside out.

He'd made love to her because of the healing.

He'd paid for her healing with sex?

She thought back to her banter, to her words—could it have sounded like she was bartering sex for services?

A slow shake of her head cleared her mind. No. No way. He knew exactly what she'd meant. He'd have told her to go to hell if he'd misunderstood her offer.

So why? Why would he say something so cruel?

She stared at his distant, flat face and instinctively knew the answer.

Because their moment together hadn't meant anything special to him, and his dick aside, he wasn't interested in taking the relationship any further. The sex must not be worth the hassle and with Aiden as his new roommate, she could make things very uncomfortable between them.

As if she'd ever do something like that. But then he had no intention of getting to know her and finding that out for himself. Instead, he'd taken the easy out, and tried to drive her away.

The stupid bastard.

"That's overkill, don't you think?" She swung her legs to the side of the couch and stood. The dampness chilling her skin didn't feel sexy any longer. It was uncomfortable, unclean.

"What?" He stepped to the side, skirting the coffee table to give her more room, maintaining a cautious distance between them.

Probably afraid she was going to rush him, declare her undying love.

The stupid, stupid, moronic bastard.

"Throwing up that big red stop sign." She forced her voice to levity, even though every muscle in her body, including her throat, wanted to shake.

She tried to ignore their nakedness, and the wetness staining her body as well as his. "I told you I wasn't looking for a relationship."

Too bad her foolish emotions hadn't believed that any more than he had.

He frowned, and took another step back. An emotion she didn't try to identify slipped across his face. "So we're on the same page."

She reached up and caught her hair, lifting it up and over her back. When his gaze dropped to her breasts and froze there, she drew her shoulders back and thrust them out. Let him take a good look at them. Memorize them.

Because he was never going to see them again.

"I'm going to take a shower. You know where the door is." She didn't try to hide her nakedness as she stalked across the living room toward her bedroom and the master bath. She had nothing to be ashamed of. Nothing.

Well, with the possible exception of wasting even one brain cell on the asshole standing naked in her living room.

"That's it?" Something dangerous threaded his voice. Apparently he didn't appreciate the dismissal. Wasn't that just too bad?

She paused in the mouth of the hallway leading to her bedroom and half turned, shooting him a sarcastic smile. "Well, unless the healing doesn't work, in which case I should probably pay you."

His thick, black eyebrows snapped together and a storm gathered across his face.

"At the very least, I should thank you," she added with another insincere smile.

She suspected, from the way his eyes darkened to thunderstorm gray, that he thought she was referring to the sex. She hadn't been.

She'd meant that since he'd so completely gutted her childish crush, she could move on with her love life. Stop measuring every man she dated by the yardstick of Marcus Simcosky.

"You know where the door is," she said again, since he didn't seem interested in dressing and leaving.

Without looking at him again, she headed down the hall toward her shower.

Aiden accused her of being too picky. He claimed the romance novels she enjoyed had instilled within her an unrealistic expectation of men.

Bullshit.

Her favorite books hadn't stopped her from accepting third or fourth dates. The memory of Marcus Simcosky had. Every time her past relationships had deepened, Cosky would creep into her mind. She'd compare the intensity of her attraction to her current flame, to that brief interlude in the doorway of Aiden's hospital room. The attraction had been so incredibly intense. So she'd ended up comparing every man she'd dated to Lt. Marcus Simcosky and the sparks that had flared between them—and her dates had all fallen short.

She adjusted the taps in the glass-enclosed shower and stepped beneath the spray, tilting her face to the hot rush of water.

Finally, she'd discovered the man behind those closed, silver eyes.

Well, she wasn't impressed. Oh yeah, the sex had been mind-blowing, but the sex wasn't worth the effort of putting up with the jackass.

As she closed her eyes and let the hot spray cleanse the sweat from her body, she pretended the heated, salty wetness washing her cheeks was from the shower rinsing the sweat away.

Chapter Five

Sunlight bounced off the concrete, momentarily blinding Jillian. She grimaced, her pace slowing, the silver haze stinging her eyes. A few frantic blinks later, and the shimmering gauze coalesced into a beam of radiant white, haloing the child before her in a bubble of incandescence.

Collin.

Her sweet Collie Bear.

His gold hair looked almost silver in the spotlight. The flop of his curls more pronounced as the stroller rattled over cracks in the concrete. A thick, sobbing wail drifted back to her.

That familiar cry flooded her heart.

Collin, Collin, does Collin ever stop bawling? Russ's ghostly singsong voice echoed through her mind.

Don't cry, baby, don't cry. Mama's coming.

Jillian increased her pace. When the stroller suddenly stopped in front of one of the restaurants, Jillian slammed into the tall, thin woman behind the handle. She reeled from the collision, catching herself by bracing a hand against the hot glass of the window beside her. The thick smell of barbeque cramped her stomach.

"Oh, I'm so sorry," a female voice stammered. "I didn't know anyone was . . . are you okay?" The woman's tone shifted from apologetic to concerned. "You're white as a ghost. Did I hurt you? Maybe you should sit down?"

"Collin." Jillian's voice was rough from lack of use. She stepped around the blurry feminine figure, every cell in her body focused on the chubby body strapped in the stroller.

Round arms, giving sticky hugs. Cupid mouth burbling kisses. "Where's mama's kiss, Collie Bear? Mama wants her kiss."

"Who? You're crying." The woman's voice was a faint buzz behind her. "Do you want me to call someone?"

"Mama's here, Collin. Mama's here." Jillian bent over the stroller. Her hand shook as she stroked a plump, wet cheek.

"Her name's Emma." The voice behind her tightened and the stroller inched back. "Look, why don't you let me call someone for you. You don't look well."

Jillian took a step after the retreating stroller, and reached for the straps holding the child in place.

"Whoa." This time the stroller took a big leap back. "What the hell are you doing?"

The child let loose with another hiccupping sob.

"It's okay, Collie Bear." Jillian lurched forward, reaching for him. "Momma's here."

"Her name's *Emma*. And you're *not* her mother. You need to leave. *Now*." The woman's voice rose shrilly as Jillian reached for the child. "I'm serious. If you don't leave right now, I'm calling the cops."

"Dance with Mama, Collie Bear. Mama wants to dance." Swooping down, with tickles and kisses. Lilting burbles of laughter. The shimmering flop of golden curls while the living room twirled around them.

Her arms aching to hold that warm, heavy weight again, Jillian unlatched the buckle connecting the stroller's straps.

A shrill scream pierced the air and the stroller jerked back hard. "Help. Someone help. She's crazy. She's trying to take my baby."

Jillian's thin arms strained to hold the stroller in place long enough to lift its precious cargo free.

A tall, slender body shoved her aside and wedged itself between Jillian and the stroller. "She's not yours! What is wrong with you?"

Hands clamped onto Jillian's arm and yanked. Already off balance, the tug swung her headfirst into the wall of the restaurant. An ugly crack sounded as her forehead made contact, and then everything went silent—a hushed, marshmallow-thick silence.

She straightened slowly, her body swaying, that odd cotton fuzziness in her head expanding until her entire mind felt stuffed with white fluff. Within that dense numbness a faint buzzing grew, an electronic whine that seemed to come from everywhere at once. A brilliant white light shimmered at the edge of her vision, undulated like waves against the sand.

The buzz grew stronger, but within the steady hum words rose and fell.

"Tried to take my baby. She's crazy. Somebody call the cops."

"I'm calling an ambulance, she's bleeding pretty bad. What the hell's she wearing? It's eighty-five degrees out."

Jillian focused on the steady drone, recognizing more and more words with each passing second.

"You alright, lady?" a male voice rumbled. "Your head's bleeding. Why don't I take that wool cape off you? You're courting heatstroke with that thing." His voice wavered in and out, growing more distant with each word.

She glanced around vaguely, her body feather light, and realized a small crowd had gathered.

"The police are on their way," someone said.

Police?

The word flushed the haziness from Jillian's mind. The police couldn't be trusted.

The crowd around her shifted and a stroller came into view. Jillian strained to focus on it, only to find the seat empty. A soft, stuttering sob drew her attention to the right, to a slender dark-haired woman rocking the chunky body of a child. A child with tousled gold hair.

Collin.

She took a small step forward, but something tightened around her wrist, holding her in place. The woman twisted, speaking in rushed fragments to someone on her right and the child's face came into view.

The haze blanketing her mind dissipated. The bright white light surrounding her darkened. The ground went hard and icy beneath her feet and the truth crashed over her in all its ugly, unbreakable agony.

The child was blond. Blue-eyed. Stocky. A wailer.

But it wasn't Collin.

It wasn't her baby.

Collin.

His name whirled in her mind.

He was gone. Her sweet Collie Bear all gone. Just like the rest of her babies, never to come home again.

The reality almost drove her to her knees; the agony felt so fresh and raw that blood-drenched night could have taken place only moments before.

She bent at the waist, a low groan breaking from her.

"Hang in there," the man beside her said, with a quick squeeze to her wrist. "The ambulance should be here any minute."

"Yeah, so should the police," someone else said.

It was only then Jillian realized the man beside here was holding her arm—a chain anchoring her in place, ready to hand her over to the police.

The bastard—he couldn't be trusted.

None of them could be trusted.

One violent yank of her arm and she was free. She fled toward her car, her heart beating so hard it pounded in her ears, drowning out the sounds of pursuit. If she was being pursued. After a moment, when hands didn't close over her shoulders, she slowed to a walk and half turned, glancing behind her. The small knot of people next to the stroller had thinned, but nobody was following her.

A couple of deep breaths pushed the panic aside and her mind went to work again.

How long had she been lost in that awful haze? She glanced toward the far right of the parking lot, but Marcus Simcosky's truck was gone.

Damn it. Damn it. She'd lost her chance.

Another deep breath. Followed by another.

She pushed the frustration aside. She'd have to start over. Waiting along Silver Strand Boulevard for one of those bastards to pass by was still her best bet for tracking them down. Her strategy had worked once; it would work again. She just had to be patient.

She'd head back to her original parking place and wait.

A police cruiser pulled into the mall's entrance as she pulled out. She held her breath, her hands tight around the wheel, and kept her eyes straight ahead. The cruiser passed by without slowing down and Jillian dared to breathe again.

With luck, everyone had been too far away to get her license plate number, or a description of her car.

She backtracked along the same route Marcus Simcosky had taken her, hoping against hope that she might catch sight of his vehicle again. When a black Ford truck in an apartment parking lot came into view, she slowed. Simcosky had been driving a similar truck. She pulled into the lot, and eased up behind the vehicle. The plate numbers were the same. Sheer disbelief gripped her. Unbelievable. She'd found him again. What were the odds of that?

A grim smile bloomed.

Did he live in the apartment complex? Or was he visiting someone?

Not that it mattered. All she had to do was park where he wouldn't notice her and wait. Sooner or later he had to come out.

Robert Biesel's hand tightened around the Coke bottle until the plastic crackled, as he watched Jillian Michaels's monstrosity of a car pull into the parking lot of one of the ritzier apartment complexes in town.

What the hell was the damn woman up to now?

Earlier, she'd tried to kidnap a baby. A baby, for Pete's sake, as if that would go unnoticed. To top the insane behavior off, she'd tried to snatch the infant in front of the child's mother, or nanny, or whoever was pushing the stroller.

Really? Was she that much of a bimbo? His cell rang as he pulled over and parked along the side of the boulevard to keep an eye on her. He glanced at the caller ID and scowled. Phillip. His tag partner must have finally realized Simcosky wasn't going to show. Time to put on his dancing shoes. He hit the talk button.

"Hey," he said casually. "You put our baby to bed?"

A snort sounded on the other end. "I wish. Where did you drop him?"

"Third and Orange, he was headed your way." He sharpened his tone. "You lost him?"

"I didn't lose him." Phillip's voice tightened defensively. "He never showed."

"Son of a bitch." Robert let the words hang there. "We better start a grid. You take Orange east. I'll take west."

Sending him on a fruitless search east of Orange Avenue would keep Phillip both busy, and distant.

"How much longer are we supposed to keep up with this waste of time?" Phillip asked, his voice still defensive, but annoyance had crept in as well. "We've been at it for months. It's clear the poor bastard's life revolves around doctors' appointments and physical therapy. He's not meeting deep throat in the middle of the night. If any of these poor bastards had an inkling of what the bosses have in the works, we'd know by now. There's a ton of money being wasted on these clowns."

Robert would have agreed with him thirty minutes ago, before Jillian Michaels had attempted to hook up with one of the SEALs they'd been assigned to monitor.

"Not our money, not our worry," Robert said. "Besides, the job's putting your kids through college, so what are you complaining about?"

"It's getting old, that's—"

"Tell you what," Robert snapped. "You explain that to the bosses, and see what their take is."

Dead silence greeted the suggestion.

"Yeah, I thought so. Call if you spot him." Robert ended the call as Jillian stopped behind a black truck and idled there.

He couldn't see the make or model of the pickup truck from his vantage point, but the color and frame looked too much like Marcus Simcosky's to be a coincidence.

What the hell this meant was another big black question mark. Phillip was right, they'd been watching the guy for months and this was the first time he'd visited this place. And then there was Jillian.

She pulled forward and disappeared behind a cluster of parked cars. He eased back into the street to get a better look. As he drove past the entrance to the parking lot, he caught a glimpse of her backing into one of the last parking places at the very end of the lot. He slowed his sedan to a crawl, watching intensely. Her car didn't move.

He glanced at the black truck and frowned. It looked like she was staking the truck out, which meant she'd hang around until Simcosky appeared. He scanned the entrance to the apartment building; lots of people were going in and out, but none of them were Simcosky.

The number of people hanging around the parking lot made it impossible to grab Jillian and force her into his car . . . but then again . . . he didn't need to.

He could use her car instead.

She'd set up her stakeout next to the tennis courts. But the parking lot curved around to the left and behind the apartment complex. A side street flanked the building ahead. There was a good chance that side street had access to the parking lot as well. If he pulled around the block, he could park back there, and use the trees next to the tennis courts for cover as he made his way to Jillian's sedan.

All the windows in Jillian's monstrosity were rolled down, so it would be easy to access her car. It made more sense to slip into the passenger seat beside Jillian, stick a gun in her ribs, and force her to drive away—rather than drag her, kicking and screaming, out of her car and into his, while every eye in the neighborhood watched.

He accelerated, scanning the building's entrance as he drove past. Still no sign of Simcosky.

Considering how slow the man moved these days, Robert would be in Jillian's car and well on his way to clearing this mess up before Simcosky made it back to his truck.

There was still the question of why the two were meeting. But he could cut that explanation from Jillian before he took the last of her lives.

It took maybe a minute to drive around the corner and pull into the driveway behind the parking lot. He grabbed his weapon from the glove box, and shoved it behind his belt, draping his T-shirt over it. No sense in alarming the natives.

Exiting his car, he crossed the parking lot to the tennis courts and casually headed south along the winding sidewalk toward Jillian's car. With luck she'd be focused on the apartment entrance instead of the park and wouldn't even realize he was on scene until it was too late.

He was twenty feet from Jillian's parking space when he realized the car was empty.

Where the hell was she? He stopped, did a slow scan of the area, and found her sitting on a bench along the side of the building.

Damn it, this new development totally blew any shot his plan had of working. She'd see him the minute she headed back to the car. What the hell was she doing over there anyway? But he realized the significance of her positioning, moments later, when a young couple strolled into view, crossed the parking lot, and climbed into a souped-up sports car.

Anyone who left the apartment complex for either the park or their car was likely to pass her. If they were headed to the park, she'd be right there waiting. He glanced toward the black pickup. However, if they were headed to the parking lot, they'd also pass her.

If this wasn't a friendly meeting—which judging from Lt. Simcosky's face earlier and her positioning now, it wasn't—than her position was key. If she waited in her car, she'd be directly in his line of sight. However, if she waited on that bench around the corner, when he passed her, his back would be to her, which gave her a slight advantage.

The strategic position surprised the shit out of him.

Who would have guessed the terrified little mouse he'd grabbed all those months ago even knew how to implement such strategy.

Just what the hell did the woman have planned for Simcosky?

Cosky watched the sexy sway of Kait's ass as she stalked across the living room.

Long after she disappeared down the hallway, he continued standing there, his dick at full mast, the smell of sex, sweat, and roses heavy in the air. His heart raced as though he were caught in an Op gone south, sprinting five klicks to the evac chopper while live rounds and mortar shells lit the hills around him.

He felt off balance. Changed. Different in a way that couldn't be seen, only sensed. Because of her. Because of what they'd shared on that damn couch.

Because he wanted her again. Already. Only worse, much worse than he had before.

This raw urgency wasn't like any kind of need he'd experienced before. He was thirty-five years old for Christ's sake. He'd wanted women before. But not like this. Not with such primal craving. This urgency pushed past lust into obsession.

"Fuck." He breathed the word more than spoke it and scrubbed his palms down his face.

He was almost afraid to take a step, afraid his legs would just keep walking and follow her into the shower, where his hands would take over, exploring that wet, lush body with soapy fervor. Afraid his brain would give leave to his body's insistence and he'd pin her to the shower wall, hammering into her until they were both spent and sated. Until the need was assuaged.

If it could be assuaged.

And that question—whether this obsession could even be satisfied—was what kept his feet planted. What kept his dick in the living room when every muscle in his body ached to follow her into that shower.

His first taste of her hadn't eased the need. It had only made the craving worse. Showed him what he was missing. How much worse would that craving be after a second taste? A third? If he followed her into that shower, would he ever make it out again, at least without her by his side?

The last thing he could afford was a second obsession. The teams were enough.

Besides, there were other considerations.

She was Aiden's sister, Commander Winchester's daughter. She was one of their own, which made her off limits to drive-bys.

And he wasn't willing to offer anything more.

Sure as hell not now, while his life was in the shitter and he had a big red DOJ bull's-eye taped to his back.

She'd grown up in the shadow of team life. His mind flashed back to the drawn mask of her face at Winchester's funeral, to the worry and exhaustion in her eyes when she'd visited Aiden in the hospital. She'd lost her father to a mission gone wrong. Almost lost her brother. Could still lose her brother. He wasn't going to give her another person to spend her life worrying over.

Memory after memory flashed through his mind. Of his mother. Of her tight, tense silences every time Dad was on duty. Of the fear in her eyes the two times somber-eyed police officials had rung their doorbell. He'd spent his childhood watching constant worry drain the exuberance from someone he loved. No way in hell was he spending his adulthood knowing he was doing the same to some other unlucky woman.

The teams had been his choice. His alone. He'd known the sacrifices they'd require. It was bad enough knowing his mother feared every deployment. He wasn't going to commit to a woman, knowing she'd spend more of her life with him in fear than in ecstasy.

Kait already had Aiden to fret over. One was enough.

Of course from the way she'd stomped out of the room, she sure as hell wouldn't be worrying over him anytime soon. Cosky grimaced as he headed for his clothes. She hadn't deserved that nasty crack. He needed to apologize. But he'd do so at a distance, through a text message, where he couldn't see her or smell her or touch her . . .

It didn't occur to him until he was tying his shoelaces that his knee wasn't aching. He rose slowly to his feet, surprised to find it stable beneath him. None of that chronic stabbing pain, or frustrating wobble. After a few tentative steps, he stared down at it in disbelief.

Hell, it felt downright normal.

Preapocalypse.

He turned slowly, staring at the hall that led to the bathroom.

Was it possible . . . no, she'd barely massaged it. Hell, she'd spent ten times as much time on his back. It was after he'd turned over and she'd started working on his knee that things had gone south. She'd spent maybe two or three minutes tops massaging the joint before they'd completely lost track of why he was stretched across her couch.

Another step and still no pain.

Maybe the massage had simply loosened the muscles, so the joint wasn't as tight and thus less achy. After all, Aiden claimed it had taken weeks of massages for his back to heal. Weeks.

Except, it was more than the absence of that constant throbbing ache. It was the absence of that piercing, molten agony and the leg's sudden stability. Neither of which could be explained by loosened muscles since they'd had nothing to do with musculature.

Jesus Christ.

Was it possible?

He turned to stare across the room. He could hardly ask her if this was normal. At least not now. Not with the way things stood between them. Wouldn't that be just his luck, to drive away the only person who might be able to set his life back on course?

Fate definitely wasn't done fucking with him.

The smartest course of action would be to vacate her apartment and let things settle down. He'd call her in a couple days, apologize, and feel her out about getting another massage. Maybe he wouldn't even need another. Maybe this first one had fixed him up just fine.

It sure felt great at the moment. He'd forgotten what it felt like to take a step without that debilitating pain, to put his foot down and trust it was going to stay there and prop him up.

He was almost to her apartment door when it occurred to him that he had no idea if she expected payment. And if so, how much. He froze with his hand on the apartment's doorknob. After that crack of his, leaving her cash was likely to be misconstrued. He made a mental note to broach this subject too—later, from a safe distance.

Or better yet, he would ask Aiden when he got home. Assuming his new roommate wasn't already wheels up.

It seemed to take forever for the elevator to reach the lobby. By the time it arrived the interior smelled like roses. The damn smell was so strong his eyes watered, not that the two young women who smiled at him and giggled as he walked through the door seemed to mind.

One sniffed the air and smiled to her friend. "Don't you love the new air freshener they're using?"

The honeymoon stage with his knee lasted all the way through the lobby. There was no doubt Kait had helped his leg, it hadn't felt this good since before he'd awoken in Sacred Heart's intensive care unit.

If it felt this much better after one massage, how would it feel after two? Three? Half a dozen?

Assuming—after what had happened between them, which was followed by his asinine comment—she'd be willing to *give* him another massage. He sure as hell wouldn't blame her if she slapped him silly and told him to stay the hell away. And if, by some chance, she was more forgiving than most women would be under the circumstances; what were the odds they could keep their clothes on once those hot, sexy hands of hers touched down? Judging by what had happened today, not very good. There was a damn good chance he'd end up on top and inside her again.

Which would pretty much negate any chance of avoiding this growing obsession.

Bloody hell.

Talk about damned if you do, damned if you don't.

The heat hit him like a hook to the jaw the moment he stepped through the lobby doors. Either he was getting soft, or the temperature had skyrocketed since he'd parked his truck.

He grunted in response to the coffee girl's breathy good-bye and strode—*strode, by God, instead of limped, or hobbled*—down the hot pavement while the sun baked the top of his head. The first twinge struck as he stepped off the curb into the parking lot. But even then, as twinges went it was light. Okay, so her massage hadn't had a lasting effect. It was already regressing. But from Aiden's account, this was normal. It took multiple massages to heal the injury completely.

He'd almost reached his truck and was craving air-conditioning and a cold beer, when quick, soft footsteps sounded behind him. A woman. Closing fast. Probably Kait determined to give him some well-deserved hell. But when he turned, he found the strange, unkempt woman from the Coronado Ferry Landing's mall.

What the hell?

How had she even found him?

She was headed directly for him; there was no question of that. He dug in his pocket for his keys, and backed slowly toward his truck.

On his second step, his foot landed on a rock and his knee buckled. That familiar stabbing agony pierced the joint, and his knee wobbled beneath him. Apparently the honeymoon was over and at the worst possible time.

He glanced at her hands, or at least where her hands should have been, as he worked his keys loose and hobbled back another couple steps. They were stuffed inside that oddball cloak she wore, which set his instincts humming.

It was pure insanity to wear a wool garment in the middle of a heat wave. But her face wasn't red or sweating. It was white, drawn, and resolute.

Unlike his face, which was sweating like hell. He ignored the urge to swipe at his stinging eyes and glanced at her hands again, his danger sense screaming as the wool garment tented slightly above her waist, as though she'd raised the hand in her pocket.

She had something in that pocket.

And it was pointed at him.

Without taking his eyes off her, he slid the key into the driver's door of his truck by touch and eased the door open. He'd locked his Glock in the glove box before heading up to Kait's, so the gun was out of play—unless he wanted to turn his back on this strange woman and lean across the seat.

She stepped closer as he opened the door farther.

"Lieutenant Simcosky?" There was a dark, ugly rasp to her voice.

He stepped behind the open door. Every nerve on alert, he watched her. "You are?"

The tented portion of her cape rose again.

In the old days he would have rushed her, taken her to the ground, and pinned her there while he searched those woolen pockets. Frustration surged, throbbing in his head. He would have chanced such an offense earlier, too, before he stepped on that rock. But damn it, his knee was too unstable at the moment. It could collapse on him any moment, leaving him vulnerable to attack. Focusing on the woman, he shoved the frustration of what he couldn't do aside and concentrated on what he could do.

A gust of wind brought the stench of unwashed clothes and flesh.

Her brown eyes were fixed on his face—livid with something close to rage, or maybe hatred. Or maybe both.

This was personal. But why?

"I don't know you," he said slowly, afraid the slightest thing could set her off. The door was little protection against a bullet and he'd bet his trident she had a gun in that pocket.

"I know you. I know what you are. A lying, murdering bastard." Her voice thickened, deepening with rage as she took a giant step toward him. "This is for my babies."

That last step had brought her within range of the truck's door. The thick metal would act as both shield and weapon. He shifted his weight over to his good leg, and dropped as low as he could, watching the tension grip her shoulders. As the hem of her poncho lifted, he slammed the car door into her.

"And for Russ," she added just before the door rammed into her, eliciting a breathless *oomph*.

A shot rang out along with the simultaneous *plunk* of a round striking the car door. Cosky drew the door back and drove it into her again, as hard as he could. If he could break an arm or shoulder she wouldn't be able to lift that gun.

Another muffled gunshot. The metallic *plunk* as the bullet hit the door. Burning cloth scorched the air.

From the report, and the lack of penetrating power, the weapon sounded like a .22. But Christ only knew how many rounds she had left. If she went for a head shot, or stepped around the door he was fucked.

She must have read his mind. With another ragged scream, she took a couple of steps back and sidled toward the front of the door.

Son of a bitch. Cosky shifted to meet her. No choice now, he'd have to take a leap of faith and hope he took her down before he took a round. He gathered himself and lunged as she cleared the door.

His knee chose that moment to buckle, throwing him off balance.

Goddamn it!

As he went down, he made a mad grab for the door handle. The gun coughed. Glass exploded above and behind him.

Across the parking lot, toward the tennis courts, someone shouted. The woman started violently and turned. Cosky got his good leg under him, shoved himself up, and gathered himself to take her down.

Suddenly she backed up fast, hustling out of his range. Still staring across the parking lot, she shrieked. It was a scream unlike anything he'd heard before. A wild, raw cry of primal agony and sheer, vicious rage. She raised the gun, pointing it toward the tennis courts. Shot after shot rang out.

The scream died. In its wake came the hollow clicks of an empty barrel, as she continued pulling the trigger.

Bracing himself against the door, Cosky hobbled forward, swearing when he stepped on another pebble and his leg twisted beneath him. The woman started and spun to face him.

Her face was twisted, lips slightly apart. Huge, wild eyes locked on him. Her mouth opened wide, but nothing emerged but a hoarse, ragged puff of breath. The gun rose, centered on his chest.

Click.

Click.

Click.

Cosky let go of the door and lurched forward. She jumped back. *Click. Click.* He chanced another wobbling step. With another of those soundless, breathless screams, she threw the gun at his head. He ducked, and it whistled harmlessly overhead.

By the time he straightened, she'd taken flight. Horns blared, tires squealing as she dodged traffic and sprinted across the boulevard in front of the apartment complex. She entered the park across the street at a dead run, her woolen cape, or cloak, or whatever it was, flapping behind her like a muddy flag.

Bending over, he kneaded his screaming knee. That freakishly strange episode had just unraveled every damn bit of good Kait's healing had done. He was back to stage one again: throbbing, stabbing, and unstable.

As helpless as an infant.

He watched her cut across the park and disappear down a side street. Frustration joined the furnace billowing away inside him, until he felt like he might explode from the pressure.

"Hey, Mister," a weedy voice yelled from his right. "Are you okay?"

Cosky lifted his forearm to swipe the sweat from his forehead and eyes. A tall, gangly kid barely out of high school jogged up to him, and skidded to a stop in front of the pickup.

"I'm fine." Cosky scanned the side street the woman had disappeared down. She was probably long gone by now. This time he didn't bother to shove the irritation aside. It solidified across his chest, in a seething quagmire that threatened to suffocate him.

Damn it, he should have had her. She'd been an amateur. Bum knee or not, he should have been able to subdue her.

Scowling, he flapped his shirt a couple of times to try to cool his overheated body. "Who was she?" Mr. Chatty bounced from foot to foot, excitement boiling off him. The heat didn't seem to affect him in the slightest. "Why was she shooting at us?"

Us? Cosky gave the kid a quick once-over. This was who his mystery attacker had turned her rage on? Why? The kid was as harmless.

"You see her before?" Cosky asked.

"No. You?"

"No." As he dug in the pocket of his sweats for his cell phone, he ran through the encounter in his head. She sure as hell seemed to know him, though. Or thought she had. She'd called him by name, accused him of being a *lying, murdering bastard.* She'd said the attack was for her *babies.*

What the hell did he have to do with her babies?

He frowned, absently rubbing his temple against his shoulder to wipe away an annoying trickle of sweat.

She'd mentioned another name too. She'd said *Russ.*

He froze as the name finally registered. *Russ*?

Had she been talking about Branson? Russ Branson was the only person he knew who went by that first name. Could this strange woman be connected to Branson?

"This is for my babies."

Her voice rang in his head. The livid rage. The echo of loss. Of grief. Had Branson been the father of her children?

He mulled her words over as he dialed nine-one-one and reported the shooting. Another question occurred to him as he disconnected the call and settled against his truck, waiting for the cops to arrive.

Why hadn't she attacked in the mall's parking lot? Maybe the delay had to do with her approach. At the mall they'd been face-to-face. Here, she'd been closing on his back. Maybe she'd wanted the advantage of his vulnerable position, so she'd eighty-sixed the first attack and redeployed when the circumstances were more advantageous for her.

"I've never been shot at before," the kid said, exhilaration lighting his face and shining in his eyes.

He was so bouncy it made Cosky's knee ache just watching him. Christ, he couldn't remember ever feeling this euphoric because someone had painted a big red bull's-eye on his back—not even in the old days when he'd been the greenest banana in the skiff.

"No kidding," Cosky said, giving his shirt a couple more cooling flaps.

From the quick look the kid shot him and the sudden stillness to his feet, he must have picked up on the dryness in Cosky's voice. Suddenly he felt about as jaded as a man could feel.

"Hey," the kid took a step and bent. "She dropped her gun."

"Leave it." His voice must have emerged sharper than he'd realized, because the kid jumped back. He tempered his tone. "The cops will want to pull prints. We don't want to smear them or add our own."

"Oh, okay. Why do you think she shot at us? Just crazy?"

"Hell, who knows?" Cosky said, although the question was plaguing him as well.

The kid suddenly stopped moving long enough to sniff the air. "I wonder if she wore perfume. I keep getting this whiff of flowers."

Cosky eased a step away, heat touching his face. He needed a shower.

In the distance the scream of a siren pierced the air.

If she was connected to Branson, why go after him? He hadn't been the one to kill Branson; Zane had. Maybe she'd gotten the two of them confused. They were the same size, the same build, the same dark hair. It would be easy to confuse them.

Which would have made sense, except she'd called him by name. Obviously, she'd known who he was. The papers had identified Zane repeatedly as being the trigger man, so she must know Zane had taken the kill shot.

Why hadn't she gone after Zane?

Probably because she'd known she had no chance of taking Zane down, so she'd gone after the easiest target, the gimp.

He swore beneath his breath and glared down at his knee. If he'd grabbed her, he'd know the answers to all these damn questions.

What a disaster.

If she was connected to Branson, she was the first lead they'd had in months. Their one shot at tracking down Branson's true identity. If they could identify the man, they could zero in on his movements, find his associates, and maybe even lock on the people who'd funded the Sea-Tac Airport operation.

She just might be their only chance at clearing their names and exposing Chastain and McKay's murderers.

And he'd let her get away.

Chapter Six

THEY'D FOUND HER.

Those bastards had found her again.

A long face, with a gleaming dome of a head and muddy dead eyes swam across Jillian's vision.

He'd been one of them . . . one of the men who'd kicked in her door and kidnapped her family. One of the men who'd dragged them into the woods and turned the guns on them. One of the men who'd stolen her life from her, who'd left her empty and aching and zombified.

Jillian darted across another street, ignoring the clash of horns and squeal of brakes, and fled down the adjacent alley. An army of green trash containers flew past her.

She shied away from the images reeling through her mind.

The cool dampness of the forest. The sharp scent of pine and decomposing vegetation. A huge, gold harvest moon gleaming overhead. The cough of guns. A child's cutoff scream. Burning pain.

She shook the memory aside and tucked her chin, coaxing another burst of speed from her exhausted legs.

Was he behind her? Following? She strained to hear. Were those footsteps pounding behind her? Or her own heartbeat?

But her own gasping breaths plugged her ears. The urge to glance over her shoulder was overwhelming. She ignored it, focused on her body, and forced more speed from her burning legs and laboring chest. Looking would slow her down. Slowing down would give him the opportunity to grab her; and if he caught her, she was dead.

Which couldn't happen.

Not yet.

Milking every ounce of strength she could muster, she raced across another street, flew down another alley. Another street. Another alley. Startled faces skidded past her peripheral view. She ran until her legs went numb and her heart threatened to explode. When she couldn't run another step, she stumbled to a walk and glanced behind her.

Nobody was behind her. The street was empty.

To the west a siren started screaming.

Jillian stopped and braced her palms on her knees, drawing great gusting breaths. It slowly occurred to her, as she fed her starving lungs, that the siren was getting louder. Closer. Straightening, she staggered toward the mouth of another alley. Halfway down the alley she spotted an industrial garbage bin bristling with broken-down cardboard boxes. She forced her numb legs toward it. The container was huge and positioned at a slight angle, which created a wedge of space between the back of the bin and the brick wall behind it. The space would provide plenty of cover, clean cover, since it was stuffed with cardboard rather than restaurant refuse.

She took a second to shove broken boxes over the back of the container so they fell against the wall. Then she dropped to her knees and crawled into the space, pulling a couple of the loose boxes in behind her to close off the entrance. Once she was certain she couldn't be seen from the alley or street, she rolled over onto her back, and dragged more cardboard over her prone body. Once she was settled, she fought to catch her breath.

It wasn't long before dampness chilled her back. She ignored the discomfort and worked on regulating her breathing. If someone had followed her, they could pinpoint her hiding place through her gasps. She needed to concentrate on calming herself and quieting down.

A dozen deep steady breaths later, and the panic dissipated. She'd fled on instinct and taken streets and alleys without paying attention to where she was going, so she had no idea where she was. She hoped *they* wouldn't know where she was either.

She'd only seen the one killer, but the rest of them had to be near. They traveled in a pack, or at least they'd been together when they broke into her home, and . . . and . . . and . . .

. . . crack after crack of gunfire. Her babies falling beside her. The smell of spent fireworks . . .

No. No. No.

She flinched, dragged her mind back from the abyss, focused on the here and now.

The same five had staked out Russ's condo, and swarmed the hospital looking for her. If the bald killer was in Coronado, the others must be too.

She'd been lucky. Four times lucky. If she hadn't given in to the nurses' insistence and taken a lap around the ward, she would have been trapped in her room when those bastards showed up at the hospital. If she hadn't knelt to tie her shoe next to the nurses' station, they would have spotted her in the hall. If she hadn't stopped to greet Russ's elderly neighbor, she wouldn't have known her brother's condo was being watched, and she would have walked into their trap. If she hadn't turned at that young boy's shout, she wouldn't have seen that bald monster skulking by her car.

Yeah, she'd been lucky.

If you could call living with this endless abyss swallowing her from the inside out, lucky.

Wouldn't lucky have been dying alongside her babies in that forest? Or drowning in the cold, murky depths of Lake Katcheca and sharing her children's resting place?

What was lucky about living, when all the people who made life worth living had been taken from her?

If she were truly lucky, one of those bullets would have stopped Marcus Simcosky's heart. And another would have killed that bastard next to her car. If she were truly lucky, they would both be dead now.

She frowned at the icy bite sinking into her spine and rolled to face the brick wall. Once the gun ran out of bullets she should have looked for another weapon instead of running. There must have been something she could have used against those two bastards.

The rumble of an engine entered the alley. She tensed and rolled to face it, peering beneath the bottom of the garbage bin. Had they found her?

Tires stopped in the middle of the street, just down from her hiding place. But they looked too big to be a police car, maybe a van or some kind of truck. Simcosky had been driving a truck, but from what little she could see from beneath the garbage container, this vehicle was a rusting white; his had been black.

Too bad she hadn't had a bulky vehicle like this available to her in the parking lot. It would make a deadly weapon, and cause crushing, agonizing injury. They'd feel every second of the pain death dealt them. Like her babies had. Like Russ had.

Like she was feeling now.

Doors opened. She watched boots hit the pavement. But the engine continued purring.

"After this haul, let's hit Barney's. This day deserves a beer," a deep male voice said as he slammed the driver's door and walked around the front of the vehicle.

She relaxed when she didn't recognize it.

"No shit," another man responded. "What are we hauling, anyway?"

"A freezer."

"You sure it'll fit in the van?"

"Piece of cake, we'll just have to slide it in on its side."

The sound of a fist hammering against metal was followed by the creak of a door opening. Jillian stirred.

"You're late," a woman snapped. "You were supposed to be here an hour ago."

Jillian cocked her head and smiled. So far there had only been the two voices, and both were going into the store. What were the chances the van was unattended? It was worth checking out; if someone else was in the van, she'd slink away. Pushing the cardboard aside, she backed out from behind the container.

"We're here now. You want it moved or not?"

Keeping low to the ground, Jillian crept toward the running vehicle.

"Just hurry it up." The door creaked again. "I was supposed to be home thirty minutes ago." The voices faded.

Afraid to breathe, Jillian went up on her tiptoes and peered into the cab. Empty. Carefully she eased the driver's door open, climbed inside, and gently closed it behind her. So far, so good. She stomped on the parking brake to release it and shoved the gear into drive. As she rolled down the alley, it occurred to her that she might not have lost her opportunity to take out Marcus Simcosky after all. From the volume of sirens, the police had been called. Which meant he could still be somewhere around that parking lot, answering their questions.

As a bonus, he wouldn't be expecting her to strike again, at least not so soon. Nor would he be on the lookout for a van. Maybe that bald bastard would still be there too.

She hunched down in the seat to make herself less visible as she turned left at the end of the alley. The fact she'd found both Simcosky and her kidnapper in the same parking lot was proof the SEALs were involved in what had happened to her family. The men who'd killed her brother obviously knew the men who'd kidnapped and killed her babies. They'd probably been having a meeting. If she hadn't rushed Marcus Simcosky, maybe she could have taken them both out at once.

Not that it mattered. If they were still there, she'd take them both out this time.

And if they weren't, well, she knew where to find them now, which was more than she'd had when she'd awakened that morning.

Cosky tuned out the gangly kid next to him. Mr. Chatty hadn't stopped talking long enough to take a breath in over a minute. If luck was with him, which it sure as hell hadn't been so far today—hell during the past four months—his new buddy would pass out from heat and asphyxiation and give him some damn peace.

Not that the temperature seemed to be bothering the kid.

"She sure did a number on your truck."

Cosky transferred his glare to the bench seat of his truck, which hosted half the glass from the windshield. The hood carried the rest. Damn it. He needed to call a tow truck.

Almost afraid to see what damage his crazy stalker had done to his door, he pushed the sucker closed and winced at the collection of dents marring its previously pristine condition. Swearing softly, he ran his palm over the dimpled metal. He'd have to send it through the body shop too, which meant days, if not weeks before he got his ride back.

Shaking his head in disgust, he shot a quick glance toward the back of the parking lot, where the monstrosity the crazy bitch had driven hid behind a cluster of trucks, Jeeps, and convertibles. He should put a couple bullets in it and see how she liked driving without a windshield and some new venting in the door. But then again . . . his gaze lingered on the rusting red paint; considering the vehicle's condition, she probably wouldn't care.

He itched to check the car out. Maybe there was something there that would confirm his suspicion that she was connected to Branson. Worst case, they'd be able to pull prints from the steering column and her name from the registration. Find out who they were dealing with. Hell, maybe she was even stupid enough to circle back and try to claim the damn thing.

If so, he'd be waiting.

Assuming she didn't try it after the cops showed up or before the new buddy he'd acquired crashed from his adrenaline rush and staggered home for a nap.

He forced his attention away from the back of the lot. It was doubtful the kid would pick up on his interest, but there was no sense chancing it. He needed to search that vehicle before the cops impounded it, so he couldn't afford Mr. Chatty mentioning it to the locals. He'd throw the cops off its scent by claiming the woman had been on foot. After they'd conducted their investigation and taken off, he'd check the car out. He just needed to be patient.

And he hoped the cops didn't discover it first.

When the first responder to his nine-one-one call arrived, he parked in front of the entrance to the parking lot, partially blocking it off. Cosky waited for them to approach him, then identified himself by rank and name and alerted the flat-faced, tired-eyed officer of the Glock locked in his glove box. The cop didn't blink, just took Cosky's driver's license and military ID and went back to his black and white. Cosky leaned against his truck's bed, shifting his weight onto his good leg, and ignored the crowds of interested gawkers on the sidewalks ringing the apartment complex.

What he wouldn't give for an ice pack, a cold beer, and an even colder shower.

The officer who'd taken his information returned as a second cruiser pulled into the parking lot, parking nose to nose with the first responder, which blocked the entrance completely. Cosky accepted his license and military ID back and took the cop through what had happened. Or at least most of what had happened. Certain tidbits he kept to himself—like the piece-of-crap sedan and the name she'd shouted at him. No sense in alerting them to his suspicion that she was connected to the events in Seattle. It was pretty obvious the men behind that clusterfuck had long arms. If word reached them that Branson's wife was down in Coronado making trouble, they'd come looking for her.

Cosky intended to track her down first.

The kid actually made himself useful and unknowingly backed Cosky's account. He'd apparently seen the woman following him down the sidewalk, which tailored with Cosky's claim of her being on foot.

He'd just finished giving his statement when Zane's dark-blue minivan pulled around the back of the parking lot and headed toward him. A patrol officer stepped in front of it, waving it off.

Groaning beneath his breath, he shot the apartment entrance a quick look, praying that Kait wouldn't decide to check into all the commotion downstairs. But then again, he eyed the chattering crowds of people watching the police from the lawns and sidewalk; half the apartment building was already on scene. Maybe the boys wouldn't notice Kait if she did put in an appearance. Assuming she didn't duck under the crime-scene tape for a howdy-boys-let's-make-Cosky's-life-hell round of payback.

And assuming the cop who'd taken his statement and her name didn't decide to mention her.

The groan deepening, he turned back to the van, watching it swerve into a parking space several spots down from the eyesore Cosky was trying to ignore. Three doors opened and three pairs of boots hit the ground. That's when it occurred to him that his teammates had just given him the perfect excuse to get closer to his target, and get one of them inside the sedan for a quick look-see.

He pushed away from the truck. "My Lieutenant Commander's here," he told the officer who'd taken his statement. He nodded toward the minivan. "I need to fill him in. If you have more questions you can catch me there."

He didn't wait for the officer's permission, simply started walking—or hobbling was more like it. Mr. Chatty's verbosity worked in Cosky's favor this time; the kid was so busy yakking at the officer taking his statement, he didn't notice Cosky's escape.

If he'd suspected his teammates had warped to his rescue because they feared he couldn't take care of himself, he would have been pissed beyond endurance. But that wasn't why they'd come. They'd hotfooted it over because they *were* his teammates and they had his back. Dry dock or not, whether he wanted the support or not. He would have done the same if the circumstances had been reversed.

Such instant support was the plus and minus of team life.

"How the hell did you hear about this so fast?" Cosky called as he limped over.

"We would have been here ten minutes ago." Rawls reached over to punch Zane's shoulder. "If our pregnant mama here didn't keep pulling over to hurl his lunch." He paused and grinned. "Thank sweet Jesus, we're not on deployment."

Zane grimaced, his face turning slightly green. "It was once, damn it."

Cosky fought a smile. There was no end to the entertainment value of watching Zane mirror Beth's pregnancy. "Hell, she's four months along. Isn't morning sickness supposed to ease by this stage?"

"Morning sickness?" Zane released a disgusted bark of laughter. "Try morning, noon, and night."

"Do you think we can stop talking about your delicate condition long enough to concentrate on why we're here?" Mac snapped, with a glare at Zane. He transferred his scowl to Cosky. "Radar said shots were fired." He gave Cosky a quick up and down before turning to survey the shattered windshield of the truck. "Glad to see your ride took the hit. What the fuck happened?"

Cosky shrugged and limped closer. "Some crazy bitch walked up to me and started shooting."

Rawls quirked an eyebrow and grinned, although his eyes were shadowed and serious. "I keep tellin' you, if you'd treat the little ladies right they'd leave their trigger fingers home."

Mac snorted and swung toward Rawls. "Cosky? Fuck no. He's smart enough to avoid entanglements. If some pissed off ex-girlfriend is gonna start shooting, it'll be at you."

Kait's huge brown eyes, liquid with shock and hurt, flashed through Cosky's mind. No doubt she'd disagree with Mac's statement.

Rawls's mouth fell open in exaggerated shock. He lifted a hand to his chest. "*Moi*? I'm hurt ya'll think so little of my people skills."

Zane's gaze zeroed in on Cosky's face. "You didn't know her?" He frowned at the shake of Cosky's head. "She say why she attacked?"

Cosky frowned. "Nothing that made sense."

He turned slightly to glance behind him. The cop who'd interviewed him had closed his notebook and was scanning the pavement. The officer who'd waved the van off had returned to bag the gun, and Mr. Chatty was keeping the third suit busy.

Turning back to his teammates, he lowered his voice. "She said, 'this is for my babies and for *Russ*.'"

Bodies stiffened and eyes sharpened. Zane glanced toward the cops in front of Cosky's truck and lowered his voice as well. "Branson?"

"Hell if I know." Cosky wiped a hand down his face, sudden exhaustion hitting him.

"You didn't ask?" Mac demanded.

"When was I supposed to ask?" Cosky snapped, fighting to keep his voice low. "While I was dodging her bullets? Or after she took off across the street?"

Rawls's lips twitched. But that shadow still darkened his eyes. "Doesn't make sense. If she's connected to Branson, why target you? Zane's the one who took the bastard out. You were too busy bleeding all over the ER."

"Let's back up." Zane stepped in calmly. "How did you end up here?"

Cosky took a deep breath, and shot the rusted sedan behind them a quick glance. So far, so good. His crazy stalker hadn't arrived to reclaim her car, the police had no interest in it and Kait—thank God—hadn't exploded onto scene.

"I picked up a tail on Silver Strand, just outside the gate. Female. White. Total amateur." He paused, shook his head. "I thought she was a reporter at first."

Mac swore, disgust touching his face, and a round of sour looks passed between the four of them. They'd all had their run-ins with reporters.

"What clued you in that she wasn't after a story?" Zane asked, with a quick cock to his head.

"Her ride," Cosky said dryly. "It shouts vagrant rather than reporter." He shot a look toward the sedan and stared—hard—before glancing back at his teammates to see if they'd picked up on the silent message.

Mac's gaze sharpened. He took a step closer, his voice dropping even lower. "Shouts?"

"It's the ugliest, loudest piece of red rusted crap you've ever seen." He glanced toward the sedan again and lifted his eyebrows.

"Do tell." Rawls linked his fingers behind his neck and did a slow stretch to the side. He shot a quick glance in the direction Cosky had indicated. When he turned back to Cosky again, surprised amusement sparkled in his blue eyes. "That must have been quite the tail."

"Hard to miss," Cosky agreed.

"You didn't tell the cops about this?" Mac's voice was so low Cosky barely heard it.

Cosky silently shook his head. There was a moment of silence.

"They could stumble across it any moment," Zane murmured softly. "We need access before it's impounded."

"No shit," Cosky drawled under his breath, his temper spiking as a wave of heat rolled through him and a cramp ripped into his thigh.

"Is it locked?" Mac asked without glancing in the sedan's direction.

With a deep breath, Cosky locked his irritation down. "No clue."

Zane shot him a hard look. "You need to sit down?"

Yeah, he did. Badly. He ignored both the question and the need.

"Rawls." Zane tilted his head toward the rusted sedan.

"On it, Skipper." Rawls casually moved off.

Cosky, Zane, and Mac shifted their bodies until their huddle was directly between the cops and the sedan, although so far the officers were so busy cataloging the crime scene, they weren't paying attention to the parking lot.

Zane and Cosky launched into a round of banal bullshit while they waited for Rawls's return.

The minutes ticked by. A burst of radio static sounded behind them, and one of the cops climbed into his cruiser and barreled out of the parking lot.

Rawls finally returned. He shifted, turning his back to the remaining officers, and dropped his voice to a low rumble. "No registration, no pictures, no identification. Negative on weapons. No cell phone either. The inside's trashed. Food cans, utensils, clothes, blankets . . . looks like she's living in there."

"Fuck." Mac thumped his knuckles against his hips. "In other words, we got squat."

"Just the plate number." Rawls's voice held a shrug. "Which is useless if the beast's stolen."

Zane frowned. "We need to pull the prints off the steering wheel. It's our best shot of IDing her." He glanced at the cops behind them. "And we better do it fast. Sooner or later they're going to realize that piece of shit doesn't belong in the lot."

"Sure. We'll just grab a fingerprint kit at the corner market." Mac turned to glare at the sedan.

"We don't need a kit. Just some tape. Like strapping tape," Rawls said. When everyone turned to stare at him, he shrugged. "Sue me. I like CSI."

"Any chance you have some tape in your med kit?" Cosky asked dryly. As ST7's corpsman, Rawls carried a medical bag everywhere—both on and off deployment. And Christ knows that that damn bag seemed to have an unlimited supply of every piece of shit known to man.

"Just duct tape," Rawls said regretfully.

Which apparently wouldn't work?

Great.

Cosky turned to stare at the entrance to the apartment complex. "They might have tape at the front desk in the lobby."

Rawls whistled. "This place has a front desk? Classy. What brought you here anyway? You said you noticed her on Silver Strand? That's three klicks west."

Mac nodded slightly. "You better take us through everything. Where were you headed?"

Uh, yeah . . . Cosky tried for a casual shrug, no way in hell was he filling them in about Kait. And not just because Aiden had asked him to keep her abilities quiet. It made his skin crawl to think of them realizing how desperate he was.

And if by some chance they found out about those heated moments on the couch—he winced.

Kait was the sister of a teammate, the daughter of a superior, and off limits to drive-bys. Everyone on the team understood that code. You couldn't concentrate out on deployment if you were worried about wives, girlfriends, sisters, or daughters getting screwed over.

"I was headed to the Coronado Ferry Landing." He spit out the first destination that came to mind.

Zane, Rawls, and Mac rocked back on their heels in unison and stared.

"Come again?" Zane asked, his voice ringing with disbelief.

"*Coronado Ferry Shopping*? You were going *shopping*?" Rawls choked on a sputter of laughter. "Sure you were."

Ah hell, he should have picked a more believable destination. Resigned, he soldiered through the explanation. "Not that it's any of your damn business, but Mom's birthday's coming up. She likes touristy shit. And that damn mall is full of touristy shit."

Rawls nodded solemnly, but his eyes were laughing like holy hell. "That's why you've bought her gifts online, at the same place, for the past ten years."

"I got bored," Cosky snapped, his face heating. He hoped to hell they thought the flush was temper. "You want to hear this or not?"

"Absolutely." Rawls's grin was huge, his teeth bright white in his bronze face. "Do go on."

Cosky took a deep breath to regroup. "I noticed her just past the gate on Silver Strand. After suspecting she was following me, I took evasive maneuvers. She mirrored them. So I pulled in here to confront her."

"Why here?" Zane took a slow look around, like he was trying to see the appeal.

"It was close," Cosky said through gritted teeth. "And I didn't want her keying my truck or some shit, while I was looking for Mom's gift."

Zane shot the black truck behind them a sympathetic glance. "Keying would have been a step up."

"No shit." Cosky relaxed slightly.

"So she followed you in here," Zane said, glancing toward the rusted sedan.

Cosky simply nodded.

"From the damage to your truck, it looks like you waited for her there?" Zane continued in an even voice.

Stiffening again, Cosky waited; the sheer reasonableness of Zane's tone set his instincts humming. More than once he'd heard his buddy rip a plebe a new asshole without ever altering that even, reasonable tone of voice.

"So you got out of your truck to wait for her." He paused, held Cosky's gaze, and lifted his eyebrows. "Without your weapon."

It wasn't a question. It was a statement. And a pretty damn obvious one since Cosky hadn't gotten even one round off.

Dead silence hung for a second or two.

Hell.

Cosky glowered at the three of them. "I thought she was harmless."

He tossed the explanation out halfheartedly, already knowing they wouldn't buy it.

He wouldn't have.

Zane turned to stare at the apartment complex. "There's no way in hell you'd climb out of your truck without your weapon unless she wasn't around. Unless you were visiting someone and you didn't want to show up armed." He turned back to Cosky, something close to sympathy gleaming in his eyes. "So how 'bout we try this again. Without the mall. Because we all know how fond you are of shopping."

"Son of a bitch." Cosky clenched his fists and split his glare between his three ex-buddies.

Rawls wheezed, struggling to hold the laughter back. He leaned toward Cosky and took an audible sniff.

"We've been too polite to mention this, brother, but your new aftershave is kinda girly." He pulled back before Cosky's elbow could hit him in the face and turned curious eyes toward the apartment complex. "Who do you think his mysterious rose lady is?"

Oh, for Christ's sake. Cosky shot him a dirty look.

"Fine." Cosky shoved a hand through his hair, sighed, and filled them in on what had happened.

"How did she track you down again?" Zane asked.

"Hell if I know." Cosky raised a hand, gave an abbreviated chop, and let it fall again.

"It occurs to me," Rawls drawled, his voice innocent, "that you still haven't explained what you're doing here."

"Because it's none of your damn business." Now if Kait would just keep her curvy little ass inside. He sure as hell didn't want to explain *that.*

And on more than one level.

"Well, sweet Jesus, Cos has a secret lady." Rawls turned to Zane, his blue eyes dancing. "I told you he was spending way too much time in physical therapy."

"If you three are done having your fun, maybe we can concentrate on"—he shot the cops behind him a quick look—"the situation. If this woman is connected to Branson, she's our first solid lead in four fucking months."

The reminder doused smiles and hardened faces.

"Take us through the rest of it," Mac ordered.

Nobody interrupted again until he recounted her reaction to the fresh-faced kid she fired upon.

"Him?" The sheer incredulity in Mac's voice matched the look on Zane's and Rawls's faces as they watched Mr. Chatty trailing after one of the uniformed cops. "You're sure she was shooting at him?"

Cosky paused; he'd been too busy covering his own ass to check out who the crazy bitch had been shooting at. "That's what he says."

Zane rocked back on his heels, glanced at the kid, and shook his head. "It doesn't make sense. If he was across the tennis courts, a twenty-two wouldn't have the range."

"You're assuming she knew that," Mac pointed out with a snort. "Fuck, she threw the gun instead of reloading."

With a shrug, Cosky glanced across the park. "She took off that way. We should head out, track her down." Sweat trickled down the back of his neck, and his temper jumped. "Then we can ask her all these damn questions."

Zane gave him a long, slow look. "Half the force is out looking for her. If she's smart, she'll go to ground. If she's not"—he shook his head and shot a quick glance at the police cars behind them—"the cops could already have her. We need to pull the prints off that car, and find out if the cops have her before we start running the streets."

"I'll get the tape." Rawls paused to shoot Cosky a wicked grin. "Unless you want to call your honey. I bet she has tape."

"If you don't shut the hell up," Cosky snapped, "that tape will be going over your yapper."

Rawls fluttered his eyelashes. "So protective. It must be love."

Cosky stepped forward, his fists cocked.

"Go get the tape." Zane stepped between them. After Rawls had jogged off, he turned to Cosky, his green gaze concerned. "You need to get off that leg and cool down. Go wait in the van." When Cosky set his jaw and glared back, Zane took a threatening step forward. "That wasn't a suggestion, Lieutenant. Go. Sit. Down."

Knowing better than to argue with that flat, cold tone, Cosky turned without a word and limped for the Chrysler. With each step he fought the urge to glance over his shoulder and see if Kait had decided to see what all the fuss was about.

If his buddies discovered that Kait lived here, they'd flash back to all the opposition he'd raised when they'd proposed Aiden take Zane's place in the condo. They'd put two and two together and arrive at a billion and one. He'd never hear the end of it.

Because you didn't mess with a teammate's sister. Not unless you were serious. The marrying kind of serious. The kids kind of serious. Two things he'd sworn off years ago.

Chapter Seven

KAIT HEARD THE FIRST OF THE SIRENS AS SHE RELAXED BENEATH the steamy, pummeling spray of her shower. When the scream of the sirens got louder and louder—until they were so loud they had to be somewhere along the block—she turned off the water. The sirens suddenly ceased as she stepped out of the bathtub. She dried off, did a quick braid of her wet hair, and threw on some clothes before padding barefoot to the huge bedroom window that looked out over Trident Park.

Two cop cars, their lights still flashing, were parked along the sidewalk, a few feet to the left of Demi's coffee cart. Worry stirring, she leaned forward, peering down, trying to get a look at her friend, but the angle was wrong. All she could see was the flash of stainless steel. Swearing, she glared down at the sidewalk. All she wanted was to curl up on her bed and watch some silly movie like *Galaxy Quest*, until the memories of the last hour faded.

Instead, because Demi refused to become cell phone dependant, she was going to have to venture outside to make sure her friend was okay. Which meant entering the living room . . .

No sweat, she promised herself, taking a deep, fortifying breath. Cosky had to be gone by now. She'd wallowed twenty minutes or more in the shower. Plenty of time for him to dress and make a speedy retreat. Besides, she had to head out there sooner or later.

It took two seconds to shove her feet into Crocs and head for the bedroom door. As she'd hoped, Cosky was long gone. But the smell of roses and sex slammed into her the moment she stepped into the living room, halting her in her tracks. To her complete dismay, the traitorous flesh between her thighs clenched at the reminder.

Good God, she needed to strip the sheet from the couch, and throw it in the washer, then open a couple of windows.

First things first though—making sure nothing had happened to Demi was priority one. She grabbed her cell phone and her keys and slipped them in her pocket.

As she stepped out of the elevator, blue and red strobes greeted her. They oscillated faintly through the sunny lobby, reflections of the strobes flashing behind the glass entrance doors and windows facing the street.

Would the cops even let her outside? What if they had the street cordoned off? She spied a blue-suited officer next to the double doors and stopped momentarily, but started walking again with a shrug. If they'd closed the street off, they'd let her know, but best not to assume anything.

The thick-bodied officer next to the doors responded to her smile with a flat, unfriendly stare. Alrighty, she wouldn't be asking Officer Unfriendly any questions. Good thing Demi was on hand. She turned to the coffee cart to the right of the doors, relaxing as she caught sight of her friend.

Not only was Demi fine, she was also busy. Apparently the advent of cops and milling throngs of bystanders had given her business a good, hard shove. A line of customers snaked along the side of the building. Kait frowned as her friend finished steaming a carafe of milk and poured it into a grande cup. She was too busy at the moment to answer questions. Sighing, she turned away just in time to watch the cop next to her punch the button for apartment 607. She froze, her mouth dropping open in shock.

He wanted to talk to her? Why?

"Excuse me," she said, stepping closer to the cop to let someone slip past.

The officer turned heavy shoulders toward her, his gaze cold and expression withdrawn like he was too fricking busy for her. Irritation flickered.

"I'm Kait Winchester," she said without bothering to smile.

He glanced at the buzzer he had punched. "Apartment 607?"

"That's right. Can I do something for you?" She glanced up the sidewalk. A dozen or so clusters of bystanders clogged the pavement. There were plenty of witnesses to whatever had happened. Why come to her? "I was upstairs, so I didn't see anything. In fact, what the heck happened?"

"Do you know a Lieutenant Marcus Simcosky?" the cop asked, reaching into his breast pocket and removing a small notepad and nubby pencil.

Kait froze. "Cosky? Did something happen to him?"

"Lieutenant Simcosky is fine," he said tersely. "I need you to verify his timeline. What time did he arrive and depart your apartment?"

"What? Why?" She could feel her face heat.

Cosky had told the cops about them? Why? Talk about embarrassing. But after a second she frowned and shook her head. Cosky might be an absolute asshole in some respects, but he wouldn't have dragged her into whatever was going on, unless he had to. And he sure wouldn't have given them private, personal information about their activities of earlier.

"What's this about?" she asked.

"It's *about* when Lieutenant Simcosky *arrived* and *departed* your apartment," the cop said with gritty shortness.

Kait's shoulders stiffened. Abruptly, she'd had enough of all the macho, alpha posturing surrounding her.

"Jeez, you don't have to get your panties in a twist," she snapped back.

His face tightened. Served the asshole right.

"He was supposed to arrive at nine. But he was a little late, so maybe quarter past nine."

His face still tight, Officer Unfriendly jotted that down in his notebook. "And what time did he leave?"

Kait shrugged. "I don't know. I didn't look at the clock."

"Estimate." He didn't glance up.

"Fine." She blew out an irritated puff of air. "Maybe quarter of ten. Around there."

The cop jotted that down. "And the reason for his visit."

Darn if her face didn't heat again. The cop looked up, his brown eyes knowing, and suddenly she was furious—with herself, with this asshole in front of her, and with the bastard who'd barged into her life, given it a good shake, and left her to deal with the fallout. Like annoying questions from irritating cops.

Why not? The cop was already thinking it and judging her.

"He came for sex. It's a standing arrangement."

Besides, no way was she telling him the real reason for Cosky's presence. She could just imagine his snarky reaction to *that.*

Officer Unfriendly stared back, completely expressionless. "Lieutenant Simcosky stated he came for a massage."

"Of course he did." Kait kept her face bland. "I thought everyone knew *massage* was a euphemism for *sex.*"

A dry expression touched the cop's face. "Do you charge for these *massages*?"

"Of course not," she said righteously. "That would be illegal." When the officer simply stared back at her, his face unreadable, she shrugged. "Ask Cosky. He'll tell you he didn't pay a dime."

At least not in money. The bastard.

Temper flashed through her. "Are we done here? Or do you want a rating on his performance? Because that would be a big fat zero."

Or at least his after-sex performance had been severely lacking.

"Yet you have a standing *arrangement*," the cop responded, his tone suddenly dry, clearly indicating that he knew she was feeding him a line of bullshit.

Kait released a deep, put-upon sigh. "I really do have things to do today. Are we done?"

The officer snapped his notebook shut and slipped it back in the breast pocket of his uniform. "For now. If I have any more questions, I'll be in contact."

"Lovely," Kait said with as much sarcasm as she could muster, scowling as he walked off.

She still didn't know what had happened. Whatever it was, it obviously involved Cosky. But Officer Snippy had said he was fine. Frowning, she turned to the coffee cart. The line had dwindled to a handful of people. Demi must have heard what had happened. Once business died down she could ask her . . . or . . . she glanced down the sidewalk, recognizing familiar face after familiar face. Half her neighbors were milling about, watching. She could get the story from one of them.

Her cell phone rang as she headed toward the group closest to her. She fished it out of her pocket and glanced at the caller ID, which stopped her in her tracks.

You had to be freaking kidding . . . she stared down in disbelief . . . it must be a coincidence. There was no way in hell Wolf could have known . . .

Aiden's voice whispered through her mind. *"We ran into a snag on our last insertion. Got stuck between floors. Wolf swept in and unstuck us."*

Okay, so all things considered, he probably *did* know.

Turning around she headed back into the relative quiet of the lobby. The phone rang repeatedly as she walked. She could swear the shrillness increased with each ring, until it seemed to buzz with sharp frustration.

Once she was in the relative silence of the lobby, she took a deep, calming breath and punched talk. "Wolf. What a surprise."

"Are you okay, *bixoo3etiit*?" a deep voice asked.

"I'm fine."

"What the hell was Simcosky doing at your apartment?" he demanded, his voice losing some of its velvet smoothness.

Kait was so surprised she almost dropped the phone. "You know him?"

There was a distinct pause. "I know of him." His voice hardened. "Even more importantly, I know he's mixed up in some pretty ugly shit. You need to steer clear."

Another fricking alpha male, butting into her life.

"Didn't we just have a conversation regarding you staying out of my personal life?" Kait snapped, her fingers tightening around the phone until they ached. "Good God, you're worse than Dad ever was, worse than Dad and Aiden combined."

Dead silence hit the line. She could almost feel the frustration throbbing in that silence.

"I worry, *hico'ooteehihi,*" he said simply, his voice gruff.

Her irritation melted. "I know. But I'm twenty-nine, Wolf. I've been taking care of myself for years."

"You don't know what you're getting yourself into with Simcosky," Wolf said, steel creeping into his voice.

"Yeah, well. You don't need to worry about that. I'm not getting into anything with him."

"You're not involved with him?"

She could hear the frown in his voice.

"*God, no.*" She tried to convince herself that the emphasis was due to relief, rather than disappointment.

"Then why . . ." Silence, followed by, "His leg. Did the healing work?"

She frowned and nudged a clump of grass in a crack in the sidewalk with her toe. "I don't think so."

"Just as well," he said gruffly.

Kait's eyes widened. He was glad the healing hadn't worked? Glad that someone who'd been critically injured in service to his country—a true hero—wasn't going to get the chance to recover from a possibly crippling injury? That didn't sound like Wolf at all.

Wow, he must be extremely worried.

She'd heard there was some deep crap revolving around Zane, Cosky, Mac, and Rawls—a pending Department of Justice investigation for one thing. But she'd assumed they'd be eventually cleared of the charges against them. They'd acted in good faith, by all accounts. The hostages they'd rescued had come out in support of them. Hell, the news reports had been overwhelmingly supportive too.

The DOJ wouldn't actually charge them, would they?

And how could such an investigation be dangerous to her?

"How much trouble are they in?" she asked quietly.

His silence tightened the muscles across her chest.

"Surely the DOJ isn't going to actually charge them? A slap on the wrist, maybe. But not actual charges . . ." The silence on the other end of the line went on and on and her belly clenched. "It's not just the Department of Justice, is it? What's going on, Wolf?"

"Stay out of it, *nebii'o'oo*." His voice was harder, more uncompromising than she'd ever heard it. "You aren't equipped for this kind of shit. And so help me, if he's dragged you into his mess, I'll skin the *heebii3soo* myself."

Good God . . . There was no doubt in Kait's mind that he meant it. Her mind flashed to Cosky's lean strength. Not that her brother would have such an easy time doing it . . . but then again, Cosky was disabled to a certain extent.

She swallowed hard, and instinctively stepped in to diffuse the edge in Wolf's voice. "Well, it's a good thing that the"—she dropped her voice slightly, although there wasn't anyone close enough to hear—"healing didn't work. He won't be back."

At least this was something she could be sure of.

He must have read the certainty in her voice, because his tone relaxed. "Good." He cleared the gruffness from his throat. "So how goes the new line of glass birds?"

Kait scowled, turning to glare out the window at the fluttery green branches of the oak tree in the park. The tree was probably full of birds, and birds were the bane of her life at the moment. Well, after Cosky.

She glared harder. "I'm not getting the proportions right. I'm not blowing the glass thin enough. So the sculptures look thick. Clumsy. Too heavy to fly. But when I try to blow it thinner, the glass shatters." She rolled her shoulders, trying to shake off the frustration. "I should stick with a dodo bird or something."

It was a throw-away comment, but an image flashed through

her mind—a fat, colorful, awkward bird. She frowned thoughtfully as the image clicked. Maybe she'd been approaching the subject wrong.

A chuckle came down the line. "You're too impatient. Too hard on yourself, *nii'ehihi'*," he said indulgently. "Give it time."

Kait snorted and rolled her eyes. Easy for him to say.

"I'm headed to the studio now." The image of a clumsy, fat bird with an oversized beak, and bold, clashing colors had taken root in her mind, and she was eager to get it down on paper, and then birth it in glass.

He laughed. "Why am I not surprised?" He paused. "Have you given more thought to that gallery's offer?"

Kait frowned. "Not really."

The gallery owner who had handled her Aunt Issa's work had dropped by the workshop without invitation and taken a shine to Kait's pieces. She'd apprenticed under Issa, so her aunt's shadow was still upon her own pieces, although the similarities lessened every year. But she still wasn't sure she wanted to open her art to the rest of the world and invite comparisons and criticism.

"Let it rest. You'll know when you're ready." Wolf's voice fell into that deep-throated sageness she found so fascinating and annoying. "I've got to run. Another call's coming through. You have my number if you need it."

With his customary lack of good-bye, he ended the call.

By the time Kait stepped back outside, the line in front of the coffee cart was gone and Demi was standing around watching the crowd, looking bored.

"Hey," Demi said, straightening. "It's about time you showed up."

"If you had a cell phone, you could have *called* me and filled me in," Kait said, stopping in front of the milk steamer.

"But then you wouldn't have been in the position to gaze at the eye candy standing on the corner." Demi nodded toward the parking lot with a smirk. "Although, from what I heard earlier, it sounds like you may have been doing more than gazing at one of them earlier today."

Kait groaned beneath her breath. She was absolutely certain she knew what, or more like whom, Demi was referring to. But she had to step up a few paces and crane her neck to look around the clusters of people clogging up the sidewalk to verify her suspicions. Sure enough, she got a quick glimpse of three familiar men.

Cosky, Zane, and Commander Mackenzie. Rawls had to be around somewhere too. If Zane and Cosky were here, Seth Rawlings would be too. The three were inseparable, tied to each other's shoelaces according to Aiden.

Of course, if Aiden hadn't gone wheels up, he'd have been over there too, or scratch that, he'd have been over here, interrogating her.

She was just about to turn away, before they caught her staring, when the cop who'd interviewed her approached the trio on the corner and pulled out his handy-dandy notebook.

Uh-oh.

Her stomach dropped and crawled down to her toes. Somehow she just knew this didn't bode well, at least for her. The cop said something to Cosky, who scowled. All three men turned to stare down the sidewalk, where they caught her watching.

Resigned, she waved.

Mac apparently had a seizure, at least of the verbal kind. He grabbed Cosky's arm and his mouth started going a zillion miles an hour.

Cosky's face grew darker by the second, until it looked like he was going to shed lightning bolts and hail, maybe unleash a dust devil.

The look he leveled on Kait would have flattened a corn field.

A pang of hurt shot through her and then she stiffened. What? She wasn't allowed on her own sidewalk when he was hanging around with his buddies? Well, screw him—at least figuratively.

He was too far away to hear her verbal response, so she gave him the middle-fingered abbreviation.

Demi snickered at the byplay. "So who's Mr. Tall, Dark, and Grouchy?" Demi asked, stepping out from behind the coffee cart to give Kait a sly nudge.

Great. Kait sighed and braced herself for a full inquisition. Wolf had nothing on Demi when it came to digging for juicy details. And she could hardly play dumb. The coffee cart was close enough to the security buzzer for Demi to have eavesdropped on the conversation through the speaker. Knowing her friend, she'd caught the entire conversation and committed it to memory so she could quiz Kait later.

"He's a friend of my brother's," Kait said as a white van with the logo Haven Hauling stenciled on the side cut across the street and pulled up next to them.

Demi turned to glare at the van as a cloud of diesel fumes enveloped them. "What a moron." She waved a hand in front of her face. "She's nose to nose with oncoming traffic. And the place is full of cops. She's just asking for a ticket."

Kait glanced at the vehicle and shrugged. "Must be dropping something off or picking it up." She turned back to Demi. "So what happened, anyway? Why all the cops?"

"You didn't hear?" Demi asked, her brown eyes lighting up. There was nothing Demi loved more than telling a story. "So Tall, Dark, and Irritable comes out of the lobby—hey," she dropped her voice. "You must have done a healing on him? He limped his way in, but not so much on his way out."

"Really?" Kait rocked back on her heels in surprise. "I didn't think it worked."

"Oh, it worked. He was barely limping on his way out." Demi grinned, and made a smacking sound with her lips. "And believe me, I watched him walk all the way to his car. An ass like that? It's begging for eyes on it."

Kait didn't doubt her for a moment. Demi did like her eye candy. And Cosky certainly fit the bill.

"So what happened?" Kait prompted.

"Yeah." Demi shook her head. "It was the craziest thing. Some crazy lady tried to shoot him."

"*What?*"

"Yep." With a grimace, Demi waved away another plume of diesel exhaust. After an irritated glare toward the idling van, she nodded. "Tried to shoot him like three or four times."

Another cloud of diesel fumes rolled toward them, and Demi spun toward the van. "Come on, lady." She stalked over to the driver's door and pounded on the window, going up on her tiptoes to glare through the glass. "Either shut the damn thing off or park somewhere else. I'm choking on your fumes."

The woman behind the glass turned her head with mechanical precision and stared at the two of them, and then just as slowly faced front again.

Demi stepped back, suddenly silent. "That's weird," she said after a long moment.

Kait raised her brows at the odd tone in her friend's voice. "What?"

Demi backed up even farther. "The woman in the van. I think it's her."

"Who?"

"The crazy lady who shot up your friend's truck."

Kait turned, in what felt like slow motion, and stared at the woman sitting hunched over in the driver's seat. "Are you sure?"

With a slow nod, Demi backed all the way up to her cart, as though she were afraid the woman was about to thrust open her door, jump out of the van, and attack. "I only saw her from the back, but she has the same wild brown hair and heavy beige coat. I mean how many people wear wool coats in a ninety-degree heat wave." She shook her head. "Crazy."

Kait took a cautious step forward, peering through the driver's window. The woman was staring straight ahead with absolute concentration. Kait followed the woman's gaze. One of the clusters of people down the sidewalk turned around and headed back into the lobby, which opened a path down the sidewalk. Cosky, Zane, and Mac came into view.

Ice slid down the back of her neck, and the hair on her arms lifted. The woman was staring with fixed intensity at the three SEALs. There was something chilling about her unwavering focus. Something sinister. It was enough to convince her Demi was right.

Turning, she headed at a fast clip toward the nearest cop, who happened to be halfway down the sidewalk, talking to a group of bystanders. If she yelled a warning, it might alert the woman, spook her into running. Better to notify the cops quietly and let them handle things.

But she'd barely covered ten feet when the ominous roar of a revving engine rumbled behind her, and she knew with absolute certainty she didn't have time to reach the cop. Instead she stopped dead and took a deep breath.

"It's her. In the van. The shooter," Kait screamed the warning as loud as she could, hoping it would reach both the cops and the three men on the corner.

And then she watched, with her heart in her throat, as the van swerved around the cop cars parked beside her. The scream of brakes and blare of horns from the oncoming traffic drowned her cry of warning. She cupped her hands to her mouth and yelled again.

Swerving, the van's front left tire hit the curb and popped with an explosive hiss of escaping air. The vehicle jolted onto the sidewalk, the front tire flattening with every rotation of its wheels. As it straightened out, its tail end swung left and clipped the front end of the first cop car. The cruiser bounced hard and pivoted on its rear tires toward the building, where Kait stood amid clusters of bystanders.

As she leapt back, people scattered in all directions. Screams and curses lit the air. The van accelerated, riding the sidewalk with its left tires. A greasy cloud of diesel exhaust slicked everything, obscuring the van beneath a smoky veil.

But Kait didn't need to see the vehicle to know it was barreling toward Cosky, Zane, and Mac.

"So you're saying it's a coincidence," Mac roared, his eyes flashing black and livid. "It's pretty fucking obvious you were visiting some damn woman in this complex, and now Aiden's Goddamn sister just happens to be sharing the sidewalk with you? Yeah, that's some motherfucking coincidence."

Cosky gritted his teeth and took a limping step forward until he and Mac were chest to chest, squaring off. "I said," he snarled back, "that it's none of your business!"

"Bullshit." The words hit the air with a lethal rattle, until it sounded like Mac had swallowed a hive of wasps. "I'm still your fucking commander and you—"

"No. You aren't," Cosky snapped back, immediately wishing he could strangle the words out of existence.

Dead silence fell.

Son of a bitch. That had been a low as hell blow. But the words were out now. Hanging there. No calling them back.

He should have stayed in Zane's van, instead of joining Zane and Mac's huddle in the corner of the parking lot, while Rawls attempted to pull prints off the sedan.

Cosky stepped back and ran tense fingers through his hair. *Shit.*

With a slow shake of his head, Zane frowned. "There's something else going on here. Cos knows better than to target one of our own for a drive-by booty call." He turned to Cosky, cocked his head, and scrutinized him with a quizzical glance. "Just spill it."

Like hell. His chest tightened. The thought of letting his teammates in on his desperation, and just how far his desperation had driven him, made his skin itch.

"There's nothing to tell." Cosky bit the words out, as a heavy-duty engine revved somewhere near the apartment complex's glass entrance.

Mac opened his mouth, the disbelief stamped across his face, and Cosky braced himself for another tirade. But a shrill scream drowned out the new spate of overkill and overreaction.

What the hell?

He turned in the direction of the scream. The clusters of bystanders clogging the sidewalk along the side of the building swung around too. The crowd shifted slightly, and Kait appeared. From the hands still cupped to her mouth, it was pretty obvious she'd done the screaming. As he watched, she screamed something again, but the roar of an engine hijacked the words.

"What the fuck," Mac said.

A white delivery van parked in front of the coffee cart suddenly squealed forward, swerving into oncoming traffic. Brakes squealed. Horns blared. The two cars on a collision course with the van swerved into the other lane. More brakes squealed. More horns blared.

The van shot past the two cop cars parked in front of the lobby doors. As the hood cleared the last police car, the vehicle jerked to the left, its rear clipping the cruiser's front end. The squad car bounced.

"Kait," Cosky shouted, lurching forward, ice pooling in his stomach as the cruiser spun toward the tall, frozen blonde standing mere feet away.

Kait leapt back as the cruiser swung toward her.

Zane grabbed his arm, hauling him back. "You won't—"

The words choked off, and Zane froze, his hand clenching around Cosky's bicep.

Cosky shot him a quick look. *Un-fucking-believable. A Vision? Now?*

The van barreled toward them, the left front and rear tires riding the sidewalk. Clusters of people dove out of its way, their screams competing with the roar of an overtaxed engine.

"What the motherfuck—" Mac reached for the weapon stashed at the small of his back beneath his T-shirt and dropped into a shooter's stance.

Cosky caught a glimpse of scraggly brown hair behind the oncoming vehicle's windshield, and knew immediately who had their asses in her sights. Jesus, the crazy bitch had come back for round two.

"Stand down," he yelled at Mac. "We need her alive."

Mac lowered his weapon slightly, targeting her tires and engine compartment; which wouldn't stop the damn thing before it smeared them all over the pavement, sure as hell not with Zane's feet frozen to the pavement.

Cosky wrenched his arm free, grabbed Zane's left arm, dragged it over his shoulders, anchoring it in place with his left hand, and wrapped his right arm around his buddy's waist. With Zane pinned to his side, he swung them both around and hobbled as fast as his knee would allow toward the cop cars blocking the parking lot's entrance.

A cop, weapon drawn, raced past him screaming, "Police. Police."

A cacophony of shots lit the air behind him. The van kept coming. He could hear it gaining on them. He focused on the barricade the cop cars made.

He wasn't going to make it.

"Cos," Mac roared, and another volley of shots peppered the air.

At the last possible moment, with the heat of the van's engine compartment steaming his ass, Cosky shoved Zane as hard as he could to the right and threw himself to the left. A huge white bullet skimmed past him.

Jesus, had he pushed Zane far enough out of the way?

He hit the ground and rolled. Pain ripped through his shoulder. And then his knee collided with the pavement. There was one moment of gut-wrenching agony. His head went light and dizzy and then his leg went numb.

A horrendous crash exploded in front of him—the screech of metal striking and then sheering. Glass fragments peppered him.

He rolled again, and tried to rise to his feet, only to fall back to the pavement, his left leg useless.

Hard hands grabbed him beneath his armpits and hoisted him.

"She hit the police car," Rawls said grimly.

"Zane?" Cosky spit the grit and blood from his mouth, and chanced an urgent glance in the direction he'd thrown his LC.

"Here," Zane said as he shoved a bloody shoulder in a shredded T-shirt under Cosky's armpit and caught him around the waist.

Rawls drove his shoulder under Cosky's other armpit.

"No." Cosky tried to knock Rawls's arm away. "Go after her."

Where the hell was Mac? The cops?

"No." Zane's voice was sharp. "We need to get you out of the way."

Son of a bitch.

The vision. Had to be. He must have seen Cosky's death. Again.

Goddamn son of a bitch.

Cosky winced as an ear-splitting screech sank like a spike into his pounding head. He glanced toward the cop cars and his crazy-ass stalker. She'd hit the first cruiser head-on, so hard it had collided with the second one, pushing both vehicles back twelve to fifteen feet. Mangled metal now bound all three vehicles together. Not that the metal tether was going to keep her in place for long. She was gunning the van so hard it was dragging both cop cars backward.

The van jolted back as the two cop cars separated, and shed a roll of tread from its front tire like a snake shedding skin. With another cacophony of tearing metal, it ripped the front bumper loose from the cop car still attached. Dragging the bumper along with it, the damn thing barreled backward toward them.

Ah hell.

Mac raced past them, his arms scuffed and bleeding, his Sig outstretched in torn hands. As though the gun would do any good. Zane and Rawls rocketed forward, dragging him away from the action at breakneck speed.

More shots behind him. The rattle and roar of the van's straining engine was fainter now, from a distance.

Another horrendous, metallic crash.

Another volley of shots.

Rawls and Zane dragged him behind his pickup truck. In unison they turned, but the corner of the apartment building blocked their view.

"I've got Cos," Rawls said, as if he was some infant they had to babysit, and Zane took off at a dead run.

He could tell from the metallic screeches of sheering metal and the sharp report of shots fired, that the bitch had targeted the front of the building this time.

His blood froze in his veins, and his chest went as cold and numb as his knee.

The front of the building.

Where Kait had been standing.

Chapter Eight

Kait watched Cosky's batshit crazy attacker accelerate, in reverse, down the sidewalk in pursuit of Commander Mackenzie. Holy crap, any second she was going to hit the cop car that sat with its nose facing the apartment building. If this impact mirrored the collision in the parking lot, she and Demi would be crushed when the police car went flying.

With one last glance at her brother's CO, who was in a flat-out run, but losing ground by the second, she turned, grabbed Demi's arm, and thrust her toward the recessed entrance to the lobby. Demi, thank God, shook off her paralysis and leapt for lobby entrance.

The clusters of bystanders, which had congested the sidewalk earlier, had scattered at the van's first run at the SEALs. Most of the men and women had crossed the street, seeking shelter in the park beyond. Several of the injured, who'd been clipped by the van as it barreled down the sidewalk, had been helped into the apartment building. Luckily, none of them had been hurt too badly.

However if she, Demi, and Mac didn't get to safety pronto, they wouldn't be as lucky. Apparently realizing that himself, Mac exploded in a last-ditch burst of speed. He vaulted the sideways cop car and ducked into the recessed alcove right behind them. Once behind the cover of the building, he spun and slammed his back against the wall, his scraped and oozing arms tucked at his side, the gun pointed up. He shot Kait one assessing, flat glance and jerked his head toward the lobby doors. A silent, but clear order to get her butt inside.

Sounded good to Kait.

She reached for Demi, who'd frozen again, but before either of them could escape into the lobby, the van struck the cop car.

The crash was so loud the sound seemed to swell in her ears until all she could hear was that horrific *boom*, followed by ringing. The ground shook beneath her feet. The windows and glass doors behind her shattered. She didn't hear the collision; she felt it instead as stinging fragments of glass rained down on her.

Amid that percussion ringing in her ears, the squad car slid past them, pushed by the van's blunt tail end. It hit the coffee cart, which crumpled beneath the impact. A spray of coffee jetted into the air, but vanished almost immediately.

The van's sliding door came into view.

Mac leapt for it and tried to wrench it open. When it didn't budge, he dove for the driver's door.

"Shoot her!" Kait screamed, the memory of that maniac driving directly into a crowd of people fresh in her mind.

He had his gun out. Why wasn't he using it?

The driver's door didn't budge either. The van slowed, but inexorably rolled forward, shoving the cruiser along in front of it.

Using the butt of his pistol as hammer Mac shattered the driver's window and leaned forward, halfway through the shattered window, reaching for something—probably the keys. The woman slammed her elbow into his face, wrenched the wheel to the left, and gunned the engine, angling the nose of the van toward the building.

Mac rocked back as her elbow struck his face, but held on with silent, grim determination. If he didn't let go and jump back, the van would crush him against the side of the building when the recessed alcove ended. Kait leapt forward and grabbed the back of his shirt, yanking as hard as she could.

The shirt split beneath the force of her pull, but he staggered back out of range just as the van accelerated backward again, and the shattered window slammed into the edge of the building.

"What the fuck do you think you're doing?" Mac roared, swinging toward her, frustration and fury flashing like black lightning in his eyes.

His words wavered, first loud, then hushed, then loud again.

"Saving you from getting crushed," Kait snapped back.

He turned a grim look on the van and the edge of the building, before snapping at her. "Get in the lobby."

This time his demand was crystal clear as her hearing adjusted.

Kait pushed Demi through the shattered doors, broken glass crackling beneath their feet, and into the lobby as what sounded like a hundred sirens started wailing in the distance. The officers on the scene must have called for backup, and judging by the increasing volume of the screaming, their brethren were coming fast.

Thank God.

Through the empty lobby doors, Kait watched the van come to a sudden jolting stop with only its nose visible. Mac stood there in the middle of the alcove, waiting, his body tense. He fired twice at the front tire and brought his weapon up again.

"Why doesn't he do something?" Demi whispered in a shrill voice.

Good question.

Why wasn't he targeting the driver instead of the car? It made no sense. It was drilled into first-year plebes to take out any potential threat immediately. This woman was a definite threat. To Mackenzie, Cosky, Rawls, and Zane, but also to the dozens of bystanders. She apparently didn't care who she hit or crushed in this insane vendetta against Cosky and his teammates. Commander Mackenzie *knew* better. So why wasn't he stopping her by any means necessary?

Just what was going on here?

Of course there wasn't much he could do at the moment. If he bolted in front of the van in an attempt to line up a shot, he ran the risk of her hitting the accelerator and running him down before he could hit his mark.

But there had been plenty of opportunities before this to bring her rampage to a quick end. Why hadn't he taken them?

Was it because she was a woman?

Because she was a civilian?

The front tires cranked to the right.

And the van shot forward again, its sides scraping against the building as it cut hard toward the street; once its back doors faced the lobby entrance, it screeched to a stop and shot backward, roaring straight toward Mac.

The woman would have crushed him too, if she'd judged the distance better. But rather than sliding between the two sides of the alcove, the van slammed into the right wall. It stopped dead and jolted forward.

The building shook. The floor bucked beneath Kait's feet.

Mac aimed for the back tires and fired.

The screams of sirens pulled closer.

Mac edged slowly back, into the lobby. Kait and Demi backed up as well, easing to the right, out of the line of fire and behind the safety of the lobby's wall.

Another massive collision. The building shook again. Plaster rained down from above. A crash sounded behind, along with the crackle and tinkle of falling glass. Kait spun around. A chandelier had hit the ground maybe fifteen feet behind them. She glanced up at the chandelier swinging wildly overhead and grabbed Demi's arm, dragging her back.

Some of the sirens were close now. Very close.

The van's engine revved again, barely audible beneath the wail of the approaching sirens, and then it shot past the lobby window.

Kait just stood there, shaking, staring hard at the window to see if it came back, while Mac bolted for the street.

"Do you think she's gone?" Demi whispered in a quivering voice as a black-and-white cruiser went screaming past the lobby window.

"I think so," Kait whispered back as her arms and legs started trembling. Suddenly she went light-headed and weak as a newborn.

Mac appeared in the window, his fists on his hips, staring in the direction the van had hurtled. Another cruiser screamed past him, flashers painting the lobby walls blue and red, before vanishing, still screaming, into the distance.

Zane skidded to a stop next to Mac. Talking intently, the two turned and jogged back down the sidewalk toward the parking lot.

Kait took a deep breath. Regrouped.

Zane and Cosky had hit the ground hard and while Zane seemed little the worse for wear, Cosky had flopped back down to the pavement when he'd tried to rise. It had taken both his buddies to drag him to safety.

While the man put "ass" in the word asshole, and she had no intention of ever opening herself to him again in either a physical or emotional capacity—that didn't mean she wanted to see him physically hurt, certainly not crippled.

If Demi had been right, and her abbreviated healing had helped his knee enough to alleviate his limping, maybe a second, more intensive healing would provide some benefit, give his leg a healing boost she feared it was desperately going to need.

Because God help her, from the way his leg had flopped so uselessly beneath him as Zane and Rawls dragged him to safety, he was going to need all the help he could get.

Cosky braced his palms against the hood of his Ford, watching the sidewalk. The unmistakable shriek of the van's engine was fading, a clear indication the vehicle was in flight. A cop car, its siren wailing, raced past them.

"Go check on Mac and Zane," Cosky ordered Rawls, without tearing his gaze from the sidewalk.

Kait was back there. So were Zane and Mac. His chest tightened. He couldn't see a damn thing with the building in his way. All three of them could be crushed. Dying. Because of that crazy bitch's vendetta against him.

He'd brought this danger to Kait's door. Him.

He needed no further evidence that his profession, along with the shit he was currently swimming in, made it unwise in the extreme to establish a relationship. He had no business getting involved with anyone. Let alone Kait.

"Let's wait a second," Rawls said, his Southern drawl absent, tension radiating from his long, lean frame.

He wanted to go. Cosky could feel Rawls's need vibrating in the air between them. But he wouldn't. At least not yet. Because he was intent on protecting Cosky instead.

Frustrated rage exploded through Cosky, and seared him from the inside out, leaving him raw. "Goddamn it, I don't need a babysitter. Go!"

"Not yet." Rawls's voice was calm.

"She's gone," Cosky snarled, his fists clenching on his truck's hood. "Hell, Mac riddled her tires and engine block with bullets. She's got half of Coronado's police force after her. She's not coming back."

Rawls shot him a flat, unbending look. "You know damn well it takes time for air to leak out of tires. Same with the radiator fluid. She could double back. You can't walk, let alone run. Mac and Zane know what they're doing."

Cosky's face tightened. Kait didn't have the kind of training his CO and LC had. But Rawls was right, he couldn't walk, which meant he couldn't go check on Kait himself. He'd just opened his mouth to ask Rawls to go look for her, when Zane and Mac came into view.

"Kait?" he shouted at them as they headed across the parking lot toward him.

Rawls went still at the shouted name and turned to stare at him.

Great. Now he had Rawls on his back too. Still, Kait was bound to come up sooner or later. Rawls hadn't been on hand when that bastard of a cop had informed them Kait had substantiated his timeline, but with Mac's mouth running a thousand miles a minute he would have heard the reason behind Cosky's presence at the apartment complex sooner or later.

"She's fine," Zane said. He turned to Rawls. "Have you checked him out?"

Rawls shook his head. He waited until his two commanding officers were closer, glanced at the cops headed their way, and dropped his voice. "I pulled some prints off the steering column. But then the excitement hit. In the interest of joining the fun, I stuck it to the back of Zane's van as I passed."

"Go," Mac said simply.

"I'll get my kit," Rawls said loudly enough for the approaching cops to hear, and took off for Zane's minivan.

"You look like roadkill," Cosky said dryly, staring at Zane's bloody shoulder and scraped right arm. Mac hadn't fared any better. Both his arms were skinned and oozing, so was his right cheek.

"You don't look much better," Zane said just as dryly; his gaze dropped to Cosky's right leg. "How bad is it?"

"Bad," Cosky said after a minute, his throat closing.

Mac swore. "I'll call for an ambulance." He made a grab for his belt and came up empty. "Fuck." He glanced around the pavement, swore again, and headed off to intercept the cops.

Aware that Zane was watching him, Cosky glared down at the pavement.

"You should be on the ground," Zane said after a too long pause.

No doubt. Cosky scowled harder at the pavement. "When Rawls gets back."

Once he went down, Christ only knew how long before he'd be able to get back on his feet.

"Thanks for saving my ass back there," Zane said, breaking after another long, throbbing pause.

"Yeah." Cosky cleared his throat, knowing damn well the comment had been thrown out as a distraction. Ass saving was priority one for the team. Taken for granted. Unless you were newly finned and fresh from BUD/s, you didn't thank your teammate. Odds were you'd return the favor sooner or later. "The ass saving went both ways today."

Zane grunted, no more comfortable with the gratitude than Cosky was.

"Let me guess." Cosky looked up, raising his eyebrows. "You had another of those damn visions."

With a hand swipe down his face, Zane nodded.

Cosky swore, shaking his head in disgust. "That damn *gift* of yours about turned us *both* into roadkill."

A frown gathered on Zane's forehead; he glanced around the parking lot, his gaze lingering on the metal and glass littering the pavement. "This scene resembles the flash."

At least that was something; he didn't have to worry about imminent death from a different direction. Although, considering how determined that crazy bitch was, he couldn't completely rule it out either.

The cell phone clipped to Zane's belt rang as Rawls loped back over, the black bag that housed his personal medical kit in hand.

Zane checked the caller ID and lifted the cell to his ear. "Hey, babe. Everyone's fine." He glanced at Cosky and moved off.

"That must have been hard," Rawls murmured, stopping next to Cosky.

"What?" Cosky asked, shifting slightly to ease some of the pressure on his back, which ached. His scraped and bloody elbows, on the other hand, stung like they'd been skinned, which they had. His left shoulder hurt more than his arms and back combined—a deep, constant throb and burn, like it had taken a major pummeling; which wasn't far from the truth considering how hard he'd landed on it.

His left leg, however, didn't hurt at all. Not even a twinge. Or a tingle. The damn thing was locked in numbness. He swallowed hard, forcing himself to look down. It just dangled there, useless. The extent of the injury was hidden beneath his ripped and dirty sweats.

Pain he could ignore, but this frozen, thick numbness scared the shit out of him.

"Beth," Rawls said. "She must have picked up on what happened through that bizarre connection she shares with Zane." He continued at Cosky's blank look. "But she didn't call. Not until after the attack was over. It must have been hard to wait until it was safe, until she could be sure she wasn't distracting him. I don't envy either of them after we go wheels up."

Assuming they saw another deployment.

Rawls must have been thinking the same thing. A shadow crossed his face and he shook his head. "Let's get you on the ground, so I can take a look at your leg."

Cosky had pushed away from the truck, balancing on his good leg, when he caught a flash of blond hair on his right. Rawls, who was blond, was to his left.

Instinctively, he tensed, twisted to look, and sent up a silent, urgent prayer that their visitor was a blond cop . . . or a blond curiosity seeker . . . or any blond other than . . .

Kait.

Son of a bitch.

Cosky watched her come closer with a scowl, hoping she'd get the message and vamoose. No question she picked up on his silent discouragement. Irritation swept across her heart-shaped face. She tucked a swath of damp hair that had worked loose from the braid dangling over her shoulder behind her ear, lifted her chin, and stared back, a sudden tight kick to her stride.

Just perfect.

"Kaity," Rawls said, "it's been what? Four years?"

Kaity? Cosky turned his glare on Rawls, acid suddenly churning in his belly.

"More like five," Kait greeted Rawls with a smile.

"Makes my day." Rawls flashed her a blinding smile. "Tell me we're going to see more of you now that Aiden's taken the spare bedroom."

The acid grew claws and climbed Cosky's throat.

She laughed. "Still the charmer, I see."

"Apparently not much of one. I never did convince you to paint the town with me," Rawls said in a teasing, rolling drawl.

Cosky's hands fisted.

Rawls glanced down at the movement and did a double take. His gaze raced up to Cosky's face, and pure devilment danced in his eyes. He turned his attention back to Kait.

"We're 'bout due for a second assault, don'tcha think? And I won't be whisked away before you say yes, this time."

With another laugh, Kait stopped in front of the truck. "Who knows, I may even say yes this time. I could use a night of dancing."

Separated from Cosky by more than the width of his truck, she scanned his body, her gaze lingering on his leg. The teasing flirt disappeared.

"You're obviously hurt." She cocked her head, watching him steadily, her message and offer clear. "Maybe I can help."

Her words caught Cosky off guard, and something inside his chest softened. Considering the rift he'd carved between them, her offer was incredibly generous. And unexpected. And untimely. She'd wanted her gift to remain private, which wouldn't happen if she worked on his leg in public. He swore beneath his breath, glanced at Rawls, and found his buddy glancing back and forth between him and Kait, a thoughtful look on his face.

"Later," Cosky said gruffly.

When they didn't have an audience.

Although . . . hell, maybe an audience was exactly what they needed. At least he wouldn't end up on top and inside of her.

A frown crinkled her forehead. "The sooner the better, before the injury has a chance to set."

"What, exactly, can you do under the circumstances?" Rawls asked slowly. He turned to Cosky, his face determined. "Obviously you were here to visit Kait. Why?"

Cosky gritted his teeth and glared back. "Not your business."

"He came for a massage," Kait said. She shot Cosky a dry look at his growl. "Zane and Mac know, they'll tell him soon enough."

True enough, but that didn't stop him from wanting to break a few of Rawls's teeth. Maybe that would stop his mouth from moving.

"A massage," Rawls repeated, a distant look on his face.

With a cocked fist and faltering control, Cosky awaited his buddy's response. *One flirty comment, or sexual reference . . .*

"The kind of massage you were giving your brother every time I visited him in the hospital?" Rawls asked, no hint of teasing in his voice. Hell, he'd even lost his Southern drawl.

Surprised, Cosky released his fist.

"Pretty much," Kait said, pulling back, wariness in her eyes.

Apparently coming to some silent decision, Rawls turned to Cosky and took hold of his arm. "Let's get you on the ground, so I can check that leg out."

Cosky tensed. With Kait watching. Like hell. "Just get me to the ER."

Admittedly, his reluctance to bare his leg in front of Kait didn't make much sense. She'd worked on the damn thing maybe an hour earlier. Hell, she'd seen a lot more of him than his bare leg . . . but there was something too pathetic about lying on the ground at their feet, with everyone towering over him.

"Lie down." Rawls's tone flattened.

With a slight hop of his good leg and a twist of his torso, Cosky faced him down. "Just get me to the ambulance. It's fine."

Which was an asinine thing to say. Everyone could see it wasn't fine.

"I've got eyes," Rawls snapped, his voice turning hard. "Sit. Down."

"Oh, for God's sake." Kait blew out an exasperated breath. "Is he always this stubborn?"

"No—" Before Rawls had a chance to continue, Mac's gritty voice broke in from behind them.

"What the fuck's he doing on his feet? Sit down."

Hell.

If he kept stonewalling, everyone was going to question why. Frustration a hot, pulsing knot in his chest, he eased himself down to the ground.

Mac stepped around him and stalked up to the hood, his cold gaze locked on Kait's face. "Go back to the lobby."

For one sweet moment Cosky hoped . . . until Kait ignored Mac, and leaned forward, watching Rawls open his medical kit.

Swearing, Cosky lowered his shoulders and head to the pavement and closed his eyes. From the determination on her face, and the stubborn tilt to her chin, it would take a nuclear explosion to budge Kait from her position.

"Sorry, buddy," Rawls said, as a ripping sound reached Cosky's ears. "Your sweats are toast anyway."

"How's he doing?" Zane asked from above him.

"We're about to find out," Rawls said. The sound of more cloth ripping filled the air.

"Goddamn it, Ms. Winchester," Mac rumbled. "You aren't—" His voice simply died.

Silence fell.

Dead. Pulsing. Helpless silence.

The teams had a name for this silence. The death watch. It was the silence of watching helplessly, while your teammate bled out in your arms.

He grimaced. His buddies had obviously just discovered what he'd instinctively known the moment he'd tried to climb to his feet and found a numb, useless husk of flesh where his right leg used to be.

He wasn't going to bounce back from this injury. Not enough to rejoin ST7. Hell, he'd be lucky to walk without crutches.

Barring a major miracle, his career was officially over.

Chapter Nine

ROBERT WATCHED JILLIAN SPEED OFF IN THE VAN, WITH HIS mouth hanging open.

Holy hell, he could not believe, *could not believe,* that little milquetoast had just attacked all four SEALs. *All four*. At once. In front of their fucking watchers.

It had been bad enough watching her go after Simcosky earlier, without being able to do a damn thing about it. He sure as hell couldn't intervene back then, not with Simcosky's eyes and ears engaged, or with so many witnesses around, which nixed any possibility of taking out both his targets at once.

So he'd watched from behind her car, fuming, as the stupid bitch ruined *everything*.

It would be one thing if she'd actually managed to take Simcosky out. At least one of his headaches would be removed. It wouldn't matter what she'd told the asshole, if the bastard was dead.

Except she'd fucking missed.

And her attack had caught the SEALs' attention.

She must have told Simcosky something, because when Robert had returned from his fruitless search for her, Rawlings had been inside her ragtag car.

He took a shallow breath as a cop car went screaming past him, in obvious pursuit of the woman who'd turned his life into a living hell. He should have just bit the bullet and taken off after her following her original attack on Simcosky. Hell, if he'd been thinking, he could have staged the pursuit, remained behind her until they were out of sight. Once the witnesses were behind them he could have eliminated her without anyone being the wiser.

But instead of a foot pursuit, he retreated to his car and followed the direction she'd taken. Which had proved pointless. There'd been no sign of her. But then she'd probably already stolen the van and returned for a second shot at the poor bastard. Only this time all four of the SEALs had been there.

Along with several of their watchers.

He swore sickly beneath his breath and ran an unsteady hand down his face. Well the cat was out of the bag now. From where he sat parked, he could see both Mackenzie's and Rawlings's tails. They'd witnessed the whole damn thing. He'd best own up and hope like hell the bosses were in a charitable mood. It wasn't like he could go to ground and avoid the issue.

They'd controlled Russ when he'd tried to abandon the Sea-Tac operation by kidnapping Russ's sister and her brats. But the poor bastard's attempted desertion had bit everyone else on the ass too.

Following that fiasco, the bosses had made sure no one could ever escape them again. He shuddered as he thought of the toxic shit they'd pumped through his veins, which would track him no matter where he went, or how hard he tried to hide. As he stared down at his tanned forearm, he almost expected to see it glow.

When his cell phone rang, he jolted and just looked at it a moment.

Had they already heard?

Slowly, he picked it up and checked the caller ID, relaxing to find Jonese's number flashing across the screen, rather than headquarters'. Maybe he could talk Jonese and Reeves into giving him a few hours to lock down the situation. Although it was doubtful. His ass wasn't the only one headquarters had in a sling.

"Did you fucking see that?" Jonese's excited voice huffed down the line.

"Yeah, it was hard to miss," Robert said tightly.

"Man, wouldn't it have been sweet if he'd taken the four of them out. *Boom*, and our job here's done. And without us lifting a finger." His voice turned wistful. "Too bad he missed them."

Robert froze. *He.*

Slowly, he turned his head to study his teammates' vehicles. Jonese had parked way down the street, behind a line of cars, which was standard procedure to avoid detection. However, as luck would have it, the van had headed in the opposite direction. Jonese wouldn't have had a clear view of the action . . . or the driver.

Twisting in his seat, he glanced toward the back of the parking lot. Reeves's position was closer, but still too far away to see into the van. In all likelihood, he hadn't seen the driver either.

Was it possible neither of them had recognized Jillian?

He coughed the nerves from his voice. "You didn't see him?"

"Who?"

"The driver?" Robert took a shallow breath and tried for a casual tone. "Ya have to wonder who the hell's targeting them, well—besides us."

"Considering they've pissed off most of the terrorists in the world, it could be anyone. It was bound to happen sooner or later, what with the way the media's been plastering their names and faces over the news," Jonese said, a shrug in his voice. "This is probably what headquarters had in mind all along. Feed their faces and names to the sharks and let the sharks take care of them."

"True," Robert said. After a few casual exchanges, he hung up.

He wouldn't have called Jillian a shark. More like a guppy. Harmless. Ineffectual. Prey rather than predator.

His frown turned into a grimace. Well at least until today. She'd been one unwelcome surprise after another today. A guppy didn't walk up to someone twice their size, with a thousand times their experience, and start shooting. They sure as hell didn't escape unscathed and return in a stolen van to take on the whole fucking team at once.

The terrified and frozen Jillian Michaels of four months ago bore little resemble to the woman who just tried to run down four highly trained SEALs.

Too bad the new Jillian hadn't done a better of job of targeting her quarry and taken out at least a couple of them. Hell, all four of them would have been nice. Because now he was left with the unpleasant headache of finding out what she'd told them, and without his team being any the wiser.

He needed to interrogate them. He glanced toward the glove box. That detective's badge he'd stashed in there would come in handy. The police would open an investigation. One more cop asking questions wouldn't raise suspicions. But he couldn't do much now with half his team still hanging around, and more and more cops arriving by the moment.

He'd have to hunt them down later and swing by for a visit.

With a quick glance in his rearview mirror he pulled onto the street, heading in the direction Jillian had taken. In the meantime, he needed to find the damn woman and put an end to her interference.

Before the cops found her.

Before Mackenzie and his crew found her.

Hell, maybe he should just take care of the SEALs now too. Why bother waiting to find out what they knew? The timing would be perfect. If he could get to Jillian before the cops, and she disappeared, nobody would know she wasn't behind Mackenzie's and his men's deaths. The murders would almost certainly be attributed to her—third time's a charm and all that.

He wouldn't have to worry about any of this shit leaking back to the bosses.

Another squad car roared around him, and Robert's heart jumped into overdrive. Everything hinged on getting to the damn woman before the cops found her. Or at least before so many cops surrounded her he couldn't handle the officers himself.

What was another murder or two pinned on the woman?

She wouldn't be around to insist on her innocence.

Kait didn't need a sense of *knowing*, like her father and brother and possibly Wolf, to recognize that Cosky didn't want her brand of help.

Or at least, judging by his muttered *later,* not at the moment.

Not in front of his teammates. Which was fine with her, she didn't particularly want to expose her gift to Mac, Zane, and Rawls either. Setting herself up for ridicule wasn't a favorite pastime.

Nor did the thought of doing a public healing thrill her. If word of her abilities got out, she'd be inundated with requests for help, and from people in much worse shape than Cosky or Aiden, or even Demi for that matter. But her gift was too damn unreliable for people to pin their hopes on. Her mother's death had proved that. So had Aunt Issa's.

A shadow of grief slid through her. Losing them no longer held that suffocating, raw edge—but the ache was still present, just as it was for the loss of her father. It would probably always be present."

The first knifing agony death brought didn't last long. It was impossible to generate such intensity for any length of time. The mind couldn't cope with such constant, agonizing pain. Eventually the grief settled into a constant, dull ache, which became less constant and duller with the passing of each day, until sooner or later you realized you hadn't thought about them for the whole day.

She'd accepted her mother's death years ago. She'd been so young at the time—just turned ten—with the healing ability barely manifested. She'd recognized the fact she hadn't been strong enough to make a difference.

But Issa . . . this time the shadow of grief held an edge of anger, the sting of frustration. She should have been able to help her. She'd been twenty-two for God's sake, no longer a child. She should have been strong enough to take the cancer from her.

What was the use of such a gift if you couldn't count on it?

If you couldn't use it to help the ones you loved.

She shook old frustrations aside as Rawls removed a knife from his kit and split Cosky's sweats. The leg had to be in pretty bad shape, not just because of how limply it had hung there, but because Cosky had made no effort to go after his attacker.

Still, from the dead silence that froze everyone's tongues when the sweats finally fell away, exposing his distended, grotesquely misaligned knee, she wasn't the only one shocked by its sickening condition.

Not only was the joint horribly swollen, but the patella had shifted to the right and was occupying territory that looked plain *wrong*. Kait's gaze flew to Cosky's face. He'd laid his head on the pavement and closed his eyes. Lord, he must be in tremendous pain.

Except . . . she frowned, studying his face closely. He showed no signs of pain. His expression had hardened into grimness tinged with resignation, but not pain. Of course, he was probably an expert at masking pain by now. He'd been dealing with his injuries for months. And if his career on the teams paralleled her brother's, there would have been plenty of other, smaller, injuries he would have been subject to as well.

Rawls sheathed the knife he'd used to split Cosky's sweats, dropped it into the square bag next to his knees, and removed a vial and syringe. "I'm going to give you some Demerol."

"Don't bother," Cosky said, his voice vibrating with the same grim resignation that was on his face. "It doesn't hurt. I can't feel a damn thing from the knee down."

Mac swore, and turned to glare across the parking lot. "Where's the fucking ambulance?"

"Keep the cops off us too," Zane called, as Mac strode off.

He couldn't feel his leg?

She didn't know much about the mechanics of the knee joint, but numbness didn't sound good. In fact, it sounded downright *bad.*

She drew a shallow breath, her stomach tightening. A wave of heat flooded her. When her hands started tingling, she glanced down, discovering she'd clenched them so tightly her fingernails were cutting into her palms. She relaxed her grip, but the tingling grew stronger. Grimacing, she rubbed her hands against her jeans hoping the stimulation would relieve the discomfort.

"What happened?" Zane's voice was so gruff it verged on raw and shaky.

"I smashed it against the pavement when I hit the ground." Cosky's voice was actually the steadier of the two.

But then, if his leg was numb, he'd known the extent of the damage much longer than his teammates. Long enough to accept it, even resign himself to it.

Another wave of heat and tingling swept through her. Suddenly an intense urge to drop to the ground and reach for Cosky's knee gripped her.

Okay, this was new.

And unwelcome.

Her body rigid, she stepped back, trying to ignore the building urgency. This wasn't the time or place. He'd been very clear about that. She needed to wait until they had some privacy.

The tingling in her hands graduated from uncomfortable to painful.

She tried to step back, to walk away. But her body refused to budge.

Possibly she could have ignored the building urgency to do something, if Cosky hadn't looked down at his knee, and then up at Zane. Their eyes only connected for a second or two, but it was long enough for Kait to catch the shared bleakness.

The next wave of urgency shoved her forward and drove her to the ground. She was reaching for his knee before she even realized she'd moved.

"Goddamn it," Cosky roared, jackknifing up, his hands reaching for hers as Zane stepped toward her. "I told you no."

An electrical shock jolted through her the instant his hands settled over hers. Stunned, Kait watched the hair on her arms stand straight up. It felt like the hair on her head might be doing the same.

"What the hell?" Cosky's eyes opened wide. From the sharp edge of disbelief in his voice, he'd felt that shock too.

Okay . . . This was getting weirder and weirder . . .

A thick surge of heat swallowed her. It built in her chest, flowed up her shoulders, and down through her arms. This she recognized—the heat and flow of the energy when she was channeling it fully.

But she'd never channeled so much before.

Kait blinked to clear the haze from her eyes. Cosky was looking down at his arms, where the hair was standing straight up. Slowly, his head turned; his gaze locked on Kait's face.

His face was red and sweating. Wet patches were already dampening the neck of his T-shirt and under his arms.

Her eyes stung and went blurry. Sweat trickled down her scalp and the back of her neck. Between her breasts.

"Kait," Zane said from above and behind her. Hands settled over her shoulders. He hissed, and the hands fell away. "Son of a bitch."

"What happened?" Rawls rose to his feet.

"She shocked me," Zane said.

He'd felt it too? What in the world was going on? This was beyond bizarre.

"Shocked you?" Rawls repeated thoughtfully. "Leave her be," he added sharply and moved to Kait's side.

"What's going on?" Zane asked.

"Best guess is we're getting a demonstration of why Cos came to see her."

Kait was vaguely aware of Rawls taking a quick look around. "Keep everyone clear. They won't want witnesses."

Cosky looked up, but without letting go of her hands. His face was streaming with sweat now, and getting redder by the moment. "How the hell did you figure it out?"

"Aiden," Rawls said simply. "She was giving him a back massage every time I visited. Dozens of them. It was weird. So when his X-rays did a complete three-sixty, and he requalified for the team, I wondered."

"What are you two talking about?" Zane asked.

Their voices blurred into a steady drone, lifting and falling, like waves on the ocean.

When Cosky's hands tightened over hers and pressed down, grinding her palms into his knee, Kait lifted her head. Sweat was running off her chin, hitting the pavement in a steady spatter. She'd never been this hot before in her life—never sweated so heavily in her life—and she wasn't the only one.

His face was streaming too and even redder than before.

Unhealthy red.

Her hands felt raw beneath his, swollen and numb.

This was wrong. Everything about this was wrong.

Cosky groaned and his hands tightened, squeezing hers. She could barely feel the pressure.

He groaned again, his voice thick. Agonized.

She blinked the haze and sweat from her eyes. His face wavered before taking shape, and then wavered again. When it finally solidified, it was twisted and lobster red.

Oh God, she was hurting him.

She couldn't feel her hands at all anymore. They were completely numb. Maybe she was pressing against his knee too hard, putting too much pressure on the smashed cartilage and torn tendons. She tried to pull back, but his hands tightened, grinding her palms back down against his flesh.

His head lifted. Platinum eyes glowing like polished silver latched on her face.

"Don't let go." The words were slurred, his voice drunk.

What the heck was happening to them? Between them?

"I'm hurting you," she gasped, going light-headed and nauseated at the simple task of talking.

"I can feel the cartilage shifting." Cosky's voice was as breathless as hers. "Jesus, I can feel it working."

No way. Her healings didn't work that fast. It took weeks of massages. Sometimes months.

None of this was possible.

Yet it was happening.

She groaned, her head swimming, nausea climbing her throat.

Oh lord, she was going to be sick. Leaning over, she retched.

The hands covering hers vanished.

"Rawls." This time Cosky's voice was sharp. "Pull her off."

"You should let this run its course."

"Off. Now," Cosky roared, and her hands were knocked loose. He dragged himself back away from her.

"Cos—"

"For Christ's sake, look at her," Cosky snapped. "She's about to pass out."

He was right. Kait tilted forward, her vision graying.

"Grab her!" Cosky's voice echoed through her head.

"Son of a bitch." Hands caught her, eased her back into a sitting position, and back even further until the pavement cradled her shoulders and spine. "Jesus, she's burning up."

"Goddamn it, do something." Cosky's voice sounded strange. Frantic.

"We need to get her temperature down." Rawls on the other hand, sounded grim. "Is this normal?"

"How the hell should I know?"

Her head swam, their voices undulating around her, swelling and receding, rising and falling.

"What happened before?"

"None of this," Cosky said tightly. "She just massaged it. Now shut up and help her."

"Zane, take off your shirt and flap it over her. We need to get some air flow going."

Her shirt lifted and a wonderful breeze wafted over her face and down her chest. Something icy and square pressed against her forehead. A second and third were placed against both sides of her neck, and more on her chest and between her breasts. She groaned, concentrating on the cold. It felt so good.

"The ice packs should help." A long pause. "Her heart rate's slowing." A long, soothing couple of minutes of silence followed before Rawls spoke again. "I think she's cooling."

"You think!" Cosky's voice cracked like thunder.

"I didn't get a baseline temperature." For the first time there was a snap in Rawls's voice. "She doesn't feel as hot. Neither do you."

Kait's head steadied. She concentrated on taking deep, slow breaths until her stomach calmed.

"I'm okay," she said once she was certain talking wouldn't launch the nausea again. She kept her eyes closed though. No sense in pushing things.

"Don't try to move," Rawls murmured.

She hadn't planned on moving. Ever. Kait sighed, enjoying the lovely breeze caressing her face.

"Sweet Jesus," Rawls suddenly said, sounding stunned.

"What?" Cosky and Zane asked together.

"Look at her hands!" A long throbbing pause. "Sweet Jesus, Cos, your knee."

The sheer disbelief in Rawls's voice made Kait open her eyes. The sky was brilliant and blue and dizzying overhead. She started to raise her hands to her face, her arms feeling like they weighed a thousand pounds apiece, but her forearms were caught and forced back down to the pavement.

"Hey," she said indignantly and tried to raise them again. This time nobody stopped her.

"She must be feeling better," Cosky said, his voice still rough, but calmer. "She's getting huffy."

Huffy? She'd show him huffy.

She tried to sit up, only to find she had no strength, so she concentrated on her arms instead. When her hands came into view, she blinked repeatedly to clear the film from her eyes and then simply stared. The back of her hands were lobster red and swollen. Slowly she rotated them until her palms faced her.

A hiss split the air. She wasn't sure if it came from her, Zane, or Cosky.

"Holy . . . crap," she said, drawing the words out as she stared in pure disbelief at her red and blistered palms. She closed her eyes and then peeked again. They looked even worse the second time—swollen, raw, blisters upon blisters—like she'd cupped her hands and reached into a volcano scooping out a pool of lava.

"Well, this is new," she said out loud, to no one in particular.

Only then did it occur to her that her hands didn't hurt. They should. Considering how much a small burn hurt, something this major should have her screaming in pain.

"How come they don't hurt?" she asked, looking up at Rawls.

His forehead wrinkled and he squatted next to her. "Can you feel them at all?"

She frowned, staring hard at the blistered skin. "They feel numb, kind of like that cotton-wool feeling you get when you're on heavy-duty pain killers."

A flash of concern darkened the blue eyes above her, but he just shook his head and shuffled over to Cosky. Which reminded her . . .

If her hands looked like she'd been cradling a nuclear-powered iron, what did Cosky's knee look like? Without considering the ramifications, she jolted up. Her head swam for a second, but steadied. Her stomach, thank God, stayed put.

"I'm okay," she said when hands settled on her shoulders.

"Well, she's not throwing off sparks anymore," Zane said.

Kait turned her attention to Cosky's knee. This time her stomach did try to climb her throat. "Oh, Cosky, no. I'm so sorry."

"Don't be," he said gruffly. "It helped."

"*It helped.*"

How in the world could he claim that? The twisted look on his face from earlier flashed through her mind. No wonder he'd been in pain. His knee was in the same shape as her hands—swollen, covered in livid blisters. She'd been burning the skin off him.

"I don't understand what happened," she said, and her throat closed up. She swallowed hard and simply shook her head.

"This isn't normal?" Rawls asked.

Silently, she shook her head again. He squeezed her shoulder and gently took hold of her right wrist, raising her hand. Squeezing a generous dollop of white cream out of a tube onto her palm, he carefully spread it over her entire hand and then wrapped it from fingers to wrist in white gauze. He taped the bandage at her wrist and repeated the procedure on her left hand.

Once he'd tended to Kait's burns, he shuffled over to Cosky's leg.

"How bad is it?" Kait asked thickly, nausea rolling around in her belly again as she focused on his blistered knee. It was the color of tomato soup now, a deep, angry red.

Rawls squeezed a puddle of cream from the tube onto Cosky's knee, recapped it, and dropped it into his black bag before gingerly smoothing the white substance over Cosky's fried skin. "It's hard to tell beneath the swelling, but . . ." His voice trailed off and he shook his head.

"What?" Kait asked on a tight breath. Her chin dropped and tears stung.

What a disaster. She should never have tried to help him. She'd just made things worse. Much worse. Now he had third-degree burns along with his other injuries.

"I'm not sure yet."

The evasiveness in Rawls's voice brought Kait's head up. Had she caused even more damage than she'd realized?

Cosky scanned her face and his eyes softened.

"The blisters are superficial," he told her, his gentle tone more comforting than his words. "The real story is what's going on beneath the blisters." He glanced at Rawls, his gaze challenging. "Isn't it?"

Zane walked over to Cosky's side and stared. "What are you talking about?"

"The cartilage," Cosky said when Rawls didn't respond. "It's aligned again."

Zane's breath hissed out. He squatted, staring hard at Cosky's cream-smeared skin. "That's impossible."

"Is it?"

Rawls's quiet question had all three men turning to stare at Kait.

Kait sucked in a breath, a sense of unreality hitting her. Her head went light and dizzy, only this time the sensation didn't go away. A wave of exhaustion washed over her.

"Yes, it is. It doesn't happen that fast. It takes weeks . . . even months," she whispered.

Rawls shrugged and squatted beside Cosky's leg with a roll of gauze. He passed the roll through the space between Cosky's knee and the pavement as he wrapped the joint. "We'll know more after the X-rays. The blisters could be screwing with our perception."

Cosky didn't look convinced.

"I can give you some Demerol."

"Don't bother." Cosky's eyebrows pinched together and he shifted his gaze to Kait's gauze-wrapped hands. "It's numb . . ." he said slowly. "Like cotton wool."

He was repeating what she'd said about her hands. She shook her head, too exhausted to try to figure out what that meant.

"The ambulance is here." Mac's voice joined them. "What happened to her?"

The sound of tires on pavement filled Kait's ears, and the ground seemed to roll beneath her.

"We'll fill you in later," Zane said.

"Fine." Mac didn't sound like he cared. He stepped closer to Zane and dropped his voice. "Across the parking lot. The dark-blue hatchback. Do you see him?"

Zane shifted. "Yeah. So?"

Mac dropped his voice even more. "I recognize the motherfucker. He was on my ass for a while. But just when I thought I had a tail, he pulled a Casper. What about you, have you seen him around?"

His voice had dropped again. Or maybe it wasn't his voice. Maybe the buzzing in her ears was just drowning him out.

So tired she couldn't keep her eyes open a second longer, Kait let herself fall back to the pavement. She'd rest for a moment.

"Kait!" Cosky's roar echoed down a tunnel, from an immense distance.

She tried to answer him, but exhaustion rolled over her like a tsunami, dragging her down into a sea of nothingness.

Chapter Ten

COSKY GLARED AT THE PRIVACY CURTAIN, WINCING AS THE HIGH-pitched whine on the other side of the cloth rose higher and higher, adding fuel to his growing frustration. His neighbor barely stopped talking long enough to draw breath, before she was off again.

Swearing, Cosky shoved the ice packs off his knee and swung his legs to the side of the ER bed. Kait was somewhere in this damn place, unconscious, possibly fighting for her life. He glanced around the room for something to serve as a crutch. An EKG machine on a rolling cart fit the bill. He was just about to swing out of bed and make a hop for it, when his curtain separated and Rawls pushed his way through.

"Hold your horses, what do you think you're doing?" Rawls snapped, launching forward and shoving Cosky back against the pillows. While Cosky struggled to sit up again, Rawls swung Cosky's left leg onto the bed. He took much more care with the right leg and went to work covering the bandaged knee with the discarded ice pack.

"I was going to check on Kait," Cosky snarled back, giving the curtain separating him from his irritating ER neighbor a fuming glance.

"She's fine," Rawls said, frowning down at Cosky's knee. He adjusted one of the ice packs and stepped back.

"So she's awake?" Cosky asked, his muscles loosening. She'd been out like a light since she'd fallen back to the pavement, not even waking up during their trip to the ER in the ambulance.

"No, but the docs say she's just sleeping."

Rawls stepped back from the bed, but he looked tense, and he was balanced lightly on his feet, like he was ready to leap on Cosky and pin him to the bed if need be.

The asshole.

"Sleeping?" Cosky's voice gained volume and velocity. "That wasn't sleep, damn it."

He swung his legs to the side of the bed again. Ice packs went flying. "I want to see her."

Rawls shook his head in disgust and threw up his hands. "Fine. We sure as hell wouldn't want you to exhibit any common sense and stay off the leg until we know how extensive the damage is."

"Are you gonna help me, or stand there like an ass?" Cosky asked, the impatience and worry thickening inside him until his lungs felt compressed beneath the pressure.

Damn it, he shouldn't have pushed her. She'd tried to pull away, tried to stop, and he hadn't let her. He'd forced her to channel that damn energy, as she called it, much longer than she should have, much longer than was apparently safe.

"You've got five minutes," Rawls said, stepping up to the bed and presenting his shoulder. "I'm not shitting you, Cos. Five minutes, so you can see for yourself that she's fine. Then back to bed. Got it?"

Cosky slid to the side of the bed, grabbed Rawls's shoulder, and pulled himself up, using his left leg to stabilize himself. He slung his arm over his corpsman's shoulders. With his lungs in a straightjacket, he slowly hopped alongside Rawls out into the emergency room and down the length of curtained cubicles. They stopped in front of the last curtain and slowly swung around. As they pushed their way through the cloth, Cosky could suddenly smell her. Oranges or lemons. The sweet scent lingered beneath the sharper smells of disinfectant and blood. Something inside him eased, and his lungs started working again, drawing that sweet, clean scent in with deep, desperate gulps.

Her curtained-off area looked identical to his except the bed seemed bigger, maybe because she looked so small and fragile within it. His chest tightened at how innocent she looked lying there like that, her face softened in sleep. Her braid glowed like molten honey against the hospital white of the pillow. It snaked out from behind her head and down the length of her body, in a gilded rope of gold.

Cosky hopped closer and reached for the chair beside her bed, dragging it over to him. She didn't stir at the dull scrape of metal against linoleum. Letting go of Rawls's shoulder, he collapsed onto the cushion and used his good leg to drag himself, chair and all, next to the bed.

"You call this sleep?" he asked in a tight voice, watching her lie there as still as death, her dusky eyelashes dark shadows against her pink cheeks.

"Yeah, I do. So do the doctors." Stepping up to the bed, Rawls scanned her face himself. Then, as though he couldn't help himself, he pressed his fingers to the side of her neck. "Heart rate is normal. So is BP. She's breathing fine. Pupils are reactive, and she's responsive to stimuli." He shook his head, dropped his hand, and took a step back, his face puzzled. "Granted, it's unusual, but she appears to be in a deep sleep. They're going to admit her to transitory care and wait for her to wake up."

Unusual?

Yeah, well that pretty much described every single event of today.

Unable to help himself, Cosky took hold of her bandaged left hand. It just lay there in his palm. Lifeless. There was no heat. No rampaging lust. Just guilt.

And respect—she put her life on the line to heal him. Hell—considering what an ass he'd been less than an hour before, that kind of generosity was unusual to say the least. And look what her good Samaritan act had netted her?

A night in the ER.

Because of him.

As if he needed another example of why he had to steer clear of female entanglements.

"So you've seen her," Rawls said as he hauled Cosky to his feet. "Now it's back to bed. That leg should be elevated."

Cosky allowed Rawls to guide him from Kait's bedside and back to his little section of the emergency room. But her pink, still face haunted him every step of the way. And he couldn't help obsessing about this strange deep sleep of hers. What if she didn't wake up in a couple of hours? What if she didn't wake up at all?

"You're borrowing trouble." Rawls sent him a sympathetic look as Cosky levered himself up and dragged his legs onto the bed. "Look at what she did. Is it any wonder she's exhausted? She expended a tremendous amount of energy. Maybe this deep sleep is simply part of the process, like refilling the well." Turning toward the chair beside Cosky's bed, he settled into it and glanced at Cosky's bandaged leg again. "Any feeling yet?"

Cosky simply shook his head.

Rawls frowned. "What did the doc say?"

Cosky thumped his head against the thin pillow behind him and scowled. "Nothing. He hasn't been in yet. They have a call into X-ray. The nurse said the doc may be in before X-ray shows up."

When Rawls's cell phone rang, Cosky breathed a sigh of relief; it was annoying as hell being out of the loop. Zane and Mac had headed out to comb the streets for her, while Rawls had accompanied him and Kait in the ambulance.

"Any luck?" Cosky asked as soon as Rawls lowered his phone.

"No. Mac called in"—Rawls glanced at the curtain and lowered his voice—"some of the guys. They'll keep at it through the night."

A few minutes later someone from radiology showed up with a wheelchair to take him down for X-rays. Lying there, with the icy metal of the table biting into his spine and the back of his skull, Cosky waited for the technician to ask about the bubbled and blistered skin of his knee, but she ignored the injury. No doubt a couple of third-degree burns and a shattered knee were small potatoes compared to the more traumatic injuries that wheeled in and out of her X-ray room.

The X-rays only took a few minutes and then he was helped back into the wheelchair. As they wheeled him away, he absently checked out his exposed knee.

At first he thought he was focusing on the wrong leg.

He blinked and looked again.

What the hell?

He jolted forward so hard he almost fell out of the wheelchair—would have if he hadn't grabbed hold of the armrests.

"Easy there," the tech said. A hand came down on his shoulder, easing him back against the backrest.

Cosky muttered something incomprehensible and just sat there in frozen disbelief.

After a moment of staring, he closed his eyes, counted to ten, and opened them again. The view hadn't changed.

The blisters were gone, so was the swelling. Healthy pink skin greeted his incredulous gaze. He leaned forward, staring in astonishment. The knee itself looked better than it had since before that flameout in Seattle. Christ, the bruising was all but gone. Even the surgical scars were thinner, lighter, and less visible.

No wonder the technician had exhibited such unconcern—the injury looked months old.

Suddenly it occurred to him that he felt amazingly good considering he'd hit the pavement at full speed. He'd landed on his shoulders, which had been aching like hell . . . at first. Not so much now. He rotated his arm. In fact, not at all now. And then there were his elbows and the back of his arms, which had received an extreme exfoliation. They'd been burning like a son of a bitch.

He extended his arm and twisted it to get a look at the skinned elbow, which had plenty of dried blood, but no scabs. He probed his right elbow with his left fingers. Smooth skin glided beneath his fingertips.

The burning sting from his collision with the pavement was gone too. Shaking his head, he pushed up the sleeve of his hospital scrubs and checked out his shoulder. More dried blood and smooth skin.

Un-fucking-believable.

Still unable to trust the evidence of his own eyes, he settled back and waited.

Rawls scanned his face as the tech rolled him toward his hospital bed, and sat up with a frown. "What's wrong?"

Cosky jerked his chin toward his exposed right knee and waited. He didn't have to wait long. Rawls glanced at it, did a double take, and shot out of his chair so fast it toppled over.

Yeah, apparently he wasn't hallucinating. Rawls saw the rejuvenation too.

"What? How?" Rawls stumbled closer. He went down on his haunches in front of Cosky's wheelchair and skimmed the faintly red skin with his fingertips. "Sweet Jesus."

"Is there a problem?" the technician asked, confusion on her face. She glanced between Rawls and Cosky.

"Not now." Rawls rose slowly to his feet.

Cosky wasn't quite as sure. The joint looked good. The kneecap had shifted back into place. The blisters and burns were gone. In fact, all the injuries he'd sustained earlier in the day had vanished. But there was still the matter of the earlier injury. Had Kait's healing had any effect on the fracture to the tibial plateau?

"When will I get the results of the X-ray?" Cosky asked.

"Dr. Phillips has a call in to your orthopedic surgeon," the tech said. "I'm sure he'll be in as soon as he's had a chance to view the films and consult with your attending physician."

When the tech set the brake on the wheelchair and moved in to help Cosky over to the bed, he waved her away.

Rawls waited until the woman had pushed her way through the curtain, before squatting in front of Cosky again. This time he did a thorough probe of the joint, from left to right and top to bottom. Once finished he just squatted there, staring, disbelief still shining in his eyes.

"Well?" Cosky prodded.

"Maybe the patella didn't shift after all. The leg was pretty swollen; maybe it just appeared that way."

Right.

"Like it appeared to be blistered?" Cosky asked dryly as he lifted and bent his arm, offering Rawls a look at his elbow. "And like my arms and my shoulder appeared to be skinned and leaking?"

Rawls's forehead wrinkled. Walking around the wheelchair, he grabbed the handles and pushed Cosky toward the curtain. Cosky didn't bother to ask where they were going. He could guess.

Kait was still sleeping when they entered her room, but she'd rolled onto her right side and tucked her hands beneath her cheek. The knot in Cosky's chest loosened. It loosened even more as her eyelashes quivered, and her lips twitched. Her sleep looked much more natural now. Normal.

She stretched—a long, lazy arch of muscles and bones beneath the covers. Her breasts lifted, and the sheet slipped down to her waist. Suddenly Cosky was left staring at the round, ripe curves that were all but falling out of her loose hospital gown.

A flash of heat rolled through him.

Only this fire had nothing to do with healing.

Tension flooded his groin. His cock swelled.

And then he realized Rawls had noticed those tender, exposed curves too. This time the tension that flooded his blood and knotted his muscles had nothing to do with lust and everything to do with rage. When Rawls leaned forward, his hand reaching for Kait's chest, Cosky shot out of the wheelchair, his hands cocked, every muscle in his body rigid and begging for action. The only thing that stopped his fist from breaking every bone in his buddy's face was the sheet Rawls dragged back up to Kait's collarbone.

Son of a bitch.

Still reeling from the adrenaline rush, Cosky collapsed back into the wheelchair. Only then did he realize he'd shot up on both legs, and his right leg hadn't crumbled beneath him. Not only had it taken his weight, it had done so without pain.

He was still processing that when Rawls captured one of Kait's hands. She frowned and muttered grumpily. With a soft *ssshhhhh,*

Rawls waited for her to settle again, before unwrapping the gauze. Once the bandage lay in a creamy puddle on the thin blanket, he simply stood there. Frozen.

Finally, with a befuddled shake of his head, he stepped to the side.

Cosky leaned forward as Rawls moved out of the way, and Kait's hand came into view. Her perfect, slender hand, with its perfect, pink skin.

Not a blister or burn in sight.

"Fuck." Mac snapped his cell closed and scowled through the windshield at the steady stream of traffic, while he tried to get his heart rate and respiration back under control.

He wanted to chalk his tension up to frustration and rage, but he'd never lied to himself, and he wasn't going to start now. Nor did frustration and rage explain the missile that had sprouted in his pants the second Amy Chastain's voice had marched down the line. What the fuck was it about the damn woman that pushed his buttons like this?

Damned if he could figure it out.

Trying to focus on something beyond his redheaded albatross, he turned his attention back where it belonged—on their tail.

How many weeks had it been since he'd noticed that cocksucker and his navy-blue hatchback, only to shrug the bastard off? Six weeks? Two months?

"Goddamn fucking—" He set his mouth and sucked back the rest of his rage.

Throwing a tantrum accomplished nothing. Next time he'd trust his fucking instincts and act on them regardless of how paranoid they seemed. If he'd grabbed the asshole back then, they'd have a six-week head start.

They might actually have a clue to pursue by now.

Zane pulled into the stream of traffic, before glancing across the van at him. "Amy didn't know?"

"Amy," Mac said through his teeth, ignoring the way his dick twitched at her name, "isn't aware of any DOJ-ordered surveillance on us."

Zane stopped at a red light. "You're sure she'd know?"

"She says she'd have heard." Mac glared out the window as he concentrated on dragging in deep, calming breaths.

If there was no surveillance on them, then the guy in the parking lot was either a coincidence, or a nonagency tail.

He caught Zane's lingering glance in the rearview mirror. "Anyone back there?"

"No blue hatchback," Zane said after a long pause.

"But?" Mac prompted, hearing the qualifier in his LC's voice. Twisting in his bucket seat, he studied the traffic behind them.

"There's a silver Accord eight cars behind us. I've seen a silver Accord off and on, never close enough to get a look at the driver, or plate. No distinguishing marks on the vehicle." His eyes were grim as he touched Mac's gaze. "It could be nothing. Lots of Accords on the road, and silver's a common color."

Which would make it a perfect surveillance vehicle.

"See what happens if you go evasive," Mac said.

Two turns later the Accord turned left and sped out of sight. Which could mean the car belonged to someone who lived and worked in Coronado—or, it could mean the driver of the car had realized he'd been made and broken the tail.

Frustrated, Mac faced forward and ground his shoulders against his backrest. "If we *are* being followed, we can't afford to lead them to Cosky's attacker. Head back to the ER. I'll call Hollister and Russo in. They're on standby; they've got time to cruise for her."

"We need to get some surveillance on ourselves," Mac continued, as he texted Russo and Hollister to call him. "See if we're being tag teamed."

If someone was tag teaming them with three or more cars, it would be nearly impossible to identify the tails. The vehicles would trade out before being made.

"Tag teaming would be as expensive as hell," Zane said slowly. He frowned and shook his head. "Hell, if they had a team on each of us, we're talking fifteen to twenty men."

"Judging by their operation in Seattle, the fucking money's there."

"Or maybe it's a coinci—" Zane glanced in the rearview mirror and broke off, frowning. "I'll be damned," he said slowly, staring in the mirror, before jerking his eyes away and focusing on the line of traffic in front of them. "A blue hatchback just pulled in behind us. Seven cars back, too far away to make the driver or plate."

Now that was one lovely coincidence.

"What do you want to do?" Zane asked, glancing in the rearview mirror again.

Mac frowned. "Don't tip him off. Keep your eyes open. See how many repeating vehicles we can identify. When we have more intel, we'll set a trap. For now head to the ER."

Zane nodded in agreement and took the next right. "What about the prints Rawls pulled? We sending them to Amy?"

Yeah . . . tension flooded his muscles and sizzled through his blood as Amy's name hit the air again—which was all the more reason to limit his interaction with the fucking woman.

"I already texted them to Radar." He scowled at the questioning look Zane sent him. "Amy would have to call in a favor to get the prints run. We know Seattle's FBI field office has a mole. We don't need her reaching out to the wrong person."

Which was all true, but had nothing to do with the reason he'd contacted Radar.

Amy knew better than to contact anyone in Chastain's old field office. There was no doubt in his mind she'd get the result back without alerting their mole. The real problem was that sending the prints to her meant interacting with her, repeatedly. Fuck, he was still hard from their thirty-second conversation earlier.

How the hell a Goddamn voice could light such a fuse to his libido was beyond his understanding. But he'd already gotten his exercise today thanks to one fucking woman. He didn't need another one sending him out for a minimarathon in the middle of the night.

His cell phone rang as Zane pulled into the ER's parking lot.

"The plates came back stolen." Radar's crisp voice informed him.

"Location?"

"Portland. A month ago."

In other words, it was another dead end. Mac expelled a frustrated breath.

"Fucking perfect." He drew a ragged breath and regrouped. "Look, I hate to ask, but we're up a creek. I'm having a strip of tape brought in to you. Will you find someone to run the prints on it?" He smiled tightly at the immediate agreement. "Thanks, we owe you."

Before he even dropped his hand, his cell rang again. He checked the caller ID. Russo. Thirty seconds later Echo Platoon's lieutenant commander had agreed to meet him at the ER. "Radar's going to take them?" Zane asked.

Mac nodded and picked up the length of tape Rawls had left curled in the cup holder. Rawls had stuck a second length of tape to the side with the smudged prints, thereby sealing the prints in plastic. "Not much of a shot here. Rawls smudged them just sealing them for mailing."

Zane shrugged. "It's worth a try."

True, although they had another avenue to pursue now as well. A hard smile spread across Mac's face as the hatchback and Accord came to mind. Not to mention Cosky's crazy stalker.

"Has Rawls heard anything on the scanner?" Zane asked as he set the parking brake and pocketed his keys.

"She's still in the wind." Mac pushed open the passenger door and climbed out of the van. "Probably gone to ground."

Which was to their benefit, because the longer she avoided the police, the better their chance of nabbing her.

"I'll wait here for Russo," Mac said, waving Zane toward the emergency room. As he waited, he scanned the parking lot for familiar vehicles. No blue hatchback or silver Accord. Several minutes passed and a gray Civic pulled into the parking lot. It parked in the very back. Nobody got out of the car. He shifted against the van, trying to get a better look without giving his interest away.

More minutes passed and a Jeep Cherokee pulled up beside him. The door opened and Russo climbed out. His dark gaze swept the parking lot and settled on the Civic. "You got something?"

"Not sure," Mac said with another glance at the car in question. The driver looked like he was eating lunch. "Swing by it on your way out and text me the plates."

Russo simply nodded and turned to stare at the entrance to the ER. He ran a lean hand through crisp black hair. "How's Cos?"

Mac shook his head. "Doesn't look good. He caught the same fucking knee when he hit the ground. Smashed it to hell and back. *Again.*"

"Damn." Russo wiped a hand down his grim face and took the tape Mac handed him, then swung back to his Jeep. "Tell Cos I'll be by later. We'll do a couple more grids for his lady, unless the cops run her down first."

Mac watched him climb into the Cherokee. The engine fired and the jeep took off. Without waiting for Russo to cruise past the Civic, Mac headed for the ER. His phone chimed several minutes later indicating that he had a text message. He forwarded the plate number onto Radar with a request to check it out.

He stopped at the front desk and received directions to Cosky's room—or curtain was more like it. A low murmur of voices sounded behind the cloth, so low he couldn't hear what was being said. Which meant whatever they were discussing was sensitive. His hunch was confirmed a second later when he pushed his way through the curtain and the voices stopped in mid-drone. Zane turned back to the bed as soon as Mac closed the curtain behind him.

"So when are they releasing you?" Zane asked.

"Hell if I know." Cosky exchanged an odd look with Rawls. "They want to take more X-rays."

The comment was delivered without the irritation or frustration that Mac expected. In fact, Cosky seemed strangely satisfied and relieved. A marked departure from his attitude as they'd loaded him into the ambulance.

"Have they scheduled surgery?" Mac asked, stepping up to

the bed. Cosky's knee was covered in ice packs, but considering the damage it had sustained, surgery seemed not only likely, but imminent.

"Yeah." Rawls coughed. "The leg didn't take nearly the hit we thought. Surgery won't be required."

"No shit," Mac said slowly, watching another round of looks pass between his men. His bullshit meter flexed. "It looked pretty bad to me."

"Yeah." Rawls coughed again, a dead giveaway a lie was to follow. "It looked worse than it actually was."

"Really?" Mac's bullshit meter warped into the red zone. What the fuck were they lying about? And why? He reached for an ice pack. "You don't mind if I take a look?"

Cosky didn't blink. "Knock yourself out."

The casual response should have eased Mac's suspicions—would have—if Rawls and Zane hadn't traded sidelong glances.

What the fuck was going on?

Before Mac had a chance to ask, or to clear the ice packs and get a look at Cosky's knee for himself, the curtain separated. A tall man in a tired suit, with a shoulder holster clearly visible against his white dress shirt, stepped into the room.

Flat brown eyes locked on Cosky. He cocked his head, the skin of his bald head gleaming beneath the overhead lights. "Marcus Simcosky?"

Mac scowled. Motherfucker, just what they didn't need. A cop. Sure, the locals were bound to show up sooner or later. He'd been hoping for later.

"Yeah?" Cosky said. The word climbed toward the end, turning it into a question.

The stranger moved into the middle of the room, his gaze drifting from Cosky to Rawls to Zane and finally coming to a rest on Mac's face.

"I'm Detective Pachico, with the Coronado Police Department. I have some questions."

Of course he did, the bastard wouldn't be here otherwise.

"You got some ID?" Mac asked, more to be an ass than from any real suspicion. He ignored the warning glance Zane sent him.

Pachico reached into his jacket pocket and pulled out a leather wallet. He flipped it open, exposing a silver badge. He held the badge up to Mac's face for a count of five, before silently pocketing it again.

"This woman who attacked you, did she give any indication as to why?" Pachico asked, his flat brown gaze returning to the bed.

"I went over this with the officers at the scene," Cosky said, staring steadily back.

With a slight inclination of his head, Pachico acknowledged Cosky's comment. "I find it helpful to conduct interviews myself rather than relying on the officer's report."

Mac snorted. More likely he conducted the interviews himself to compare against the officer's report. Discrepancies in the witnesses' accounts would raise flags.

The detective flicked Mac a look, but ignored the nonverbal commentary. "Did the woman say anything?"

Cosky shrugged. "She claimed she knew me. Called me a lying, murdering bastard and then pointed the gun at me and screamed 'this is for my babies.'"

The detective frowned. "She accused you of killing her children?"

"No." Cosky countered. "She pointed the gun at me and said 'this is for my babies.'"

"And she didn't say anything else?" Pachico's voice dripped disbelief.

"No. She didn't."

"You expect me to believe, that this woman—who targeted you not just once, but twice—didn't explain why she wanted to kill you?"

Cosky stared steadily back. "I can't help what you believe. What I *can do* is tell you what happened, which I've done."

"And you've never seen this woman before?"

"No."

"Take me through what happened. Both times."

Mac listened to Cosky recite the events leading up to the first attack, including the woman following him and the aborted showdown at the mall.

"And she just walked away?" Pachico asked, only he sounded thoughtful rather than disbelieving.

"That's right," Cosky said. "I thought she'd mistaken me for someone else. When she didn't come back, I took off."

The detective nodded slightly and motioned for Cosky to continue. At the end of the recital, Pachico stirred. "And she didn't say anything more? Anything at all?"

Mac crossed his arms and set his feet. "How many fucking times does he have to tell you—no, he doesn't know her, and no, she didn't say anything else—before the words sink in?"

With a slow swing of his hips, Pachico turned on Mac. "See, here's my problem. If he didn't know her, if *none of you* knew her, then why are members of your team canvassing the streets?"

Mac shrugged. "She tried to take us out. Cosky the first time. All three of us the second. Call us curious."

"Really?" Pachico cocked an eyebrow and regarded Mac levelly.

"I would have thought the fallout from the last time you took the law into your hands would have cured you of such curiosity."

Mac's hands clenched. "We have no intention of apprehending her." He pushed the lie through his teeth. "If we spot her, we'll call it in." He paused and sent the bastard a gritty smile. "Christ knows your boys can't seem to find her."

Pachico held his eyes, his cold face knowing. The bastard wasn't buying a damn word of it. Luckily, he couldn't prove a thing.

"So, if you find her, you'll turn her in?" he asked point-blank.

Mac bared his teeth. "Absolutely."

Not. You motherfucker.

Pachico matched him toothy smile for toothy smile. He'd give the bastard one thing: He had balls. Mac didn't find that quality particularly appealing under the circumstances.

"Is that all, Detective?" Cosky broke into the pissing match.

"For now." Turning toward Cosky, the detective reached into his jacket pocket, pulled out a white business card, and flipped it onto the bed. "You find her, you call. If she contacts you, you call. If you remember anything new, you call."

Without waiting to see if anyone picked the card up, he pushed back through the curtain. Dead silence claimed the room. After a few minutes, Mac poked his head outside. The corridor was empty.

Which didn't mean dick; the bastard could be listening from the curtained-off rooms to their right or left. From the watchful looks on Cosky's, Rawls's, and Zane's faces, they realized the lack of privacy too.

Guess he wouldn't be getting the answer to the big puzzle of the day, which was what the *hell* his men weren't telling him.

Twenty-four hours after she'd ditched the van, a transformed Jillian slunk out of the house she'd broken into. She'd whacked her hair off just above her ears and dyed it a deep, rich auburn, courtesy of the Clairol package she'd found in the master bathroom's medicine cabinet. Sunglasses and a baseball cap swallowed her head and most of her face. She'd traded the poncho for loose jeans, blue-and-white pinstriped sneakers, and a red University of California sweatshirt. The sweatshirt's huge middle pocket—which extended from the right to left—was the exact length of the butcher knife she'd sheathed inside.

Everything was a size too big, but she wasn't picky.

With luck, the owner of the house wouldn't return anytime soon and alert the cops to the broken window and missing clothes. At least not until Jillian had finished what she'd set out to do.

She kept to the main streets as she walked, trying to mimic the easy confident stride of someone who didn't have anything to hide, who belonged here, who didn't have murder on their agenda. Apparently she was a better actress than she'd thought, because she passed three cop cars and not one of them looked at her twice.

A baseball game was underway in the park across from the apartment complex she'd tracked Simcosky to. She took a seat in the middle of the steel bleachers and settled back to stake out the building. Within fifteen minutes, four cop cars had cruised past the baseball diamond. The police were certainly making their presence known, but she didn't see anyone actually guarding the front entrance.

Of course they could be waiting inside the lobby, out of sight.

On the bench below her sat a trio of tanned, toned, and chatty Barbies. Jillian ignored their theatrical falsettos, concentrating on the apartment complex across the grass.

"It was terrifying," Blond Barbie said, her voice rising to compete with the cheer that shook the crowd as the bat connected with the ball. "That psycho tried to hit me. I barely jumped out of the way in time."

Psycho?

Jillian's head snapped down. She shrugged the sting off and scanned the back of the Barbies' heads. They looked like an ad for Clairol—silky, soft hair in blond, brunet, and strawberry hues.

If she'd almost hit them the day before, they must have been on the sidewalk, which meant they probably lived in the apartment complex. There had to be some way she could use them to get to Simcosky.

Another cheer rolled through the bleachers, and the steel bench shook. Jillian grabbed hold of the metal seat and fought back a surge of nausea. She should have eaten something before leaving the house, ransacked the fridge as well as the closets. But the thought of food had turned her stomach inside out.

"Check out all the cops. They must not have found her," Brunet Barbie said. "I wonder how Kaity's boyfriend's doing?"

"A lot better than if she'd actually shot him or hit him with the van," Strawberry Barbie said.

"Did you get a look at him?" There was avid interest in the brunette's voice. "Talk about eye candy. Kaity has all the luck."

Jillian leaned forward.

"No kidding," the blonde said. "Now that he's seeing Kaity, maybe his friends will start hanging around. Did you see his blond friend? Oh. My. Fucking. God." She made kissing sounds. Interesting.

Apparently Marcus Simcosky didn't live in the apartment complex. His girlfriend did. She frowned, rolling that information around in her head. A girlfriend would come in handy. She could use this Kaity to get to Simcosky. Assuming she could find out what apartment this Kaity lived in and what the woman looked like.

Turning, she stared across the park at the towering apartment complex. The place was huge. At least seven or eight floors. What were the chances the women below knew everyone who lived there? Not very likely.

Clearing her throat loudly, she scooted down a bench, until she was directly behind her quarry. "Excuse me, I couldn't help overhearing. I'm new here. Just moved in over the weekend. What happened yesterday? I heard all the sirens, but by the time I got downstairs, all the action was over."

Blond Barbie fluffed her hair and twisted to look behind her. Pale-blue eyes scanned Jillian's face, and then dropped to her clothes. "Some crazy homeless person tried to kill Kaity's boyfriend."

Jillian released a relieved breath as contempt rather than recognition flooded the sharp angles of the blonde's face. She sniffed and turned back to her friends, dismissing Jillian.

Leaning down again, Jillian pressed her luck. "Who's Kaity?"

The brunette answered without turning around. "The tall blonde in apartment 607."

Blond Barbie gave the brunette a shoulder nudge and then the three huddled together, whispering.

Jillian tensed, certain they'd recognized her, waiting for their cry of alarm.

And then their voices drifted up to her.

"*. . . freak . . . my God did you see her fingernails?*"

Lifting her hands, Jillian stared at her ragged, filthy fingernails and smiled. The whispering had nothing to do with recognition or fear. It was simple cliquishness and bitchery.

The trio ignored her for the rest of the baseball game, which was fine with Jillian. She had the information she wanted. Now she needed the opportunity to put the information to use. That opportunity came sooner than expected. When the game ended, the Barbies hooked up with a couple of the baseball players. Amid flirting, teasing, and some shoving among the guys, the group meandered across the park toward the apartment complex.

Jillian followed them. From the group's backward glances and snide laughter, there was little doubt they knew she was behind them. Just before they crossed the street, Jillian closed on them, trailing so closely she hoped it looked like she was with their group.

The glass in the entrance doors and side windows was still missing, thanks to her grand opening with the van. A blue-suited security guard stood against the wall inside the lobby. He glanced at the chattering group as they passed and nodded politely. Jillian forced herself to smile back and held her breath as she followed her adopted herd across the lobby.

Any minute someone was going to recognize her and scream.

Any minute the guard would rush her.

But with the exception of snide laughter and snarky sotto voce comments about Jillian's clothes, hands, hair, and parentage, the lobby remained quiet. As her group approached the elevators, one of the doors opened, and the Barbies, along with their entourage, piled inside.

When Jillian tried to follow, Blondie blocked the entrance. "We're full." She cast her friends an exaggerated eye roll and laughter lit the elevator.

Jillian silently stepped back. Their laughter rang in her ears long after the doors closed. Four months ago that level of bitchiness would have infuriated her. But her priorities had shifted since then. She'd discovered what was worth investing energy and emotion into—and it wasn't Barbie dolls.

What mattered were the people you loved.

What mattered was vengeance when they were stolen from you.

What mattered was getting to Marcus Simcosky's girlfriend, who lived in apartment 607.

Chapter Eleven

Exhaustion weighed on Kait the following morning. The simple task of grocery shopping had wiped her out completely. Giving into her craving for Butter Brickle ice cream may not have been the brightest thing she'd ever done. She should have rested a couple more hours at home, after being released from transitory care, before heading to the store—although how she could still be tired after sleeping for eighteen hours straight . . .

She'd never had such an extreme reaction to a healing before. But then again, she'd never done such an extreme healing before. Her lobster-red, blistered hands flashed through her mind. The memory felt like a dream, which had a lot to do with the lack of evidence to back up the memory. Her hands looked picture-perfect this morning. According to Rawls, so did Cosky's knee, which brought another surge of disbelief.

How was that possible?

It had taken six months for Aiden's back to fuse.

A constant stream of people interrupted her journey from the parking lot to the lobby, so it took twice as long to reach the elevator. In between visits with her neighbors, she compulsively checked her caller ID and voice mail, even though she would have heard her cell phone ringing.

Wolf hadn't called, neither had Cosky or Rawls.

Cosky's silence was understandable. As was Rawls's. Before she'd checked herself out of transitory care, Rawls had stopped by her room to tell her Cosky's orthopedic surgeon had admitted him for a boatload of tests: X-rays, MRIs, CAT scans. The sudden improved condition of the knee had raised all sorts of speculation.

Since they didn't want to drive the speculation her way, they felt it was safer to avoid her—at least at the hospital. Rawls had only stayed a moment and limited his questions, simply telling her they'd be in contact after Cosky was released. Kait had no doubt Rawls had an enormous list of questions he intended to ask her then.

Questions she wouldn't be able to answer. She had no idea what had happened in the parking lot and no idea how that one enormously freaky session could have improved Cosky's leg to the extent his orthopedic surgeon had actually noticed. She was as puzzled by the whole thing as the doctors were.

She glanced at the clock between the elevators. It was just after eleven a.m. How long would it take them to run all those tests? Had Cosky been released yet?

God, she hoped not. Facing him in the parking lot had been one thing. Adrenaline and concern had overpowered the awkwardness, and then that freaky healing had hijacked the moment. There hadn't been time to think about the last time they'd been together, aka their naked, sweaty, passionate encounter on the couch.

But the memory of that encounter had haunted her the moment she'd returned home. Even with the windows open, the place still reeked of roses and sex, courtesy of the sheet she'd left tucked into the cushions of the couch the day before. That sex-stained sheet was the reason she'd clandestinely checked herself out of the hospital rather than accepting Demi's offer to drive her home—Demi would have insisted on seeing her settled.

Dealing with that sheet, and the memories surrounding it, had launched her craving for Butter Brickle ice cream too.

One more grievance to toss at Cosky's feet.

In the elevator, she checked her voice mail again, just in case she'd gone inexplicably deaf and hadn't heard the phone ring. Still no message. Cosky would call before coming over, wouldn't he? It was common courtesy. But something told her the man didn't put much stock in courtesy, especially if he wanted something—like answers.

She swore and glared down at her phone. Maybe it was broken. She punched the talk button and frowned at the resulting dial tone. It *sounded* like it was working, just like it had the other dozen times she'd checked it. Plus it had connected just fine with her home phone the last time she'd tested it.

So why hadn't Wolf called?

Kait sighed, nudging the plastic bags with her toe. Wolf's silence was causing her heart palpitations on two levels. He'd known about the first attack on Cosky within the hour. Within half an hour was more like it. He should have heard about the second attack by now. He should have heard about her trip to the ER too. Considering how overprotective the man was, he should have been burning his way through her minutes as he charged to her rescue. If he'd decided to forgo calling, and simply headed down to Coronado, he should have arrived by now.

Unless he'd been reeled in for deployment.

God knows the SEAL teams could be called into rotation at a moment's notice. If Wolf was part of a covert ops team too, which seemed pretty obvious, he could have been called out. He could be in the heat of battle in some godforsaken country—or something could have gone wrong with Aiden's deployment and Wolf was on his way to the rescue . . . again. Which meant both of them could be in danger.

Considering what her brothers did for a living, they were *always* in danger.

She should have learned by now that worrying accomplished nothing, well, besides giving her an ulcer. With a deep breath, she concentrated on the image of a colorful, cartoonish dodo bird. She painted the creature so clearly in her mind it pushed everything else out. Soon she could see it with total clarity, smell the burnt metal of blown glass. Her mind emptied of everything but her creation.

It was a trick she'd learned years ago. If she concentrated hard enough on her craft, filled her mind with her creations, she could push aside the worry, the fear, the uncertainty that went hand in hand with life on the edge of the teams.

By the time the bell to the elevator dinged, the exhaustion had given way to a burst of creativity, and Kait was itching to get started on the image in her mind. She glanced down at the plastic bags at her feet, swore softly, and bent to pick them up. The glass would have to wait until she put the groceries away.

Her purse dragged at her left shoulder and the two bags felt like they weighed a ton a piece as she stepped out of the elevator and headed toward her apartment. A slender figure down the hall, next to Martha Chamber's door, caught her attention, and she swallowed a groan. Martha was an absolute sweetheart, but by God, the woman liked to talk. And talk. And talk.

If she got waylaid by the woman, she'd never get to her studio. But as she drew closer, she realized the person in front of Martha's door was too thin and too tall to be her next-door neighbor. In fact, she wasn't even sure the figure was a *she.* Anorexic-thin, with shorn hair, sunglasses, and a baseball cap, the figure was the very definition of androgynous.

She smiled absently at Martha's visitor as she approached her door. The smile faded when the figure suddenly headed toward her.

"Kaity?"

Her smile fell away completely. The woman—or at least the voice sounded like a woman's—obviously knew her. She smothered a sigh and turned to face the stranger. There was something vaguely familiar about the pitch of the cheekbones and shape of her chin, but Kait couldn't quite place her.

"Yes?" Kait summoned another smile.

The woman came closer, her right hand tucked inside the center pocket of her sweatshirt. The cocked tension of that arm caught Kait's attention, and a sliver of ice pierced her. There was something off about that arm. Something strange about the way her hand was tucked inside the pocket.

"You'll have to forgive me," Kait said, widening her smile, which had no effect on the tight-lipped woman across from her. "I'm afraid I don't remember you."

"Why should you?" There was an ugly vibration to the question.

Kait took a cautious step back, which was useless since the woman took two steps forward. "Do I know you?"

"No. But you will." The cold edge to the stranger's voice was so sharp it echoed down the hall.

Kait's gaze flew up; she studied the steep cheekbones and sallow skin, the narrow pointed chin.

The sense of familiarity sank deeper. Set off alarm bells.

She'd seen this woman, and recently.

"What can I do for you?" Kait asked, working hard to keep the unease from her voice. She lifted her shoulder slightly and felt her purse slide down to the crook of her elbow. If she needed it, there was Mace in her purse.

"You can call your *boyfriend* and tell him you need to see him." The woman's inflection of the word *boyfriend* was infused with something stronger than contempt, closer to hatred.

What the heck?

"I don't have a boyfriend," Kait said, losing the smile. She held her ground as the woman took another step forward.

"Liar!" A hiss replaced the cold snap in the woman's voice.

As Kait stared at the face across from her, the sense of familiarity clicked into place. An avalanche of ice hit the pit of her belly.

Was it possible?

She scanned the woman's face again. The long ratty brown hair was gone. Either cut off or stuffed inside the hat. But the shape of the face was the same, so were the cheekbones and the chin.

Wasn't this just perfect? Cosky's crazy stalker was after her now.

"I *know* Marcus Simcosky is your boyfriend," the woman said, her voice so thick with rage it didn't sound human.

"You're misinformed. He's not my boyfriend." Kait's gaze dropped to that red sweatshirt with its open pocket.

"Liar!" The woman's voice climbed. "I know you're involved with that lying, murdering bastard. I know he was visiting you yesterday. I know you're important to him."

A bulge formed, pressing against the fabric of the woman's pocket, like she'd clenched her hand around something. A gun? She'd had a gun the first time she'd gone after Cosky.

"What's in your pocket?" Kait asked. She had Mace, but it was zipped inside her purse and her hands were full. If the woman had a gun, by the time Kait dropped the right bag, unzipped the purse, and retrieved the Mace, she'd be dead.

"A knife." The woman's voice was insanely calm. "Which I am going to use on you unless you convince your boyfriend to come over."

A dozen self-defense moves her brothers had drilled into her spun through her mind. Not one of them was applicable under these circumstances.

"Call him. Now." The woman bobbed her head for emphasis and her sunglasses slid down her nose and hit the floor.

The wild brown eyes locked on Kait's face, and the hair on Kait's arms rose. The woman was completely batshit crazy, as Aiden would say.

As though she'd conjured him up, Aiden's calm voice whispered through her mind. *"Use whatever weapons you have on hand. Strike fast. Strike hard."*

On pure instinct, she stepped forward and swung the bag of groceries in her right hand as hard as she could at the woman's head. Luckily, it was the bag with the carton of ice cream and bottle of Miracle Whip.

The woman wasn't expecting the attack. She didn't have time to field the blow or shield her head, and while the carton of ice cream might have softened on the trip home, the bottle of sandwich spread still packed quite a punch. A dull crack sounded as the bag connected with the woman's temple.

The plastic bag split. The ice cream and Miracle Whip hit the floor with a muffled thud.

The woman just stood there, her eyes wild, her hand still clenched inside that huge open pocket. And then her eyes rolled back until the pupils were gone and all that was left was white. She tilted back and just kept going, falling to the floor with a thud that oddly enough didn't sound any louder than the ice cream or sandwich dressing.

Without taking her eyes off her fallen adversary, Kait unzipped her purse and found the Mace. The woman didn't stir.

A frizzle of concern went through her. Maybe she shouldn't have swung so hard, what if she'd killed her?

The memory of countless horror films, where the supposedly dead monster suddenly got all grabby, reeled through her mind as she crept forward. With her Mace aimed at her stalker's closed eyes, she bent down, took hold of the woman's wrist, and carefully eased it out of the pocket.

A huge butcher knife followed.

Holy crap, the crazy lady hadn't been lying. And that knife was *huge*. She could have done some major damage with that sucker.

She pried rigid fingers lose from the knife's handle and tossed the weapon toward her apartment's door. The slow but steady rise and fall of the woman's chest assured her the woman was still alive.

Thank God.

Common sense dictated that Kait lock herself in her apartment and call the police. But what if the woman awoke before the police showed up. What if she disappeared? What if she killed someone before she was captured again?

She was unconscious for the moment—begging to be tied up.

Kait snatched up her purse, found her keys, and unlocked her apartment. After a quick peek behind her to make sure the woman wasn't stirring, she grabbed the butcher knife and raced for her kitchen. She dropped her purse and the knife on the kitchen counter, grabbed her cell phone from her purse and a roll of duct tape from the kitchen drawer, spun around, and headed for the hall. She wheezed with relief on finding her would-be attacker still prone and unconscious.

She'd bound the woman's hands and feet with duct tape before it occurred to her that she should have called for help. She could have stood guard over her captive with the Mace, while her neighbor went for the duct tape. Obviously, she hadn't been thinking as clearly as she'd thought.

The woman still hadn't stirred by the time Kait punched in nine-one-one. Kait hovered over her, worry stirring again as she reported the incident to the dispatcher. She winced as she got a look at the damage she'd inflicted. The bag must have caught the woman's left eye, along with her temple. It was already swelling and turning red. Ice would slow the swelling and with the crazy lady's feet bound, she didn't have to worry about her taking off while Kait was grabbing an ice pack.

She answered the dispatcher's questions as she returned to the kitchen and pulled a bag of mixed vegetables from the freezer. Her stalker was still out cold when she returned to her side and carefully laid the frozen vegetables across the woman's eye, which was already showing light streaks of blue.

The dispatcher gave her an ETA of five minutes for the nearest cruiser and asked Kait to remain on the line until the officer's arrival. Seconds later, her call waiting buzzed. She checked the window for the incoming call. Cosky.

Perfect timing.

She could thank him for dragging his mess to her door.

Cosky held off the impulse to call Kait and make sure she was "just hunky-dory"—as Rawls claimed—until he was settled in Zane's van, safe from unwelcome eyes and eyes. Or at least ears and eyes that weren't privy to the explanation behind the inexplicable complete recovery his knee had undergone. His orthopedic and emergency room doctors were still scrambling to figure that one out.

While the original damage to the tibial plateau hadn't healed to the same degree as his injury from the parking lot—hell, if you could even call it an injury since there was no evidence of recent trauma according to his X-rays—there had been significant evidence of boney bridging between the bone grafts.

The surgeon had used words like *significant* and *excellent*, even *unbelievable* a time or two. He'd gone on to say that he would have expected the volume of boney bridging on the X-rays to coincide with the seven- or eight-month post-surgery mark. Not the four-month mark, and certainly not three days after the last set of X-rays, which had indicated nonhealing.

Rawls had calmly questioned the accuracy of the X-rays from three days earlier, suggesting that the quality of the machine or staging of the leg explained the discrepancy. While the orthopedic surgeon had conceded that Rawls's suggestion was a possibility, he hadn't looked convinced.

"I've been thinking," Rawls said in a thoughtful voice. He twisted to stare at Cosky, who was stretched across the bench seat behind him. "Perhaps the injury in the parking lot was easier to heal because it was fresh. There was no scar tissue that had to be reversed. The fracture to your tibial plateau, however, is four months old. There's scar tissue, advanced trauma to the muscles, nerves, ligaments, tendons, and bone." He paused and ran a hand through his hair. "Not to mention all the hardware they added during surgery. Maybe that's why she wasn't able to heal it."

Cosky paused with his cell phone in hand. He hadn't told his teammates about the previous diagnosis. Hell, he hadn't told Aiden, either. The bastard had guessed. At the time, the thought of their pity had made his skin itch. But the situation was different now. Not only was the fracture healing—it was healing at an accelerated rate, almost double normal. There was a very good chance he'd be able to rejoin his team.

Because of Kait.

He looked down at the cell phone in his hand. "She did heal it," he finally said. "You saw the X-rays from three days ago. The fracture wasn't healing. These new ones show serious improvement. That has to be because of her. Because of what she did in her apartment and in the parking lot."

Rawls waved his hand dismissively. "I meant completely heal. Like the blisters. Your knee was toast, Cos. We all saw it. The patella was in the wrong damn place."

"Maybe it wasn't as bad as we thought," Zane said as he pulled out of the ER's parking lot. "There was a lot of swelling. The swelling could have affected our perception."

Rawls pinched his chin, his thoughtful gaze dropping to Cosky's leg, which was stretched across the backseat of the van and covered in ice packs. "Maybe." But he sounded skeptical. "How's it feeling? Still numb?"

Cosky dropped his cell onto the seat, leaned forward to pick up the ice packs, and folded his knee to his chest. He slowly extended it again. For the first time since he'd hit the pavement, a twinge went through the joint, but the small pain was nothing compared to the jolts he'd experienced before.

"It twinges, nothing serious," he said, stretching it across the seat again. He draped the ice packs back over it and picked up his phone. After highlighting Kait's number, he hit talk and lifted the phone.

"I'll admit one thing has me pretty worried," Rawls said after a moment, his voice so serious Cosky's phone paused on the way up. "You seem to have developed an unnatural affection for the emergency room."

Cosky responded by shooting him the finger. He caught Zane's grin through the rearview mirror as the call went through.

She answered on the first ring. "Wow, your timing is perfect."

Caught off guard, he pulled back slightly. "Come again?"

"Well, I just wanted to *share* with you how much I appreciate being attacked and taken hostage in order to draw you into your crazy stalker's snare."

"*What*?" Cosky straightened so hard his spine popped. "She attacked you? Are you hurt?"

A pause waltzed down the line. "Attacked might be a slight exaggeration. Attempted attack would be more accurate."

What the hell?

"Goddamn it, Kait!" His voice rose with each word until it thundered through the van. "Did she hurt you?"

He was vaguely aware that Zane had pulled the van over to the side of the road, and both he and Rawls had twisted in their seats and were staring at him.

"No, actually, I'm the one who did the damage."

He took a deep breath, let it out carefully, and worked on slowing his racing heart.

"What happened?" he asked as calmly as he could manage.

"She was waiting for me when I got back to my apartment. She had a knife."

His heart stopped. He could feel it. It literally stopped beating for a second or two. A wave of heat drowned him. He dragged in a couple of deep breaths and grabbed hold of his control. She was obviously fine. In fact, she was pretty damn sassy. That Goddamn bitch must be long gone.

"How did you get away?" he asked tightly, the calmness a thin veneer.

"I knocked her out."

His hand tightened around the cell. Slowly, oh so slowly, he pulled it from his ear and stared at it in disbelief.

"*You knocked her out,*" he repeated, his voice sounding slow and stupid. He saw Zane and Rawls exchange glances.

"Yeah." She paused and then added in a careful voice, "With my bag of Miracle Whip."

There was another pause, longer this time, and then a giggle burbled down the line. With a hard swallow, he closed his eyes. That last comment had made no sense. She had obviously been more affected by the encounter than she was letting on. He opened his mouth to assure her that they were on their way and would keep her safe. She broke into the silence before he could get the assurance out.

"Oh, thank God. She's waking up. She's been out so long I was getting worried."

The blood froze in Cosky's veins.

"*She's what? She's still there?*" he roared, jolting forward. "What the hell are you thinking? Get out of there."

Dead space pulsed down the line and then she coughed. "Ah, yeah. Did I forget to mention that I duct taped her feet and hands? She's not going anywhere."

Of course she had. *Son of a bitch.*

Cosky bent forward, his fingers so tight they started to cramp and his lungs so tight they started to wheeze.

"Are you alright?" she asked, sounding concerned.

His shoulders started to shake. Unable to help himself, Cosky started to laugh. Zane and Rawls exchanged grim glances, a clear indication his laughter sounded more frantic than natural.

"She knocked our crazy lady out and tied her up," he told his worried buddies, knowing they'd see the irony in the situation.

She'd done, by herself, what the four of them hadn't been able to do together. Respect spread through him. Kait was one capable and clever cookie, that was for sure.

"Shit," Zane said. "Tell her not to call the cops. We're on the way."

The laughter died. He should have thought of that.

"Look," he said roughly, the urge to laugh still tickling his throat. "We need to talk to her. Don't call the police."

Dead silence echoed down the line.

Ah hell. She'd already called them.

"The cops have her?" he asked, the urge to laugh gone.

"No, but they're on their way." She sounded cautious, as though she didn't like the direction the conversation had taken.

"We need to talk to her," Cosky said, and waited.

"I'm sure the police will—"

Cosky broke into her determinedly cheerful voice. "Alone. Without eyes and ears on us."

She swore. He could almost hear her mind working.

"What's going on? She called you a lying, murdering bastard. Why does she want you dead?"

He took a deep, careful breath. Let it out as silently as possible. "That's what we need to find out."

"And you can't do that at the police station?"

"No."

"She's connected to what happened in Seattle, isn't she?"

It was his turn to swear. Christ, he didn't want her sucked into this. She must have picked up on his reluctance and guessed at its cause.

"I'm already involved," she reminded him quietly. "You can't keep me out of it now."

"Damn it." He pressed the phone hard against his ear and closed his eyes. "We don't know if she's involved, that's what we need to find out."

For a moment all he heard was her breathing and then she sighed.

"Fine. I'll take her down the back stairs. The cops will be coming through the lobby and up the elevator. Pull around to the back of the building. I'll be coming out the last door. We don't have long. The cops will be here in about four minutes."

"We'll be there," he promised. But the line was already dead.

As soon as he lowered the phone, he remembered their possible tail. He swore, and shoved tense fingers through his hair. With the cops all but on scene, they didn't have time for evasive maneuvers. They'd have to hope their eyes and ears were lagging so far back they wouldn't see the exchange.

Chapter Twelve

HER HEAD SWIMMING AND NAUSEA CLOGGING HER THROAT, Jillian stumbled down the stairwell. She tried to balk on the next step, but was forced forward by the insistent hand wrapped around her elbow. Marcus Simcosky's blond bitch of a girlfriend was stronger than she looked. Or more likely, Jillian was weaker.

The repeated collisions the day before had taken a toll on her body. She'd been tired prior to her rampage in the van, chronically malnourished and exhausted. But after her vehicular attack on those four bastards, things had gone from bad to grim. The dizziness and nausea, which she'd been flirting with for weeks, had become a constant companion.

And that had been before Simcosky's bitch had whacked her upside the head with her grocery sack. The impact had knocked loose some crucial connection between her brain and her body. Her legs felt like they were walking down the stairs by themselves, without the necessary sensory input from her mind—numb and clumsy, they misjudged distances and depths. She'd lost track of how many times she'd missed a step and almost pitched down the stairwell face-first.

The only thing keeping her upright and moving was the determined woman by her side. Considering who the bitch was delivering her to, the support was less than a blessing.

And to think she'd been so hopeful when the bitch had cut the duct tape from her ankles, certain that she'd be able to free herself. Escape.

The hope had lasted until Simcosky's girlfriend yanked her to her feet and force marched her toward the stairway. Stumbling, shaking, fighting back the vomit, Jillian had realized all too soon that she'd lost the battle. Lost the war. Lost any possibility of exacting revenge.

With her hands bound, barely able to see or stand, what chance did she have of escaping?

A rush of despair flooded her, weighed down legs that already felt like they were encased in cement and slogging through quicksand.

She'd failed.

She'd failed her babies and her brother and herself. She was about to die without making one ounce of difference, without avenging the murders of her children or her twin, and without setting the record straight and clearing her brother's name.

Grief consumed her, mixed with the despair. Dull lethargy numbed her heavy body and even heavier heart. She should have closed her eyes and drifted into death four months ago. At least she'd be resting at the bottom of Lake Katcheca now, along with her babies.

Her babies, who'd been stolen from life before they even had the chance to live.

She missed the next step and pitched forward. Kaity pulled her back, stabilizing her.

"We're almost there."

Kaity's voice came from a distance, down a long, echoing tunnel.

Jillian leaned against the stairwell's wall and gave her eyes permission to close.

"I hit you pretty hard. I think you have a concussion. Plus, your eye's swelling shut. I brought the ice pack. It will slow the swelling if you can keep it on your eye."

"Just kill me and be done with it," Jillian said, without straightening or opening her eyes. "They'll shoot me as soon as you turn me over, so you'll be as guilty as them when I die."

"They're not going to kill you. They just want to ask you some questions."

"Is that what they told you?" Jillian found enough strength to laugh. "And you believed them? They're lying. Everything that comes out of their mouths is a lie. They'll kill me as soon as they have me alone. Just as they tried to do before. Just as they did to my brother. Just as they did to my children."

Kaity's hand tightened on her arm and drew her forward and down. Jillian concentrated on remaining conscious and upright. Although why bother? She should let go. Let her head spin up to the stars and her body tumble down the stairs. If she was lucky, Kaity wouldn't be able to cheat gravity.

If she was lucky, the fall would kill her.

And then lady luck stripped that final hope from her.

"We're there," Kaity said, drawing Jillian to a stop and holding her upright by slipping an arm around her waist.

Jillian felt a breath of despair, before it evaporated beneath the lethargy. She opened her eyes, fought to focus. The blurred image of a metal door took shape.

"Who killed your family?" Kaity asked, stopping in front of the door.

Jillian stared at the gray metal, watched it disappear in a flock of dancing black dots. "Your boyfriend and his buddies."

"When? Where?"

The questions came from a distance. Vaguely Jillian felt the arm tighten. She stared at the ground and watched her blue-and-white pin-striped sneakers shuffle forward.

"The guys didn't kill your family," Kaity said. "I don't know what happened, but I know them. And they don't kill innocents."

"Then you don't know them as well as you think," Jillian whispered, the effort draining the last of her strength.

The grating *screech* of metal being wrenched apart sounded.

The black tunnel that had dimmed her ears moved into her eyes. Blue sky and grass spun around her, and was swallowed by a bright white haze. The white haze shrunk, framed itself with black.

"Rawls! Thank God! She's in bad shape. I barely got her down the stairs."

Jillian's arms were lifted and something hard pressed against her belly. Suddenly she was light as breath, floating.

"I think she has a concussion, and her eye's almost swollen shut. Here's the ice pack. You're going to check her out, right? She should see a doctor."

Jillian wanted to laugh. But it was too much effort. A doctor? Like these lying, murdering bastards would tend to her before they killed her.

"I'm handing her off to Cos and staying to help you with the Five-0," a different voice said. A male voice with a soothing Southern twang.

"No. You need to go with her. You have the medical training."

"Now Kaity—"

"You're going with her, Rawls. I'm dead serious. She needs medical treatment. I can handle the cops on my own."

"Cos will keep an eye on her until—"

"You go with her, or I'm calling the cops and telling them you have her. I'll give them Zane's plate number. At least I know the cops will take her to a doctor."

"Christ, Kait, we don't have time for this." The Southern twang was gone, sheer male exasperation throbbed in its place.

The unmistakable sound of a minivan's sliding door opening sounded and memories engulfed her.

"Take those cleats off Wes. You ripped chunks out of the carpet last time you climbed in."

"Are we going for ice cream, Mom? Kenya's dad took us to Baskin-Robbins."

"That's the plan. Buckle your sister in."

"She won't stop wiggling."

"Lizzy—"

"Oh God, she's crying!"

That lovely, floating feeling abruptly stopped. Something hard wrapped around her waist.

"What the hell's taking so long?"

She recognized Marcus Simcosky's hard voice and struggled to open her eyes. The bench seat of a minivan came into view.

Flash.

The slow sway of Wes's hanging head, the flash of his white-gold hair.

"*No. No. No.*"

The sudden searing agony cleared her head.

"Rawls, do something!" Kaity sounded panicked.

Wes's blond hair morphed into black. The chubby cheeks of childish innocence shifted into the hard, sculpted face of pure masculinity.

Marcus Simcosky.

And he was reaching for her.

No! Adrenaline hit. She swung her bound hands at his looming head.

"Son of a bitch." The words were bit out, and then her arms were caged and she was dragged into the van and anchored beside him. "I've got her," he snapped. "Go."

To her right, from her good eye she saw a flash of movement, and a familiar-looking man with blond hair and blue eyes swung into the van, settling on the bench seat beside her. The sliding door slammed shut.

"What the hell, Rawls?" Simcosky's voice rose. "You were supposed to stay behind."

"Tell that to Kait. Go, damn it. The Five-0've arrived. We need to ghost it."

The van started to move. Jillian's head spun.

"Stop the van," Simcosky yelled from her right.

The roar slammed into Jillian's head and sparked a throbbing so vicious it brought the nausea surging up. She jolted forward, dropped her head between her splayed knees and heaved. And heaved. And heaved.

She heard swearing, and a hand cupped the back of her neck, lingered there.

"This is why I came," the blond, blue-eyed man with the Southern twang said.

He had a name. Jillian knew he had a name, but she gave up trying to remember it.

"Kait was worried about her, with reason, I might add. She said she'd call the Five-0 and give them our plates if I didn't come along to take care of her."

"Kait spends so much time worrying about other people, she forgets to worry about herself," Marcus Simcosky snapped. "Zane, stop the van. I'll wait with Kait."

The van kept moving.

"Goddamn it," Simcosky's voice rose again. "Zane—"

"The cops are already here," a calm voice broke in. "We can't chance them catching sight of her. Besides, the doc told you to lay off that leg for a couple of days."

Swearing broke out to her right.

"Zane, hand back your water. She's dehydrated as hell. We need to get fluids in her. Hey there, sweetheart." The voice took on a gentle, crooning tone. "Let's sit you back so I can check out that shiner."

Hands took hold of her shoulders and eased her up and back.

"You called Mac? Right?" the man with the gentle hands and soothing voice said, his voice growing more distant with each beat of her heart. "Call him back; tell him to get hold of Radar. I need . . ."

She awoke slowly, skimming along consciousness to the drone of masculine voices.

"How do we know she's not faking it?"

"Because I can tell, and she's not."

She recognized the one voice, the Southern one. Although it was missing the gentleness and croon. The other voice—the cold, hard, and brutal one—was not familiar. She wanted to keep it that way. Best to keep her eyes closed and head down. Simcosky's girlfriend had said they wanted to question her. Since she wasn't dead, the blond bimbo must have been right, which meant the longer they had to wait for their answers, the longer her lifespan.

So she lay there, still as possible, as the urge to move, to stretch, to ease her battered muscles became a constant itch.

"Did Kait make out okay with the five-oh?"

"Yeah." It was Marcus Simcosky's voice. But less loud and angry. "She covered for us."

"Told you. She's quick on her feet."

"When the fuck's she going to wake up?" the hard, gritty voice demanded, and Jillian knew he was talking about her.

Fingers touched her neck, lingered. Jillian fought to regulate her breathing. Could he tell from her pulse she was awake? The thought sent her blood crashing through her veins. Certainly he could feel *that.* Panicked, she tensed, ready to launch herself up and at him, when the hand fell away.

"She's awake. You might as well open your eye, sweet cheeks. We're not going to hurt you."

Liar.

His voice might be gentle and his hands soothing, but he was one of them. A murdering, lying bastard like Zane Winters and Marcus Simcosky.

Still, it was useless to keep pretending. Best to face her fear and enemy. With a deep, ragged breath she opened her eyes. Or eye. Her vision cut off to the left of her nose.

She was lying down, something soft beneath her head. Her right eye, which was still working, although blurrier than normal, had a hazy view of brown leather—maybe the back of a couch. She couldn't see anything to her left. When she tried to force her left eye open, a molten poker pierced it. She froze, and the piercing pain settled into a deep, raw ache. After a moment, she released her pent-up breath, reached up, and gingerly touched her eye. The cold of an ice pack chilled her fingers. Holding the ice pack in place, she rolled her head until she could see to the left. A tall blond man with concerned blue eyes came into view. She recognized him from the television and papers. He was one of the men responsible for Russ's death.

That concern was just another lie. Like the lies they told about her brother to the FBI and the reporters.

An IV stand caught her attention. Frowning, she forced her blurry gaze to focus on it, to follow the plastic line that ran from the clear bag down to her arm and into the needle that penetrated the vein beneath her elbow.

She jolted up and swayed. Once her head stopped swimming she tried to tear off the tape that held the needle in place.

"Easy." The blond SEAL stepped around the IV and behind her head. A hand came down on her shoulder and pushed her flat, then he caught the hand scrabbling at the IV needle and pinned it against the couch behind her head. "It's just fluids."

And she was supposed to take his word for that?

"Take it out!" Her voice rose shrilly.

"No." His voice was calm. "You're dehydrated."

She tried to reach the needle with her other hand. He caught that one as well.

"Don't make me bind your hands again." While his voice might have been calm and gentle, there was no give there.

Her breath locked in her throat, Jillian subsided. What was really in the bag? Some kind of poison? Would it make her death look like an accident?

"I promise you. The only thing in that bag is fluids. To hydrate you. We aren't going to hurt you."

Tilting her head back, she bared her teeth at him. "And I'm supposed to believe you? A murderer?"

"Yeah." He frowned down at her, the fake warmth of concern still firing the blue of his eyes. "About that. Kait says you told her we killed your kids and your brother. What makes you think that?"

She glared back. "Because you did."

"When?" A second voice asked in such a calm tone it sent a rift of unreality through her. How could he be so calm while talking about the murder of her babies?

Rolling her head to the left, she tried to get a look at the monster who spoke so casually about the murder of children and found herself face-to-face with Zane Winters.

The bastard who'd killed her brother.

"You!" She tried to tear her hands from the blond SEAL's grip and bolt up, but he easily held her down. "You bastard. You bastard. You killed them. You killed my babies."

Zane Winters stepped closer, his green eyes shadowed. He exchanged a grim look with Marcus Simcosky. "We had nothing to do with whatever happened to your children."

"Liar." The word vibrated with her rage.

"Why are you so certain we killed your kids?" the man who'd murdered her brother asked.

"Because you admitted it. On the television. In the newspapers. You admitted you killed them," she hissed at him, struggling to free herself from the hands binding her wrists.

"There's no way in hell I admitted to killing your kids. Not on television. Not to the papers."

"You admitted to killing Russ," she threw at him. "You told all those horrible lies about him. Made him out to be some kind of a monster. Your buddies kidnapped me and the kids on the same day! The *same day* you killed Russ. That wasn't a coincidence."

A long pulsing silence fell. She could literally feel the tension squeezing the room. Yeah, they couldn't deny that now, could they?

"You're talking about Russ Branson."

"No." Her voice broke. She hardened it. "His name wasn't Branson. That's just another of your lies."

Zane spun to look at Simcosky, and then turned back to Jillian and took a step closer. "What was his name?"

She tried to jerk her hands loose, every cell, every muscle, every atom in her body wanting to hurt him. Rip out his eyes. Make him pay for what he'd done—what he'd taken from her. "You don't even know the name of the man you murdered?"

Did he hear the hate in her voice? The rage. She'd never wanted to hurt anyone as badly as she wanted to hurt him. All of them. Right here. Right now.

"We knew him as Russ Branson."

"So you admit you killed him?"

"Yes, I killed him—"

His admission shocked her so much she missed the rest of his sentence.

"—my fiancée. If I hadn't taken him out first, he would have killed me, Beth, Amy Chastain, and Christ only knows how many others."

"Liar!" The word emerged on a shriek.

Zane Winters winced, squared his shoulders, and took another step forward; but before he could say anything, another man pushed him aside and pointed a lean, tanned index finger at her.

This new threat was leaner than the other three, and older. His short black hair was graying at the temples. Eyes as black as a cloud-shrouded midnight locked on her.

"Lady, I'm getting pretty fucking tired of you calling us liars. You obviously don't know a damn thing about your brother." The thunderstorm masquerading as a man snarled as he repeatedly chopped the air with his extended index finger. "In Seattle alone he was responsible for the attempted hijacking of flight 2077, for the kidnapping and rape of Ginny Clancy and Amy Chastain, for the murders of Todd Clancy and Agent Chastain. Your brother was a Goddamn sociopathic—"

"Mac, you're not helping," the blond SEAL holding her hands behind her head growled.

The thundercloud wheeled on him. "She's the one throwing the fucking lies around. Let her get a dose of the truth."

"Look." The blond leaned over the couch's armrest behind her head and stared down. "We own taking out your brother. We had no choice. But we had nothing to do with what happened to your kids."

"Right," she sneered the word up at him. "And I suppose it was just a coincidence that the bastard who shot me and killed my"—her voice hiccupped and went watery before she infused it with venom—"was hanging around your lame buddy yesterday?"

Pure shock brought Cosky to his feet. "The hell you say?"

The woman who'd tried to kill him—twice—twisted beneath Rawls's grip. Her good eye locked on Cosky. The wild, brown depths were brimming with rage. But there was something darker beneath the fierceness—the raw desolation of someone who'd lost everything and had nothing left to live for.

Christ, if she'd witnessed the murder of her kids, no wonder she was halfway to insane.

He gritted his teeth beneath his own surge of anger. If what she claimed was true, if that bastard had killed her kids . . . Christ, he deserved the slowest and most excruciating death imaginable. Cosky would be happy to hand it to him.

He thought back to her first attack on him. She'd been determined to kill him. Driven by hatred. Yet, she'd turned away from the perfect opportunity to take him out. He'd been down on the ground, defenseless. All she would have had to do was step around the pickup's door and empty her pistol into him. Instead, she'd spun and fired across the parking lot.

It hadn't made sense then, why would she target that chatty kid? Well, it made sense now. She hadn't been aiming for Mr. Chatty. She'd been aiming for someone else entirely.

"This man who shot you." Cosky left out the fate of her children. The reminder of her loss had to be unbearable, and he needed her coherent. He needed answers. "He was at the back of the parking lot yesterday, wasn't he? He's the one you were targeting."

Her lips curled into a combination snarl and sneer. "You think I'm so stupid I wouldn't recognize the bald bastard who shot me . . . and—"

Raw agony crumpled her face and darkened her eye. But almost instantly the agony bled into savage wrath. She shook her head and the ice pack took flight. She looked almost malformed at that moment. Her left eye was swollen shut and shadowed with blue. Her face twisted into a mask of primitive ferocity.

It took a few seconds for her description of her shooter to sink in. *Bald bastard.*

Son of a fucking bitch.

"Goddamn motherfucker," Mac said, his face livid. "Cos, give me that business card."

Cosky dug into his pocket and pulled out the business card that antagonistic bastard of a detective had given him in the emergency room.

That bald, antagonistic bastard of a detective.

"The world's full of bald men," Rawls said. When his captive suddenly slumped against the pillow, her muscles slack, he let go of her hands and bent to pick up the ice pack.

"Yeah, but this particular chrome dome was far too interested in what she"—Cosky jerked his chin toward the woman stretched across his couch—"said to me."

"And he didn't show up at either crime scene," Mac said with his cell phone plugged to his ear. "What are the odds of that?" He lifted the business card and glared down at it. "Radar, I need another favor. Check with the Coronado PD. See if they have a Detective Alejandro Pachico in house. Get a description if they do, and buddy, keep this on the down low. Yeah, ASAP."

Zane ran a tense hand through his hair. "If this guy's a ringer, and he's involved in what happened to her"—Zane said with a nod toward their captive—"then it's a good bet he can lead us to whoever was behind that mess in Seattle."

Mac's lips stretched into a predatory smile. "Which will lead us to who financed McKay's hit."

Rawls perched on the armrest above the woman's head and laid the ice pack across the left half of her face. "We can't keep calling you her or she," he said with a non-threatening smile. "What's your name?"

She arched her neck to stare up at him, a frown wrinkling her bruised forehead. Suddenly she winced and her face smoothed out.

"Jillian," she finally said, the delay so long Cosky didn't think she was going to answer at all.

"And what's your last name, Jillian?" Rawls persisted.

She pressed her lips together and glared. Caution registered on her face. Her gaze twitched from Cosky to Zane and over to Mac.

"Michaels," she said grudgingly, apparently deciding that providing her last name wouldn't give them an advantage.

Zane frowned, and took a step closer to their guest. "Was your brother's last name Michaels too?"

"You know it wasn't," but her voice lacked heat.

She looked exhausted, lying there. Fragile. The half of her face not covered by the blue ice pack was a sullen gray against the rich mahogany of their leather couch.

"We knew him as Russ Branson," Zane said, his voice quiet.

Cosky and Rawls exchanged glances and waited. Knowing Branson's real name was the first step to tracking his bosses down. Although now, thanks to Jillian, they had another, even more promising lead. Before she had a chance to answer, Mac's phone rang.

Mac lifted the cell to his ear. "Yeah. There is? What does he look like?" He listened for a moment, and scowled. Disappointment touched his face. "Fuck. Can you get me a picture? Thanks." He lowered his hand and shrugged. "The description fits; he could be legit."

Of course, the smart ringer would impersonate the person in the department who resembled him the closest in case someone called the department to verify his identify.

"Did Radar get a photo?" Cosky asked.

"He's sending it to my phone," Mac said. "We'll know for sure in a minute." He turned to Jillian. "Did she give up Branson's name?"

"Not yet." Zane turned toward the couch and scowled. "Damn."

Jillian's face had gone slack and her good eye was closed.

"She's faking it." Mac stalked forward and glared down at her as though he could get her to open her eye with sheer force of will.

"No, she's not," Rawls said. "She's malnourished, dehydrated, and exhausted. The only thing keeping her awake is adrenaline and rage, but she can't maintain that kind of intensity for long in her condition."

Mac didn't look like he believed the diagnosis. But before he could grill their sleeping hostage, his cell buzzed.

He lifted it to look. "Radar sent the pic." A couple of finger punches later and he grinned, that predatory anticipation back in full force. "We have a ringer. And our first lead."

"I need to let Kait in on this," Cosky said, picking up his cell from the coffee table.

"Bullshit." Mac made a chopping motion. "This intel is need to know. And she doesn't need to know."

Ignoring the order, Cosky highlighted Kait's number and hit dial. She was in the thick of this fucking mess, thanks to him. No way was he leaving her vulnerable to that bastard.

"Goddamn it, Cos—" Mac's voice rose.

Cosky flatly stared back, listening to his phone ring and ring and ring. "If he has a contact in the Coronado PD, which you can bet your ass he does considering how well informed he is, then he knows Jillian attacked Kait. I'm not leaving her vulnerable. That asshole could swing by her place at any moment to question her about Jillian."

It bothered the shit out of him that they'd left her alone to deal with the cops. Damn it, someone should have stayed for support. Although, considering the way his body tightened in anticipation of hearing her voice, not to mention his sudden intense craving for his fingers on her smooth, hot skin, it was probably a good thing he hadn't bailed from the van to help her out.

There was a good chance he'd still be in her bed.

The call quit ringing and her husky voice came on line. "Hello?"

Bingo, his dick jolted straight up.

"Hey—"

"You must have gotten my message," she broke in.

He frowned in confusion. "What message?"

She snorted. "The one where I thanked you for dragging your mess to my door."

Cosky drew back, the confusion deepening. She'd said something similar when she'd called him originally, back before they'd picked up Jillian. Before he had a chance to question her, she started talking.

"I'm fine. But your stalker got away again."

"You have someone there with you?" Cosky asked, his confusion vanishing.

"Yeah," she confirmed his suspicion in such a casual voice, it made him wonder how much experience she had in lying. Because she was pretty damn good at it. There was no tension in her tone, no hesitation, nothing to give the lie away.

"There's a detective here now, as a matter of fact. But he says they still haven't found her."

Cosky froze, an ugly suspicion stirring. Ice broke out over his back, and prickled down the nape of his neck. "Would this detective's name be Pachico?" he asked, the words coming out low and hard and dangerous.

For the first time she paused, and he could sense her surprise. "It would—"

He swore viciously, his heart slamming against his ribs like he'd just finished CQB training.

Damn it, he shouldn't have caught her off guard. If Pachico was half the professional they suspected, he'd pick up on her surprised reaction.

Cosky's own ineptitude had just put Kait in danger. Serious danger. A cold, black pressure rose inside him. He recognized it instantly. Fear.

He'd never had trouble caging it before, forcing it into the background. This time it insisted on taking the driver's seat.

He forced himself to concentrate, and realized she was talking.

"But dinner alone isn't getting you out of this," she said in a half-laughing, half-flirting tone. She paused as though listening. "No, I'm not turning you down. I never turn down a free dinner."

Cosky tried to calm his surging blood pressure. "You didn't tell him anything?"

If Pachico knew they had Jillian, he'd know Jillian had told them about him. He could decide to grab Kait and use her as a bargaining chip. Previous experience proved the bastard's pawns didn't have the life span of a fruit fly after he was done with them.

Every muscle in Cosky's body clenched. Not Kait. No way in hell was he losing Kait.

She laughed again, this time with an edge of irritation. "Of course not." Her voice smoothed. "What time are you picking me up?"

"Get rid of him," Cosky said tightly, aware that Zane and Rawls were watching him with absolute stillness. "We'll be there ASAP. Do *not* go anywhere with him. Do *not* challenge him. Do *not* question him. Get him out of your apartment. Hole up inside until we get there."

"Yeah," she said dryly. "Like you have to tell me that. I'll be here. Is your knee up to this?" Kait asked. The softness in her voice told him the question was out of actual concern, not window dressing for Pachico's benefit.

His chest tightened. Christ, considering his abysmal treatment of her earlier, the last thing he deserved was her concern. She had a good heart, Kait did. Better than his, that was for sure.

"My knee's fine," he said gruffly.

She humphed beneath her breath. "Sure it is."

He tried to breathe around the knot in his chest—around the tug-of-war of fear and something he didn't want to examine too closely. "Call me as soon as you get rid of him."

"I will." She sounded exasperated. "I'll see you in fifteen."

The phone went dead.

He swore viciously, started to hit redial, but then his brain kicked in.

Calling back and keeping her on the line would be too fucking suspicious. He wasn't supposed to know that Pachico, or whoever the fuck the bastard was, didn't work for the Coronado Police Department, so there should be no concern for Kait's safety.

Zane grabbed Cosky's arm as he wheeled around. "I'm driving."

Cosky followed his LC through the kitchen and into the garage, the fear a volcanic vent threatening to rip him apart. He went to work tamping it down, covering it with ice, chilling it out.

"You okay?" Zane asked, with a sharp sideways glance as they approached the van.

"Yeah," Cosky said, his voice so tight it cracked.

They climbed into the van in silence.

Zane waited until they were out on the road before glancing down at Cosky's fisted hands. "You can put those away."

Cosky looked down in surprise; he hadn't even realized his fists were cocked. Finger by finger, he forced them to relax. When his hands were uncurled again, he pressed them against his thighs, shocked to find them shaking.

"So, you finally ready to admit it?" Zane asked.

Cosky slowly turned his head toward the driver's seat. The world seemed off-kilter, warped, reeling.

"What?"

Zane shot him a wry sideways glance. His expression was a cross between sympathy and amusement. "That you have feelings for her? That you've had feelings for her from the moment you ran into her outside Aiden's hospital room."

The earth shifted beneath Cosky's ass. He sat there in the passenger seat, a lump of disbelief and denial. "Bullshit. I'm not a Winters. I don't have a soul mate."

"I'm not talking soul mates. I'm talking feelings. Serious feelings."

Cosky snorted and fought to keep his hands from fisting again. "Beth's pregnancy's turned you hormonal."

Zane shook his head. "Cos, you're a cold bastard. Always in control. You never let fear rule you—or if you do, you hide it well. Yet, your hands are shaking. A guy like you? Yeah, that ain't going to happen unless you got feelings for her. Strong feelings."

Cosky folded his arms and set his back. "Bullshit. I'd be just as worried about Beth if she was in that apartment with that bastard."

With a quick grin, Zane shook his head. "Jesus, you're a stubborn ass. You haven't been avoiding Beth for the past five years. And then there's Aiden. Hell, you threw up every fucking roadblock you could think of to keep Aiden from moving in. What the hell was that about?"

Cosky scowled. Hell, he should have known Zane would notice. The asshole noticed everything.

"I don't deny I'm attracted to her. But that's all. Hell, why do you think I've been avoiding her?" He turned his scowl on Zane. "She's one of ours. I'm not about to screw her and walk away."

But wasn't that exactly what he'd done?

The scowl vanished beneath a surge of shame.

Turning his head, he stared out the window and tried not to imagine what was happening in Kait's place. "Can't this damn thing go faster?"

Kait was alone with a killer. A cold-blooded murderer who'd shown no mercy to Jillian or her children.

The minutes ticked by slower and slower as he waited for her all-clear call.

Life could end in a heartbeat. He'd seen it happen too many times to count. One moment someone was laughing, talking, living—the next their eyes were fixed and they were cooling in your arms.

That black shadow inside him expanded again, tried to squeeze the breath from his lungs.

He closed his eyes and willed Pachico from her apartment. Life would be a hell of a lot less livable without Kait in it.

Chapter Thirteen

KAIT HIT THE DISCONNECT BUTTON AND PIVOTED TO FACE Detective Pachico, or whoever the man was. The change in Cosky's tone when she'd mentioned her visitor had been disconcerting. He'd gone from easy to edgy in an instant. Obviously, Cosky believed this man was dangerous. And if Cosky, who had gone up against the most dangerous men in the world, felt her visitor was a threat, she'd be wise to pay heed. She needed to get him out of her apartment.

But how?

"Lieutenant Simcosky?" he asked, arching thin, pale eyebrows.

"Yeah." Kait tried out a light laugh. "I may have overreacted and left him a nasty message after his stalker attacked me."

Her visitor just watched her—cold intelligence glittering in his dark eyes.

"At least I get a free dinner out of it." She tried another smile on him, which had no effect at all. "Are we done? I need to change clothes and put on my face."

He took a step toward her. There was something predatory and taunting in the movement. Kait held her ground.

"So this woman said nothing to you?" he asked, his voice polite, his face even politer, yet a chill worked its way up her spine, leaving an entire army of goose bumps behind.

Every instinct she possessed whispered caution, warned her that this man was deadly.

Too bad those instincts hadn't kicked in while he was on the other side of her locked door.

She'd answered his question before, multiple times, but Cosky's warning echoed in her mind. *Don't challenge him.*

So she answered his question again, with as much patience as her edgy composure could manage. "She said she was going to use me to trap Cosky. She thought he was my boyfriend."

He cocked his head, his dark gaze watchful and . . . mocking? "Having dinner with him does give the impression of intimacy."

She shook her head. "He's not my boyfriend. This dinner's an apology. He's a friend of my brother's."

"A friend of your brother's," he repeated, and yeah—there was open mockery on his face. He was toying with her. "Who just happened to be visiting you yesterday, when he was first attacked?"

"I told you," she forced an irritated edge into her voice, as though she was tired of going over the same ground. Which she was. "He was here for a massage."

"You told the police he was here for sex."

She rocked back and tried not to look surprised. *They'd put that in their report?*

"I was just messing with them," she said, and saw disbelief in his eyes. "His knee and thigh have been bothering him since he got out of the hospital. Cramping and stiffness. I told him I'd massage it for him. Massages promote healing," she added self-righteously.

At least sometimes.

Other times? Not so much.

"You're not a masseuse," he said flatly, as close to calling her a liar as he'd come so far.

"Not licensed." She shrugged, held his gaze, and took a step toward her purse, with its can of Mace tucked inside. He matched her step, blocking her. Kait's scalp tightened and tingled. She fought to keep her voice steady. "But I took a course in massage therapy."

His hand dipped into his jacket's pocket.

"Your brother can verify this?" Those cold, intense eyes scanned the room.

Tense, Kait watched him. What was he looking for? Even more important, what was in his pocket?

"Ms. Winchester?" he prompted, swinging back to her.

She jolted and silently scolded herself. "I'm sure Aiden would, if he were available. But he isn't. He deployed yesterday."

His lips curved, but not with humor. "Of course he did."

She held his gaze. "I don't see why it matters. What difference does it make why Cosky came? Or whether we're involved?"

"Because involved women lie for their guy."

So did uninvolved women, but she was certain he already knew that. "Was there anything else you wanted to know?"

"Did this woman say why she's so interested in Simcosky?" he asked, watching her with unblinking, single-minded focus.

She'd already answered this question. Repeatedly. She took a deep breath and answered it again. "She said he was going to pay. That they were all going to pay. She said she was going to make sure of it."

The pasty skin of his forehead crinkled. "For what?"

Kait shrugged and reached up to brush back a strand of hair. She didn't try to hide her puzzlement. "I don't know. She said they killed her children. But Cosky wouldn't hurt children. She must have confused him with someone else."

A strange intensity darkened his eyes. He cocked his head and studied her face with the concentration of a predator just before it pounced.

A whole herd of centipedes skittered around in her belly. Nervously she went over what she'd said. Had something given her away? She hadn't told him anything that she hadn't already told the police.

Suddenly he turned to the teak bookshelf behind him and picked up a fragile, multi-jeweled glass square. Kait went rigid and breathless, watching him rotate the object between his palms.

He caught her gaze and smiled, a cold, knowing smile, and then he lifted the glass square with one hand, holding it high. The jeweled panels sparkled beneath the sunlight streaming in through the living room.

"It's quite beautiful really, exquisite how the pieces fit together. Like a puzzle. Your aunt's work?"

Except it wasn't a question. He was telling her he knew it was important to her. He was telling her he could see through her, as easily as he could see through the object in his hands.

Her mouth dry, she simply nodded.

"Your father's sister." He idly rotated the glass cube in his palm. "She was an artist? Stain glass, blown glass, ceramics?"

Who was this guy?

Locking her reaction down, she pretended that she believed an ordinary detective could have collected such detailed information about her family in the space of an hour or two. "That's right. It was her last piece."

And as such, of immense emotional value to her.

Which this bastard knew.

He held her gaze with eyes utterly cold and flat and devoid of humanity. "It's astonishing how quickly beautiful things can shatter. One moment here"—he leisurely scanned her body—"the next gone."

He wasn't talking about the glass cube. Kait's skin went cold. Her muscles rigid.

She braced herself, certain he was going to release the cube and let it shatter against the floor.

Which would force her to confront him—force her to step beyond this pretense that hung between them like a thin veil.

Ice churned in the pit of her stomach.

Cosky's stalker might have been crazy, but she'd been an amateur compared to this guy. This guy had the eyes of a killer.

For the second time that day every self-defense move her brother had taught her reeled through her mind. Except, he'd counter all of them. She knew it, as surely as she knew she wasn't going to be able to defeat him as easily as she'd taken care of Cosky's stalker.

A thick silence throbbed between them. She watched him, waiting for him to drop Aunt Issa's last gift. Waiting for him to pounce.

And then a knock sounded on her door. She jolted. He didn't. Instead, he casually lowered the glass square.

The knock sounded again.

It was too soon to be Cosky. Her visitor had to know that. But he turned, with an odd mesmerizing grace, and set the glass cube back on the bookshelf. He turned it slightly, returning it to the exact position it had been in before he'd picked it up.

Without a word he turned and headed down the hall toward the door. Kait watched him, still frozen in the living room.

He turned with his hand on the door handle, looked at her, and smiled. "Tell Simcosky I'll be seeing him."

When he opened the door, he bowed slightly to Martha and

stepped to the side, inviting her into the apartment with a sweep of his arm. And then he was gone.

"What a nice man," Martha said, sending a beaming smile in the direction he'd vanished. "You don't see manners like that these days." She closed the door and shuffled down the hall toward Kait. "I was worried about you, girl. What with all the happenings around here lately."

"I'm fine," Kait said automatically. Although her hoarse voice and shaking legs gave lie to the assurance.

"You don't look fine. You're shaking like a leaf," Martha said.

She could hardly tell the woman the truth. She wasn't even sure what the truth was. Maybe she'd blown the last five minutes out of proportion.

More likely, she was damn lucky to be alive.

"I think the adrenaline from earlier is wearing off," Kait said, suspecting her smile was as wobbly as her legs from the concerned look Martha settled on her.

She glanced at the wall clock and urged Cosky to hurry.

Funny how facing her death had suddenly made Cosky's company so much more palatable. Although, this latest scare could be tossed at Cosky's feet too.

If his crazy stalker hadn't attacked her, she wouldn't have caught the attention of this empty-eyed killer.

She'd make sure to remind him of that, when he showed up at her door.

It seemed like hours before Cosky's cell rang again.

"Kait?" His voice sounded like he'd gargled glass. All he heard was choppy breathing, and then a voice cleared.

"I'm okay. He's gone."

Cosky closed his eyes, his arms going weak. Christ, he'd never been so thankful for the sound of a voice. "We're almost there."

"He's not a detective, is he?" Her voice shook, but just for a moment, and then it steadied.

His hand tightened around the phone. "No, he's not."

Her breathing grew choppy again.

"Is he the one who killed her family?" she asked in a thin whisper.

How in the hell had she figured that out? Had that bastard told her? Christ—Cosky took a deep breath and banked the flash of rage.

"I bet he enjoyed it," she continued in the same thin whisper.

Cosky shook his head to clear it. "Enjoyed what?"

"Killing children." He heard her take a deep breath. Her voice grew stronger. "He gave me a message for you. He said to tell you that he'd be seeing you."

"I'm looking forward to it." Cosky bared his teeth. Kait's apartment complex came into view. He pushed back the ferocity and remnants of terror. "Pack enough clothes to last a few days."

No way in hell was he leaving her on her own.

A ghost of a laugh rolled down the line. "I'm doing that right now. I'll meet you in the lobby."

Like hell.

"We're coming to your door," he said in a flat voice.

"There's no need. If he'd wanted me"—her voice shook—"he'd have me. He's probably long gone now. You should rest your leg."

Fuck his leg.

"We'll meet you at your door," he said again, his throat burning beneath the urge to shout. Christ, Kait was strong, but she'd been through enough today. She didn't need him bellowing at her, regardless of how much he needed to release some of this fury.

Because she was right. If that bastard had wanted her, Kait would be gone and there wasn't a damn thing he could have done to stop it.

He shoved his door open and swung out of the van, wincing as his leg struck the curb and knives sank into his knee.

Son of a bitch.

Apparently, Kait's healing was wearing off. Although the pain wasn't nearly as bad as it had been before, it was enough to catch his attention and adjust his stride.

His next step was much more cautious.

Zane, of course, picked up on it. "Your knee giving you hell again?"

Knowing where an affirmative would lead, Cosky ignored the question. He wasn't waiting in the damn vehicle like an invalid while Zane escorted Kait downstairs. This was his mess. He'd clean it up.

Zane started to say something and suddenly stopped dead. He bent over and groaned.

Oh, for Christ's sake.

Cosky stopped to glare. "Beth needs to get a handle on this damn morning sickness. This has lost its entertainment value."

"Go ahead and tell her that," Zane said, straightening, a green tinge to his face. "Jillian won't be the only one with a black eye."

With a scowl, Cosky stalked into the lobby. The elevator was open; they took it to the sixth floor. Kait opened the door within a second of his knock. He took one look at her white face and huge eyes, and pulled her into his arms.

For an instant she pulled back, but then she folded against him. Her arms stole around his waist.

"I'm okay," she said, her voice quavering. "He didn't hurt me."

Cosky felt her arms tighten around his waist. The bastard may not have hurt her, but he'd scared the living hell out of her. He felt a shiver shake her and forced down another surge of fury. Every instinct he possessed urged him to hunt that bastard down and put a bullet in his brain.

"We need to get moving," Zane reminded him from behind.

Kait took a deep breath, her breasts rubbing against his chest, and a frizzle of heat teased the ice encasing him. Her arms loosened and she stepped back. Briskly she swung to the side, bent down, and picked up a suitcase.

"I'm going to stay with a friend for a while," she said, stepping into the hall and closing the apartment door behind her. "You really didn't need to come. The security guard could have walked me to my car."

Uh . . . yeah . . . Cosky exchanged grim glances with Zane and ran a tense hand down his face. It was a good bet she wasn't going to appreciate what he was about to tell her.

"You can't use your car, Kait." He didn't try to sugarcoat the news. "You're in their sights now, and these guys are connected. They can track you through your car."

She took one step and froze. Slowly she pivoted to face him. "They? How many are there?"

His hand started to rise, to brush her ashen cheek. He forced it back down. "We don't know."

"Okay . . ." She didn't argue, didn't protest, just stood there with her brow furrowing. "Renting a car is out then. If they're as connected as you say, they'd find out the rental info."

Zane's eyebrows lifted. "That's a good bet."

Kait's nod was decisive. "I can't go to Demi, either. Not if there's the slightest chance I could be followed."

"You're coming back with us," Cosky said flatly.

She absently nodded, but the furrow in her forehead deepened. "If they can find me, they can find you."

True enough.

There was little doubt in Cosky's mind that those bastards had identified the condo months ago.

Considering the effort and resources Russ's bosses had expended in order to grab those mysterious passengers from flight 2077, it was likely they'd assigned eyes and ears to the men who'd scuttled the operation. They couldn't afford not to. They'd need to make sure he, Zane, Rawls, and Mac weren't about to tank their entire operation. They'd want to know exactly how much information Russ had let slip, and how much intel they'd gathered on their own.

No doubt those bastards would have taken much stronger, permanent action if the media shitfest hadn't swirled around the incident with the velocity of a tornado. To eliminate Cosky and his buddies now, while they were shouting conspiracy at the top of their lungs—yeah, that would have raised too many questions.

So they were probably biding their time, watching from a distance, ready to strike instantly if need be. No doubt he, along with the rest of the men involved, would have unwelcome eyes and ears inside their homes too, if Radar hadn't gotten his hands on the prototype of a combination audio jammer and high-tech electronic scrambler. Not only did the device jam both external and internal microphones, but it recognized and allowed authorized electronic signals to ring through. Like their cell phones. Thank Christ. Having to leave the house to make a call or check voice mail would have gotten old pretty damn fast.

"We're set up," Cosky said simply. "You're not. You'll be safe with us."

As a unit, the three of them headed for the elevator.

"I have a friend," Kait said, the worry lines still creasing her forehead. "I'd be safe with him."

Him?

Cosky stiffened. "You'll be safer with us."

He caught Zane's amused glance at his brusque tone. Kait, thank Christ, didn't seem to notice it.

She gave a ghost of a laugh, affection in the sound. "Believe me; I'll be just as safe with Wolf."

Wolf?

What the fuck kind of name was that?

"You're staying with us," Cosky said through his teeth.

Zane's lips twitched, but he didn't say a word, just held the elevator door open.

Kait waited until the elevator doors slid shut before leveling a steady look on Cosky's face. "Thank you. I'll take you up on your generous offer—"

Cosky relaxed.

"—until Wolf comes to get me."

A strangled laugh escaped Zane. He tried to disguise it with a cough. Which didn't fool either of them. Cosky shot him a murderous glare. Kait's gaze held confusion.

"I don't think you understand the danger." Cosky tried for a reasonable tone, but the words emerged gritty and hostile.

A shadow darkened her eyes. She stiffened slightly, her face cooling. "Believe me; I'm well aware of the danger. Five minutes alone with your detective Pachico was all the lesson I needed."

Cosky winced, the memory of her white face and huge eyes flashed through his mind. She was right; she knew exactly how much danger she was in.

So she must have a fuckload of faith in this *friend*, this *Wolf,* to put her life in his hands.

The burning acidic rush that sank into his bones and blood shocked the hell out of him. It wasn't his business how much faith Kait put in this guy. He was happy she had someone she could depend on. Someone she obviously trusted completely. It took the responsibility off his shoulders.

Silence accompanied them down to the lobby.

Halfway across the lobby, Kait seemed to notice that he was limping. Some of the chill vanished from her face. She slowed, matching her gait to his, and glanced around.

"So the healing didn't last?" she asked softly.

Cosky glanced at her and shrugged. "It's a hell of a lot stronger than it was before yesterday morning."

He hadn't meant to remind her of those frenzied moments on her couch. But the comment did. It reminded both of them. The memory heated her dark gaze, and his blood responded—thickened and slowed, flushed with languid heat.

It wasn't hard to pinpoint when she remembered what had followed the sex. The arousal vanished from her eyes.

He jerked his gaze away. He still needed to apologize for that, but before he had a chance to jump into it, Zane interrupted them.

"Why don't you take the front passenger seat? Cosky can stretch his leg across the backseat."

Damn. He'd actually forgotten Zane was with them. Talk about pathetic.

As Kait climbed into the van, he caught her arm and her attention. She turned to face him, one leg in, one leg out of the vehicle, her face as smooth and expressionless as glass.

"Thank you," he said gruffly, indicating his knee with a sweep of his hand.

Her gaze softened, but she simply nodded and turned away.

Curiously off balance, Cosky climbed into the rear seat and settled back. Stretching his leg across the bench seat, he stared at the cool perfection of Kait's profile.

The urge to apologize grew stronger and stronger, but Zane—the bastard—was listening to every word they said. Apologizing would alert the asshole to the fact Cosky hadn't been completely honest about what had taken place in Kait's apartment the day before.

The apology would have to wait until he had Kait alone.

Kait tried to call her *Wolf* twice during the trip across town. It suited Cosky just fine that both calls went to voice mail. With luck the bastard wouldn't call back until they reached the safety and electronic scrambling of the condo.

"Looks like you have company," Zane said, parking beside Russo's Dodge Ram.

Hollister's and Trammel's vehicles were in view as well. Which meant Taggart was probably on scene too, since Tram and Tag roomed together.

They entered the condo to the rumble of Mac's voice. Cosky was familiar with the tone and cadence—he'd spent hundreds of hours listening to it during mission briefings. He exchanged glances with Zane and headed for the dining room. Something was in the wind.

Jillian was still out like a light on the couch, the IV feeding fluids into her veins. But the dining room looked like central command. Maps, diagrams, and photographs were pinned to the drapes and walls.

The six men in the dining room turned. Mac's voice stalled as he caught sight of Cosky and Zane. He shot one irritated glare toward Kait and turned to Zane.

"We're setting a trap for the bastard," Mac said.

"How the hell did you manage all this?" Zane asked, closing in on the maps. "We weren't gone even thirty minutes."

"The wonders of the Internet," Rawls said, turning to Kait. "Glad to see you in one piece, darlin'."

Tag stepped forward, pulling her into a bear hug. "Good to see you, Kaity girl."

Cosky stiffened, his eyes narrowing. Their hug looked far too natural and . . . tight.

Something had happened between Tag and Aiden, nobody knew exactly what it was—except maybe Tram, and the bastard wasn't talking—but it had been bad enough to send Aiden packing. Had the rift been because of Kait?

Wasn't his business.

Kait and Tag were adults, if they'd had a fling that was their affair.

Too bad he couldn't convince his fists of that.

Mac interrupted the lovefest by grabbing Kait's arm, thank Christ. "What did you tell that bastard while he was at your place?" Mac asked, dragging her from Tag's arms. The look he shot Taggart held a clear warning.

Releasing a breath he hadn't even been aware of holding, Cosky relaxed.

"Nothing," Kait said. "At least nothing that I hadn't already told the police."

"Which was what? Exactly?" Mac demanded.

"That she wanted me to call Cosky and tell him to come over. Then I hit her with my grocery bag and knocked her out. I told the police I went into my apartment for some duct tape to tie her up, and she took off while I was gone."

A grin tugged at Tag's lips. "That was some grocery bag."

"Yeah." She coughed out a laugh, humor gleaming in her eyes. "It had a jar of Miracle Whip in it."

Rawls laughed. "Talk about irony."

"So what's the plan?" Zane asked, bringing everyone back on track.

"I'm going to call our bald friend and tell him we picked up Jillian, give him an address to pick her up at," Mac said with a hard grin.

Zane's gaze narrowed as he scanned the maps and diagrams. "And we'll be waiting for him."

Mac's smile was cold. "That's the plan."

Kait turned to look at the woman lying on the couch. "How can you be sure they don't know you have her here? What if Pachico followed from my place when you picked her up?"

"You said you didn't tell him we have her."

Cosky stiffened at the accusatory bite in Mac's voice, but Kait just frowned.

"I didn't." She paused and added softly, "But I think he knew."

Zane turned toward her, his eyebrows raised. "What makes you think that?"

She shook her head. "I don't know. Instinct?"

With a snort, Mac turned away.

"You posted Millian two blocks to the west," Zane said, which brought Cosky's head around. Hell, he hadn't even seen Millian's beat-up truck. "Who did you post to the east?"

"Brenton," Russo said, without taking his eyes off the map on the wall. "We have the all clear. Nobody appears to be watching."

Appears, being the operative word. If they'd staked out the place through a neighboring condo, they wouldn't be watching from the road. And while neither he, nor Zane, nor Rawls had identified any unfamiliar faces hanging around, or unfamiliar vehicles in the parking lot, that didn't mean much. Professionals would know how to mask their presence.

"Let's pack up, and set up," Mac said. His icy gaze settled on Cosky. "You sit out."

"Make sure you wake her every half an hour," Rawls said with a chin jab toward the woman on the bed. "If her pupil is dilated or pinpricked, get her to the ER. You can remove the IV once this bag's drained."

Cosky nodded, watching as an arsenal of weapons were checked and rechecked, and then stashed behind belts or waistbands or tucked in boots. Watches were synchronized. Cell phone batteries checked.

Kait's gaze locked on Rawls's cell phone, which obviously reminded her of her good buddy, Wolf.

She dug into her purse, her hand emerging with her cell. Cosky pretended he didn't see her punching buttons, and wondered what Tag thought about her pet *Wolf.*

Rawls—Goddamn him—got entirely too helpful.

"Here, you'll need it green-lighted to place or receive calls." Rawls took the phone from Kait, connected it to the scrambler's port, and hit a couple of buttons. "It will take a few minutes, and then you should be good."

A few minutes later the door slammed and silence reigned. Cosky scowled, frustration rising like a tidal wave. He should have been headed out with them, damn it. Would have, if not for his damn knee.

He transferred his glare down to his leg. He'd better get used to babysitting detail, because that's all he'd be good for if his knee didn't recover one hundred percent.

His scalp itched like crazy beneath his toupee as Robert aimed the Oldsmobile sedately along the street in front of the development Simcosky and Rawlings lived in. He chanced a quick glance at their condo as he passed, relaxing at the sight of Mackenzie's and Rawlings's vehicles. There were several unfamiliar vehicles as well.

Another indication they had Jillian and that the bitch had told them more than he could afford.

By now they had to know Jillian was related to Russ. It was also a good bet that the bitch had described Robert to them and filled them in on his role in that previous debacle.

Luckily none of that mattered, because they were all about to become very dead.

The fatalities would be higher than the six he'd planned on. But that was for the best if Mackenzie was filling the rest of his team in on Jillian's intel. Everyone in that damn condo needed to be silenced. And this was his best shot of silencing them.

Without a twinge of regret, he picked up the handset to the old-school analog cell phone with its enormous battery packs. The damn think took up half of the passenger seat beside him.

There was one serious disadvantage to the high-tech toys Simcosky and Rawlings were guarding their castle with. They were all geared toward digital signals, not the old analog one. So if you wanted to—oh, say, arm a bomb from a distance—without their fancy jammers and scramblers and whatnot interfering with the signal, well you just had to step back into the 1970s and go old school. An analog signal from an old-school cell phone, sent to a pager that was powered by tapping into the electrical wiring of the house itself, would do the trick.

Without anyone in the house being the wiser.

Of course, all their high-tech toys had been aimed at jamming unwelcome eyes and ears. They hadn't been trying to guard against the arming of a bomb. Why would they? Up until, well, now, they hadn't been threatened with any actual physical harm. The bosses had been targeting them through the legal system and the Naval Special Warfare Office itself.

The bomb beneath the condo had simply been insurance.

If things got out of hand and those bastards poked their noses into sensitive shit, well, instant and utter obliteration was available. But the bomb was meant as a last resort.

The bosses didn't want additional attention given to their story. And an explosion taking out four decorated Naval Special Warfare officers who just happened to be screaming conspiracy—well that was bound to attract far too much interest and speculation.

So in thirty minutes, when the bomb beneath the condo detonated and incinerated everyone within the house, the bosses were going to be dangerously pissed and armed for retribution themselves. He needed to make sure he aimed that venom in the right direction.

He glanced at the clock embedded in the dashboard of the Oldsmobile. He had fifteen minutes, give or take, to intercept Phillip and put plan B into action. It shouldn't be that hard to hide the old analog cell phone in Phillip's car, along with other incriminating items.

His best bet would be to take Phil out and stage the scene. Convince Manheim that Phil had attacked him when Robert had tried to bring him in.

He was working the strategy out in his mind when his cell phone buzzed. He checked the window and found CALLER UNKNOWN. Probably one of the crew, since everyone was using prepaid, untraceable cells.

If his luck held, the caller would be Phillip. He'd talk him into meeting him for lunch, and then lure him out to the park on some pretext or another. He'd stash everything in Phil's car after he'd eliminated him. He felt a twinge of regret, but only a twinge. While Phil was a good guy, there was only room for one when it came to self-preservation.

"Yeah?" he said.

"Detective Pachico?" a gravelly voice asked.

It took a second for the name to kick in, which was the last fucking thing you wanted when you were running an alias. Jesus—he needed to screw his head on straight. This kind of a slip could get a guy dead pretty damn quick.

"Who is this?" he demanded, although he'd finally recognized the gritty baritone. He put the cell on speaker while he scrolled through his phone's tool kit and started the recorder so he could listen to the conversation later.

"Mackenzie. You said to call if we tracked your girl down."

Robert's eyebrows rose. Well this was unexpected, and suspicious as hell. "You found her?"

"Yeah, we've got her."

"And where, exactly, do you have her?" Robert asked, keeping the dryness out of his voice. His eyebrows climbed higher at the address Mackenzie rattled off. The bastard sure as hell wasn't directing him to the condo.

Pulling over to the side of the road, he punched the address into his GPS system. Mackenzie's coordinates would take him clear across town, into the industrial corner. Plenty of secluded spots to set a trap in that neck of Coronado.

"Huh," he injected surprise into his voice. "That's clear across town from the last sighting."

"Explains why nobody's had any luck finding her," Mackenzie offered blandly.

Oh yeah, the bastard was good. He hadn't even paused.

Robert scowled, pinching the bridge of his nose as it occurred to him what a colossal monkey wrench this development had thrown in his plans. Mackenzie wouldn't have called unless they were already in place and waiting to spring the trap. So half his targets were across town. They must have taken one vehicle and left the others. Which explained why he hadn't seen Winters's van.

How many men had Mackenzie taken with him? The van fit eight, with the size of those bastards it would be a tight fit, but SEALs were used to more cramped quarters than a minivan.

It was likely they'd leave the women at the condo, along with one, possibly two guard dogs. At least Jillian would be off his back. Still, most of his targets would be left standing, with blood in their eyes and revenge on their minds.

He toyed with the idea of telling Mackenzie he couldn't get there until later. That might get them back to the condo in his thirty-minute window. But after a moment, he shook his head in disgust; postponing the meet was certain to tip them off, and he sure as hell didn't need them all abandoning the condo.

What a fucking pity he couldn't deactivate the bomb.

"Pachico?" Mackenzie demanded.

"I'm en route," Robert said.

"We'll be waiting," Mackenzie said.

Which was probably the only true thing the bastard had said so far.

As soon as Mackenzie hung up, Robert dialed nine-one-one. Okay, so he wouldn't be eliminating all his targets at once, that didn't mean he couldn't pile a heap of shit on the rest of their heads.

"Nine-One-One, what's your emergency?" a nasal female voice asked.

"Yeah." Robert coughed and worked a shake into his voice. "I just drove past the old Pontaine Produce plant; you know, where all those druggies hang out? Well, the gate's down and there's a bunch of big guys with guns shooting the place up. Thought I should call it in, because, you know, there's a lot of screaming and everything going on . . ."

He hung up while the dispatcher was still asking questions, and then just sat there and smiled.

That should keep them busy for a while.

Chapter Fourteen

KAIT SHOT COSKY A QUICK GLANCE AS THE DOOR SLAMMED behind Commander Mackenzie and the rest of Aiden's teammates. The silence that fell was thick, tense, and uncomfortable. Of course this was the first time Cosky and she had been alone—aside from the sleeping woman on the couch—since she'd stalked naked across her living room.

"So that's what it's like," Kait said the first thing that came to mind.

"What?"

Cosky turned his head, but his shadowed gaze barely brushed her face before he turned and limped into what had to be the kitchen, judging by the Formica countertops.

"One of your super-secret strategy sessions." Kait turned in a slow circle, checking out Cosky and Rawls's living room.

Her gaze lingered on the stark white walls. Not a picture, a clock, or a knickknack in sight. The rest of the room was just as bare. A coffee table, a leather couch, a couple of recliners—both upholstered and leather. A huge television in an entertainment center tucked into the far corner. The shelves in the entertainment center held a collection of electronic boxes. She recognized a Blu-ray DVR system and a cable box, along with the electronic scrambler Rawls had fiddled with earlier. But that only identified half of the electronic gadgets stashed on those shelves.

So this was Aiden's new home. Considering he'd still had boxes stacked in the corner of his bedroom at Tag's place when he'd moved out—four years after moving in—this place would suit him just fine. As long he had a spot for his guns and his clothes, and a place to watch the ball games he'd be happy as a clam.

Her brother sure didn't have much to show for his healthier than average bank account.

Cosky still hadn't responded to her comment, but then there wasn't much to say. She'd thrown it out as an icebreaker, rather than a conversation starter. Not that it had worked in either capacity. She listened to the sound of a fridge opening. After several seconds of rustling, the fridge closed again.

There was a long pause and then Cosky asked, "Do you want a beer?"

Her lips quirked, now that question was what you'd call an afterthought. "Thanks, that sounds good." Maybe the beer would relax her.

The fridge opened again and closed in short order. She headed over to the couch as his uneven footsteps progressed across the kitchen floor. Jillian was completely out of it, her mouth partially open, barely audible nasal snores mirroring the rise and fall of her chest.

Kait took a seat on the edge of the couch beside her and lifted the ice pack covering Jillian's eye. She flinched at the swollen, blue flesh that was revealed. Oh God, the injury looked a thousand times worse than it had looked earlier. Her stomach tightened. She shouldn't have hit her so hard. A little less force would have still given her the opportunity to escape.

"You handled that well," Cosky's quiet voice said from across the room.

It took a couple of swallows before Kait trusted her voice to remain steady. "What?"

"Her," he said simply. "You used your head. You didn't hesitate. You picked the best weapon you had available."

There was approval in his voice.

Kait strangled back a laugh. Here Cosky was praising her for the very thing she was kicking herself for.

"Has Rawls checked out her eye? I mean, the eye itself. I didn't do any damage, did I?"

"He says she's fine." There was a shrug in Cosky's voice. "Or she will be once the swelling goes down."

His voice was right behind her shoulder, and then the icy chill of cold glass touched her bare arm. She jumped a bit and looked up, watched him twist the cap off and accepted the bottle he passed her.

Another awkward silence fell between them. They filled it by drinking their beers. After a few sips, Kait set her bottle down on the coffee table in front of the couch. Shimmying her body closer to Jillian's head, she reached out and settled her hands on Jillian's swollen eye and temple.

"Hell no!" Cosky's disbelieving voice cracked across the silence.

There was the sharp *click* of glass hitting wood, and hard arms locked around her waist, dragging her up and back.

"Hey!" Indignant, Kait twisted, trying to break his hold.

"You are not doing a healing on her." His voice was flat, adamant.

"That's not your call," she snapped. When his arms didn't loosen, she tensed. "If you don't let go of me right now, I'm going to knock your nuts up into your skull."

His arms loosened, but they didn't let go. To Kait's dismay, a flash fire started where his hot arms chained her. Intense heat radiated out from their point of contact, flooding into her abdomen and coursing down her legs. Her breasts went tight, her nipples drawn. The core of her went liquid and melting. This wasn't the heat of healing. It was the unwelcome heat of arousal.

Something she had no intention of experiencing again.

Ever again.

At least with him.

His arms tightened again, drew her against his chest until she felt the hard, urgent beat of his heart against her back, and the insistent press of his erection against her lower back.

No. Way.

She stiffened. Acting on instinct she stomped as hard as she could on his left foot.

"Son of a bitch." His arms loosened.

She twisted to face him and aimed for his crotch with her knee. He blocked the attack at the last second, taking the blow on his thick thigh, instead of his crotch.

"Jesus Christ," he roared, letting go and stepping back.

Kait drew a shaky breath and tried for an unconcerned shrug. "I warned you."

He glared back at her, dark red highlighting his cheekbones. She couldn't tell whether it was the flush of arousal or anger. Maybe both.

After a couple of deep breaths, he unlocked his jaw. "It hasn't even been twelve hours since you were released from transitory care, after your *last* healing. Don't you think it's a little soon to try *another* one?"

His voice sounded hoarse and gritty, like he was trying not to yell at her.

Kait stuck her chin up and glared right back—although he did have a point. Not that she was going to admit that to him. "And don't you think it should be up to me to decide whether I'm up for another healing? I've had a lot more experience with this than you have." She delivered the lie in her best it's-none-of-your-business voice.

And hoped he didn't pick up on the little fact that the healing in the parking lot had been a first for her—the first time she'd ever channeled so much heat, or so much energy, the first time she'd healed an injury in one session, and the first time she'd passed out. None of which he needed to know.

The red faded from his face, and suddenly he just looked tired. Swearing beneath his breath, he ran a hand through his hair and turned around to hobble toward the closest recliner.

He was limping much, much worse than he had been earlier.

Had she hit his knee when she'd gone for his crotch?

"I'm sorry," she said taking a step toward him. "I wasn't aiming for your bad knee."

His short crack of laughter wasn't amused. "No shit."

It was Kait's turn to color. Okay, possibly she'd overreacted.

"Anyway"—he eased down into the recliner and pulled the lever that lifted the footrest—"I should be apologizing, not you."

His voice sounded as tired as his expression looked.

"There's no need," she said, shying away from the direction the conversation was headed. Instinctively, she knew he wasn't talking about their altercation of a few minutes earlier.

"Yeah, there is." There was dogged determination in his voice. The kind of gritty determination that came with completing an unpleasant task as quickly as possible. "Look, I'm sorry for that crack I made at your place, you know . . . after . . . well, after the—yeah."

Kait's lips twisted. He couldn't even say it? The coward. "You mean the sex?"

Let him fumble around that.

He shot her a bad-tempered glare.

She braced her hands on her hips and stared him straight in the face. "When you called me a whore?"

He straightened in the recliner like she'd shoved a red-hot poker into his shorts. "What the . . . ? I didn't call you *that*."

She raised her eyebrows and matched him glare for glare. "What do you call exchanging sex for services?"

"Ah hell." Shame edged into his scowl. He opened his mouth and she could almost smell his contrition, could almost hear his coming apology. And then he scanned her face. Suddenly he frowned. "You know I didn't mean that."

She cocked her head and stared back. "Do I?"

His face softened and a hint of amusement touched his face. "Yeah, you damn well do. You're just busting my balls." He paused, and then added wryly, "Not that I don't deserve it."

She almost caved at his dry admission, but braced herself against the weakness.

"Finally, something we can both agree on."

He settled back against the recliner, his lips quirking, and regarded her steadily. "You've got a serious mouth on you, anyone tell you that?"

There was a softness to the question she wasn't expecting, a tone close to affection.

"Just Aiden and Wolf—" Which reminded her, she picked up her cell phone from the coffee table and tried Wolf's number again. It went straight to voice mail.

Obviously her big brother was off . . . somewhere . . . and she had no idea when he'd be back. She was going to have to rethink her exit strategy from Cosky's condo.

"Still no answer?" he asked, sounding oddly satisfied.

Frowning, Kait turned to stare at him. He was slumped back in the recliner, legs up, half asleep. She must have been mistaken about that odd tone in his voice. He had to be as anxious to get her out of his home as she was to leave. There was nothing more awkward than a one-night stand that dragged on past the one night.

Or in their case, the morning.

"I want you to know," he said, and his silver gaze snared her eyes, so brilliant it was close to mesmerizing, "I'm sorry for what happened at your place. For the way things played out. For being such an ass."

For the sex.

He didn't say it, but it was clear.

Kait ripped her eyes away. "Forget it."

"Kait—" he said, sudden tension in his voice, and the leather beneath him squawked as he sat up in the recliner.

Swinging away from him, Kait headed to the couch and took her previous seat beside Jillian. She didn't want to discuss what a mistake those heated, heady minutes with him had been. Or at least, she didn't want to hear him characterize them as a mistake. She didn't want to hear him tell her they couldn't happen again. She didn't want to hear his list of excuses as to why he couldn't be with her, when it all boiled down to one thing.

He didn't want to be with her.

What she wanted was to pick up with her life and carry on, without the memory of him apologizing for not having feelings for her.

"Let's just chalk it up to a massage that got out of control and move on, shall we? No harm. No foul." She laid her hands across her victim's swollen, discolored eye.

The tension radiating from him morphed into disapproval, but this time he didn't try to interfere.

As it turned out, there wasn't anything to interfere with. After several minutes of sitting there, awkwardly twisted to the side and hunched over her reclining patient—nothing happened.

Not even a spark of heat. No hint of healing energy. Absolutely nothing.

Frustrated, she sat back. Maybe she'd burned herself out in the parking lot and needed some time to recharge. Or maybe Jillian just fell into the seventy percent she couldn't help.

And then another possibility occurred to her. A worrisome possibility. What if channeling such extreme energy had burned her out completely? What if she'd fried the circuit in her brain or body that allowed the healing in the first place?

"What's wrong?" Cosky asked.

"There's nothing there," Kait said slowly, the paranoia building hard and fast—could she have lost the ability completely?

He was silent for a moment. "Aiden said your ability didn't work all the time. That you couldn't help everyone."

"Yeah, but—" She paused, briefly debated, and then shrugged. There was only one way to assure herself that she hadn't lost the healing ability—and his participation was essential to her test—so he needed to understand her concern. "The healing on your leg yesterday, the one in the parking lot?"

His gaze narrowed and locked on her face. "Okay?"

"It wasn't normal." Rising to her feet she shoved her hands into the sides of her loose braid, and felt some of the strands pull loose.

"How so?" Cosky asked absently, his gaze locked on her hair.

"I've never channeled so much energy before. It's never gotten so hot. For God's sake my hands blistered, so did your knee." She paused and dropped her voice. "I've never healed an injury in just one sitting before, either. And I've never passed out." Her voice dropped even lower. "What if I burned the ability out? What if it's gone now?"

With a shake of his head, he transferred his gaze to her face. "It's more likely she isn't someone you can help, or—you just need to recharge the energy. Maybe your ability is like a battery. You have to give it time to recharge after exhausting it."

His gaze drifted back to her hair and took on a platinum glitter she found distracting as hell. She forced herself to focus. "I want to test it. See if it's still there."

He cocked his head and his face went still. The glitter in his eyes dimmed, suspicion taking its place. "How?"

Cosky was a smart guy; Kait was certain he'd already figured out what she was about to propose. "By doing another healing on your knee."

"No." The denial came instantly.

Oh yeah, he'd known exactly what she was going to ask.

"I *know* the ability works on you. If it works again, I'll know it's still there."

"For Christ's sake, Kait, you were burning up. Rawls had to use ice packs to get your temperature down." He shoved the lever to the footrest down and jolted to his feet. "How do you know another healing so soon after the last—which you yourself characterized as abnormal—isn't going to burn you out? How do you know it won't do permanent brain or organ damage? It's not worth the damn risk. Give yourself a couple of days."

"I won't do a full healing. I just want to see if it's still there," she said in her most persuasive voice. "I'll stop immediately as soon as I sense it's working."

He didn't look convinced.

"It could be the last chance I'll have to do another healing on your leg," she said, changing tactics. "Who knows how long it will be before I get back after Wolf comes for me."

His lips flattened. Folding his arms, he planted his feet. "No."

Okay . . .

She frowned; there had to be a way to convince him to let her try. She flashed back to Aiden after his spinal injury, to his frustration and fury with the shortcomings of his body, not because of what it meant to his own life, but because of what it meant to his team.

Because he'd felt like he'd let down his team.

The team. That was the key.

"Look, your leg's a liability to your team right now." When he flinched slightly, she knew she was on the right track. "You need to be as close to one hundred percent as possible."

"We're not on a damn rotation," he growled back, his voice gravelly and hard.

But his argument lacked conviction, and Kait knew she'd found his weak spot. Without hesitation, she dug into it. What she was suggesting would benefit him anyway. There was no reason for him to be stonewalling her.

"You may not be on rotation, but you are in the middle of a battle," she reminded him quietly, letting the weight of her words get to him instead of the volume. "Your team could have used you today."

He went still, intense—his gaze focused inward.

"And what happens if Mac misjudged? What happens if this

Pachico ringer circles back? Attacks here instead of falling into Mac's trap? Is your leg strong enough if you need to rely on it?"

He twitched at that. Swearing beneath his breath, he raked his hands through his hair and swung around to face her. "I'm carrying. We'll have to rely on that."

But then he swore again and threw himself into the recliner. From the frustrated anger on his face, she knew she'd won.

"Fine. You want to burn yourself out. Be my guest." He watched her approach, sheer bad temper flashing in his eyes. "And don't think I didn't catch how you manipulated me there."

She shrugged. "Everything I said was the truth. You wouldn't be letting me try this if it wasn't."

He just glared back.

Settling on her knees in front of him, she pushed his sweatpants leg up, exposing a compression sleeve over his knee. Since she needed bare skin, the sleeve had to go. But it was too tight to roll up over his thigh, so she unlaced his boot and took it off, then rolled the compression sleeve down his hairy calf and off his broad foot.

An unwelcome tingling sparked in places she didn't want to concentrate on. This felt far too much like undressing him. Her gaze drifted up his legs; the material of his sweats didn't look nearly as loose in the crotch as they had before. And then she saw his hands clamp onto the armrests of the chair. His fingers turned white and dug into the leather.

The thick sultry charge of arousal crackled in the air around them. Her muscles tightened. So did his. The hair on her arms lifted. So did his.

Okay . . . this was obviously one of the stupidest ideas she'd ever had.

"Problem?" There was pure challenge in his rough, aroused voice.

Yeah, stupid. Stupid. Stupid.

"Not"—she paused to cough the huskiness out of her voice—"at all."

She laid her hands on his knee, and heat instantly swamped her, which would have been reassuring, except it was the wrong kind of heat.

There was no gradual build to the hunger this time. Her body knew exactly what it felt like to have the hot, hard length of him lodged inside her. Exactly what it felt like to feel him on her and in her and driving her to the stars.

And it wanted to feel him again. Inside of her. On top of her. Wrapped around her.

Lust exploded, dragged her into an inferno of hunger, a fierce red mist that incinerated everything in its wake. Her reservations, her hurt, her caution—all were consumed by the eruption, until the only thing left was fervent need.

Raw urgency.

Heat swept up from her hands, into her arms and raced through her body in an electrifying, carnal flood, finally pooling in the throbbing, wet valley between her legs.

Her core clenched, aching for the hard, fiery length of him.

He groaned, his hands wrapping around her arms. One moment she was on her knees and the next she was straddling his lap, the bulge of his erection grinding into her mound, exactly where she needed the pressure the most. His fingers slipped into the loose strands of hair along the sides of her face, combing them out and then sliding around to the back of her head, and went to work unraveling the braid itself.

The urgent press of his lips found hers. His tongue swept into her mouth as he pulled her down on top of him and rocked her against his erection.

She opened her mouth wider, her tongue rubbing against his, and sank down, trying to appease the unbearable urgency by riding his erection.

He groaned into her mouth, his musky, masculine scent swelling until she felt cocooned in it.

Tearing his mouth from hers, he nipped the side of her neck and then soothed the sting with the stroke of his tongue.

"Jesus. I want you. Worse than before."

Distantly, an alarm sounded. He didn't sound pleased by that need.

Another nip, higher up her neck. Another wet, languid stroke of his tongue. "You're like a Goddamn drug. I'll never get enough."

The alarm shrilled louder, harder.

Pure frustration had been in that last comment, maybe even a hint of accusation.

She started to pull away, but his arms tightened, dragged her closer. His hands swept up her back, inside her shirt. Their callused, hard strength launched an entire fleet of goose bumps in their skimming, skating wake. And then his teeth closed over the lobe of her ear and tugged. She quivered at the caress. When he drew the lobe into his mouth and suckled, she groaned and ground herself against his crotch.

Somewhere behind her a metallic *crash* sounded.

Lost in his taste and the feel of his mouth and hands against her skin—the sound barely registered in Kait's passion-soaked mind.

Cosky responded instantly.

One second she was in his lap. The next they were both on their feet. He picked her up and set her to the side.

Off balance and reeling, Kait shuffled to the left. Her unfocused gaze fell on the IV stand. It was lying half on, half off the coffee table.

Cosky was already halfway across the living room, quickly gaining on a fleeing Jillian.

Oh God.

Embarrassment flooded her. She'd forgotten the other woman was even in the room.

Cosky caught Jillian just as she reached the living room door. If the woman hadn't knocked over the IV stand as she fled, she would have gotten away. God knows they hadn't even noticed her get up.

She could just imagine trying to explain to Commander Mackenzie how they'd let their prisoner get away. The humiliating image was still prickling in her mind when her cell phone started ringing.

Cosky swung Jillian around as Kait picked up her phone.

She checked the caller ID. WOLF. *Thank you, God.*

Kait could hear Wolf shouting something as she raised the cell to her ear. But she couldn't make out the words.

"Wolf? What? I didn't catch—"

"Get out of the house." His voice was a thunderous roar. "Get out now."

She didn't question the command. Just dropped her arm and leapt for Cosky and Jillian.

"Run," she screamed.

Robert had Phil on the line and was arranging to meet him for a quick bite—a very quick bite, in Phil's case, since he'd be dead before consuming his last meal—when his caller ID started bleeping. After apologizing to Phil, he switched lines.

"Gather your team and head back up to Seattle." The voice was flat, completely expressionless.

Robert froze, his blood chilling and chugging through his veins. "Sir?"

The bomb hadn't even gone off yet. How the hell had Manheim found out about it so soon?

"Chastain's widow has been digging into the lab explosion. She's asking questions we don't want answered. She needs to be silenced."

Robert released the breath he'd been holding and pinched the bridge of his nose, his mind scrambling. "Okay."

Sometimes lady luck dropped a diamond in your lap. When that happened, you grabbed it and ran.

"We may have a bigger problem," Robert said, trying to project a thoughtful tone. "Several of ST7's members just converged on Rawlings and Simcosky's condo. At least seven, possibly eight members. If Amy Chastain's been in touch with Mackenzie . . ."

He let his voice trail off. Let the inference work on Manheim, rather than pushing the connection and inviting suspicion.

"You think they heard about the lab from her and they're planning something?" Manheim asked, his voice jumping from flat to sharp.

"It would make sense and explain this sudden convergence on the condo. We've never been able to get ears inside. But we have eyes outside, and they looked pretty damn grim going in. Reads like a strategy session. I was about to alert you."

Manheim hissed, the serpentine sound rolled down the line, thick with icy censure. "We cannot afford their interference."

"Yes, sir," Robert let his voice fade, as though he were thinking. "We do have the fail-safe beneath the condo and with them all on site . . . perhaps—"

"Do it."

Well, look at that. He'd barely had to bait the request.

"You have the trigger?" Manheim asked, his voice returning to its habitual chilly flatness. "The bomb will silence the core group. You'll still need to take your team to Seattle and handle Amy Chastain."

"Yes, sir, I'll take care of it."

"See that you do." The line went dead.

For one long moment after the call ended, Robert just sat there, staring out the windshield in disbelief.

Just like that, and he was back on top again.

The bosses would never know that Jillian had resurfaced, because she'd perish in the explosion they had *approved.*

As for Phil, well, hell, his buddy had just had a reprieve. Not that he'd known how close he'd come to spending eternity in an unmarked grave.

He glanced at his watch. The bomb would detonate any moment. The timing would be off, but he could whitewash that easy enough—bombs could be tricky, they didn't always arm exactly as planned.

As for the SEALs who would escape the explosion . . . easy as pie to explain that screw up, he'd just tell Manheim the truth. The bastards had left the condo before it exploded.

The bosses wouldn't be pleased, but they could hardly blame him for that piece of unfortunate luck.

He whistled, grinning out the windshield. Euphoria bubbled inside him. He could kiss Amy Chastain for handing him this out.

Maybe he would, just before he killed her.

His erection throbbing like a Goddamn abscess, which wasn't exactly conductive to sprinting, Cosky grabbed Jillian and lifted her into his arms. She started to struggle, but seemed to think better of it. Freezing, she curled into his embrace instead.

The good news was the door was right behind him. The bad news was his knee wasn't up to running with his own weight on the line, let alone one hundred–plus pounds of extra weight clinging to his chest.

He didn't question Kait's warning though. She'd proved to be unflappable, with a steady head on her shoulders. If she screamed *run* and bolted for the door, there was a reason behind it.

So he flung open the living room door and took the steps two at a time, praying his knee wouldn't explode beneath him. When he reached the sidewalk, Kait appeared beside him, her cell phone still clutched in her hand. They separated as they hit the driveway, racing between the cluster of cars and the sparse grass.

To Cosky's surprise, his knee held up just fine, not even a twinge as he abused the hell out of the healing joint. Likely that had a lot to do with the surge of adrenaline. No doubt he'd pay for this stunt later, after the adrenaline crash.

He turned his head toward Kait as they converged again behind Aiden's Mustang, and raced for the street. "What's—"

The condo exploded behind him.

The force of the blast lifted him, flinging him forward. He twisted in midair and tried to take the impact with the pavement on his back, so he wouldn't crush Jillian. He didn't quite make it. He hit the pavement hard on his left shoulder and heard the *pop* of the joint dislocating. An instant later burning, gutting agony hit.

Still, he managed to shield Jillian. She landed safely on top of him. He rolled as soon as he got his breath back, locked the agony in a compartment inside his mind, and pushed Jillian beneath him to protect her from the fiery chunks of debris raining down around them.

The condo was ablaze behind them. The windows and door were gone. Burning debris rained down all around him.

"Are you okay?" he asked Jillian, barely waiting for her shocked nod before struggling to his feet and pulling her up alongside him. They needed to get out of here, before whoever had set the bomb came back to finish the job.

"Kait?" he roared, his body chilling as he caught sight of her several feet away. She lay prone on the pavement, her braid frosted with ash and smoldering.

"I'm okay," Kait gasped, pushing herself up on scraped hands and knees. From there she rose, although with quite a wobble, to her feet. Once upright, she turned to look behind her.

She froze in shock, horror creeping over her face.

Her right cheek was scraped and oozing pinpricks of blood. She was missing one shoe, and her shirt was all but shredded.

Still, the sight of her upright and moving was the most beautiful thing he'd ever seen.

They'd been lucky. Two or three seconds longer in the condo and they'd be dead. And then there was the percussion blast. It could have easily broken their backs or necks. Not that they were out of the woods yet.

The house hadn't exploded on its own.

Someone had planted a damn bomb.

He went to grab his Glock from his waistband, only to remember he'd removed it in the condo. Which meant it was toast, along with the rest of his belongings.

Rage sizzled through the shock. Son of a bitch. Some motherfucking asshole had just detonated everything he owned. Everything.

Leaving him unarmed and vulnerable with two women to protect.

And a fucking bum knee, although it was holding up remarkably well under the circumstances.

He locked the shocked fury behind another compartment and focused on what needed to be done.

They needed to retreat, and hole up somewhere safe.

"Let's go," he yelled at Kait, but the command was consumed beneath the famished roar of the fire.

Giving up on verbal communication, he wrapped an arm around Jillian's waist and urged her forward. On reaching Kait, he touched her arm, choosing a spot that wasn't oozing blood and scraped all to hell. She jolted at the brush of his fingers and swung to face him. Shock still rounded her mouth and eyes. She probably hadn't even noticed the myriad aches and pains yet.

"Oh, Cosky," she said in a hushed, numb voice. "Your house." Her gaze had the bright glossy look of shell shock. It dropped to the awkward drape of his arm and suddenly sharpened. "You're hurt."

He brushed her concern aside. "We need to go. *Now.*"

Kait finally seemed to come alive. She spun, but before they'd taken three or four steps, a black Escalade with tinted windows screamed to a stop beside them.

"Go. Go," Cosky roared, shoving Jillian toward Kait. He turned, determined to hold off whoever was in the SUV.

The glossy black passenger door flew open.

Chapter Fifteen

MAC RAN A TENSE HAND OVER HIS HEAD AND BRACED HIS HANDS on his hips. Rocking back on the heels of his boots, he scowled across the deserted parking lot. The place had been a produce shipping station before it had gone bankrupt and then was abandoned. Now it was a popular hangout for the addicted or homeless. The chain-link fence and dilapidated buildings dotting the property offered protection from the elements and the police.

While the property was raided every once in a great while, and the filthy, lice-infested inhabitants hauled off; for the most part, the city of Coronado pretended the property didn't exist.

Which made it perfect for his purposes.

The crumbling sheds, with their peeling white paint and termite-infested walls, were perfect for clandestine surveillance. His men were obscured by the teeming interior shadows.

Detective Pachico, or at least the bastard pretending to be him, wouldn't see his team until it was too late.

If he showed up.

Lifting his hand, Mac scowled down at his watch. The asshole should have been here by now.

"The bastard's blown us off," Mac said grimly.

From the somber expression stamped across Zane's habitual calm face, his LC was thinking the same thing.

But Zane, being the optimistic bastard he was, offered excuses. "Could be caught in traffic. Could have gotten a phone call."

"Yeah." Mac didn't believe it, but he glanced at his watch anyway. They could afford to hold steady a while longer.

Silence beat the air between them as they waited. One minute. Three. Seven.

The bastard was in the wind. Mac was sure of it. "If he made us, they've probably pulled the eyes."

Which meant they wouldn't have anyone to grab and shake down for answers.

Fuck, they'd been unceremoniously dropped back down to square one. Or close enough. Although they still had Jillian; maybe she'd prove more helpful once they had a chance to question her.

"Goddamn son of a bitch." Swiping a hand down his face, Mac gritted his teeth, fighting to hold the frustration in check. He could feel it swelling inside his chest, until he felt like a balloon on the verge of popping.

If Pachico's fucking ringer had bolted, if they'd pulled their fucking tag team, if Jillian didn't cough up some answers that would lead somewhere—well, hell, they'd lost their three best chances of clearing their names and serving justice to the men responsible for McKay's murder.

When his cell rang, he plucked it from his belt and gave it a quick once-over.

Caller unknown.

It could be anyone from Pachico calling to gloat, to Cosky asking for an update. That was the price of dealing with prepaid, untraceable cells, the caller ID sucked.

Raising the phone to his ear, he hit talk and barked into the mouth piece, "Yeah."

"Commander Mackenzie?" A controlled feminine voice marched down the line.

His fingers went rigid. So did his cock.

If he hadn't recognized her voice, he would have known exactly who was on the line by his dick's instant reaction. *Jesus fucking Christ,* the damn thing had locked onto her voice like Pavlov's dog had locked onto that damn bell. And now that he thought about it, the two shared other elements in common too—not only were they both man's best friend, they were both driven by primal, instinctive impulses.

Impulses that couldn't be reasoned with.

When his chest started to burn, Mac realized he'd forgotten to breathe. Just another of those annoying, frustrating reactions she incited in him.

"Mackenzie?" she asked, her tone not altering from that cool control.

Mac's mouth tightened. He hated, absolutely hated, the way he felt around her. Like he was back in eighth grade, the underprivileged, underdeveloped class laughingstock, getting ground beneath the prom queen's high-heeled shoe.

"Kinda busy right now," he snapped, his hand so tight around the phone his fingers burned.

"Too bad," her voice cooled. "I was going to fill you in on some recent developments concerning a couple of the first-class passengers on—well, maybe later." The line went dead.

Son of a fucking bitch.

He punched in her phone number and hit dial. It went straight to voice mail.

He dialed again. Voice mail.

"You grind your teeth any harder, and you're going to need some serious dental work," Zane said. He paused, and then asked dryly, "Amy?"

Mac froze. He hadn't realized anyone else had noticed his unwelcome reaction to the damn woman. "What the fuck makes you think that?"

Zane snorted. "She's the only person I know who'd hang up on you. What did she want before you pissed her off?"

Mac relaxed, the last thing he needed was his frustrating—in more ways than one—reaction to the damn woman to become common knowledge among his men. Hell, among anyone.

"Apparently there's been a development with some of the passengers from flight 2077."

With a relieved whistle, Zane scanned the silent grounds. "That's damn good news, because this little party's looking more and more like a bust."

No shit. Mac tried Amy's number again. Third time was apparently a charm, because she relented and answered.

"I take it you've freed up some time?" she asked with no deviation in her cool, collected tone.

Mac locked his instinctive response down. The fucking broad would almost certainly hang up on him again, and who knew how long she'd punish him next time before taking his call.

"We're in the middle of a stakeout," he told her tightly, instead.

"Really? Did he fail to show?"

"No, he didn't—" Mac's voice rose.

"You wouldn't be talking to me if the stakeout was successful," she interrupted, her voice so calmly reasonable it made Mac want to shake her and then kiss her fucking senseless—until she lost every ounce of that enormous self-containment.

Which was, yeah—completely insane—and why he needed to make sure three states and 1,250 miles continued to separate them.

He took a deep breath and released it carefully. "What about these passengers?"

"A lab exploded four days ago. Twelve people assumed dead. Eight of the twelve were booked into first class on flight 2077."

Mac thought that over. "What are your FBI contacts saying?" he asked. "They checking into it? They questioning the coincidence of these scientists being on the plane four months ago?"

She snorted, a mixture of frustration and derision in the sound. "Coincidence. That appears to be the operative word. At least in the FBI's eyes."

So they weren't checking into it.

Mac wasn't surprised. If the lab bombing was connected to the attempted hijacking, the men behind the two events sure as hell wouldn't want them linked. Which meant whoever was working for them within the FBI would make sure the lab bombing didn't draw any attention.

Their lack of initiative could work in his team's favor, though. The local investigation wouldn't be trying to link the two events, nor would they be searching for anything beyond the scope of a normal arson investigation.

He and Zane had speculated that the original hijacking had been an attempt to acquire the team of scientists, along with the research they'd been carrying with them. Maybe some of that research had survived the blast, even if the scientists hadn't.

Assuming the scientists had been in the building when it went *boom*.

He nudged a rock with the toe of his boot as another possibility occurred to him. "The place was totally razed? Was there anything left?"

"According to the reports, not much survived the blast," Amy said.

"They have bodies?" Mac asked.

"A good dozen. Charred beyond recognition. They'll have to pull dental records for identification."

"And if someone were to swap dental records . . ."

"You think they kidnapped the scientists before torching the place." Amy didn't sound surprised by Mac's suggestion. No doubt she'd already questioned that possibility herself.

Mac shrugged. "We can't discount the possibility. They sure as hell have the resources to pull off an op of this magnitude. And if they wanted those scientists bad enough to stage a hijacking . . ."

Amy made a soft sound of agreement that traveled through Mac's system like falling dominos. First his skin went tight, then his muscles clenched, his blood heated, his chest tightened—*fuck*—he gritted his teeth at the ache that took up residence in his groin.

"So you're coming up?" Amy asked, but there was no question in her voice.

She'd banked on the certainty they'd hightail it up to check that lab out.

Scrubbing a hand down his face, Mac glanced at the entrance to their trap. Still nothing. Pachico was way late now, too late to be anything but a thumbed nose. If Amy was right, though, and these scientists were the passengers Russ had been after, then another window had opened up before them.

It was worth checking into.

"What's the name of the lab? The scientists?"

Silence echoed down the line. "I'm going with you to check the place out."

Like fucking hell.

He kept his voice easy. "Sure. What's the lab's name?"

More silence. And then, "I'll fill you in when you get up here."

Mac's mouth tightened. Goddamn it, couldn't the woman be reasonable for one fucking second?

Of course, you could always go over, or around, a stone wall, or a stubborn woman.

"It will be a couple of days before we can make it. We're right in the middle of something."

"Your stakeout."

"That's right. We'll head up as soon as we're done here."

Which would be in seconds, but she sure as fuck didn't need to know that.

"I'll fill you in when you arrive."

He couldn't tell whether she believed him or not. She hung up before he had a chance to, which irritated the hell out of him all over again.

"We're headed to Seattle?" Zane asked, waving the rest of the team in.

"Yeah, I'll fill you in on the way up." Mac punched in Radar's speed-dial number as he turned toward Zane's van.

How hard would it be to locate a lab that had recently burned? Shouldn't be that hard, particularly if the explosion had claimed lives. The drive from Coronado to Seattle took approximately twenty hours, depending on traffic and weather. Radar would have scrambled up an address and the necessary intel before they arrived. They could be in and out of the bombed-out husk before Amy got suspicious.

A strategy that was interrupted by the half-dozen police cars that suddenly barreled into view. They took the corner leading into their trap in a single line and headed straight toward them on a cloud of dust.

"Fuck," Mac said grimly, his hands on his hips as the cruisers approached. Somehow, he just knew this was not going to be fun.

Or quick.

Cosky advanced on the Escalade, his heart racing like a damn greyhound. How the hell was he going to hold them off long enough for the women to escape?

"Kait!" a deep, rich baritone bellowed from inside the shadowy interior.

Kait skidded to a stop and spun. Dragging Jillian with her, she bolted for the Escalade.

What the hell? Cosky moved to intercept her.

"It's Wolf," she yelled at Cosky's approach.

Another explosion sounded behind them, followed by the shriek of tortured metal. It was the cars, Cosky realized. The gas tanks were exploding.

"Get inside," Wolf ordered.

Cosky wanted to slam the order back down the bastard's throat. But damn it, they needed the ride. Leaping forward, he jerked open the back door, boosted Jillian inside, and followed her through the door. Kait dove into the passenger seat.

The asshole behind the wheel floored it before the doors were even closed. As Cosky dragged the door shut—thank Christ he'd dislocated his left shoulder, rather than his right—he was aware of a dark head and a huge, broad body behind the steering wheel.

A series of smaller explosions rocked the condo as the Escalade raced away. Probably the ammunitions lockers. They'd had a shitload of weapons and ammo in the place.

Cosky twisted in the seat, scanning the road behind them. No other cars were in sight. Or at least in play.

But the condo was a giant fireball, flames clawing fifteen feet into the air. A dense black cloud boiled overhead.

"Everyone get out, *bixoo3etiit*?" Wolf asked.

A square face with the chiseled cheekbones of one of those shirtless, moronic male models that graced the covers of his mom's romance novels turned toward Kait. Pitch-black eyes scanned Kait's face.

He must not have liked what he saw, because he swore grimly and faced forward again, tension tightening the muscles of his huge shoulders.

"Yeah, we all got out." Kait's voice was hoarse. "You have the best timing."

The compliment tightened Cosky's lips. Now that his adrenaline was flatlining, suspicion kicked in. How had this asshole known where Kait was? She hadn't talked to him. And while she'd called him—repeatedly—the only message she'd left had been of the "call me" variety.

"Almost too good to be true," Cosky agreed in a tight voice. When the bastard cocked his head slightly, Cosky knew he'd picked up on the subtext.

Inscrutable obsidian eyes caught and held Cosky's gaze in the rearview mirror. But then the tanned skin of his forehead wrinkled.

He reached up with a huge, square hand and adjusted the rearview mirror, tilting it down and to the left.

Cosky twisted slightly, following the new angle of the rearview mirror. It was centered on Jillian, who'd pressed herself against the door, as far away from him as it was possible to get. She'd curled in on herself, her arms wrapped around her belly, her cropped hair spiky. Her left eye was completely swollen shut and the color of a robin's egg—while her right eye, brimming with wary hostility, shifted between Cosky and the driver's seat.

She looked fragile, and more than a little pathetic. But she was alive, and relatively unharmed.

Which was more than Cosky could claim for himself.

Grimacing, he faced forward again, his shoulder sending bolt after bolt of throbbing agony into his brain. Now that they were safe, it was getting harder and harder to lock the pain down. He needed to get hold of Rawls. As the corpsman of ST7, his roommate had plenty of experience manipulating dislocated joints back into place.

But before he reached out to Rawls, he needed to get hold of the cops. Call the bombing in. The amount of ammo stashed in the Condo made it a serious threat to both bystanders and firefighters.

He reached for the cell phone holster on his belt. It was empty.

Son of a bitch, he'd left the damn thing on the coffee table—which no longer existed. "Kait, call nine-one-one," Cosky said, leaning forward to take the pressure off his shoulder.

They needed to get hold of Zane, Rawls, and Mac too. Let the team know everyone who'd been inside the house was safe.

"Already done," Wolf said, in that deep, smooth baritone Cosky had already come to recognize and hate.

"Really?" Relieved to have something to concentrate on besides his damn shoulder, Cosky didn't try to hide his suspicion. "When was that? Before the damn bomb went off?"

"No," Wolf responded, his rich tone not quite disguising the menacing challenge lurking beneath the smoothness. "Before the bomb went off I was too busy saving your worthless ass."

That's when it clicked. Kait had received a call just before the bomb had detonated. He went rigid with rage. That call almost had to have armed the damn thing. The electronic jammer would have scrambled any other incoming signals.

"You called Kait?" He worked to keep the aggression out of the question, but knew he hadn't masked it well.

"I did." Challenge vibrated in the bastard's voice. He twisted the rearview mirror back to the right. Glittering eyes brimming with hostility raked Cosky's face. His lips twisted dismissively. "To warn her to get out of the house."

"How the hell did you know she needed warning?" Cosky demanded, his muscles bunching, tensing for battle.

He reeled the enmity in. Damn it, he needed to use his brain. They were trapped in an SUV, going at least forty miles an hour. He had a fucked-up shoulder and knee. It would be impossible to get Jillian and Kait out of the vehicle at this speed, in his condition.

He needed to keep the big bastard from pulling anything, at least until the Escalade was parked and he could neutralize him.

"You don't have the clearance for that answer." Ebony eyes gleaming with hostility caught and held Cosky's gaze.

The bastard made no attempt to hide his wrath. Which begged the question—what was he so angry about? Had Kait told him about those hot-as-hell moments on the couch? If the two were involved, yeah, finding out Cosky had made love to her would explain the anger.

"We need to stop by a hospital," Kait interrupted the building skirmish. She twisted in her seat and leaned around the backrest of the passenger seat. Worried brown eyes raked Cosky's awkwardly hanging left arm. "Cosky broke his shoulder."

"Dislocated," Wolf said in an unconcerned voice before Cosky could correct her. "I'll take care of it."

Like hell.

From the menacing vibes, the big bastard was more likely to rip Cosky's arm off and garrote him with it than manipulate it back into place.

Kait must have picked up on the tension, because she frowned and turned toward the driver's seat. "Wolf—"

"You should have stayed away from him, *nebii'o'oo.*" The affection in the comment was clear, so was the frustration and anger.

"You have no idea what happened," Kait snapped, her shoulders stiffening.

"I know you're my *netesei* and he almost got you killed." Steel laced the smooth baritone.

Cosky's body twitched. What the hell was a *netesei*? And what the fuck was Kait to him?

Not his business, damn it. Not his business.

Kait was off-limits to him.

She was also a beautiful woman. Of course she was going to have male companionship. It was just a hell of a lot easier to ignore that fact when her *male company* wasn't breathing down his neck.

He took a deep breath, tried to relax. But it became trapped in his constricted chest.

The Escalade took a hard right into an abandoned parking lot next to a high school football field and screeched to a stop next to the chain-link fence. Those hard black eyes met and held Cosky's own through the rearview mirror. He caught the open challenge in the big bastard's gaze.

Every muscle in his body locked onto that challenge, reciprocated it.

The driver's door flew open. Wolf slid out of the SUV.

Cosky thrust open his door and stepped out to meet him, his adrenaline firing like rocket fuel.

The bastard wanted to have at it?

Bring it on.

He was vaguely aware of Kait exiting the SUV behind him, but the bulk of his attention was locked on the huge bastard stalking around the corner of the Escalade.

They met up next to the taillights.

While Cosky wasn't expecting a friendly handshake, neither was he expecting the battle-ax of a right hook to his jaw. The blow slammed into him like an anvil and would have knocked him on his ass if the Escalade's rear door hadn't caught his back.

His face numb, ferocity a violent red mist blanketing his mind, he shoved off from the back door and launched himself at Kait's *nebe'ib.*

The bastard was going to be her ex-*nebe'ib,* if it was the last thing he did.

"As I've explained," Mac said for the tenth time as he leaned against the hot metal of the shift sergeant's black-and-white cruiser. "We had a report that the woman who attacked Lieutenant Simcosky and Kait Winchester had taken refuge inside—"

"And you wanted to check the premises yourself before calling it in." The stocky patrol sergeant who'd spent the last twenty minutes interrogating him broke in, repeating verbatim what Mac had told him.

"Exactly," Mac said with a tight smile, one that showed his teeth and building annoyance. "We wanted to make sure she was in there, instead of wasting your time if it was a false positive."

He raised his arm and wiped a stream of sweat from his temple with his shoulder, then twisted slightly to check on his men. They'd been taken to individual cruisers for questioning.

Luckily, they'd had time for a quick strategy session before the first cruiser had pulled up. At least everyone would be reciting the same information.

"While we appreciate your concern for the department's time management," the sergeant drawled back, his voice both dry and disbelieving, "the *question* is whether you actually intended to call the situation in, or whether you're here to apprehend the woman yourselves." His voice dried and slowed even further. "As I'm sure you're aware, it's against federal statute for anyone in the United States military to act in a law enforcement capacity."

The smug, self-righteous motherfucking asshole. He knew fucking well that was the exact statute they'd been accused of breaking by the DOJ back in Seattle.

"Yeah," Mac drawled back, cinching in the retort he wanted to make—something along the lines of *if you'd do your fucking job in the first place* . . . "We had no intention of apprehending the woman. We were going to leave that to you boys."

The sergeant dipped his head, his eyes and face unreadable. But

Mac knew the bastard didn't believe a word that had come out of his mouth.

Not surprising really, they were trained to recognize bullshit.

He was just hitting on the wrong steaming pile of shit.

Mac had to hand it to Pachico's ringer. Sending the police out on this wild goose chase had been a brilliant move.

Albeit a fucking annoyance and waste of time.

"Look," Mac tried to sound reasonable, which was damn hard to do when his entire body was shedding urgency. They needed to get on the road. He caught himself before glancing at his watch. The bastard questioning him had caught him checking it twice already. One more time and he'd start wondering why Mac was so obsessed with the time. "You've checked our weapons. Regardless of what your nine-one-one caller claimed"—nice touch, you motherfucker—"you can tell from the smell that they haven't been fired." He paused and gave the sergeant a hard smile. "If the woman was in there, she's probably long gone by now. How 'bout we call this a bust and move on?"

"There's still the matter of permits for this arsenal you and your men are carrying." He held Mac's impatient gaze with cool eyes. "And why you had such an arsenal in the first place."

Mac lost his smile. "You know damn well we have permits. As for the volume of weapons, sue us; we're used to being armed. The volume may seem a little much to you boys in blue, but believe me—it's light for my team."

With a frown, the sergeant opened his mouth, but a sudden burst of static, followed by the urgent babble of a rushed voice, distracted him.

Leaning against the hood of the cruiser to the left, Zane cocked his head and listened, only to suddenly straighten. Tension gripped his lean frame. He leapt toward Mac, his face tight. Grim eyes locked on the sergeant's suddenly wary face. "What's a ten eighty-nine and an eleven seventy-one?"

The sergeant turned and pointed toward the last two cruisers, waving them off. The officers dove inside, cranked their wheels, and took off in a cloud of dust.

"Damn it." Zane caught the guy's elbow and jerked him around, then stepped up almost chest to chest. "What the fuck does that code mean?"

The sergeant jerked his arm free, glancing between Mac and Zane. "Why?"

"Because that's our place," Rawls said, closing in on them at a run. "And we left friends back there." His face was hard, his voice urgent. "What happened?"

Swearing, the sergeant took off his hat and ran a hand over his head, then glanced at the dissipating dust storm.

"Goddamn it." Zane was already dialing his cell. After a minute he turned back to Mac, shot a look at Rawls, and grimly shook his head. "His phone's going to voice mail."

"What's going on?" Mac roared, his voice getting louder by the second.

A chasm opened up inside him. From the sergeant's reaction and reluctance to tell them, it had to be bad. Very bad.

Well, fuck him.

"Let's go," Mac yelled, gesturing toward the van. Not that the order was necessary. Tag, Tram, Russo, and Hollister had abandoned the cruisers they'd been escorted to, and were headed toward the van at a dead run.

"You won't be allowed in," the sergeant said flatly, grabbing Mac's arm.

Ignoring him, Mac yanked his arm free and turned toward the minivan.

The sergeant swore, grabbed his arm again, and swung him around. "The whole block will be cordoned off. It's standard procedure after a bomb threat and a fire."

Bomb? Fire—

Jesus.

Mac's legs went weak. He saw horror twist Zane's and Rawls's faces.

Grabbing his phone, he punched in Cos's number.

It went straight to voice mail.

For a moment Kait simply stood there, her cell phone still clenched in her hand, her mouth open, shock freezing her feet to the ground as Cosky and Wolf tried to beat the life from each other. With fists, knees, boots, or shoulders—anything that could deliver a solid blow.

Blood misted the air as fists connected with noses and mouths and ears.

They locked the rage in tight throats and rigid faces, with an occasional breathless grunt as a particularly vicious blow knocked the air from their lungs. But there were other sounds: the dull, hollow thud of a fist hitting home, the gravelly scrape of boots on pavement, the muffled thud of solid muscle hitting the Escalade's rear door.

She was amazed at Cosky's strength and skill. He was holding his own, even though he was down an arm and a leg. Although—Kait watched him pivot and kick, his boot catching Wolf under the chin—the leg didn't seem to be handicapping him.

Male aggression soaked the air, so thick and heavy she could almost smell the metallic, musky heat of it. They weren't going to stop on their own. Not until one or both were seriously injured. She slipped her cell phone into her jeans' pocket and prepared to interfere.

As Wolf stumbled back, Kait found her legs and darted between them. If they wouldn't end this stupidity themselves, she'd end it for them.

"Stop it, both of you." She held up her arms, a palm braced against each laboring chest. "I mean it. Stop it, right now."

Wolf was the first to step back. His thick, black braid streaked with blood and partially undone, he swiped swollen, scraped knuckles against the trickle of blood sliding down from his split lip.

For a long moment Cosky's chest pressed against Kait's hand. His heart hammered against her palm. A large knot was already forming on his left cheekbone, just below his eye. Which was turning faintly blue and starting to swell.

Kait wavered on her feet, staring at his face, a sense of déjà vu crashing over her—the injury looked identical to Jillian's. Which reminded her . . . what were the odds Jillian had remained in the car?

She scanned the parking lot and found the other woman headed for the gate leading onto the football field. Dropping her arms, she eased to the left, intending to go after her.

Both men moved forward as she backed off, their predatory gazes locked on each other.

Oh, for God's sake. This was ridiculous.

"Cosky," she said dryly. "Jillian's getting away."

At least that news made a dent in his hormone-sopped brain. He turned.

"You touch her again," Wolf said in a soft, dangerous voice that sent chills up Kait's spine, "not even Kait will stop me from killing you."

Turning, Wolf loped toward Jillian who broke into wild, uncoordinated flight.

When Cosky took a step forward, like he was going to follow, Kait grabbed his good elbow to hold him back. They stood side by side, watching as Wolf's longer strides quickly caught up with the fleeing woman. When he was close enough to touch her, she skidded to a stop. He ducked the fist she swung at his head and caught her around the waist, hoisting her struggling body over his shoulder like she weighed nothing.

He turned around, slowly walking back with Jillian anchored in place by a thick arm around her calves and his hand on her back. Except . . . the hand on her back seemed to be moving.

Kait squinted, to get a better look. Sure enough, his free hand was stroking her back. He'd also turned his head, which put his lips right next to her ear, and he seemed to crooning something to her over and over again.

In fact, his attitude and the way he held her was gentle, even protective. Hardly the grasp of a jailer. Suddenly his warning to Cosky echoed in her mind.

You touch her again, not even Kait will stop me from killing you.

Suspicion tickled.

She turned her attention to Cosky's eye. It was almost swollen shut now, and turning the same lovely shade of blue that Jillian's eye sported. The same injury to the same eye . . .

Even considering the brutality of the fight, the odds of Cosky being hit in the exact same spot as Jillian . . . well that didn't seem very likely, did it?

And now that she had time to think about it, what exactly had caused Wolf's explosion anyway? Sure he took his big brother duties seriously, but to attack Cosky with such ferocity over something he *knew* wasn't actually Cosky's fault? And to attack him when the odds were so uneven. For God's sake, Cosky couldn't even lift his left arm.

That didn't sound at all like the man she'd come to know during this past year.

"You know, your *friend* has to be behind the bombing," Cosky said in a tight voice.

Yeah . . . Kait frowned. It was pretty obvious what had generated Cosky's hostility. And lord, she could actually see his point. He didn't know Wolf's background, so the timing would look pretty suspicious.

"He didn't have anything to do with the bomb," she said, wishing she could fill him in on how her brother had known about the explosion. But to do that she'd have to explain their relationship and tell him about the gift her father had kept hidden all his life, and the one Aiden was hiding now.

Although, her father and Aiden's version of the *knowing* revolved around numbers and money.

She frowned, watching Wolf approach. Maybe his warning had nothing to do with the family gift, and everything to do with his military contacts—or whoever he worked for.

"For God's sake, Kait." It sounded like Cosky was forcing the words through his teeth. "It's pretty obvious you have *feelings* for the guy, but try to look past them and use your brain. He had to know the bomb was there in order to warn you before it went off."

Sighing, Kait simply shook her head. She could almost feel the jump in Cosky's blood pressure at her gesture. How the hell was she going to get his focus off Wolf?

At least it should be fairly easy to get Wolf's off Cosky. She just needed to fill him in on the events of the last twenty-four hours, because he'd obviously jumped to some erroneous conclusions.

She waited to confront him until after he'd eased Jillian into the passenger seat of the Escalade and cinched the seat belt around her stiff body.

"I think you may have picked up the wrong impression," she said as he slammed the door. "Cosky didn't give Jillian the shiner. I did."

Out of the corner of her eye, she saw Cosky go still.

Wolf shot Cosky a look thick with contempt. "You hide behind your woman?" Swinging to Kait, his gaze gentled. "Why do you protect him, *hookecouhu' heeyei*? He's not worthy of you."

"I'm not protecting him, nor am I his *woman*." Kait folded her arms across her chest, stuck out her chin, and glared. "Trust me; Cosky didn't give her the black eye. I did. And if you'd asked me what happened to her, instead of jumping to ludicrous conclusions—I could have told you that." Her censorious gaze shifted between the two battered men. "And saved you two from beating each other to a pulp."

Some of the aggression drained from Wolf's face. He frowned and glanced at the window of the passenger seat like he could see Jillian through the tinted glass. "She fears him. It rolls off her in waves."

"Well, sure." Kait waved a hand. "She's confused and blames him for something he had no part in. Remember the incident at my apartment yesterday morning? The one you called me about? That was her. She tried to shoot him. When that didn't work, she came after me. She must have heard he'd been visiting me, and assumed we were an item, so she decided to use me to lure him into a trap. That's how she got the black eye. I hit her." When he still didn't look convinced, Kait threw up her hands and turned to Cosky. "Tell him."

"I don't give a damn what he believes," Cosky growled, the aggression on his end still at a high boil. "I want to know how he knew about the bomb, how he knew you were at the condo, and why the bomb just happened to detonate after his call to you."

Yeah, this wasn't going well at all. Before she had a chance to step back in with some more smoothing over, her phone rang.

Ignoring the incessant chiming coming from her pocket, Kait fixed a militant gaze on her brother. "Wolf, tell Cosky—"

"You better answer it," Cosky interrupted grimly. "It's probably Zane checking to see if we're alive."

Oh crap. She'd totally forgotten about contacting Cosky's teammates to let them know they'd survived the blast. His buddies were probably worried sick.

Her hand dove into her pocket and dragged the phone to her ear. "We're okay." She rushed the reassurance out as soon as the ringing stopped.

"Winchester?"

She recognized the harsh, gravelly voice immediately. It wasn't Zane. Without hesitation, she handed the cell to Cosky. "It's for you."

From his terse responses, and the tension gripping his lean frame as he talked to Commander Mackenzie, Cosky wasn't getting the thank-God-you're-alright-we-were-so-worried-about-you speech.

In fact, it sounded like the receiving end of a reprimand.

Finally Cosky rattled off the directions to the football field, snapped the phone closed, and tossed it to Kait.

"Doesn't sound like your commander was happy to hear you survived," Wolf needled in an amused drawl.

Oh, for God's sake.

Shooting her brother a look of disgust, Kait stepped between the two again. "You aren't helping."

It wouldn't hurt her brother to play nice. Once Cosky told his teammates what had happened, they'd wonder how Wolf had known about the bomb too, and with six members of ST7 on hand, her brother would be at a distinct disadvantage.

Chapter Sixteen

By the time Zane's van rolled into the parking lot, Cosky couldn't see out of his left eye. His adrenaline surge had also plummeted, which allowed pain to register, and the combined agony of his dislocated shoulder and pummeled face verged on unbearable. He was used to pain, used to compartmentalizing it, ignoring it, reaching past it to get the job done.

But Jesus Christ it was hard to ignore the constant knifing agony piercing his shoulder and eye.

He was getting too old for this shit.

The van pulled up beside the Escalade. All four doors opened, and everyone jumped out. Zane's smile of relief vanished as he caught sight of Cosky's face.

"Rawls." Zane raised his voice, his sharp green gaze lingering on Cosky's eye before dropping to the arm Cosky was cradling against his chest.

Mac rounded the hood of the van and caught sight of Wolf's battered face. "Who's this motherfucker?"

Wolf braced his ass against the passenger door of the SUV and ignored the question.

"Simcosky?" Mac barked, swinging back to face Cosky. Black eyes, snapping with temper, locked on Cosky's face. "What the hell happened to you this time?"

Cosky spat out a mouthful of blood and scowled in irritation. Mac was acting like he was some accident-prone banana with a monthly pass to the ER.

"Did you forget the part about the condo going *boom*?" Cosky's voice emerged thick with phlegm. He coughed and spit out another mouthful of blood.

Rawls appeared next to him. "That eye screams *fist*, not *boom*." He turned to Wolf, who waited impassively next to the SUV with his arms braced across his broad chest. "So which of you was the punching bag, and which the boxer?"

"Who the fuck is he?" Mac asked, directing the question at Cosky this time, rather than Wolf.

"He's the asshole who called Kait and warned her to get out of the condo about thirty seconds before it exploded," Cosky said coldly, the rage rising again.

Gazes sharpened and swung toward the big bastard leaning so nonchalantly against the Escalade. Russo, Hollister, and Tag broke into a loose pincer formation and blocked the bastard in. Not that he seemed to notice. Or care.

Cosky scowled. Anyone with an iota of intelligence would show at least a kernel of worry at being confronted by seven pissed-off members of ST7. This bastard didn't even flinch.

Who the hell was he?

"No shit." Mac swung back to Wolf and stalked forward, his knees stiff, shoulders even stiffer. "You mind explaining how you knew that bomb was there?"

Without reacting in the slightest, Wolf watched him approach. "That's classified."

"You misunderstood me, you motherfucker," Mac snarled, his hands clenching and landing on his hips. "That wasn't a request. How did you—"

"I misunderstood nothing," Wolf said without raising or sharpening his voice. "The information is need to know. And you don't have the clearance."

"I'm Commander—"

"I know who you are," Wolf interrupted flatly. "Which changes nothing. *You don't have clearance.*"

Russo cocked his head and frowned. Slowly he stepped forward, his face thoughtful. "I know you."

Wolf simply stared back.

Surprised, Cosky glanced between Russo's thoughtful face—where recognition was registering—to Wolf's inscrutable features.

"Okay, Cos. Let's check this shoulder out. Looks dislocated, but we need to make sure there isn't a fracture," Rawls said.

Cosky grunted and kept his focus on Russo, as Rawls carefully probed the joint. After a moment, he took Cosky's left forearm and slowly stretched the arm out until it hung straight down.

Christ, Cosky gritted his teeth at the urgent, constant burn and waited. He'd dislocated enough joints to know the relocation hurt every bit as bad as the dislocation, which hurt like bloody hell. On the plus side, once the ball popped back into the socket, the relief would be instantaneous.

At least for his shoulder. His eye was another story.

"Where do you know him from?" Cosky asked Russo, trying to ignore what Rawls was doing to his arm.

"In Kunar, this past March," Russo said slowly. He scanned Wolf carefully, from hair to boots, like he was comparing the man standing in front of them against the man in his memory.

Zane looked surprised; he stared at Wolf closely. "You're talking about that insertion that went south? The one we lost Gassy and Kieb in?"

"Yeah," Russo said. "We were all headed home in body bags, until this bastard and a bunch of his buddies dropped in, cleared a path to the roof. Had a fucking Black Hawk waiting."

Silence fell. Wolf just stood there beneath their speculative gazes, staring back with that fucking inscrutable black-eyed calm.

"That true?" Mac asked as it became obvious the man in front of them didn't intend to add anything to Russo's account.

Wolf didn't say a damn word.

Before Mac had a chance to work back into his scowl, Kait stepped forward.

She shot Wolf an apologetic look. "It's true. Aiden told me he was there. That he'd 'unstuck' them, and got them off the rooftop."

"How the fuck does Aiden know him?" Mac asked, his voice thickening with frustration. "How the hell do you know him?"

Kait hesitated and finally shrugged. "Dad was Arapaho. So is Wolf," she said carefully. "They're of the same clan. Aiden and I have known him for years."

From the careful cadence in her voice and the dry glance Wolf shot her, Cosky was absolutely positive she'd left out a good chunk of information.

"Wolf," Russo said slowly. "You got a last name Wolf?" When the other man remained silent, Russo stepped forward and held out his hand. "Mighty thankful for your timely intervention there in Kunar. Never got a chance to thank you for that."

After a moment, Wolf's massive arms loosened and fell to his side, but it was another moment before he reached for Russo's hand.

"We were in the area," Wolf finally said dismissively.

Translation: no thanks necessary. The standard response following rescue. Except this time, the canned response failed to leave Cosky with the warm fuzzies.

"We? Who?" Cosky asked. He wasn't nearly as eager to fall at the bastard's feet. There was a hell of a lot that Kait and her mysterious family friend weren't filling them in on.

Like how he'd known about the damn bomb.

Wolf dropped back into his impassive routine again. Goddamn him.

"Okay, buddy," Rawls said. "We need to take care of this shoulder. Down on the ground."

Swearing, Cosky eased down to the ground and stretched out on his back. Christ, he wasn't looking forward to this. Rawls sat next to him, his chest facing Cosky's left side. After carefully straightening the arm, he braced a boot just under Cosky's armpit, extended his legs, and began to slowly, but with increasing pressure, pull on the arm.

Cosky took a deep breath, closed his eyes, and fought to relax. Vaguely, he was aware of voices in the distance. Slowly Rawls increased the tension, pulling the ball away from the shoulder joint. The pain was a constant, agonizing burn.

After a few seconds, there was a *pop*, and just like that the pain was gone. He unlocked his jaw. "It's in."

He opened his eyes to find a scraped, heart-shaped face staring down at him with huge, worried brown eyes. Without thinking, he reached for her—the urge to feel her soft lips under his hitting him hard and fast and completely unexpectedly. He was reprimanded for that moment of sheer foolishness by the knifelike pain that lanced his shoulder.

"I'm okay," he said, sitting up.

He ignored the flash of regret as she backed away. Rolling to his feet, he scanned the parking lot.

Russo, Tag, and Tram were clustered around Kait's Wolf, talking. Zane and Mac stood nearby, clearly listening.

Cosky headed for Zane. "He fill you in on the bomb?"

Zane silently shook his head, and shot Kait a frowning glance. He bent his head toward Cosky. "Something's come up," he told Cosky quietly. "We're headed up to Seattle to check it out."

"A lead?" Cosky asked, his voice just as quiet. Anticipation stirred.

Zane simply nodded. "You up to keeping an eye on Jillian and Kait?"

Hell.

The anticipation vanished. Of course he wouldn't be going with them. He was a damn liability. Hell, he was half blind, with an arm and leg of diminished capacity. No wonder he'd been relegated to babysitting duty.

That's when it occurred to him that he didn't have a place to babysit the women. He didn't have a house.

"We need a safe house," he told Zane. "Someplace those bastards won't connect with us."

"The women come with me," Wolf said from behind him.

Swearing, Cosky swung around. He hadn't even heard the bastard's approach, and then his claim sank in.

"No," he said tightly.

Wolf rocked back on his heels and raised thick, black eyebrows. "It isn't negotiable. They come with me."

Stiffening, Cosky stepped forward, but before he could say anything, Mac stepped into the fray. From the black cloud roosting on his commander's face, he was no more enamored with Wolf than Cosky.

"You want to take Aiden's sis with you? Fine. But the other one stays with us."

"No." The denial was intractable.

"You really think you can stop us from taking her?" Mac asked, his voice rising in disbelief. "There's seven of us, you stupid motherfucker. One of you."

"And the thousands of police, troopers, and sheriffs who will be on the lookout for you after I report you kidnapped two young women," he said in a flat, cold voice.

Dead, hostile silence greeted the threat.

Russo finally shook his head and glanced at Mac. "We can't take them with us, anyway. Where are we going to stash them while we're"—he glanced at Wolf and raised his eyebrows—"busy?"

Zane shot Cosky an apologetic glance and nodded toward Wolf. "There's your safe house."

Cosky's entire body tensed. Was he shitting him? "No."

"He has no connection to us," Zane reminded him.

And they were supposed to wave off the bombing of the condo?

Zane must have picked up on his thoughts. He snagged Cosky's elbow and drew him away, then dropped his voice. "Think about it. That bomb must have been lying in wait for months. Since before we brought you back from Seattle. Rawls set the cameras up the day after we arrived back, so we'd have them on tape if they'd planted it since. Yet they didn't detonate it until Jillian showed up. They know we have her, and they want her dead."

Son of a bitch, he had a point. Cosky scowled and ran a tense hand down his face.

Apparently picking up on Cosky's softening, Zane pressed on. "This is our best shot of keeping Kait and Jillian alive. Nobody knows about him, so they won't be tracking the girls through him. You said yourself we needed a safe house with no connection to us."

And then the bastard moved in for the kill. "Plus, you'll be on hand to keep an eye on him. Do some poking around. Find out what the hell he's hiding."

Ah hell.

Swearing, Cosky turned to glare at Wolf. "I'm coming."

Wolf's thick, black eyebrows bunched like a beetle. "No."

"Wolf." Kait touched his arm.

Cosky's hands fisted at the caress. "I'm coming."

After a long glance at Kait, Wolf growled beneath his breath.

After several seconds of intense negotiation on Russo and Zane's part, it was agreed that Cosky would accompany the women to wherever Wolf was taking them.

What wasn't mentioned, although Cosky was certain Wolf was well aware of the unspoken pact, was that Cosky would pass the safe house's location on once Mac and the team had scouted out the lab and learned all its secrets.

Soon enough Kait's fucking Wolf would be finding the rest of ST7 breathing down his ass.

It took over seven hours to reach the safe harbor Wolf had promised them, and Kait was exhausted by the time they pulled into the driveway.

They stopped for food, water, ice, and gas; which Kait purchased since the men's battered and bruised faces would have raised notice. Cosky iced his eye while intently watching the road ahead and behind.

An hour into the drive Wolf called someone on his cell. The exchange took place in Arapaho, which Kait had been learning over the course of the past year, but she wasn't nearly fluent enough to follow his half of the conversation.

She'd caught some of it though—the words for *food* and *clothing* and *house*. But the rest shot past her in a blur. From the annoyed expression and deepening chill on Cosky's face, he didn't appreciate her brother's reticence.

"There will be food and clothing waiting for us," Wolf told them after hanging up, but without explaining where they were headed.

Cosky didn't ask. No doubt he knew Wolf wouldn't tell him.

But Kait suspected she knew.

She was sure of it when he took the exit for Highway 99.

He caught her gaze, his black eyes gleaming with warmth and acknowledgment.

She'd been to his cabin three times now. The first, a couple months after she and Aiden had discovered they had a previously unknown sibling. During one of Aiden's rare leaves, Wolf had shown up and escorted them to his haven in the woods.

His place was somewhere deep in the forests south of Yosemite National Park. From the moment she'd seen the lodge, she'd loved it. Made from rough-hewn logs, with verandas running the entire length of the house in front and in back, the building had three bedrooms—each with its own fireplace and bathroom. The kitchen and living room were comfortable and homey, with leather couches and tables cut from logs.

But the setting and the mountain view . . . ah, both were majestic.

She'd expected a certain amount of awkwardness as they'd gotten to know each other. But it was simply impossible to feel uncomfortable at the lodge. The place was too serene, too lovely, too perfect for awkwardness, which was undoubtedly why Wolf had taken her and Aiden there for their inaugural vacation together. It had been the perfect setting to get to know each other. They'd spent the entire two weeks talking, sharing, and cementing the blood bonds between them.

She could never have found the place on her own, though. All she remembered were a multitude of unmarked, twisting, narrow paved roads, followed by unmarked dirt roads, followed by a series of narrow rutted driveways.

But even now, two years later, she could still remember that moment of pure awe as he topped the last rise and paused at the crest of the hill. Below, in a perfect bowl of a valley, a miniature lake had shimmered like topaz.

Her fingers had itched to transfer the view onto paper.

Kait's preferred artistic medium was glass, but with no kiln available, she'd switched to canvas and spent the two weeks painting—either on the back veranda or sheltered beneath the huge boughs of ponderosa and sugar pines overlooking the rocky shoreline—as she listened to Wolf and Aiden talk.

It was close to one o'clock when the Escalade finally erupted from the dark, tree-lined driveway and cruised down to the glowing house below. Every window was lit, beaming out to them with welcoming warmth. Wolf pulled to a stop in front of the stairs leading to the front veranda.

As soon as the SUV stopped, Cosky thrust open his door and stepped out. Stretching, he scanned the shadows that ebbed and flowed against the brightness spilling from the house. "Who else is here?"

"No one." Wolf headed around the hood of the SUV. "I had a friend stock the place and leave."

Kait slid out of the car and arched her back as Wolf opened the passenger door and caught Jillian before she fell out.

"You can take the room you slept in before," Wolf said, glancing at her as he lifted Jillian's still body in his broad arms.

Kait nodded. Although a shower was definitely in order before hitting the mattress.

Wolf climbed the five stairs to the veranda easily, even with Jillian's extra weight in his arms. He shifted her slightly to open the front door. Kait and Cosky followed him into the spacious living room.

With a sigh, Kait glanced around. Nothing had changed since she'd last been here. Although at the moment the rock fireplace didn't house a snapping, cheerful blaze. But the leather couch, with the colorful Navaho blankets tossed over it and the worn, butt-indented leather recliner were in the same place.

"You've been here before," Cosky said as Wolf carried Jillian across the living room. There was something sharp in his voice, but when she turned to look at him, his swollen, bruised face was impassive. "Do you know where we are?"

He probably had as good an idea as she did. Every time she'd awoken and looked at him during the ride up here, he'd been watching the road. He must have seen all the signposts.

"Just a general idea. Somewhere south of Yosemite Park."

He swore softly and scanned the room, then headed for the computer system sitting on a massive table with polished logs for legs. After a few minutes of tapping on the keyboard, he swore again.

"It's password protected." He looked at her.

She shrugged, and broke into a yawn. "Look. We're safe here. Wolf isn't going to hurt us."

He just stared back.

"I don't know the password," she finally told him. "I'm heading to bed."

It suddenly occurred to her that there were four people and only three bedrooms. And she was the least damaged of the four people currently in the house.

"Do you want to take my bed?" she asked reluctantly, hating the thought of giving up that blissful mattress for the couch. But she didn't have nearly the injuries Cosky had.

"You're not sharing his." There was such an acidic bite to the question she couldn't tell whether it was a command or a question.

"Of course not!" Kait blurted, feeling heat sting her face. "We're just friends."

Cosky cocked his head, his face watchful.

"Like we're friends?" he asked, that strange sharpness still in his voice.

Kait stared at him.

What he was really asking was if she'd slept with Wolf, like she'd slept with him. Which was none of his business.

"*Are* we friends?" she asked him quietly.

She wasn't sure exactly what they were. But she knew what they weren't. Not quite lovers. Not quite friends. Not quite acquaintances. What did that leave?

His soft curse echoed through the room and suddenly he looked tired—more than tired, exhausted and hurting.

Something inside her softened. As it always did when she thought of him in pain. "I could do another healing before we go to bed." Her gaze lingered on his grotesquely swollen, blue-tinged eye. "Maybe it will help your shoulder, knee, and eye."

A splash of warmth touched his face and his eyes softened. He laughed softly at her recital of his injuries. "Don't forget the scrapes and cuts and bruises."

His gaze dropped to her face, and then lower, lingering on her lips.

Kait felt her muscles heat and her blood awaken to pulse through her veins.

Her nipples tightened, and she basked in the sultry, spicy heat he was suddenly emitting.

After a moment he took a breath so deep, it lifted his chest. He shook his head. "I'll live, and you're exhausted. Go take your shower and hit the sack."

The soft *click* of a door opening caught their attention. They both turned as Wolf backed through the first door in the hall and closed the door behind him.

"It's the first bedroom," Kait said. "He must have given it to Jillian."

"You know your way around this place," Cosky said, only he didn't sound admiring and that peculiar sharpness was back in his voice.

His tone sounded almost jealous. Which was crazy. He'd made it all too clear he had no interest in pursuing a relationship with her. Before she had a chance to confront him about that weird tension, Wolf joined them.

He glanced at Cosky and jerked his head toward the hall. "I'll take first watch; you catch some shut-eye in the last bedroom."

Cosky stiffened slightly, his face cold, eye even colder. "I'll take the couch."

Wolf tilted his head, studied Cosky's flat face. "I'll relieve you in four hours."

"Don't bother," Cosky said, without softening.

Another long moment of testosterone flaring and masculine aggression followed.

"Oh, for God's sake," Kait stepped between them, caught Wolf's arm, and tried to steer him down the hall. "If he wants to sleep on the couch, let him sleep on the couch."

For a second Wolf resisted, but then he chuckled and slung an arm over her shoulder. "*Ooxonouubeiht.*"

"Hey," Kait said indignantly, recognizing the word. "I'm not crabby."

He laughed and gave her a one-armed hug.

"You've been studying," he said in a voice of pleased indulgence.

"I'm trying." She smothered a huge yawn behind her hand. "But it's a lot harder to learn without my tutor."

Chuckling, he followed her through the open door of the second bedroom. "Everything you need is in the bathroom. You know where—" He broke off and swung toward the open door behind them. "Problem?" he asked, his voice suddenly full of chilly threat.

"No." But Cosky didn't budge from the middle of the door. Pure ice sculpted his face.

Kait stared dumbfounded between the two men.

"You're taking the couch." It wasn't a question, and Wolf's voice was very soft. Full of command.

"And you're taking the third bedroom." Cosky's voice matched her brother's for softness and menace.

Abruptly furious with the pair of them, Kait threw her arms up and then pointed at the open door. "You're both leaving, *now*, so I can go to bed. You want to kill each other? Fine. Just close my door before you start whaling on each other so you don't wake me up."

Wolf looked surprised. "*Nebii'o'oo—*"

"I mean it, Wolf." Kait tried to shove him toward the door.

He let her shove him out the door, and she closed it empathically behind him. Then stood there listening for the muted thud of fists striking hard flesh.

Several seconds passed before footsteps sounded in the hall. A few more seconds and then Cosky said softly, "Go to bed, Kait."

She took his advice and headed for the shower, where she took the fastest one on record and fell into bed, instantly falling asleep.

Wearing the navy-blue sweats his reluctant host had shoved at him, with his hair still wet from the shower he'd taken in the bathroom adjacent to Kait's, Cosky folded one of the colorful blankets thrown across the back of the couch to use as a pillow and stretched out across the cushions. He checked the hall and immediately lurched to his feet again.

He shoved the couch across the hardwood floor a foot or so, and checked the hall again.

All three bedroom doors remained closed. Once his temporary bed was in position, he turned off the living room light and stretched out again, angling his head until he had a good view down the hall through his good eye.

The hallway was illuminated by a light shining in the kitchen. If any door opened during the night he'd see it. If anyone tried to sneak into someone else's bedroom, he'd see them.

It didn't matter how many times he reminded himself that he'd walked away from Kait—the mere thought of her entwined in that bed with anyone and the urge to maim seized him.

She deserved better than him.

But she deserved better than that bastard sleeping in the room beside her too.

There was no question that son of a bitch was Special Forces. No doubt he pulled the same kind of dirty, dangerous duty as ST7. Damn it. Kait deserved better than that.

Better than them.

She deserved a man she didn't have to worry about dying in some foreign rat hole. She deserved a husband who returned every night and spent weekends by her side.

Goddamn Wolf couldn't offer her that anymore than he could.

His gaze fixed on her bedroom door, Cosky fought the pull toward her. The impulse to get up, walk over, open her door, and bury himself in her heat and softness again.

At least until Wolf dragged him away and buried him somewhere in this pristine wilderness he called home, because there was no doubt the bastard had his ears tuned to her room, just as Cosky had his eyes locked on that hallway door.

So he spent his time listening to the quiet. Although it wasn't truly silent. In fact, the damn place sounded alive. The logs creaked and moaned around him. The wind in the trees outside sounded like whispers against the windowpanes, like eerie, raspy breathing.

It had been too dark when they'd arrived to get much of a layout of the place. But he'd recognized the huge, wavering shadows arching into the night sky as trees, the metallic sheen behind the cabin as water. Some kind of lake, or a pond. There was no trickle of rushing water, so it couldn't be a river.

But beyond the vague sense that they were somewhere south of Yosemite National Park, he had no idea where they were. If he'd had his cell phone, he could have checked the GPS locator.

But the only cell phone available was Wolf's.

Yeah, like he'd hand that over.

Sighing, Cosky tried to relax. But every single inch of him throbbed or burned—with the exception of his knee. Not even the handful of aspirin he'd taken earlier eased the pain in his hands or face or ribs. But his leg felt better than it had in months. Better than it had any right to feel considering the hell he'd put it through recently.

He'd checked it out while he'd showered, and he could swear the scar from his surgery looked fainter, less ragged and raw—less red.

Kait really had healed it. Possibly it was even still healing.

Too damn bad he couldn't say that about the rest of his injuries. Although none of them were career threatening, and while they weren't exactly comfortable, they'd eventually heal on their own.

When lying there became unbearable, he roamed the interior of the cabin, familiarizing himself with the layout of the place. The walls were rough-hewn, notched logs, varnished to a high gloss. The same wood plank floor in the living room continued down the hall and into the kitchen. Black granite with flecks of white graced the kitchen counters. Stainless steel was everywhere—in the stove, dishwasher, refrigerator, and gas grill fitted into the middle of the kitchen island, as well as in the washer and dryer tucked into the corner of the kitchen, next to the freezer: which was also stainless steel and huge.

He checked out the freezer and fridge.

They didn't have to worry about starving.

Trying to keep awake, he checked out the walls as he passed. A variety of pictures hung from them: water colors, pastels, a couple of oils. The subjects were as varied as the medium: everything from majestic mountains to pristine lakes, local animals, and flora. His favorites were the birds. There were only a couple in the house, but they caught the eye. So colorful and vibrant they seemed to be hovering there, ready to flap their wings and take flight.

Then again, maybe he was just punchy.

Daylight slowly seeped through the windows, lightening the interior of the cabin with ghostly fingers of silver and haze. On the front porch, he took a few seconds to breathe in the crisp, pine-scented air.

He'd been right about the trees. Although Wolf had cleared out the space immediately in front of the place, and layered it with gravel, monstrous trees bowled the cabin in. Towering overhead, they reached for the sky with giant boughs of emerald.

Yosemite National Park claimed that the area's weather pattern and deep, alpine soil grew some of the most massive trees in the world.

He could believe it with these suckers as evidence.

It wasn't long before he heard a door open inside the cabin, and the creak of footsteps on the plank floor. Wolf joined him on the front porch.

Leaning his arms against the rough log that formed the top rail, Wolf closed his eyes, breathing in deeply. His split lip was more swollen than ever, scabby with dried blood. The bruises on his cheeks and chin were a vivid yellowish blue. But his body and face were the most relaxed Cosky had seen them.

"I can smell the stink on you," Wolf said, with his eyes still closed, and while his face might have been relaxed, his voice sure as hell wasn't.

Cosky straightened, knowing the bastard wasn't talking about body odor.

"It rolls off you in waves. The stink of lust. The stink of jealousy. The stink of possessiveness." He opened his eyes, his gaze flat and cold. "You make no claim on her; you have no right to her. Remember that."

Turning, Wolf vanished back in the house.

Cosky stayed put, his hands clamped around the top rail, practicing some deep breathing exercises.

Hours later, the smell of bacon wafted through the house. From his position on the couch, he saw Kait's bedroom door open. She stumbled into the hallway like she hadn't quite awakened. Her bruised and scraped face was rosy and blank with sleep. She started for the kitchen, but some instinct kicked in and she stopped to glance over her shoulder. When she saw him, she turned and headed his way.

He didn't question the satisfaction that she'd come to him first, rather than that bastard cooking in the kitchen.

Slowly, he sat up as she approached, his gaze lingering on the golden, fluffy rope of hair spilling down from the shining cap of pulled-back hair. She was wearing sweats, like he was, but hers were purple.

"Did you sleep okay?" she asked on a yawn.

"Yeah." He tackled the urge to taste her mouth, taste that yawn, taste her blurry-eyed sleepiness.

"Wolf makes a mean breakfast if you're hungry," she said around another yawn. Turning, she padded back toward the kitchen.

He checked on Jillian as they passed her room, but she was still asleep, swallowed by the gigantic, four-poster log bed.

Wolf glanced up as Cosky entered the room. The granite island in front of him was overflowing with platters of crisp bacon, eggs, hash browns, and toast. Wolf went back to filling the plate in front of him, picked up a piece of toast, and plastered it with what looked like strawberry jelly. Without saying a word, he picked the plate up and disappeared into Jillian's room.

"Help yourself," Kait said, pouring a cup of coffee.

Cosky took one of the ceramic mugs sitting beside the coffee-maker and one of the plates stacked on the kitchen counter. After pouring himself some coffee, he filled the plate.

The silence was companionable as they ate. Wolf returned to the kitchen with an empty plate, rinsed it, and stuck it in the dishwasher. After heaping another plate full of bacon, eggs, and hash browns, he carried it out to the back porch. All without saying a word.

Sighing, Kait pushed aside her empty plate and followed their host out to the porch. Cosky followed, feeling like a third wheel.

Wolf looked up from the bench he was sitting on and frowned. "It's cold, *bixoo3etiit.* There's a *hookoubiixuut* next to the door."

She backtracked, put on a coat, and then sat next to Wolf on the bench, cuddling into him as he draped a thick arm around her shoulders. The black eyes that met Cosky's hostile gaze were snapping with challenge.

Cosky ignored the challenge. It was pretty obvious the pair was close. Picking a fight with Wolf because of a Goddamn hug wasn't going to win him any points with Kait. He'd bide his time and wait, and drive as many wedges as possible between the pair during the next few days.

After breakfast had been consumed and cleaned up, Kait disappeared into her bedroom and Wolf disappeared outside.

When Kait returned, she was carrying a sketch pad and pencils.

"Wolf had them delivered," she said with a joyous smile as she headed out to the back porch.

When he checked on Jillian again, he found Wolf sitting beside her bed. Their host looked up with a scowl as Cosky entered the room, the animosity as sharp as ever. Cosky shrugged and headed back out the door. It was no skin off his back if Wolf wanted to play guard dog. It would keep him away from Kait.

By the time he returned to the back porch, Kait was deep in her sketching. He sat there watching her—memorizing the absorbed look on her face, the faint frown as she tried to get the outline or shading just right, the way her thick, fat braid hung over her shoulder.

She was so beautiful, his chest ached.

At some point, he realized she was drawing a bird. It was still raw, sketched in black and white, but he recognized the ink strokes.

"You're the artist of the yellow bird in the kitchen. And the blue-gray speckled one in the living room," he said slowly, remembering how drawn he'd been to the two paintings. The birds had been so lifelike, he'd half expected them to take flight.

"The kestrel," she said, looking up with a bright smile. "It's one of my favorites. Such subtlety to its colors. Did you like it?"

He wasn't sure which painting she was talking about. But it didn't matter. They were both striking. "It's beautiful. You're very talented."

A smile lit her face, as though he'd just handed her a gift precious beyond measure. She drew in a deep, lingering breath. The smile on her face was almost dreamy.

"Isn't it glorious here? I don't paint much anymore. I've moved into glass. But Wolf had an easel along with almost every paint imaginable delivered. So I'll get plenty of painting in while we're here." A shadow slid over her face, and she shivered. But she shook the moment off, and turned the wattage up on that smile again. "You have no idea how incredibly expensive all that paint must have been."

Cosky glanced around the million-dollar setting. "I'm guessing he can afford it."

Kait's smile died beneath the suspicion in his voice. "He's not what you think, Cosky, trust me."

"If he's in Special Forces, Kait—like you say, like Russo claims—then he isn't making enough money to afford a spread like this."

She stared down at her sketch pad, her shoulders stiff. "His family has money. And he's doing us a favor by letting us stay here until it's safe."

She didn't ask the questions that were on both their minds: How long they were going to have to stay here. How they were going to resolve the danger. What the hell they were going to do.

All questions he had no answers for yet.

Right.

Cosky took a deep breath, let it out, and scrabbled for an innocuous subject that wouldn't chill her voice or stiffen her shoulders or send shadows of fear skimming across her face.

One that wouldn't mar her joy in her sketching or the beautiful morning.

"So is your artistic nature part of your Arapaho heritage?" he asked.

She laughed, relaxing. "No, my aunt Issa, my mother's sister, was the artist. She taught me."

Aiden had talked about an aunt. "She's the one who stepped in after your mother died? Raised you while Commander Winchester was on deployment?"

"Yeah." She stared into the forest surrounding them, memories chasing across her face. "At first she only stayed when Dad was gone. But after a while she moved in permanently."

"You were close," Cosky said softly.

"She was my mother in every way that counted." Kait smiled wistfully. "I barely remembered my real mother. She died when I was six. But Issa . . . she gave up her life to raise us. She was there in the mornings to make us breakfast. There at night to tuck us in. She sat up nights with me when I was sick. Held me when I cried myself sick over some stupid boy. She taught me everything I know about painting and glass—she was my mother."

There was a haunted quality to her words, the echo of grief.

"You still miss her." The words were out before Cosky could call them back.

"I'll always miss her," Kait said simply. "She died from cancer, you know. A slow, vicious slide into pain and helplessness and death." She swallowed hard, a tight mask creeping across her face.

Cosky thought of his father's battle with the disease. It had stripped his dad of everything that had made him the man he was—of his strength, his independence, his control, his ability to provide for his family. It had taken everything from him, months before it had taken his life.

"I lost my father to cancer too," he said quietly. "Lung cancer," he added at her inquiring look. "Even though he hadn't smoked in over thirty years. It's the most god-awful feeling, watching while they're stripped of their dignity and control and left helpless."

"Except I should have been able to help," Kait whispered. "I had the healing ability by then. I should have been able to heal her. Save her."

"She was one of the seventy percent?" Cosky asked, remembering Aiden telling him she couldn't heal everyone. That seventy percent of the time it didn't work.

"I guess. It didn't matter how many times I tried. None of my healings did a thing." She was quiet for a moment. "I was so angry for so long after she died. I mean, what worth is such a gift, if I can't use it to help those who matter the most to me?"

"You healed Aiden," Cosky reminded her gently. "Maybe you should focus on the people you've helped, rather than those you haven't."

She laughed, honest amusement on her face. "You're going to hate hearing this. But you sound just like Wolf. That's what he keeps telling me." She paused to smile at him. "Was your dad in the military too?"

"No, he was a cop. It's ironic. My mother spent years worrying about him every time he hit the streets, certain we were going to lose him to a bullet, or a knife . . . Which would have been kinder actually—if he'd been killed on the job. At least it would have been instant."

"You never know what's down the road," Kait said. "My friend Demi lost her husband because of a baseball. He was an accountant, talk about low-risk careers. They're living the good life one moment, the next he gets hit in the head at the company baseball game and he's gone."

Cosky frowned, shook his head slightly. "Anything can happen. Still, high-risk professions like law enforcement or"—he shot her a sideways glance—"special ops, they carry with them a hell of a lot more worry for the loved ones left waiting in the wings."

Kait scoffed beneath her breath and picked up her pencil again. "Of course they do. But if it's the right man, the worry is worth it. If you ask your mother, I bet she'd tell you she doesn't regret one moment of the life she had with your dad, regardless of how much time she spent worrying."

"You've seen what life is like for the women on the teams," Cosky said—his head suddenly light and dizzy, as though the ground had shifted beneath his feet and he couldn't find solid footing. "The constant worry, the heartache when that nightmare comes true. Hell—you experienced it firsthand with your father's death, with Aiden when we dragged him, paralyzed, back to the States."

She shrugged. "I'm not saying the worry isn't there. Or the pain if you lose someone. I'm saying life is messy. Pain is part of life. The worry I feel over Aiden and Wolf's safety, or the heartache when Dad died, that's all part of loving them. I'm proud of them. Proud of their courage. Proud that they believe in our country enough to stand up for it, to sacrifice themselves for it. I wouldn't trade one second of the time I had with Dad, or have with Aiden and Wolf, to avoid the worry when they're out on rotation or the possible pain if they don't come back."

Her words slammed into Cosky like a Zodiac had flipped and smacked him in the head.

"You love him." His voice was hoarse. Raw.

"Excuse me?" She looked startled.

"Wolf. Your *friend*. You just said you *loved* him," Cosky said through his teeth.

"Well, of course I do," Kait said carefully, her face suddenly cautious.

Cosky shot to his feet and took a tight trip around the veranda, shocked to find his hands and legs shaking.

"Jesus fucking Christ, Kait. You don't have a clue who this guy is. You don't know him. How the hell can you love him, when you don't even know who the fuck he is?" he roared, forcing the words through the knife piercing his throat.

Kait shot to her feet, the sketch pad hitting the plank floor with a solid *splat*. "I do know him, damn it. He's my brother. Okay? He's Dad's oldest son. My brother. Just like Aiden. And I'm not the only one who's been blessed with a family gift. So I do know him, and a hell of a lot better than you. So *back off*."

Turning, she stalked back into the house. The door slammed behind her.

Cosky was left alone on the porch, his mouth hanging open, relief turning his legs and arms weak.

Chapter Seventeen

MAC SHIFTED IN THE SHRUBBERY NEXT TO THE HOLE THEY'D CUT in the chain-link fence.

From the burned expanse of the metal links, the fence had been in place before the explosion had torched the lab.

Zane and Rawls were due back any moment from their recons around the sides and back of the building.

A slight rift of wind touched him. It carried with it a fresh, clean scent, like baby powder and fresh rain. His body recognized the scent before his mind did and instantly stiffened, in all the wrong places. He froze for just the barest second, while his heart suddenly jumped into overtime, and his mouth went dry. Neither reaction pleased him.

Straightening carefully, he turned toward the breeze, watching through a night vision device as Amy headed toward him in that brisk, no-nonsense stride of hers.

And damn if she didn't have a night vision device too. Just fucking great, this was exactly what he'd been hoping to avoid.

At least she had the sense to keep her mouth shut—voices carried. And while the building seemed deserted, they hadn't had a chance to check the interior yet. For all they knew there was a cleanup crew already inside.

A scowl firmly in place, he watched her weave through the shrubs flanking the fence. She used the cover like a pro. And she moved silently too. As silently as his team. If it hadn't been for that scent he'd come to identify with her, he would never have known she'd made the connections and figured out their strategy.

She waited until she reached him and raised an eyebrow. He couldn't see the color through the night vision device—the moon was all but obscured by Seattle's customary cloud cover.

"So you're not arriving for a few days, huh?" she said in a low voice, although he could clearly hear the sarcasm in her tone.

"We didn't want you underfoot," he snapped in an equally low voice.

He wanted to add a lot more, like where the hell she'd gotten the NVD and what the hell she'd been thinking heading out here on her own, instead of waiting for their arrival and if she'd lost her fucking mind to do something so foolhardy. His skin chilled at the thought of the danger she could have stumbled into.

None of which he said, because voices carried and she was already underfoot. But damn if he wasn't going to lay into her when they got out of this place.

"It occurred to me there was no way in hell you'd wait days to check out the first solid lead we've had in months."

"Assuming this place has any connection to flight 2077."

"It's connected," Amy said, her voice turning grim. "It's too much of a coincidence to be otherwise."

True, and Mac wasn't a big believer in coincidence either, but every once in a while a coincidence really was just a coincidence.

"Where's the rest of your team?"

"Recon." Mac turned slightly to scan the blackened, smoke-smelling husk in front of them. "There's no security."

"Doesn't that seem a bit suspicious?" Amy whispered.

It did, but then again, maybe the destruction within was so complete, it made a security detail worthless. Why bother guarding something if there was no worth attached?

Could be this whole trip up north had been one giant waste of time.

His cell vibrated and he lifted it to his ear.

"Nothing around back," Zane said softly. "Rawls reports the same to the east."

"Clear on this end," Mac offered quietly. "But we have a visitor."

Zane's voice didn't change, but then he'd given him the all clear. "Who?"

"Chastain's wife." He could hear the bite in his own voice.

"Amy?" Surprise echoed in Zane's voice.

"You know of any other wives the man had?" Mac tried to smooth the edge from his voice, but it was impossible.

"Copy. I'll let Rawls know. Is she breeching the interior with us?"

"No. Insert from your ends. I'm headed in from here." Although Mac suspected they wouldn't have much to do with that decision. The woman was about as hardheaded as they came, and she'd already appeared out of nowhere in the dead of night. Mac doubted she had any plans to stand around outside and twiddle her thumbs.

Of course they could always use a lookout. They were down half their insertion team since Russo, Hollister, Tag, and Tram had been called up.

Like that timing hadn't been suspicious as hell.

Slipping the cell phone back into his jeans' pocket, he turned toward her again. "You might actually prove useful; we need a lookout."

Her snort clearly expressed her opinion of that plan.

"You're not trained in insertions or close-quarter battles. You'll be in the way." Not to mention a big fucking distraction. Mac grimaced.

"Bull," Amy interrupted calmly. "I've had plenty of crime-scene experience, a hell of a lot more than you or your team has."

"And if the cleaning crew shows up while we're inside?"

She shrugged and turned to study the blackened building. "I'm pretty handy with a gun."

Why did the damn woman have to be so stubborn? Mac took a deep breath and let it out slowly. "We need a lookout."

"If you needed a lookout you would have brought one. I'm going in, and we're wasting time. Your team's moving in without you."

Without waiting for his response, she dropped into a crouch and headed toward the building, her gun extended in a two-handed grip.

Mac swore viciously, and fell in behind her.

She reached the lab's gaping front door—the entire door must have been blown off during the explosion—and waited beside it. He glanced over at her and swung through into the darkness beyond. He could feel her body heat behind him, and his skin prickled.

They moved slowly down a hall with offices and conference rooms to their right and left. Most of the doors to the rooms were missing, but every once in a while they'd come across one hanging loosely from a hinge.

After checking another charred office, Mac made a note to come back after they'd swept the place and have a look at those blackened metal file cabinets. Maybe something had survived the blast.

The smell of smoke was overwhelming. But there was another smell beneath the smoke that was all too familiar; it was the thick, pervasive scent of charred flesh, in this case, human flesh.

He glanced toward Amy. Had she picked up on the scent? Did she know what it represented?

She backed out from a room to their right and turned, catching his eye. With a small jerk of her head she slowly moved back down the hall. The last two doors on the right and the left led into conference rooms. Mac took the one to the right and Amy took the one on the left; they rejoined in the hall moments later.

An intact metal door guarded the end of the hall. He didn't bother tugging on the blackened handle, because the walls along either side of it had disappeared. The frame still stood, and the door as well, but there was nothing on either side. He stepped through the space to the right and she stepped through the space to the left.

A much larger room spread out in front of them. Full of gutted computers and office furniture and mangled desk chairs, it had obviously been some kind of computer station. She carefully moved down the wide, mostly empty aisle between the charred cubicles, pulled a screw driver and pair of pliers from her tool belt, and started pulling hard drives.

While Amy grabbed the hard drives, Mac eased into the next room.

This room was full of mangled pieces of metal, glass, and plastic. The roof was also off, so the moon bathed it in a spidery web of silver light. A huge metal contraption towered before him. How in the hell it was still standing was a mystery to him.

He was about ready to turn away, when movement caught his eye. He froze, his gaze darting back to where the movement had originated. Another slight shimmy of movement. It was coming from the floor.

He frowned, easing closer. Legs took shape, from the thighs down. The torso was underneath the mangled behemoth of a machine.

The legs were too damn slender to belong to either Rawls or Zane. Hell, they were too damn slender to belong to a man.

He studied where the torso disappeared beneath the machine. Was she stuck under there? She was using her heels to push herself deeper into the belly of the machine, Mac realized slowly. Why?

This gal was obviously up to something. It would be to their benefit to wait until she'd completed her task and find out what she was up to.

Turned out they had to wait for a while. They were still waiting when Zane and then Rawls silently appeared beside him.

He was just about ready to call it quits and yank the woman out by her feet, when she made a soft hum of triumph. Her oddly silent shimmy changed direction. She went from pushing with her heels to pulling with them.

He listened for a moment to her grunts of effort and hisses of pain. She was making progress. But by God, it was slower than a fucking snail and they didn't have all freaking day.

Scowling, he reached down to grab her ankles and yank her free. Rawls grabbed his elbow and yanked him back before he could make contact.

He stumbled, the sound loud as a bell in the silent room. The legs on the ground froze, and then jackknifed up, the heels digging frantically into the ground as the body they were attached to wiggled urgently.

Mac shrugged; at least the noise had lit a fire under her ass.

The torso grew longer; a hand emerged and caught the edge of the metal contraption. A second hand joined the first. A pair of breasts appeared, clearly visible in a skintight T-shirt. Slender shoulders. He frowned. The shirt was ripped in places from the tight fit, and blood clearly dampened the shirt. Whatever the hell she was doing under there was important enough to continue regardless of the pain.

A slender throat emerged. How the hell was she going to get her head out? Hell, how had she gotten it inside to begin with?

That mystery was answered when she started pushing up with her hands, instead of pulling herself forward. The machine lifted a fraction of an inch. There was no way she was going to be able to lift the damn thing enough to scoot out from beneath.

Mac gestured at Zane and stepped up to the left side of the machine. Rawls squatted by the woman's feet, as he and Zane leaned a shoulder against the machine and pushed up.

The woman froze as the machine started moving, a startled squeak breaking from her. And then Rawls had hold of her legs and tugged her out. The squeak escalated to a choked scream. Rawls had her flat on the ground beneath his legs with a hand clamped over her mouth before Mac and Zane had lowered the machine back to the ground.

And then all hell broke loose.

The woman grabbed a heavy chunk of pipe and swung it at Rawls's head. He ducked, but the metal connected with the side of his head. A dull thud and he slumped. She thrust him aside and rolled, sliding out from beneath him. Mac and Zane dove in unison for her, which ended up saving their lives.

The room suddenly exploded in gunfire.

Jillian was halfway through the front door, her gaze dazzled by the shimmering sunlight bouncing between the cabin and the swath of emerald trees in the distance, when a deep voice broke over her from behind.

"Ah, *nebii'o'oo,* you are awake."

She took another step, tantalized by the wood smoke scent of freedom.

"You wish to walk, *bexookeesoo*? Soon. The fresh air will do you good." His voice was right behind her—yet she hadn't heard footsteps.

With a last yearning look toward the trees and the safety they represented, she turned to her kidnapper. Or one of them. The new one.

The huge, dark-haired one with the braid who'd caught her after she'd fled the car. He was so tall she had to tilt her head to look up at him.

She wasn't quite sure what to make of this one. He hadn't been identified on the television as one of the men who'd killed her brother. In fact, he and Marcus Simcosky, one of the men she knew had been involved in the murder of her brother, seemed to detest each other.

They had the bruises and split lips to prove it.

Yet this Wolf, as Kait had called him, had come after her when she'd fled during their fight. He'd forced her back to the car.

Wary, she watched him step closer, unnerved and baffled by him.

He'd established himself as her guard, yet he'd proved to be an incredibly gentle one so far. After swinging her over his shoulder on the football field, he'd stroked her back and crooned assurances in her ear the entire way back to the car.

"You are safe, *nebii'o'oo.* No one will harm you. You are safe now."

And he'd made good on his promise, planting himself in front of the car door and refusing to let those murderers take her.

Was he some kind of a setup to gain her trust? Someone those bastards had called in to get her to loosen her guard so she'd answer their questions? While he didn't seem to be connected to the SEALs, he was obviously connected to Kaity somehow, and she was Marcus Simcosky's girlfriend.

"Come," he said, stepping to the side. "Breakfast is waiting. You must eat, and then we will walk to the lake."

She wouldn't be able to outrun him, so after a long hesitation, she finally slipped past him, retracing her steps toward the bedroom he'd given her the night before. Their arrival at the cabin was a blur. She'd awoken briefly as he'd carried her into the cabin, but had fallen asleep again before he'd put her to bed. There was a vague impression of darkness and moonlight streaming through an open window haloing a big, blocky body in the armchair beside her bed.

Other images had flickered through her dreams: a warm, sheltering embrace cradling her as she cried, a hard shoulder that smelled like wood smoke and pine beneath her cheek, a smooth, velvet baritone crooning unfamiliar words.

He touched her elbow in front of the bedroom and opened the door, silently escorting her inside. A plate sat on the bedside table. Piled high with bacon and eggs and hash browns, there was enough food for both of them.

Did he expect her to eat with him inside her bedroom, from her bed? Her feet dug in and she stopped in her tracks.

Turning, he stared down at her and lifted a heavy eyebrow. "You need to eat, *bixoo3etiit*. Eat to build strength. Your choice, kitchen or here?"

He was right. She did need to eat. She needed to regain her strength so she could escape this house and this man.

But eating in the kitchen . . . with the blond chick and Marcus Simcosky, one of the cold-faced, cold-voiced monsters who'd been responsible for Russ's murder. Suddenly the bedroom sounded like a haven.

"I'll eat here." She held his gaze, forcing herself not to look way. "Alone."

Approval lightened the pitch black of his eyes. "Every bite, *nebii'o'oo*. I will be back."

It was the same word from her dreams. Unfamiliar. But strangely beautiful.

Off balance, she retreated into the bedroom, waited for him to leave, and firmly closed the door. She picked up the plate and turned to sit on the armchair next to the bed. Only then did she realize the cushion had the imprint of a butt—a very large butt, for a large man.

Slowly, she turned to stare at the door.

The images from her dream danced through her mind. The shadowy profile of a man sitting next to the bed. Protective, sheltering arms. Sobbing into a hard shoulder. She sniffed the air and could swear she smelled smoke and pine.

She turned to study the pillows on the bed she'd slept in the night before. They'd been wet when she'd awoken.

Was it possible? Had he spent the night next to her bed and cradled her when she wept?

If so, why? To make sure she didn't try to escape? Why not just lock the door and nail down the windows? It would have kept her prisoner without eating into his sleep.

Shelving the questions, she sat down and dug into the food. As her belly filled, exhaustion tugged at her. Halfway through she was so tired, she could hardly keep her eyes open. She fought her way through several more bites before giving up.

Setting the plate down, she got up and stumbled over to the bed.

As she drifted off into sleep, a vague alarm stirred. This exhaustion wasn't normal. She'd just woken up after sleeping for hours. Had he drugged her food?

Distantly, she felt someone removing her shoes and lifting her, then setting her down again. A cover was pulled up to her neck. She rolled, cradling her head with her clasped hands, the alarm fading.

As she fell into sleep, the scent of wood smoke and pine embraced her.

"You are safe here, *wo'ouusoo*. Sleep."

Kait was lying on her bed, staring at the ceiling, picturing what she wanted to do with her abandoned sketch, when a soft knock sounded against her door. She ignored it. The man on the other side of the door wasn't Wolf. She was certain of it. Her heart didn't jump into warp drive for Wolf. Her blood didn't start humming. Her body didn't start melting.

She might not be able to see Cosky, but her body sensed he was there and was screaming *I want some of that*.

Luckily, she'd gotten pretty good at ignoring what her body wanted over the past few days.

When the door opened, and Cosky stepped into the room, closing the door behind him, she ignored him.

He walked to the foot of the bed and stared out at her.

"I'm sorry," he said, his voice quiet, strong, without that acidic sharpness that tightened her nerves and heart.

Okay. An apology was the last thing she'd expected. Sitting up, she stared at him suspiciously. "Are you? Really?"

"Yes." He scrubbed a hand down his bruised and scuffed face. "Look . . . come out to the porch. We need to talk."

"Why?" she demanded. "You either believe me or you don't. You aren't going to change my mind about Wolf. I won't be able to change yours. Talking is redundant at this point."

"I believe you."

Another surprise.

"You believe me," she repeated sarcastically, injecting every ounce of disbelief she was feeling into her voice. "Why? You sure didn't five minutes ago."

"Because he's your brother. Because before I knew he was your brother, the thought of him in your bed—ah hell, it was messing with my mind." He ran a tense hand over his head, but held her gaze squarely. "Because you wouldn't lie. Not about that. Not about something so important." Sincerity vibrated in his voice.

"So you don't think he set the bomb? You don't think he's on the take, or working for the other side, or any other of the myriad of suspicions that were running through your mind?"

He gave her level look. "Let's just say I'm willing to give him the benefit of the doubt." He paused, looking at her steadily. "Because of you."

Warmth unfurled in her chest, spread through her body in a frothing, foaming tide. He believed her. That was more than she'd ever expected.

"Now please, come back outside. Before your brother walks through that door and sees me in your bedroom." The barest hint of teasing lightened his voice. "He's the protective sort."

Kait laughed. Now that was the understatement of the year. To prove her point, a fist sounded on the wall next door.

Cosky turned and glared at the wall. "See? I'm getting to know him already."

"Overprotective." Kait raised her voice as she slid off the bed.

Another *boom* sounded on the wall beside her bed. She stuck her tongue out in the general direction of the sound before following

Cosky down the hall, through the kitchen, and onto the porch. After they'd settled onto the bench, Cosky handed her the sketch pad and her pencils.

A comfortable silence fell between them as she sat down, but she could sense his questions. His curiosity. Sighing, she dropped the pad onto her lap.

"Dad didn't know about him." She wondered if the comment sounded defensive. It felt defensive to her.

"I'm sure he didn't," Cosky said quietly. "Everyone would have known about him if your dad had. He was proud of his kids. He wasn't afraid to show it."

"Yeah." She coughed the lump out of her throat. "As near as we can figure it, Dad and Wolf's mother were childhood sweethearts. But Dad, well—his home life was pretty awful. He rarely talked about it. But Aunt Issa told me once that his father beat him. I guess there was a lot of drinking."

"Which explains why your father never drank. I don't remember ever seeing him tip a bottle of beer, let alone something harder."

"That's what Aunt Issa said. Anyway, he hated the reservation. Wanted off it something awful. And then something happened when he turned sixteen. He snapped or something. Almost beat his father to death. He went to Wolf's mother. Told her he was leaving. Wanted her to come with him." Her voice trailed off.

"She didn't go with him."

"No." Kait stared blankly out into the dazzling sunlight that danced between the tree trunks. "Dad hated his heritage. He legally changed his name from Littlehorse to Winchester. Went to school. Joined the navy. He cut his family and clan off completely. He hardly ever talked about his life before college. And never talked about the reservation. Of course we knew we were half Arapaho. But that was all. No idea which tribe. Which reservation."

"You weren't curious?"

"Of course I was. As for Aiden, I don't think he cared. He belonged to the teams from the moment he was born. But I wanted to know. So I asked him what tribe we were from. I was sixteen. I thought knowing might help me figure out my gift. That someone on the reservation—like a relative—might teach me how to use it. My dad, well, he was next to no help. He got so cold and sarcastic and angry." She shook her head, her fingers tightening around her sketchbook. "I'd never seen him like that before. I never asked again."

Cosky took her hand. Squeezed it. "How did you find out about Wolf?"

Kait stared down at their clasped hands. His fingers were warm against hers. Strong. "I took one of the earlier pictures of Dad, when he was in college, and sent it to all the Arapaho reservations asking if anyone knew who he was." She looked up. Smiled. "And Wolf showed up at my door."

He gave a bark of laughter. "That sounds like the bas—" He glanced at Kait's face. "Guy."

She rolled her eyes and snickered. Like the name switch had fooled either of them. But at least he'd made the effort. An hour ago he would have let *the bastard* stand.

"I take it he's the only half sibling you're aware of?"

"Yeah, Wolf's mom never married. So he has no other brothers or sisters."

Cosky was quiet for a while. She peeked down at their entwined fingers. Had he forgotten he was holding her hand?

"Why the secrecy? Why not just acknowledge your relationship?" Cosky asked quietly after a moment.

Kait cleared her throat. She should feel guilty for breaking so many of Wolf's confidences, but all she felt was relief. "Wolf said he has enemies. Ruthless people who would come after me and Aiden to get to him. So please, don't tell anyone else any of this. I couldn't bear it if I put Wolf's life at risk."

"You have my word," Cosky said simply.

Kait relaxed. Cosky's promise was as good as gold. She didn't need to worry about word of her new brother spreading.

"You said you weren't the only one blessed with a family gift. Can Wolf heal?"

She squirmed slightly. This wasn't her place to tell. "No."

He pinned her with a focused, thoughtful look. "But he has some kind of ability. That's what you meant."

"Look." She squirmed harder, and tugged her hand free. For a second, his grip tightened, clung, but then he released her. "I shouldn't have said anything. It's not my place to give his secrets away."

He nodded, apparently respecting that. With a deep breath of relief, she relaxed.

"Obviously Aiden can't do the kind of healing you do, but he's certainly the luckiest bastard I've ever met. Everything he touches turns golden. Is that his gift?"

Kait's mouth fell open. "How did you figure that out?"

Cosky shrugged. "It's logical. You said family gifts. Ergo, more than one. Aiden has the same heritage, but he can't heal, otherwise he wouldn't have sent me to you. He is, however, uncommonly lucky. How does his ability work?"

"I don't know, actually. He says he just knows things sometimes. Like he'll look at a stock and know it's going to rise. He'll look at a horse and know it's going to win. My dad could do the same thing."

"Handy," Cosky said absently, his voice thoughtful. "So that's how you can afford an apartment in the most expensive complex in Coronado."

"Aiden and I inherited everything after Dad died."

Cosky nodded, without looking surprised. "Just knowing," he murmured, a strangely amused look in his eye. He suddenly turned his head, focusing to Kait's right. "Is that how you knew about the bomb? You just knew Kait was in danger?"

Kait froze, and then slowly turned her head. Her stomach dropped straight to her toes at the sight of Wolf leaning against the wall to her right. Oh lord, how long had he been standing there?

"I didn't tell him, Wolf. I swear," she said in a small voice. "He guessed."

"No harm done, *netesei.*" Wolf's voice was soothing. The gaze he shifted to Cosky wasn't nearly as gentle. "I make no claims."

There was open challenge on his hard face.

"Of course you don't." Cosky stared back, his face impassive, but without the earlier aggression or animosity. "Since you seem to *know* so much, have you heard of Zane? Zane Winters?"

A frown wrinkled Wolf's tanned forehead. He straightened slightly. "So it's true?"

Cosky simply inclined his head.

Kait looked back and forth between the two men. "If you guys are talking about Zane's premonitions," she said dryly, "Aiden already told me about them."

Cosky shot her a surprised look. "How long have you known?"

Kait shrugged. "Since Aiden joined the team. Zane's the first person outside of our family who has such a gift."

"Yet Aiden never mentioned his sense of *knowing* to anyone," Cosky said dryly. "Not even after Zane's flashes had saved his ass a time or two."

"Well, his isn't quite the same thing. His doesn't save lives. To be honest, I think he's kind of embarrassed that it makes him rich instead of helps people, like Zane's does." Kait admitted, although Aiden's embarrassment sure didn't stop him from using it to his benefit.

Wolf relaxed. "You obviously trust in your LC's ability, which explains why you accepted Kait's gift."

With a roll of his shoulders, Cosky shot Kait an apologetic glance. "I didn't actually. I just figured, what the hell, it wasn't going to hurt."

Amusement lightened Wolf's dark gaze.

"Pragmatic." He sounded approving. Suddenly he straightened and turned. Opening the door, he disappeared back inside the kitchen.

Cosky shook his head, watching him go. "Not much for talking is he?"

Kait laughed, a deep, strong sense of relief rising. Cosky believed her. He wasn't just parroting what he thought she wanted to hear. He truly believed her.

He shifted on the bench until he was facing her. She smiled at him, her gaze caressing his battered face. His eye looked so terrible. So painful. "I want to try a healing on your face."

"No."

"Cosky," she said, reaching for his eye. "I know it hurts. I'm back to normal again. I'm fine. Another healing won't drain me."

He caught her hands in both of his. "The minute you touch me I go up in flames. I lose my common sense. I lose my control. All I can think about is getting you naked and under me."

Her hands started trembling. She thought it was because of his words, but then the burning started—the same heightened burn from the parking lot—and then his words sank in. Flushing, she jerked her fingers free. He didn't have to sound so frustrated about his reaction to her.

Suddenly she realized the burning had subsided.

Maybe she'd imagined it.

Before she had a chance to retreat, he leaned forward and caught her hands again. "If you do a healing here, we're going to lose control. There's a time and a place for these healings of yours. And it isn't on the porch in public in broad daylight, with your brother breathing down our necks."

Kait froze; the fire had sprung to life again the instant his hands covered hers. The timing couldn't be a coincidence. She shook his hands off. The burning vanished.

His hands had been covering hers in the parking lot too. When that immense burst of heat had consumed her and she'd healed his knee from major damage in seconds.

In seconds.

She'd channeled more energy than she'd ever held before.

"Kait," his voice rose, thick with frustration. "I'll admit to being an ass that first time. And I have no idea where this thing between us is headed. But when I thought you were in love with—"

"Cosky," she broke in and reached for his hands. Only this time nothing happened when their flesh touched. The fire didn't spring to life.

That was odd. Maybe she'd imagined the whole thing. Releasing her grip, she sat back.

"What?" He didn't wait for her response. Just reached out and settled his palms over the back of her hands again.

And the burn was back.

"You know that I want you, right?"

Instantly, the fire leapt.

She barely heard him.

Her chest heated. The energy streamed from her chest up into her shoulders and down her arms, and her hands began to burn. Transfixed, she stared down at their clasped hands and watched them redden. Felt the energy build. It felt exactly the same as it had in the parking lot. All of a sudden, he seemed to notice. With a hiss, he jerked his hands away.

They were brick red.

"What the hell?" Cosky said, shaking his hands. Spreading his fingers out, he stared down in disbelief.

The energy vanished. The burning in her hands dissipated.

"You're the trigger," Kait said slowly, the disbelief a thick haze clouding her mind. "It's because of you I was able to channel that enormous burst of power in the parking lot."

Cosky fisted his hands, which were slowly losing their lobster redness, and looked up. "What are you talking about?"

"Remember I told you that healing in the parking lot was an anomaly? I'd never channeled that much energy before. I think it was because of you. You grabbed my hands, remember? That's when everything went wild. I didn't put it together until now. When you put your hands over mine, that weird fire started up again."

Cosky shook his hands again and rotated them until they were palms up. "It must be a coincidence. I don't have any healing ability."

"I don't think it's a coincidence. It's almost like when you put your hands over mine, it supercharges my ability. Supercharges the amount of energy I can channel."

Shaking his head, Cosky leaned back. "Kait, there's been plenty of touching." His silver eyes warmed when she blushed. "If it's because of us touching, then we'd be burned to a crisp by now."

The blush still heating her cheeks, Kait laughed. "I don't think it works that way. I think the touch has to be more specific. Just now, when I touched you, nothing happened. But when you put your hands over mine, the fire soared. Remember how red your hands got. When you jerked your hands away, the burning stopped. Somehow, your hands on top of mine boosts my healing ability."

He was silent for a moment, a deep frown knitting his forehead. Eventually he looked down at his hands again. "But why?"

She smiled back, trying to mask her satisfaction. He was going to get that healing, whether he wanted it or not. "I have no idea, but it will be easy enough to test. Put your hands out." As soon as he extended his hands, she laid her palms over them. "Anything?"

"You're certainly lighting a fire, but it's not to my hands," he said with a slight quirk to his lips and a glitter to his eyes.

Flushing, Kait pulled her hands away.

He quirked an eyebrow. "I wasn't complaining."

Kait blushed again. She wasn't normally the flushy-blushy type. But this new behavior was such a departure from his earlier hands-off icy demeanor, she wasn't quite certain how to react. What if she said the wrong thing and he reverted back to Mr. Iceman?

Maybe it was best to ignore his flirting, until she figured out whether he was serious. With that in mind, she cleared her throat and held out her hands, palms down. "Now cover the back of my hands with your palms."

The instant his flesh touched down over hers, the heat hit. The fire pulsed higher and higher. Her hands started burning.

"Shit," he said, pure disbelief in his voice.

He was looking down at their hands, which were getting redder by the moment. After another second, he pulled his hands away. He splayed them out in front of him and just stared.

"See?" Kait asked quietly.

"This is what happened in the parking lot." It was half question, half statement.

"I think so. I think you boosted the energy I was channeling. I think this was why I was able to heal your knee so quickly. And why the blisters disappeared." She paused, held his gaze. "I want to try this on your eye."

Mac hit the ground on his belly to the *rat-tat-tat* of gunfire and rolled to his right, crawling beneath a scorched steel desk, which wasn't much of a shield considering the firepower those bastards had. AK-47s could pierce pretty much anything.

He glanced to the right and left, then had one breath-stealing moment of worry for Amy before he forced her from his mind. Zane was to his right behind some kind of steel mini fridge, the damn thing barely shielded him, and Rawls—Mac chanced a quick glance to his left and found his corpsman behind another fried desk, their mystery woman smashed against the wall behind him.

Mac snorted in disgust. The damn idiot had put his body between her and the shooters. Forget the fact she still had hold of that length of pipe she'd nailed him with and looked like she could use it again at any moment.

The gunfire ceased. Mac popped his head up to locate their targets, which started the rat-tat-tatting back up again. Christ, they were well and truly pinned down, like fish in a fucking barrel.

He glanced over at Zane, but his LC was as pinned down as he and Rawls were. From the heavy artillery lighting up the room, those bastards had both the men and the guns. A sense of déjà vu hit him. It looked like Amy had been right. The bastards pinning them down had the same overkill approach as the ones they'd confronted in that farmhouse all those months ago. He hoped to God they fared better this time.

Rawls was effectively stuck. There was a wall to his right and behind him, and absolutely nothing but empty space to his left. He had no place to go if he tried to make a play. Zane was in pretty much the same position. There were only a few feet between him and that monstrosity that their mystery girl had been trapped beneath though. He had no idea what was behind it. But it was time to find out.

He caught Zane's eye and jerked his head toward the towering machine. Zane nodded and leaned around his desk to fire. Mac bolted for the machine, skidded around it, and slowly made his way around the back. The area tightened the deeper he went into the room, but at least there was a solid wall behind him. Although solid wasn't the best description—riddled with holes worked better. Those holes made him nervous.

If someone was back there, he was fucked and dead.

Apparently their attackers hadn't inserted throughout the building yet, because the back recesses remained empty and silent. By the time he reached the north corner, the wall had thinned to studs and charred wire. Which didn't leave him any cover.

Talk about a bad idea.

Gun extended, he slipped through the wall and eased forward and to his right, which should lead him back to the room they had originally entered from. Should . . . which didn't actually mean it would. Christ, he could be headed away from the battle, not toward it.

His shirt clung to his sweaty back as he picked his way as quickly as was safe around debris, trying to keep his approach as quiet as possible.

Off-and-on gunfire hammered the building—his men's Glocks, as well as those damn AK-47s.

Were any of those shots Amy's? Had she caught sight of them first, or they her? If they'd shot her before opening up on them, he would have heard it. The damn place was an echo chamber.

Christ, he hoped that meant she was holed up somewhere safe and sound. And this was exactly why women shouldn't be in the military. Men spent too many fucking brain cells worrying about them.

To his right, gunfire started up again. He increased his pace, looking for cover in case his targets noticed him coming. Nothing.

Damn it to hell.

If they saw him coming before he saw them, he was as good as dead.

Chapter Eighteen

A DOOR FRAME ARCHED JUST AHEAD TO MAC'S LEFT. WHERE THE door should have been was nothing but a gaping black hole.

Another volley of shots fired.

"Fuck," he whispered beneath his breath.

His men were pinned down. If there wasn't any cover for him to set up shop, maybe he could at least take out a couple of those bastards and give his guys a fighting chance.

If he took a couple of rounds . . . well, hell, at least he wouldn't have to worry about getting goat fucked by the DOJ and NCIS. With that in mind, he ducked low and swung through the gaping hole. As luck would have it, three feet into the room was a huge metal cabinet. He slipped behind it.

Through his night vision device, he caught a glimpse of several men kneeling in front of the wall, framing the room they'd found the woman in. Movement across the room caught his eye. He tracked the movement and found Amy sliding through the open door in a half crouch, gun drawn.

Son of a bitch, unlike him, she had no cover. He needed to move now, to draw their eyes and fire, otherwise she was dead.

Stepping out from behind his cover, he took out one and then two of the targets. She took out two others. The fifth spun toward him on his knees, but Mac's round caught him in the head. He pitched forward across his dead buddies.

"Clear," Mac said as he eased forward, listening to the way his voice echoed in the aftermath of the firefight.

As he closed the distance to the mess of bodies against the steel wall, he grimaced. Christ, they needed to get the hell out of this place. If someone had reported the shots and the locals were in route, yeah, they'd be well and truly fucked this time.

Zane swung over the wall as Mac approached, and went to work rolling the bodies over and stripping off their masks and night vision devices. Someone had sure outfitted these guys to the max.

Amy started going through pockets.

"Rawls, you got the camera in your pack?" Mac asked.

Rawls nodded, thrust the girl they'd pulled from beneath the machine toward Mac, and shrugged out of his rucksack.

The girl went limp in Mac's one-arm clasp, and then twisted hard, trying to wrench free. Without missing a beat, he lifted her off her feet and simply held her there. After a moment, her struggles lessened.

"Behave," Mac told her coldly.

Rawls handed the flash camera to Mac and took possession of their unexpected guest again. This time the woman didn't bother trying to wrench free. Instead her gaze skittered between Rawls, Zane, Amy, and himself with guarded watchfulness.

She was biding her time.

Fine, as long as she kept quiet about it. So far she hadn't made any sounds other than that surprised squeak when they'd grabbed her feet and jerked her from beneath the machine.

"Son of a bitch," Zane suddenly said grimly. "Take a look at this."

Mac walked around the bodies toward the one Zane was crouched in front of. Even in the milky light of the night vision device, he recognized Pachico's face.

"Son of a bitch," he echoed Zane tightly. "He's dead?"

There went that avenue to answers.

"Not yet," Zane said slowly, rising to his feet. "Your round creased his hair. He's out, but stable."

Mac smiled. "Grab him. Let's get the fuck out."

"You know him?" Amy asked, taking a step forward and staring down at the bald man sprawled out on the bloody floor beneath them.

"Yeah," Mac said with a hard grin. "We ran into him in Coronado. He was impersonating a detective with the Coronado PD. We were trying to catch him yesterday when you called."

"Your stakeout." Amy crouched down, staring much more intently.

"Let's move, people," Mac snapped.

While Zane lifted Pachico's limp body in a fireman's hold, Mac took hold of the woman's arm, and they headed back out of the building.

"Rawls," Mac said as they moved down the hall. "Get the car. We'll meet up in front of the gate."

His LT was the fastest of them. He'd have the car back by the time they got the girl and Pachico through the fence.

Although they were still left with one big problem. Where were they going to hole up with their new hostage?

As Mac tried to shove the woman through the hole in the fence, she started struggling. "I'm not going with you."

"Look at that, you can talk," Mac said, "and yeah, you're coming with us." He grabbed her arm and yanked her back toward the fence.

"No. I'm. Not." She wrenched herself back. Only this time Mac was expecting the movement. "Unlike you, I wasn't doing anything illegal. So it doesn't matter if the cops catch me on the premises."

"It's not the cops you need to be worried about, Dr. Ansell," Amy broke in to say. She nodded at the woman's sharp look at her. "Dr. Faith Ansell. I recognize you from your DV photo. Glad to see you didn't perish in the fire like reported."

"You worked in the lab?" Mac asked.

Hell, maybe their luck was finally changing. They had Pachico and one of the scientists those bastards had been after. Two pieces of the puzzle were finally falling into place.

"Who the hell are you people?" Faith asked, her suspicious gaze shifting between Mac and Amy.

"Believe it or not," Amy said, "we're the good guys. And the bad guys, the ones with AK-47s, buddies to the three men who just tried to shoot you, could be arriving any moment. You need to climb through that fence and come with us. We'll explain once we're on the road."

"You guys need to move," Zane said, a note of urgency touching his flat tone. "We're losing our window."

"Obviously you know the explosion wasn't an accident," Amy told the scientist when it became apparent she wasn't going to respond to Zane's urging. "Otherwise you wouldn't have lain low and played dead. Obviously you know someone is after you, otherwise you wouldn't have broken into the lab in the middle of the night to look for whatever it is you were looking for."

"I didn't break into the lab," Faith said sourly. "I'm a partial owner of the property. And why the hell should I trust you? You did break in. You have night vision devices and guns. You killed those poor men." Her voice faltered.

"Oh, for Christ's sake." Mac pushed her against the fence. This time she didn't try to wiggle away, instead she bent down and slipped through the narrow hole. Amy followed her, her rounded ass swaying in the air.

"You need some help getting Pachico through?" Zane asked.

Mac dragged his hypnotized gaze away from Amy's ass and bent down to their bound and gagged prize. Pachico's eyes were still closed, which didn't mean much of anything since the bastard could be playing possum. But his breathing was slow and calm and there was no tension in his limbs. Maybe he was still out of it after all.

Mac grunted as he dragged the guy to the fence and shoved him partially though. Zane grabbed his shoulder and pulled him the rest of the way. As Mac dropped to the dirt and shimmied through himself, Rawls swung in with the van. Everyone piled in.

They stripped off the night vision devices and rucksacks as Rawls took off.

On a rough-hewn log bench, overlooking the calm blue-green waters of an alpine lake, Jillian watched through her lashes as her guardian unpeeled an orange. His huge hands were surprisingly limber, flexible, working the orange with ease and care.

They mesmerized her.

"Eat," he said simply and handed her several sections of orange and half a roast beef sandwich wrapped in a paper towel.

She'd woken from her nap to find him banging on the wall across from her bed, which should have been frightening, but barely made a dent in her conscious before she'd fallen back into a deep, grief-riddled sleep.

Her pillow had been soaked and her cheeks wet when she'd awakened the second time.

Had he cradled her again as she wept? She didn't remember any dreams this time. But she knew they were there. They were always there, waiting to ambush her the moment she closed her eyes.

Taking a deep breath, she gazed out over the mirror-like surface of the water.

The lake was shaped like a bowl, with a rocky, steep shoreline riddled with exposed boulders and tree roots.

So very similar to the one she'd died in all those months ago.

"Why were you banging on the wall?" she asked absently.

He glanced at her and smiled slightly. "I was being *hisoh'o*."

Which told her nothing. "Meaning?"

He shrugged. Reaching down, he pulled the hem of his jeans up and slid a wicked-looking knife out of a sheath strapped to his calf. "Loosely translated, it means being her elder brother."

So he was Kaity's brother. She would never have guessed it by looking at them. But then maybe he meant figuratively.

Jillian didn't even flinch as he straightened with the knife in his hand. Instead, she took a bite of her sandwich, watching as he rummaged through the plastic bag he'd brought with them and emerged with an apple. Wielding the deadly blade deftly, he nimbly quartered and cored the fruit, and handed her two sections. After wiping the blade with a paper towel, he set it on top of the plastic bag.

She dropped the apple sections next to the orange sections onto the paper towel stretched across her lap and took another bite of her sandwich.

"What language is that? It's beautiful." Which it was, in a primitive, arrhythmic way. It wasn't quite like anything she'd heard before.

"Arapaho," he said simply, taking such a huge bite out of his sandwich, half of it disappeared.

"You're Indian?"

He simply nodded.

She went back to staring at the surface of the lake, fighting the memories, fighting the loss, fighting the endless agony of grief that threatened to drown her.

"It doesn't bother you?" he asked, his gaze direct, intensely black.

Confused, she frowned at him. "What?"

"That I'm Arapaho? Indian? Many still view my people as barbarians."

Shaking her head, her gaze slid compulsively back to the water. "Have you killed?"

She knew that he had. Had known since Kaity had shoved her into the SUV and he'd turned his head to look at her. The icy hardness that allowed killing sheathed him, just like it did the four SEALs who'd killed her brother, just like it had sat upon the men who'd kidnapped her and her children all those months ago.

She'd become an expert at recognizing the face of a killer.

Would he admit to it? Or lie?

"Yes." His voice was flat. Unapologetic.

The admission shouldn't have reassured her, yet strangely, it did. "How many?"

"Many," he admitted with the same cold lack of apology.

"Do you kill children?" The question emerged on a haunted whisper.

The bark of guns . . . the stench of fireworks . . . her babies falling.

She shuddered and shook the memory away.

"Never." His voice was harsh, icy with cold, vicious rage.

Startled, she glanced at him, wondering if the wrath was directed at her, at her question. But he wasn't looking at her; he was glaring down at the lake.

"We don't kill children, *heneeceine3 betee.* We don't kill anyone who doesn't need killing."

She relaxed beside him, his words echoing through her mind. *"We don't kill anyone who doesn't need killing."*

"Who is we?" she asked, finishing off the rest of her sandwich.

Not because she was hungry. But because she needed to regain her strength; she needed to escape. She might have been captured. She might be their prisoner. But she hadn't failed yet. There was still time to make them pay.

"We don't kill anyone who doesn't need killing."

His explanation resonated within her.

The men who'd stolen her family needed killing.

"We," he echoed slowly, "are my people."

She nodded slightly. He must mean his tribe. A long, comfortable silence fell between them. She'd just finished the last of the apple and orange slices when he spoke again.

"Who do you cry for Jillian?" His voice was very quiet. Very gentle.

Frozen. She stared down into the water. Suddenly feeling like she was drowning. Drowning in the memories. In desolation. In the endless, emptiness of grief.

The echoes of childish giggles haunted her mind.

"We see you, Mommy. It's our turn to hide. You find us." The pounding of feet scattering.

"Who, *nebii'o'oo*?"

"My babies. My brother." Her voice sounded dull, wooden. "They *murdered* my brother and my children."

She wasn't telling him anything that he didn't already know. Damn them. Zane Winters and his SEAL brothers might have denied killing her kids, but they were liars. They knew exactly what had happened.

The lack of surprise at her revelation was proof he knew the answer to his question.

So why ask?

"Who?"

"You know who." She didn't look at him. "Marcus Simcosky, Zane Winters, and the other two."

"No."

The denial snapped her head around.

She started to rise, the betrayal sinking so deep it caught at her heart, snagged her breath.

"Jillian." He caught her around the waist and drew her struggling body against his side. He held her there, immovable. Inflexible. Until she collapsed exhausted and panting against him. "They do not kill children. They are not the ones who killed your babies."

"They admitted it," she forced the words out through a raw, burning throat.

"When?" There was patience in his voice.

"On the television, they admitted they killed my brother." She spat the words at him.

"Your brother, yes," he agreed steadily. "Your children, no." He paused, held the rage in her gaze without flinching. "Your brother was not who he claimed, nor who you thought him to be."

"You're one of them. Of course you'd back their story."

He shook his head, tightened his arm around her waist. "You

know this in your heart, *heneeceine3 betee.* You have always known it. Trust in your heart."

She swallowed hard, trying to ignore his words. But they dug in and clung with claws tipped in poison.

Of course she'd wondered about Russ sometimes. About his constant surplus of money. Or how he'd disappear for weeks on end and then suddenly show up again out of the blue.

But he'd always had a good explanation. His job paid well, his consulting constantly took him out of the country.

"He loved me," she said, hearing the thickness in her voice. "He loved the children."

"I do not doubt that," he said placidly as he stroked a palm up and down her back.

She could have bolted then. He wasn't holding her in place. But she stayed. The warmth of his palm felt so good against her back.

"Tell me what happened, *heneeceine3 betee.*"

She shied away from the question, and the agony that nipped at its heels.

"What does that mean?" she asked, half in curiosity—he'd called her the same thing several times now—half in procrastination.

He smiled, leaned over to press his lips against the top of her head. She grimaced in disgust. Her hair was filthy.

"It means *lion heart.*"

With a slight smile, she leaned into him. But then she frowned. "I'm not a lion. When I saw him in the parking lot, the one"—her voice quavered and thinned—"the one who shot me, who shot Wes and Brianna. When I saw him, I ran."

"He shot you and your little ones?" Wolf asked, his voice as icy as the water glittering in front of them, but his fingers were warm and gentle against her back.

Jillian shook her head, a tight, hot knot clogging her throat. "He shot me, and Wes, and Bree, but the other men, they must have—I didn't see, just heard the guns go off and," her voice died to a hoarse whisper, "Lizzy, Collie, and Katie crumpled and then, and then everything went cold and dark.

"I'm not a lion. I am not." Wrapping her arms around herself she bent and rocked. "I ran when I saw him."

His hand resumed, that soothing up-and-down caress.

"But you came back, did you not? In the parking lot at Kait's building. You came back to kill him. To kill them all." There was no disapproval in his voice. He was simply stating a fact. An accepted fact. He'd obviously heard the story from Kait. "Tell me what happened, *netee*." She sighed and leaned into his warm hand. She was still a lion in his eyes. And he didn't seem disturbed by the fact she'd tried to kill four people. Four innocent people according to him. Did he know she'd threatened his Kaity with a knife?

"This man, the one who shot you, what does he look like?" Wolf's voice had chilled, the velvet baritone roughening.

She took a deep breath, let it out slowly. "He was tall, thin. Brown eyes. No hair."

The warmth in his eyes centered her. Before she realized it, she began to talk.

"Lizzy let them in," she whispered, her mind turning inward, pulling up that horrific day. "She wasn't supposed to let strangers in. She knew that"—her voice thickened—"but she was only six, still a baby. I was in the kitchen. They pushed her into the kitchen with a gun to her head." Jillian started to shake, her throat so tight she could hardly get the words out. "She kept . . . she kept saying 'I'm sorry, Mommy. I'm sorry.'" Jillian choked on the lump in her throat, and then forced the rest of the memory out. "The other kids were in the family room, watching television. They wanted me to call them into the kitchen. They said they'd kill Lizzy if I didn't."

She wasn't aware she was crying until moisture hit her hand.

For a moment she stared down, dumbfounded. She hadn't cried while awake since coming to in the sinking van. Her tears had been reserved for the night. For the dreams.

"They made you call the rest of your kids into the kitchen," Wolf repeated, a dark, dangerous edge to his voice.

Her nod was sluggish. "They said—they said we'd be okay as long as we did what we were told. But they'd kill someone each time I disobeyed." Her voice rose until it pierced the trees, shrill with anguish. "What could I do? They would have killed my Lizzy if I didn't call the others. But by calling them, I killed them."

"No." His voice broke into her cry, inflexible in its certainty. Instantly, her voice fell. "Calling your children did not kill them. They would have found them. They would have rounded them up. You couldn't have stopped that. *This was not your fault.*"

Absolutely still, she sat there and let his assurance sink in. Let it spread out. Let it slow her heartbeat and unfreeze her lungs.

Calmer, she continued. "They taped our hands and mouths and took us to the garage. To my van. They pulled the seats out, made us lie down and then taped our feet. One drove. One sat in the passenger seat. One in the back with us. After a while, they met up with two SUVs and they split us up."

Wolf stroked her back again and pulled her closer. His big body burned against hers. But not even his heat could warm the icy hemorrhage in her mind. "What did they do with your van?"

She frowned. "They must have taken it back to the house and put the seats back in."

He shook his head, for the first time looking surprised. "Why?"

"Because after they shot us, they cinched us into the seats and drove the van off the bluff above Lake Katcheca."

He went very still beside her. His hand frozen on her back. "Your children are—"

"At the bottom of the lake," she said thickly, only this time the tears didn't fall. Her eyes burned. Her heart burned even worse. But the agony transcended tears. "I woke up when it hit the water."

"They shot you." He gently stroked the scar along the side of her head. When her hair had been long, the scar had been covered by the length of the strands above. Cutting it had exposed the thick, calloused healing tissue.

"Twice. They thought I was dead. I woke up when the van hit the water. The moon roof was open. I barely made it out."

She barely made it to shore too. Or up the rocky, endless bank.

She didn't remember much of the ordeal. The motorist who'd almost hit her as she stumbled onto the pavement said she was barely conscious. Raving and incoherent.

"I didn't try to get them out." The words erupted from her in all their agonizing frenzy. "I didn't even try. I should have tried. I shouldn't have just left them there. What if they were still alive? What if I was wrong? What if they weren't dead before it went down?" Her voice climbed higher and higher, the agony a constant, unforgiving scream inside her mind. "I killed them. I killed them by leaving. How could I have just left them there?"

"Jillian." He caught the hands that were clawing at her face and forced them to her sides. "Jillian, *heneeceine3 betee.*"

"I'm not a lion," she shrieked. "I left them there. I left my babies to die so I could save myself."

"No." He shook her. "You left to survive. You left to give them the revenge they deserved. They were already gone. You could not have saved them."

"How can I be sure?" Her voice rose again.

"Because you knew. In your heart you knew they were gone. You felt it. They were already gone." His voice was so calm, so full of certainty. "It's a mother's *betee, bixoo3etiit,* to know when their babies have left them."

She swallowed hard. "What does *betee* mean?"

"Heart. Your mother's heart knew they were gone."

Sitting perfectly still, she thought back to that moment when she'd seen them in the backseat. To the instant, incandescent anguish. Her beautiful babies. Dead. All five dead. He was right. She'd known. The moment she'd remembered, she'd known.

But somehow she'd lost that certainty through the following months.

"We'll bring them home to you," Wolf whispered, wrapping an arm around her shoulder and drawing her against his side. "After we find the ones who took them from you, after you have avenged them. We will find your children and bring them home. As they deserve. As you deserve."

Sniffing thickly she frowned. "How will I find the men who did this? You said it's not Simcosky and his friends?"

The question sounded more like an accusation and Wolf smiled slightly. But the smile quickly faded. Suddenly he bent and unstrapped the knife sheath attached to his calf. He slid the blade into the holster and dropped it into her lap.

Startled, she stared down at it. "Uh, what—"

"You need a weapon worthy of a lioness, *netee*." Shifting to face her, he took her hand and placed it on his chest, just below and slightly to the left of his sternum. "This is where you strike. When the time comes, strike hard, strike fast. Let no one stop you."

Cosky knew exactly where Kait was headed with this conversation.

He crossed his arms over his tight chest. No way in hell was he letting her near his eye.

She edged closer, so close he could smell that clean, lemony scent that had taken residence in his dreams as surely as she'd taken residence in his heart. He'd denied it to Zane, the day before. But it was a lot harder to deny it to himself. Wolf had cracked that self-delusion wide open. Pain and rage had consumed him at the thought of the big bastard sharing her bed, but that had been nothing compared to the agony of hearing Kait admit that she loved him.

A cold, numb chasm had ripped open inside him. The emptiness, the loss, had been unlike anything he'd experienced before. He'd been bleeding to death from within. Where he couldn't see it, only feel it—feel himself sliding down into that endless, empty chasm. Not even his father's death had hollowed him out so completely.

He didn't want to feel like that ever again.

He still hated the thought of her spending a lifetime worrying about him, but she'd been right that life was messy. She'd been right that worry and love went hand in hand. Christ, he'd been scared near to death because of her, for her, more than once during these past three days.

Besides, Kait had been raised by and around some of the most courageous and committed men in the world. Had he really thought she wouldn't be drawn to such men herself? Chances were she'd choose the same kind of man as her father and brothers for a lifetime commitment.

And if she was going to love a special operator, it was damn well going to be him.

Yeah, he may have been a complete and utter ass there in the beginning. But Kait wasn't the type to hold a grudge. She wasn't the type to refuse second chances. And from the way her body went into overdrive when they got together, just like his did, she still wanted him.

He could work with that.

He hadn't lost her. Not yet.

And he sure as hell wasn't going to lose her to a damn healing gone wrong.

"Give it up, Kait. We aren't experimenting on my eye." Cosky leaned against the bench and crossed his arms, trying to ignore the entreaty on Kait's face.

"Cosky—"

"No, damn it." His chest tightened. "Did you forget that channeling that much energy last time damn near killed you?"

"It didn't almost kill me. It just tapped me out." She scooted closer and touched his hand. "And we didn't know the trigger then. We know how it works now, we can control the intensity."

He snorted, unmoved. "We don't know a damn thing about how this works. For all we know, channeling so much energy again, so soon after your last crash and burn, could cause irreparable damage." He paused, leveled a stern look on her upturned face. It didn't help that she was so damn beautiful . . . and earnest. "You could end up brain damaged. Hell, your temperature spiked so high last time it about fried you."

It was her turn to snort. "That won't happen this time. We can break the connection and dump the energy just by lifting your hands."

Frustration tightened Cosky's throat. "We don't know that for sure."

"But we do." Her voice rose. "That's what happened every time we've tested it."

"You weren't doing a healing," Cosky snapped back, scowling. "We were holding hands. There's no way of knowing if the current will break if I lift my hands when you're in the middle of an actual healing."

"It did in the parking lot," Kait insisted.

Cosky wasn't so sure. "Kait—"

"Look, that's why we start small, right?" Kait suddenly changed tactics. "We'll try it for say two seconds, then quit."

Swearing, Cosky rolled his shoulders. "Two seconds?"

"Two. I promise." The smile she beamed at him was glorious and impossible to refuse.

Damn it.

"Fine. Two seconds," he said with a scowl.

She moved fast, like she was afraid he'd change his mind. Leaning over him, she settled her hands over his eye. He grimaced at the pressure. The damn thing still hurt like hell.

"Now cover my hands with your palms," she said.

"You're not feeling anything?"

"Not yet," she said.

From the hard buds of her nipples pressing into his chest, he knew that was a lie. She was definitely feeling something, the same something that was hardening his cock and tightening his balls. He could think of a dozen things he wanted to do with his hands, and helping her hold his eye wasn't one of them.

"Cosky," she said, pure entreaty in her voice.

Ah hell.

Reaching up, he settled both palms over her hands and started counting.

One. Two. Three. He lifted his hands.

"Cosky!" Pure irritation sharpened her voice. "It hadn't even started burning yet."

Which was the whole point. "You asked for two seconds. I gave you three."

"How generous of you," she said sarcastically, without dropping her hands. "And you know I meant two seconds after it starts to burn. Let's try again. You can see I'm fine. And it's clear you can flip the switch."

She had a point. Not to mention the brush of her breasts against his chest was too damn distracting.

"Fine." He reached up again, settled his hands over hers. "Two seconds."

"Three," she said quickly, which earned a snort.

The burning started at the five-second mark. He counted off three seconds and released his grip.

"Kait," he said sharply when her arms didn't fall. He could feel the heat emanating from her hands; it warmed the entire left side of his face.

"I'm okay," she said slowly. "The burning stopped as soon as you lifted your hands. But there's residual warmth radiating out, so I think it's still healing."

"The deal was you'd drop your hands as soon as I let go." Cosky reached for her wrists and pulled her hands away from his face.

She didn't fight him. "Actually, the deal was you'd let go after three seconds. Nothing was said about when I had to let go." Suddenly she hissed, and jerked back. "Oh . . . my . . . God . . . Cosky."

Freezing, he scanned her from head to foot. She looked shocked, flushed, but not in distress. "What's wrong?"

"Your eye." Disbelief rang in her voice.

Frowning, he lifted a hand to his left eye. It felt noticeably less swollen and didn't hurt like it had before.

"How much better is it?" It was hard to judge from touching.

"A lot." There was awe in her voice.

He started to get up, so he could find a mirror. But she grabbed his arm.

"I want to try it again." There was more than entreaty in her voice. There was demand. Urgency.

He blew out a tight breath. "Kait—"

"I'm fine. I'm not drained in the slightest. You broke the current the instant you lifted your hands. This is amazing, Cosky. Think of the implications! This works. We can control it. And if your eye looks this much better after three seconds, think what it could look like after five. Maybe you'll be able to see out of it again."

He pulled back until he could get a good look at her face. She looked slightly flushed, but not hot. There was no perspiration like there had been before. He raised a hand to her forehead and felt for a fever.

She felt slightly warm, but not hot.

Maybe she was right. Maybe they could control this. And damn, it would be nice to see out of both eyes again.

"Okay, five seconds this time."

"Seven."

"Five, or none," he said sternly, steeling himself against her flirty smile.

She rolled her eyes at him. "Fine. Five."

As she leaned into him again and settled her palms over his eye, there was a noticeable difference. The pressure didn't cause any pain. At least to his eye.

There was plenty of pressure in other areas, though. To reach his eye she had to lean against him. Every breath they took rubbed her breasts against his chest and hardened his cock. By the time they completed this healing; he'd be poking her in the belly with his dick.

Which wasn't where he wanted to be poking her.

"Anytime now, Cos," she said, the dryness in her voice a clear indication she'd picked up on his body's enthusiastic appreciation of her nearness.

With a grimace, he reached for her hands. He gave it six seconds this time, a compromise to her seven, and broke contact when the temperature level jumped from warm to too damn hot. His burning flesh immediately cooled.

"Kait?" he asked sharply, because the hands pressing against his eyes were still hotter than hell.

"I'm fine."

He relaxed at the sound of her voice. There was no tension in her tone. No distress in the body pressed against his. He started to slide his arms around her waist, only to stop. Would simply holding her open a channel again?

Which started a disturbing train of thought.

They'd obviously established some kind of energy channel that was activated by touching. But what would happen if they wanted to touch without opening the channel? Could he stroke her bare skin now without that insane heat rising? Could he hold her, stroke her, without worrying about the energy getting out of control? What would happen if he made love to her? Would the act of lovemaking open a channel and fry her?

It hadn't before. But they'd made love before that incident in the parking lot.

What if the parameters had changed since then?

Obviously it was time for more testing.

He slid his hands beneath her shirt and skimmed them up her bare back. She froze, her breath catching.

"Ah, Marcus, what are you doing?" Her voice quivered.

He dragged her closer and turned his head until his breath was moistening the shell of her ear. "I'm conducting an experiment of my own." He smiled at the shiver that raked her. "Is it getting hot?"

"Yes." Her voice shook.

But the hands against his face weren't getting any hotter.

He laughed softly and caught her earlobe in his teeth. "In your hands?"

"Oh." She coughed, her body going languid atop him. "Not there."

"Good to know." He skimmed his fingers down her back.

She quivered as he nibbled a path down the side of her neck, and he smiled in satisfaction. Until her face turned into his throat and her mouth found the patch of skin just below his ear. She nipped him, and then soothed the slight sting with a long, slow sweep of her tongue.

It was his turn to quiver, a splinter of pure lust ricocheting through him. His body went hard, urgency climbing. Suddenly he craved the taste of her, the press of her body against his. Tightening his arms, he drew her hard against him, until he could feel the steady beat of her heart against his chest. Lifting his hand, he caught her chin, nudging her face toward his.

He caught a glimpse of her rosy face and dreamy eyes as he leaned in to brush her mouth with his. It was a gentle caress, fleeting, which wasn't enough for either of them. Her lips opened, and her tongue snuck out and stroked the crease between his lips. He caught it with his teeth and drew it into his mouth, suckling it.

God knows where that deep, carnal kiss would have taken them. He was so damn hungry for her he'd forgotten where they were, or that there were other people in the house.

And then a voice cleared loudly above them.

Kait jumped, dropped her hands to his chest, and tried to scramble away.

Scowling, Cosky wrapped his arms around her, holding her in place. It was about time Wolf got used to seeing Kait in his arms. She was going to spend most of her free time there, if he had any say in it.

Leaning his head against the bench, he glared up.

Wolf's cold, hard face came into focus. Shock suddenly rounded the black eyes. They quickly narrowed and studied Cosky's face intently. That's when Cosky realized he could see the big bastard clear as day.

Out of both eyes.

He blinked, and his vision sharpened. Closing his eye, he gingerly explored the socket. The swelling was completely gone. So was the pain. When he opened it again, his eyesight was even clearer than before.

Son of a bitch. She'd actually done it. She'd completely healed his eye.

In six seconds.

Un-fucking-believable.

Chapter Nineteen

MAC SHIFTED UNEASILY ON THE BENCH SEAT OF ZANE'S VAN, HIS skin prickling as Amy's body heat bathed his left side.

"Can you head back to my car? I parked a couple blocks up from the lab; there's an excellent chance it hasn't been spotted," Amy said.

"You can drop me off anywhere," Faith, the scientist they'd rescued, muttered.

Rawls snorted. "Not likely, sweetheart; you're safer with us for the time being."

"Safer?" Faith's voice rose. Out of the corner of his eye, Mac saw her lean forward and twist, to get a better look at Rawls. "You killed those guys!"

It was Mac's turn to snort. "Did it escape your notice that they started shooting first? Or"—his voice hardened—"that we saved your ass? You'd be either dead, or in their hands—which is as good as dead—without us."

That shut her up.

"My car?" Amy prompted.

"It's not a good idea," Zane said after a moment. "Even if they haven't discovered your ride, they may be patrolling the area pretty heavily. We can't chance going back to your car."

Zane looked at Mac. "Call Wolf. We need a safe house. And we need Jillian to ID this bastard. Make sure he's really the one who killed her kids."

Dead silence hit the van. Mac could feel the tension that gripped Amy's slender frame.

"Kids?" she asked in a tight, soft voice.

"Yeah, we found Russ Branson's sister. It looks like her family was taken by this guy." Mac nodded toward the man slumped against the door. "Once they had no use for them, they murdered everyone. Or tried to. Branson's sister escaped."

"But they killed her kids." The look she turned on the limp body beside her was icy. "Why?"

The smile Mac turned on Pachico's limp body was hard. "Exactly what I intend to ask him, after the bastard quits playing dead."

"So how about you, sweetheart?" Rawls raised his voice. "You want to tell us what the hell you were doing beneath that machine in the middle of the night?" He paused a moment and then added as an afterthought, "And why everyone seems to think you're dead?"

At least the scientist didn't pretend the question wasn't directed at her. "No," she said politely. "Not particularly."

Rawls barked out an amused laugh. Mac wasn't nearly as amused. "Lady, we saved your fucking ass back there. You owe us some damn answers."

"How do you figure that?" Her voice didn't rise, or deepen, just kept that polite flatness. "I was minding my own business. You were the ones who interfered. For all I know, those other guys, the ones you killed, were following you; and you're the bad guys."

"Trust me, sweet cakes, we're the good guys," Rawls drawled. "It's just that our white hats clashed with the night vision devices."

Faith snorted.

Amy shifted slightly, and her elbow brushed Mac's arm. Heat flared at the point of contact, and places farther south.

"Tell me something, Dr. Ansell," Amy suddenly said in a calm voice. "Were you booked on flight 2077 from Seattle to Honolulu six months ago?"

Even from his position on the other side of Amy, Mac could see the woman go completely still.

"Yeah? So?"

"So were the two men in the front seats. Let me introduce you to Lieutenant Commander Zane Winters and Seth Rawlings, without whom you wouldn't be alive, or at least free, now."

Faith leaned forward slightly. "You were the SEALs who stopped the hijacking," she said slowly.

"Yes," Amy said simply and waited.

"Can you turn on the lights, so I can see your faces?"

Zane reached up to turn the overhead lamp on, and twisted in his seat so she could get a good look at his face.

A long moment of silence claimed the vehicle. Finally Faith cleared her throat.

"I read on the news that you claimed there was more behind the hijacking than the FBI and Homeland Security were admitting. That the men behind the hijacking weren't after the plane at all, that they were after some of the first-class passengers."

"Which the FBI ridiculed, and since we didn't have the list of names, we had no proof," Zane said, and Mac could hear the frustration in his LC's voice.

"But they were scientists," Faith said slowly. "From first class."

"That's what we believe," Zane confirmed.

"Do you know who was behind the hijacking?" the scientist finally asked.

"No." Mac's voice tightened. "Although, I'm sure our new buddy here will fill us in once he wakes from his nap."

He turned to stare at Pachico, who still lay slumped against the side window. Of course, the bastard was smart. He could be playing possum. He'd know that Rawls controlled the door locks and windows from the master switch up front. With no exit on hand, the bastard was probably keeping his chin down until an opportunity opened up.

"Well, I don't know who's behind this," Faith finally said, "but I have a good idea of what they were after. And I'm pretty sure they got it."

"You want to fill us in?" Mac growled when the silly woman didn't go on.

"Well, this is all theory," she said. "I don't have any proof."

"Sweet cheeks, looks like we're in the same club." There was more than a hint of grimness in Rawls's drawled words. "Why don't you tell us how come you're not dead? Obviously, you weren't in the lab when it exploded."

"Yeah." She coughed. "Nobody was in the lab when it exploded. At least nobody alive."

Amy shifted again; this time Mac was able to concentrate on the conversation rather than that increasing burn spreading across his skin and nagging at his groin. "There wasn't anyone in the lab when it exploded?"

"Nobody alive. They brought half a dozen bodies in, a body for each person in the lab. But they were already dead."

"Back up," Zane said. "You were there? You saw what happened?"

"Not all of it, but enough to piece together what happened," Faith said tightly. "And looking back and putting things together, it started right after the attempted hijacking.

"You see, we had two security guards. Tony and Jimbo. It isn't like our work was dangerous or required extra security or anything. So their main duty was just keeping an eye on the gate and the cameras, letting trucks into the loading dock. You know, little things like that."

"So you weren't working on anything sensitive?" Rawls asked, confusion in his voice.

Mac shared his confusion. What the hell were these bastards after if it wasn't top secret or classified?

"Well . . . yes, we were; and no, we weren't," Faith said and sighed. "Maybe I should start back even further."

"Please." There was a world of exasperated irritation in Mac's clipped entreaty.

"Okay, well. I guess this starts with Dr. Benton then. He was basically our boss, the project originator. His father had worked on the new energy paradigm as an intern with Dr. Fredric Poole sixty years ago—before Dr. Poole was murdered and his research disappeared."

"New energy?" Zane asked, the interest in his voice mirrored Mac's own.

"Yeah, the project was working on a way to access a clean, renewable source of energy. A cheap, renewable source of energy."

"Energy as pertains to what?" Rawls asked slowly.

"Everything." Her answer was flat. "It would have supplemented gas, diesel, coal, natural gas, nuclear energy, electricity. It would have powered absolutely everything that needed powering from household appliances to airplanes to cars, for a cost of next to nothing once the apparatuses had been developed."

Mac shook his head. Now that sounded like a very good reason to have a thousand security guards around, and a very good reason for mass murder, or hijacking a plane.

"Where exactly does this energy come from?" Mac asked.

"From the universe or solar system." She started to wave her arm, and hit Amy. After a muttered apology, she started talking again. "The energy is already there. It's infinite. All we have to do is tap into it."

"So your Dr. Benton was working on developing this apparatus? He was continuing his father and this Poole's research?" Mac made a note to look the name up, when something else occurred to him. "You said Dr. Poole had been killed and his research had disappeared; I'm assuming someone didn't want this research expanded on. So how did Dr. Benton Senior survive?"

"Dr. Benton's father survived because Dr. Poole was paranoid as hell." The scientist paused to take a breath. "Apparently Poole was convinced that several other breakthroughs in this technology had been made in the past, but every breakthrough triggered a crackdown and the scientists in question were either shut down and completely discredited and their research confiscated, or they were killed and their research vanished."

"That's seems a bit farfetched, don't you think?" Zane said mildly.

Faith gave a watery chuckle. "That's what I thought too, at least until recent events."

"Okay." Amy sounded interested, rather than disbelieving. "So this Poole was paranoid. How did that translate into Dr. Benton Senior surviving to continue the research?"

"Toward the later part of his research, Poole became convinced that he was being followed and watched. This was during the fifties, during Getty's reign of terror, and rumors started floating around that he was a communist and that his research was a weapon aimed at the heart of America. He urged Dr. Benton's father to not just quit, but to denounce him, so by the time they moved against Dr. Poole,

Dr. Benton had left the team and started working on nuclear energy. Dr. Poole convinced Benton to break from him so at least some of the research would survive the coming storm. Turns out his instincts were right on. His labs were shut down, his research confiscated, and he was arrested and brought before the Grand Jury on charges of treason. But before the case was brought to trial, he was found dead, hanging from the ceiling fan in his living room; and his death was ruled a suicide."

"Let me guess," Mac said dryly. "His research disappeared."

"Apparently, it was never seen again."

Zane half turned in the seat above and looked back at her. "And they never checked into Benton?"

"Of course they did, which is why Dr. Benton Senior never acknowledged the research again. Instead, he handed it off to his son. Even then, Dr. Benton Junior resumed the research under a different umbrella. As far as everyone except the immediate team knew, we were working on simplifying the transference of electricity. Nobody knew we were building Dr. Poole's solar energy apparatus."

"Somebody had to know," Mac corrected grimly. "It would take tremendous resources to fund the kind of research you're talking about. Who was backing the lab?"

"Dynamic Solutions," Faith admitted.

The news didn't surprise Mac in the slightest. Not when most of the scientists in first class that day had been on their way to the corporation's annual show and tell.

"But Gilbert—Dr. Benton," she corrected at the confused look Amy shot her, "had complete faith in Leonard Embray, Dynamic Solutions's CEO. And nobody else was supposed to know what we were working on."

Mac frowned, wondering what the chances were that Embray himself was behind the whole damn thing. Little was known about the man, but as the CEO of one of the largest corporations in the world, he sure as hell had the money and power behind him to pull off something like this.

But then again, why the hell would the man go to all this trouble? The research was already his. "Why were you flying to Hawaii?"

"Because we had a working prototype of the apparatus, and we were on our way to show it to him, but under the cover of the trade show, under the cover of attending to drum up additional funding."

Dead silence fell.

Zane was the first one to break it. "You're telling us you actually created this new energy apparatus, something that would revolutionize the world's technology and make every single way we currently power things obsolete?"

"Yes," she said quietly. "We had the prototype on the plane with us."

"Sweet Jesus." Rawls whistled and shook his head. "In other words, our suspect list just expanded to include every gas company, natural gas company, electrical . . . every single raw resource company out there."

"Look on the bright side," Amy drawled, irony heavy in her voice. "At least we have a suspect list now."

Mac shook his head with a scowl. Right, a suspect list with hundreds of the most powerful, influential men in America sitting at the top of it. The type of technical revolution they were talking about would bankrupt every single damn one of them. It sure as hell made sense why they might have combined forces to make sure the technology never saw the light of day, or combined forces to get control of it and use it to their own advantage.

"So you had it on the plane," Mac prompted when it looked like their guest wasn't going to continue.

As he waited for her to take up the story again, he shimmied himself around until he was facing Pachico and shoved the man against the passenger door so he could check to make sure the zip ties binding his wrists and ankles hadn't slipped. His new BFF tensed beneath him for an instant. He relaxed immediately, but it was already too late.

"Nice try," he told the bastard, after verifying that his wrists didn't have any wiggle room. But Pachico could wait, at least for a little while. The good doctor was a gold mine of information.

"Yeah . . ." Faith fell silent for a moment. "The attempted hijacking shook us. We didn't see how it could have been connected, but still . . . And then when your story hit the news and you insisted that the hijacking had been a cover for the kidnapping of seven of the first-class passengers on board . . . well that hit home. There were seven of us on board."

"And you didn't think that was important enough to step forward and identify yourselves?"

"How could we without admitting what we were working on, what we had created? You're aware of the ramifications now. The prototype was still in our possession. We were still vulnerable. Leonard Embray, Dynamic Solutions's founder, may have had the resources to protect us; but we were on our own and we had no idea who to trust, or where to turn."

"And you couldn't turn to the FBI, or Homeland Security because—"

"You five kept insisting they were compromised and not to be trusted," Faith finished dryly. "Nor could we combine forces with you, not with the media frenzy surrounding you. There was too big of a chance that you were being watched; and if we approached, we'd be recognized."

"So you effectively did nothing," Mac snapped. "And left us out to hang."

"Believe me, we had meetings ad nauseam about the situation," she said and Mac could hear the shrug in her voice.

"And did nothing," he returned with another snap.

"Pretty much." She didn't sound apologetic.

"Let's back up a moment," Zane said. "You said that Embray knew about your research, that he was, in fact, funding it. Why the hell didn't you get hold of him? He's got the resources to throw a security net over the whole project. Christ, he could have whisked you away to some hidey-hole."

"We did go to him, or at least we tried to. He's been 'unavailable' since the hijacking."

"Son of a bitch," Mac said, reaching up to knead his forehead where a killer headache was digging in. "Are you telling me he's missing in action, or that he's severed the connection with you?"

"We don't know," Faith said tightly. "The private number Dr. Benton was given was disconnected; when Dr. Benton tried to contact him through regular channels, we were told he was unavailable. Not only were we unable to contact him after the attempted hijacking, but there is no record of him appearing in public anywhere since."

Mac snorted. "The guy takes privacy to the extreme. He rarely appears in public."

"True," Faith said, "but he was scheduled to give a presentation at the trade show; he gives it every year. It's one of the few public appearances he makes. He canceled this year. He also canceled the keynote speech he'd promised to deliver to the University of Washington's graduating class this year." She paused and leaned back against the backrest of her seat. "Maybe it's a coincidence. I don't know. But Dr. Benton was convinced that something happened to him."

Mac frowned, shooting Pachico another glance. The guy was still pretending to be sleeping. Fine with him, at least it kept the bastard busy.

"You think he's dead?"

"I don't know. Dr. Benton thought he was."

"Then why the hell wouldn't his disappearance have been announced or his body show up?"

She sighed. "Gilbert thought it was because of the way he'd set Dynamic Solutions up and that his death wouldn't allow whoever is behind this, whoever it is trying to grab power, to actually step into his shoes."

"In other words, they have to continue the illusion that the man's alive to retain control of the corporation?"

"That's what Gilbert thought." She didn't sound like she was sure of that scenario herself though; if anything, she sounded doubtful.

Apparently he wasn't the only one who picked up on her doubt because Zane asked the question that was on the tip of Mac's tongue. "But you don't believe that scenario?"

Her sigh was heavy. "I don't know. Everything just seemed so farfetched, so . . . paranoid. But then there's what happened to Tony and Jimbo and what happened in the lab."

Tony and Jimbo—Mac backtracked to the beginning of the discussion. "Tony and Jimbo? The two security guards you mentioned?"

"Yeah, Dr. Benton had brought everyone on board personally. I mean, he recruited me from the university. I'd interned under him there. He had the same kind of personal relationship with every person he brought on board."

That made sense. He'd want to know he could trust them. "So he'd handpicked the two security guards?"

"Yeah, he'd known them since they'd been kids. They were totally reliable and trustworthy. But two weeks ago, they were killed in an automobile accident; they missed a curve in the road and sailed over an embankment. They were both killed on impact. According to the autopsy reports they both had blood alcohol levels twice the legal limit."

"And why did this raise an alarm?" Zane asked.

"Because Tony was allergic to alcohol; in fact, a couple of Christmases ago, we had to rush him to the emergency room after he ate a piece of supposedly alcohol-free fruitcake. His face swelled up like the Pillsbury Doughboy and then it was all itchy and splotchy for days afterward."

"And someone allergic to alcohol isn't going to go out and get falling-down drunk," Zane filled in. He shook his head. "Sloppy, they should have checked out whether the guy was a drinker."

"Exactly," Faith agreed. "Then a couple of days later, two new security guards showed up, courtesy of Dynamic Solutions, only Dr. Benton couldn't contact Embray to verify their employment. And when he tried to fire them, he was politely told that their employment was a condition of our continued funding."

"And your project head just accepted his?" It didn't seem likely if he was as paranoid as she'd made the guy sound. If he'd been in the poor bastard's place, he'd have walked on the spot. The only reason he hadn't resigned his commission after that fiasco with the feds, following the hijacking, was because those bastards had his team squarely by the balls. No way in hell was he abandoning Rawls, Cos, or Zane. And then there was McKay.

Somebody was going to pay for McKay's death.

"Of course he didn't accept it. He told us he was shutting the project down effective immediately and told us to start looking for new jobs. But when he gave notice, he was told that he, along with his entire team, would be persona non grata with the entire scientific community."

"So he backed down," Mac said, feeling an unexpected kinship with the researcher. The poor bastard had been forced into compliance for the same reasons Mac had. He'd been protecting his team.

"He wasn't given a chance to back down," Faith said tightly. "Later that day, the new security guards let a delivery truck in. The truck was full of heavily armed men. They rounded everyone up then killed Marcy, Angel, and Bekka, our clerical staff, and Julio, the janitor. They loaded everyone else up in the van. And then they unloaded seven bodies. Five men and two women."

Mac swore. "There were five men, two women on your research team?"

She didn't say anything, but her silence was confirmation enough. So they'd kidnapped the entire research team and then faked their deaths so nobody would look for them. No doubt they were even now altering the autopsy reports to match the people supposedly killed in the explosion.

It was brilliant in an ugly sort of way. They had the entire team at their disposal now. They could either make sure the research disappeared, or they could complete the technology and make sure they owned the rights, the patent, and the control over it.

Except, of course, they'd screwed up somehow and allowed one of the scientists to escape. "How did you avoid your teammates' fate?"

"Pure happenstance," she said after a moment on a sigh. "During lunches and breaks I like to read. But the break room is too crowded and noisy, so I have this . . . well, nest . . . behind all the supplies in one of the closets. There are a couple chairs back there and a bunch of books, some personal things. I was back there packing things up when the delivery truck came through."

"And they didn't hunt for you?" Zane asked, the same surprise in his voice that Mac was feeling.

"Gilbert dialed my cell phone as soon as they came in and hid his behind the centrifuge. So I could hear what was happening. He told them I'd left early. When they couldn't find me after they searched the building, they must have believed him. I could hear a lot of movement in the lab where he'd hidden the phone, and then one of the men said that Charlie hadn't found me at home. And the other guy said it didn't matter. If I was camped out inside the building, the explosion would take care of me. If I wasn't, they'd find me sooner or later. After they left, I snuck out the back door, took a bus downtown, and paid cash for a motel."

Mac fell silent. The kind of research she was talking about was revolutionary. Yeah, people would kill for it. They'd keep killing for it.

"There's obviously a tie-in between Dynamic Solutions and what happened at the lab, hell—what happened last spring to flight 2077. Although it still doesn't make sense. Why didn't they just grab everyone from the lab originally? Why bother trying to take the damn plane?"

Rawls glanced in the rearview mirror, his gaze lingering on the scientist. "Why did you sneak back into the lab? What were you doing under that machine?"

For a moment, it didn't look like she was going to answer, but then she shrugged. "There was supposed to be a backup disk, detailing our research, taped beneath the machine."

The frustration in her voice was a pretty clear indication that the disk had been missing, but Mac asked anyway. "I take it the backup was gone?"

She blew out a tight breath and nodded.

Zane's cell phone chimed. He fished it out. "It's Wolf, calling back." He lifted the phone to his ear and asked for Cosky then quickly filled him in with what they'd learned. After a few minutes of listening, he lowered the phone. "Cos says this Wolf is okay. Apparently he's got a place that nobody will be able to find. He's sending us the location." His phone chimed again. "Fuck," he said. "It's the Sierra Nevadas. That's at least a fourteen-hour drive."

Mac was silent, thinking. "He cleared the guy? He was trying to kill him yesterday."

Zane shrugged. "That's what he says."

"Hell," Mac said after a second. "He'd be perfect. Nobody will link him to us, so nobody would go looking for us there. Besides, Russ's sis is already there. Is he okay with us coming?"

"Apparently," Zane said. "We need to decide fast. It won't be long before your new BFF's buddies head out looking for him."

"Is that right, Pachico? You got some buddies looking for you?"

The shoulder beneath his hand didn't tense this time. But Mac knew damn well the bastard was awake. Fine, they'd let him play possum for a while and once they had him at the safe house they'd rip every bit of information they needed from the bastard.

"He's awake?" Zane asked with a glance over his shoulder.

"It's a damn safe bet, he's just feeling shy," Mac drawled and sent Zane a hard grin. "If the bastard is smart, he'll spend the next couple hours ruminating on the fact he has some pretty pissed bosses right now. I'm guessing these aren't the kind of men you want pissed at you, so it would be in his best interest to come clean and help us nail these bastards before they take steps to nail him."

Zane grunted and turned back around. "Amy, if they found your car, they know you were involved in this tonight. Your and Dr. Ansell's best bet is to come with us."

"Where are your boys?" Mac asked abruptly, glancing over his shoulder at the woman who'd been the bane of his dreams for the past few months.

She frowned, her hazel eyes shifting to meet his. "They're spending the night with a friend. Why?"

He shook his head. "You need to call someone. Send them somewhere safe. You could be gone for a while."

Amy already had her phone out and was dialing.

Zane shook his head, but continued frowning. "I've got a bad feeling about this. They know we were at the lab, they know we have Pachico, they know we have Jillian. These bastards aren't going to sit idly back and wait for us to come to them."

Mac nodded. He'd been thinking along the same lines. "They'll push back."

Zane gave a grim nod. "Hard."

Chapter Twenty

JILLIAN AWOKE FROM A DEEP, DRUGGED-LIKE SLEEP TO THE SOUND of voices.

Many voices. A jumble of tones, but no real words.

She recognized some of them: Marcus Simcosky's flat, chilly tone; Kaity's throatiness; Zane Winters's calm; even the commander's gravelly growl. But there were others she didn't recognize. A woman's brisk, no-nonsense, clipped voice. And another female voice that was slower, higher, less assured.

She didn't realize she was listening for Wolf's voice until she heard it.

"Drag him into the kitchen."

She barely recognized the feral grittiness to his voice; it was such a departure from his normal smooth velvet baritone.

"Let's just dump him on the couch," Rawlings said in that Southern twang she recognized from the condo. "He's playing possum, so he's a deadweight."

"The knives are in the kitchen. There's water for clean up," Wolf said with that earlier feral viciousness.

Boots sounded in the hall outside her door, followed by the scuffed sound of shoes being dragged across wood.

"He was kidding, right?" the woman with the brisk, clipped voice asked.

"Hell, I don't know." The commander sounded like he didn't care either.

She stretched and settled back against the pillows. She felt amazingly good, the pain in her head and eye gone. Lifting her hand, she probed at her left eye.

To her shock, the swelling was gone. So was the pain. She closed her right eye and focused on the oil painting across the dusky room. The mountain view was shadowed, but visible.

Good lord. She could actually see.

How long had she been asleep?

Apparently, long enough for the swelling to go down and her eye to return to normal. She swung out of bed, and headed for the bathroom to take a look.

She had no intention of leaving her bedroom, though.

Maybe the men who'd invaded Wolf's cabin hadn't killed her children. But they'd still killed her brother. The brother who'd loved her. Who'd loved his nieces and nephews. Who'd stepped in to fill Steve's shoes after he'd died. She would never have been able to keep the house without Russ. Or gotten the van.

It felt like a betrayal of everything he'd done for her to get chummy with his killers.

Wolf was different. He hadn't been directly involved.

"Someone should wake Jillian," Zane Winters said, his voice right next to her door. "See if she recognizes him."

Jillian stopped dead, her heart suddenly leaping in her chest. She could only think of one person Zane would expect her to be able to recognize.

She returned to the clothes she'd neatly folded on the chair beside the bed, and dressed in a daze.

Had they really found one of the men who'd killed her children? A combination of apprehension and anticipation balled inside her, settled in her chest like a cold, hard weight.

Rather than strapping the knife to her calf as Wolf had done, she held it in her hand and tugged her sleeve over it. The sweatshirt dwarfed her, so the knife disappeared.

Nobody was in the hall when she walked through her door.

"Jillian described him as tall, thin, with brown eyes and no hair." Wolf's icy voice drifted down the hall.

Jillian started walking in his direction.

"A perfect description of our fake detective, wouldn't you say?" Mackenzie said. "Grab one of those knives. Let's wake this bastard up."

With each step, the hall seemed to elongate, like one of those carnival fun-house mirrors. The kind that stretched on and on forever.

The voices in the kitchen seemed to rise and fall too, which added to her feeling that the world had slipped its axis and she was free-floating in zero gravity, tumbling head over heels without a tether.

"He's faking," Wolf said tightly.

And suddenly Jillian found her tether. Her anchor. She locked onto his voice and let it draw her down the hall.

"No fucking shit," Mackenzie snapped.

"Actually, he could have passed out," Rawlings said. "That was some chokehold you had on him when you grabbed him in the living room. I thought you were going to strangle him."

"You still have your questions," Wolf said.

A pause shook the room.

"Mightily obliged you held back," Rawlings drawled, but he sounded wary.

"It's not my place to dispatch him." Wolf's voice dropped back into that feral grittiness.

"We don't even know if this is the guy," the woman with the clipped voice said. "And no talk of *dispatching* him. He'll be turned over to the authorities once he's answered our questions."

Nobody responded.

"We agreed—" the woman snapped.

"I agreed to nothing," Wolf said in his flat, inflexible voice.

For the first time in months, her chest warmed. Flushed with heat.

When she stepped through the kitchen door, Wolf was waiting for her, his black velvet gaze locked on her face.

"*Hooku bexookee*," he said, and that feral bite was gone. "Do you recognize this man?"

"What the hell did he call her?" Mackenzie asked.

His lioness. He'd called her his lioness.

The heat in her chest spread out, infusing her with warmth.

Her hand tightened around the handle of the knife.

There was a bound man slumped in one of the kitchen chairs. He was bald. She could see the shimmer of his scalp above the white bandage ringing his head like a crown. Blood spotted the right side of the bandage and streaked the side of his face.

Her breath hitched, and her throat went dry.

Wolf caught one of the chair legs with his boot and swung the chair around to face her. The screech of the plastic feet against the plank floor swelled in her head. The man's bald head was bent, chin poking his chest.

But she recognized him.

"You do what you're fucking told and you and the brats will be fine. But one wrong step and we'll kill a kid. We'll make you choose."

Wolf reached down, grabbing the man by his chin, and jerked his head up. Hard. The guy sprang to life, fighting his bindings. He twisted his head until his chin slipped free. "Do you recognize him, Jillian?"

"Get down on the floor. Don't say a word. Not one word, understand?" His bald head gleamed beneath the garage's overhead lights. Empty brown eyes studied her face. "You're doing really good. You keep this up and everything will be just fine."

Liar.

Murderer.

"I'd say that's as close to a *yes* as a look can get," Rawlings murmured. Suddenly he frowned, stepped closer to Jillian, and stared fixedly at her left eye. "I'll be damned."

Zane Winters stared at her for a second too. He turned to Cosky and lifted an eyebrow. "Another miraculous recovery?"

"I don't know what the hell you clowns are accusing me of," the bald murderer said. Flat brown eyes touched her face and slid away. "But you just made a big mistake. One that's going to bury you. I'm undercover, working a case, and you just blew my cover."

Jillian took a step forward.

"Was that before or after you opened fire on us in the lab, you motherfucker?" Mackenzie growled.

The man's mouth snapped shut. He shot Jillian an assessing glance. "You're fucking with me, right? You believe her lies? The woman's crazy. You saw that yourselves." His gaze shifted to Marcus Simcosky. "For Christ's sake, she tried to shoot you and then run you over. She went after your girlfriend with a knife. She's got some major screws loose."

"We need some pictures, okay? Nothing scary. Just taking some pictures

to remind your brother of what's at stake. Be a good girl and tell your kids to come along."

"Is this the man who killed your kids, Jillian?" the woman with the clipped voice and short red hair said. "We need you to identify him."

Jillian opened her mouth, but the affirmation got stuck behind the locked muscles of her throat.

"You are stronger than you think, *hooku bexookee*," Wolf said softly. He grabbed the man's chin again and wrenched it over until he was facing her. "Look at her."

"She's a crazy fucked-up bitch," the man who stole her babies spat. "I can't believe you're buying into her shit. She probably didn't even have any kids."

Jillian wasn't aware of moving.

One minute she was across the kitchen. The next she was standing in front of him.

With the ground gritty and damp beneath her knees, and her children kneeling on both sides of her, Jillian watched her killer drop the camera and lift a big black gun with an extra-long barrel. "Sorry, sweetheart," he said as the first bullet struck in an explosion of pain. "Nothing personal."

Without hesitation she lifted the knife and drove it into his chest.

Just beneath and slightly to the left of his sternum.

"Sorry, sweetheart," she whispered. "It's personal."

Cosky froze in absolute disbelief, staring at the knife plunged hilt deep into their best shot at getting some answers. For an instant, shock held everyone silent and still. Faces went slack. Mouths fell open. Eyes rounded.

Pachico—they still didn't know the poor bastard's real name—looked more startled than anyone. His mouth was the widest, eyes the roundest. His face blank. Somehow the white bandage crowning his head added to the shocked look on his face. And then, oh so slowly, he fell forward. He would have kept going, fallen right out of the chair face-first onto the floor if Cosky hadn't leapt forward, grabbed the back of his button-down shirt, and hauled him upright again.

"Rawls!" Cosky roared.

Although he already knew it was too late. There weren't enough tricks in their corpsman's medical bag to pull the bastard through. Jillian's aim had been perfect. She had driven the blade straight between the ribs and toward the descending aorta. If by some damn miracle the blade had missed the aorta, it would have pierced the vena cava. Either way, he'd bleed out in a matter of minutes, maybe even seconds.

The bastard they'd pinned their hopes on was a corpse. Their best hope was that Rawls could keep him alive long enough to answer some questions before he rattled off his last breath.

"What the Goddamn motherfucking hell," Mac bellowed, his body stiff with rage as he stalked toward Jillian.

In one long stride Wolf rounded the chair, caught Jillian around the waist, and pushed her behind him. Backing her into a corner, he planted himself in front of her.

Mac stopped, scowled at Wolf's impassive, inflexible face, and without saying another word, turned around and headed toward Cosky.

Rawls squatted in front of Pachico, who was just sitting there, staring down at his chest.

"There's hardly any blood," Faith whispered. Her gaze was riveted on the knife handle and the slowly spreading tide of red seeping out around it. With each second, her face turned paler, until her freckles stood out like flecks of gold. "Maybe if nobody pulls it out, we can get him to the hospital in time."

Pachico's head slowly rose. From the stark look in his brown eyes, it was obvious he realized what the scientist hadn't—he was already bleeding out inside.

Rawls shot to his feet and turned to Kait, who was standing rigid and white-faced across the room. "Kait—"

Cosky knew immediately what his buddy had in mind. "No!" he snapped, stepping forward to block Kait's path in case she had any bright ideas.

Shoving his hands through his hair, Rawls wheeled on Cosky. "Goddamn it, she can save him. Look what she did to your knee. Look what she did for your eye."

"No," Cosky reiterated even louder, although it was more for Kait's benefit than Rawls's.

The wound was too major, life threatening. It would take an enormous amount of energy to heal something that severe. There was no way in hell he was letting Kait channel that much energy and risk frying herself for that scumbag.

"What are you two babbling about?" Mac said, shooting Cosky and Rawls a disgusted glare. He kicked the bound feet until Pachico's dull brown eyes lifted. "You're tapping out, buddy. Now's the time to make things square with whoever the hell you believe in. Who signs your paychecks?"

An ugly, amused light muddied the brown eyes below Mac. "You poor bastards don't have a clue who you're chasing. I'll let you have the pleasure of finding that out for yourselves."

Rawls swung to Cosky. "Christ Cos, if we lose him, we lose our best shot at finding out who set us up, who killed McKay. Goddamn it, we lose the teams."

Cosky's jaw tightened as the truth of Rawls's words sunk in. From Zane's account of the mission, the scientist they'd rescued in the lab had provided some new leads. But that's just what they were—leads. There was no way of knowing whether they'd pan out.

Pachico, however, he had actual names.

He had answers.

Her eyes on his face, Kait took a couple of shaky steps forward and touched Cosky's arm. "We could try—"

Looking down into her pale, willing face, he simply shook his head. There was no hesitation. He'd rather risk his career, his life on the teams—than her.

Rawls turned to Kait.

"I can't help him," she said, before Rawls even opened his mouth. She didn't look at Cosky, but he was certain she was thinking the same thing he was. To heal a wound of this magnitude, she would have to supercharge her gift, which she couldn't do without Cosky's help.

Zane's gaze bounced between Cosky and Kait, like he knew something was going on, but, shrugging, he turned to Pachico and crouched. "It does you no good to hold out," he said in a reasonable voice. "Who is pulling the strings? Where did they take the scientists from the lab?"

"Don't worry about that," Pachico said, his voice thinning. "They'll find you." His breathing grew labored and spotty. "Sooner than you think," he gasped out as his eyes glazed.

Cosky frowned. What the hell did that mean?

When Zane reached out to shake him, he was unresponsive.

Rawls pressed his fingers to the thick neck. Silence colored the room. After a few seconds, he stood up.

"He's gone," he said, frustration stamped across his face.

Cosky turned away from the accusation in the blue eyes. There wasn't even an ounce of regret over his decision.

"Motherfucker." Mac turned furious black eyes toward the corner, where Jillian stood backed up against the log walls, and Wolf's thick body shielded her. "You were looking right at her. You must have seen the knife. You could have stopped her."

Wolf stared back impassively. "She had every right to take his life. He took five of hers."

Swearing again, Mac gripped the back of his neck and spun in a tight circle, like he was trying to walk the rage off. "Nobody is debating that, damn it. But we needed to talk to him. We needed fucking answers."

Crossing his arms across his chest, Wolf shook his head. "He would never have answered your questions."

Mac scowled back. "You don't know that. We had his life to barter with, which makes damn fine incentive." Suddenly Mac tilted his head, and studied Wolf with suspicion.

"Did you get anything out of him on the trip here?" Cosky asked.

"Nada," Zane said with disgust.

"Or maybe that was your whole fucking plan," Mac said sharply. Bracing his feet, he pulled back his shoulders and stalked close to Wolf, the hostility radiating from him. "Maybe you let her kill him because you didn't want him talking. Maybe you're neck deep in this shit and this invitation to your castle was nothing more than a smoke screen to keep us close and make sure we didn't latch onto something."

"*Tei'yoonoh'o.*" Pure contempt throbbed in the word.

And then suddenly Wolf frowned. Going very still, he cocked his head, as though he were listening to something.

Zane turned to Rawls, who was still standing there, staring down at their dead hostage. "Don't beat yourself up. Nobody could have saved him."

Stiffness claimed Rawls's lean frame and Cosky knew he was thinking that Kait could have.

Zane slapped Rawls's shoulder and froze, his hand clamping down.

Cosky recognized the fixed, rigid expression.

Jesus Christ, unbelievable. The bastard was having another one of his visions.

"Ah hell," Rawls said. He glanced at Cosky and worked up a poor excuse of a smile. "Still, I suppose it's my turn in the headlights."

Yeah, right—Cosky swore. Chances were Rawls wasn't the only one in the line of fire. Wolf's strange behavior suddenly came to mind. He glanced over at their host as Zane shuddered and dropped his hand.

Wolf was still standing there, unusually still, a distant look on his face.

"What did you see?" Cosky swung to Zane, urgency stirring.

Something was about to go down. He was sure of it. To have two men equipped with a sense of *knowing*, and both hitting on something at the exact same time. Yeah, that wasn't a coincidence.

Suddenly, Wolf shook himself; spinning, he grabbed Jillian around the waist and half carried her across the room. "Everyone out of the house," he said, as he threw open the door. "Out. Everyone." His voice rose to a shout. "Kait. *Move.*"

The last time Wolf had ordered Kait to vacate a house, the condo had exploded.

His adrenaline spiking, Cosky caught Kait's shoulder and pushed her toward the door. "Move. Move. Move."

Spurred by the urgency in Wolf and Cosky's voices, Amy grabbed the scientist's elbow and propelled her forward. Cosky and Rawls brought up the rear. They sounded like a herd of bison as they raced across the porch and down the stairs. The staircase shuddered beneath their speed and combined weight.

"Head for the trees," Wolf yelled, gesturing toward the blue-black sphere arching into the night sky directly across from the kitchen porch.

"The vehicles are—" Mac shouted.

"The trees," Wolf roared.

For the first time ever, Cosky heard frustration in the deep baritone. Rage.

Faintly, in the distance came an eerie *whop-whop-whop.*

Cosky's breath caught. The sound was intimately familiar.

"Fuck," Mac breathed. He reached out and shoved Amy forward. "Run, damn it. Run."

The *whop-whop-whop* grew louder as they raced for the trees.

When the scientist stumbled over the uneven ground, Rawls swooped down and caught her around the waist, slinging her over his shoulder.

By the time they reached the sheltering branches of the forest, the sound of the blades beating the air echoed through the valley.

They crouched beneath the pine boughs just past the tree line and watched the sky.

"How many?" Amy asked, scanning the tops of the trees. She held a gun in a two-handed professional grip.

"One." Mac reached behind him and pulled a gun from beneath the belt at the small of his back.

Cosky, Zane, and Rawls did the same.

The clicking *snick* of clips being ejected and inserted filled the air.

"How did they find us?" Kait asked, her face a creamy blur as she knelt beside Cosky, her cheek almost resting on the bark of the tree trunk.

Good question. The bird had shown up on the tail of the Seattle crew.

They'll find you. Sooner than you think.

Pachico's dying words whispered through his mind.

"You guys scanned him, right?" Cosky asked, already knowing what their answer would be. Of course they'd checked him for trackers. This wasn't the first party they'd been invited to.

"What the fuck do you think?" Mac snapped, sounding insulted. He shifted on the mat of pine needles beneath the shadow of a massive pine and glanced toward the circular driveway in front of the cabin. "We need the damn cars."

The trees surrounding them blocked the moonlight—which shielded them but affected their own vision.

"Forget the cars," Wolf snapped, stroking a soothing hand down Jillian's shaking back as the helicopter broke into the space overhead.

Cosky hissed as the bird dropped down. It was a Huey.

He hadn't seen a Huey in forever. His first few training jumps had been off a Huey's deck, but soon after, they'd been pulled from commission.

"If it's full," Cosky said tightly, "we're looking at fifteen pairs of boots on the ground."

A spitting, hissing sound broke over the night, followed by an arch of light, and the cabin exploded.

Wolf didn't make a sound. But his body went rigid.

"Oh, Wolf," Kait said in an anguished voice. She reached for his shoulder, but he stood stiff and silent beneath her touch.

Another arch of light and the cars exploded.

A damn good thing they hadn't headed for the cars.

"We're screwed," Zane said grimly. As they watched, the bird was set down and a swarm of men hit the ground, their bodies dark against the hissing, spitting orange flames clawing at the dark sky behind them.

"We should fall back into the woods. Use the trees for cover." Amy's voice never lost its calm rationality.

"It's too dangerous," Cosky said, glancing at the pitch-black forest behind them. The trees were ghostly shadows lurking in the darkness. "There's no light. We'll be tripping over everything, which will lead them right to us. If they have night gear, we'll be sitting ducks."

The moon was hidden behind a bank of clouds. What little light filtered down from the sky didn't penetrate the forest canopy.

"We've got eight boots on the ground," Wolf said. "And they've got night vision devices."

Shit.

Grim silence fell.

They watched the team fan out, their dark bodies clearly visible against the backdrop of the writhing, flickering flames. They were obviously searching the perimeter of the burning cabin for survivors. The building site was ringed by trees. Maybe they wouldn't bother searching past the cleared area, which meant a lot of area to cover.

"Our best bet's to take cover in the trees," Wolf said in a whisper. "Few men are trained to look up. It will give us an advantage if they come this way."

Cosky looked up, scanning the trees surrounding them. There were several with lower branches that could be used for climbing.

The cabin was fully engulfed, the flames scratching at the dark sky. The roar, as the fire consumed the cabin, was growing louder and more urgent with each second of life.

"We need to move now," Cosky said. "The fire will mask the sound of branches breaking."

"Wait until the last man is past the first tree," Mac whispered. "Take out the target closest to you and then move out."

Cosky and Zane exchanged disgusted looks, like they needed a lesson in the basics. And whether Mac wanted to believe it or not, Wolf and Amy were hardly amateurs.

He clasped Kait beneath the elbow and lifted her to her feet. They split into teams—male and female. Kait and Cosky, Rawls and the scientist, Mac and Amy, Jillian and Wolf. Zane scaled the tree by himself.

With Kait's shapely ass climbing carefully above him, Cosky followed her up the tree. The bark was rough in places against his hands. Sticky in others. When they found branches sturdy enough to perch in, they settled down and waited.

Through the tree trunks they watched the fire climb higher and higher, until it seemed to rail at the night in a frenzy.

The insertion team regrouped in the clearing, beyond the chopper's blade. They huddled together, obviously discussing something. Cosky urged them to return to the Huey. Instead, they turned, fanning out again and heading directly toward the stand of trees they'd taken refuge in.

Son of a bitch.

They could not catch a break today. One of the bastards must have seen something. A flash of movement, a swath of clothes.

As still as possible, and far too aware of Kait's equally still body above him, Cosky waited. The preinsertion tension felt different this time. Denser. Deeper. More edgy. With Kait's life hanging above him, there was so much more riding on the success of this particular operation.

Kait didn't move a muscle, didn't make a sound as the first arm of the insertion formation passed silently beneath them with assault rifles cradled in their arms. Cosky held his breath, urging them to continue on. If they looked up, the game was over.

But Wolf had been right. The bastards obviously hadn't been trained, nor had enough experience to suspect danger raining down from above. He counted the targets off as they ghosted beneath.

Four. Five. Six. Seven.

Their formation was fairly tight, which put all eight of them within range of his team above them. They'd definitely seen something to send them so tightly grouped into this neck of the woods.

But it was the mark of tadpoles. It left the entire insertion team vulnerable at once.

Of course, just how vulnerable they were depended on how accurate the shooting was from above. As soon as the shots sounded, those bastards would know where they'd taken cover. If they didn't kill every damn last one of them almost immediately, they'd regroup and target the trees. If that happened, Cosky and his team would be facing heavy casualties.

Cosky sighted on the eighth target. The asshole was still too far out and moving cautiously, his rifle sweeping from side to side. As long as he kept that horizontal sweeping going, they were fine. But if the bastard looked up . . . yeah, best not to go there.

Come on. Come on.

When the Tango passed beneath his branch, he held his breath.

Kait must have held hers too, because he didn't hear anything above him. At least he didn't have to worry about her freaking out and getting them all killed.

Respect touched him. She had the nerves of a SEAL.

Which was saying a hell of a lot.

He waited until the Tango had cleared his tree by a dozen steps or so, steadied his aim, and gently pulled the trigger. His target hit the ground instantly.

The shot ruptured the silence and echoed through the trees. Their quarry turned and sighted up, but it was already too late. On the heels of his shot, five more rang out and the Tangos up front went down. And stayed down. Unmoving.

The two middle—unlucky bastards—spun, their heads and rifles rising.

They'd finally figured out the danger was lurking above. But Cosky had already lined up his second shot. He took down the man closest to him, and shifted his aim toward the last Tango.

Before he had a chance to squeeze the trigger, a volley of shots rang out and the bastard lurched to the left and crumpled.

His heart in overdrive, a cold sweat slicking his back and shoulders, Cosky waited. The trees remained silent. They waited some more. When nothing stirred, Cosky glanced up at Kait, held his palm up in the age-old *wait here* signal, and as silently as possible eased himself down from the tree. If a previously unidentified Tango still lurked, Cosky would be a bull's-eye in a shooting rink.

But they needed those night vision devices.

Not to mention the assault rifles.

He caught sight of Mac, Zane, and Rawls as their boots hit the ground, and headed for his target in a crouched run.

They quickly ransacked the bodies, stripping off the night vision devices and assault rifles. Cosky was about to rise when shots broke out from the far right.

As he hit the ground and rolled behind the nearest tree, he heard the solid *thunk, thunk* of someone taking hits.

His heart levitated up his throat. His temperature spiked. Blood pounding furiously through his veins, he glanced up the tree he'd stashed Kait in, instinctively finding the white blur of her face.

She'd crouched down almost flat on the branch, making herself as small as possible.

Relief exploded through him. She was alive.

Thank Christ.

But someone had taken a couple of rounds.

Who?

And Kait was still exposed. A sitting duck. All the women were sitting ducks.

Praying that she'd remain still and silent in her perch above, Cosky scanned the woods around him. He couldn't see the shooter. But he'd fired at them after they'd descended from the trees. With luck, the bastard's focus was on the ground.

Holstering the Glock behind his belt, he jerked on the night vision device, and picked up the assault rifle. He scanned the silent forest. He couldn't see shit with the tree in his way. On the other hand, the damn thing was currently the only thing standing between him and the business end of an assault rifle.

He listened intently, but the forest stood silent.

He couldn't see his team.

Fuck this. He needed some solid intel.

He chanced a quick glance around the trunk and spotted Zane and Mac behind trees to his front left and two still figures on the ground close to the tree Rawls had climbed down.

To his far left, a couple of rounds rattled off and the bark next to his head splintered.

Cosky ducked back as Zane and Mac opened fire in the direction the shots had come from, but it was doubtful their shots connected. The bastard was using the trees for cover.

He was the closest to Rawls's still body.

Fuck. Fuck. Fuck.

Let him be alive.

Chapter Twenty-One

COSKY LOCKED THE SURGE OF FEAR DOWN AND FORCED HIMSELF to think. To get to his buddy, he needed someone to provide cover. From the sounds of things, they only had the one shooter left. The bastard already knew Cosky's position. So shouting wasn't going to give that shit away.

"Cover," he yelled.

The second Zane and Mac laid into the bastard to their left, spraying the trees to keep him busy and caged, Cosky darted out. Keeping as low as possible to the ground, he reached Rawls's body as Zane and Mac hammered away at the tree their shooter had ducked behind.

Wolf didn't join the volley of gunfire.

Had he taken rounds too?

Rawls was splayed facedown on the thick carpet of pine needles, half over the guy he'd been stripping of equipment. He didn't move as Cosky rolled him over.

Cosky flinched at the sight of him. Accepted the rush of horror.

Rawls's head and chest were soaked with blood. He didn't check for a pulse before lifting him over his shoulder. Just grabbed him and ran.

But Jesus Christ . . . he didn't hear even a whisper of breath coming from Rawls's limp body. He told himself the constant shooting, as Zane and Mac covered his return, was masking his buddy's breathing.

But he couldn't quite make himself believe it.

His blood an icy lump in his veins, he raced for the nearest tree, which was several up from the tree Kait waited in.

As he laid Rawls's limp body down, shots broke out again in their shooter's direction. Then silence.

"Clear!" Wolf shouted.

Thank Christ.

Cosky's hands shook as he stripped the night vision device off and pressed his fingers to Rawls's neck. He couldn't find a pulse.

Zane and Mac appeared by his side.

"Is he alive?" Zane asked, the question hitting the air like a bullet. Quick and fast.

Without waiting for Cosky's reply, the two men dropped their rifles and ripped their shirts off, balling them into compression pads. Zane dropped to the ground as Cosky shifted his fingers, and pressed down again, praying for a pulse.

Please. Please. Please.

Come on, buddy. Come on.

Kait suddenly dropped to her knees beside Rawls's still figure.

"Which is the worse wound?" she asked urgently.

"Chest," Zane said, sounding breathless and hopeful as he shifted out of her way.

A weak flutter pulsed against Cosky's fingers, and his breath exploded in relief. "I got a pulse."

It was barely there. But it was a pulse.

"Goddamn it, get her out of the way," Mac roared, bending and reaching down. Zane shoved him back.

"Cosky," Kait said, her hands pressing down hard on Rawls chest. "I need you."

Jesus. Jesus. Jesus.

Cosky ran shaking fingers through his hair.

They weren't talking about a simple healing. The parking lot in front of Kait's complex flashed through his mind. Her white face and limp body as she collapsed to the ground.

"Cosky," Kait said. Calmly. Clearly. "He'll die without it."

The decision was made without even thinking. He dropped to his knees and covered Kait's hands.

One.

Come on, damn it. Come on.

Two.

Please.

At three, the heat flared.

Cosky closed his eyes. Swearing softly in relief.

"What the fuck are they doing?" Mac asked.

"Trying to save his life," Wolf said from behind them.

The heat exploded as the channel opened. Their hands got hotter and hotter. At the seven-second mark, Cosky hesitated, started to release his grip.

"No," Kait said. "I'm fine. We need to go longer."

At ten seconds, sweat started flowing.

At fifteen seconds, there was a collective breath being exhaled from the crowd watching above.

"What . . . ?" Faith said, her voice awed. "They're glowing."

At twenty seconds, the burn in his hands was close to unbearable; he gritted his teeth and rode it out. Watching Kait closely, he hoped like hell he was judging the effort she was expending correctly and wasn't letting her fry herself.

Even in the darkness, he could see the red in her face and hands. And Christ, she *was* glowing. An ethereal silver glow emanated from her entire body. But she wasn't the only one glowing. So was Rawls. That same silver glow cocooned his body.

Was he glowing too?

He didn't have the breath to ask.

The glow wasn't static, he realized slowly. It seemed to be shivering, or pulsing.

At forty seconds, Kait's breath grew choppy and labored.

They couldn't chance anymore. This had to be enough. He released his hold on Kait's hand and within seconds the white glow surrounding her diminished.

He relaxed, realizing he had concrete evidence he'd broken the channel.

She continued pressing down, but the white shimmer surrounding her was fading with each second.

Vaguely aware of the shocked circle of people ringing him, he reached for Rawls's neck; but his fingers were so swollen and raw, he couldn't feel Rawls's skin, let alone a pulse.

"Zane," he wheezed, his breathing raspy and thick. "Check for a pulse."

Christ, let the forty seconds have been enough.

He waited with tense muscles and a knot in his chest for Zane's report.

"We've got a pulse," Zane announced after a moment. Another couple of seconds passed and then—"It's getting stronger."

Kait continued pressing down, but the glow surrounding her had faded to a haze. Ten seconds later, the haze looked like more of a smoky film.

And then it was gone.

Cosky dropped to his ass, leaned forward, and caught Kait around the waist, dragging her into his arms. She felt hot—way too hot, and wet as hell—but her breathing was already returning to normal.

Amy knelt next to Rawls's still body and struggled to work the blood-soaked T-shirt up over his torso. Zane dropped down beside her and lifted Rawls up. Cosky closed his eyes—sweet relief flowing at the rise and fall of Rawls's chest.

The memory of that still chest and feeble pulse was an icy shadow in his memory.

He turned to Kait, feeling her forehead. She was too hot. Damn it, they needed ice, or something cold to get her temperature down.

She pressed her body against him. "I'm fine."

She wasn't fine; she was too fucking hot. Worried, he scanned the crowd of faces above him, but Wolf was missing.

While they didn't have ice, they did have an alpine lake on hand; if he could get her down into the water, they could probably cool her off.

Even as the thought crossed his mind, Wolf appeared beside him, handing him a cold, wet T-shirt. He gave a second one to Amy, who went to work wiping down Rawls's bloody chest.

Cosky gently bathed Kait's forehead, rolled her sleeves up as far as they would go, and bathed her arms, then worked the cold, wet cloth beneath her sweatshirt and bathed her abdomen and chest.

She signed, cuddling into him, and he kissed the top of her head.

"He's not bleeding anymore," Amy announced, her voice thick with disbelief. She paused and shook her head, the T-shirt still in her hands. "In fact, I can't even find any wounds."

"How the fuck . . ." Mac's voice trailed off.

Cosky's lips twitched. It was the first time Cosky could ever recall hearing the commander at such a complete and utter loss for words.

A long silence fell.

And then Wolf cleared his throat. "Looks like we've inherited a chopper. Anyone know how to fly?"

Chapter Twenty-Two

THREE DAYS LATER, JILLIAN SETTLED ONTO AN EMERALD SWATH OF grass above a meandering stream. Drawing her knees to her chest, she stared down the steep bank. The water below was so calm and clear she could see the rocks and tree roots that studded the gravel bed. Every so often, a flash of silver would catch her eye as small fish darted from nook to cranny.

This new haven Wolf had brought them to was similar to his log cabin in some respects. Not so much in others. Rather than a lodge-style home, their current hideout consisted of one huge room full of well-worn sofas and leather chairs, a sturdy dining room table, and a gigantic, well-stocked kitchen. It was surrounded by a loose cluster of rustic cabins—some with one bedroom, some with two, some with three.

Cosky, Zane, Mac, and Rawls had shared one until Zane's fiancée had arrived, after which they'd moved into a smaller one. Amy and Faith shared another. She and Wolf a third. Kait had taken the smallest, although Jillian suspected from the way Kait and Cosky couldn't keep their eyes or hands off each other, she wouldn't be alone in that cabin much longer.

Like the ashes of Wolf's beautiful log home, this hidey-hole was deep in the mountains, surrounded by forests, only this time in Washington State, nestled in foothills of the Cascade Mountains.

Their flight from the burning cabin remained a haze in her mind. She vaguely remembered Wolf calling someone and a hard-faced man, with cropped black hair and the eyes of a raptor, arriving in a battered pickup. There'd been hurried moments while he and Wolf had scanned the helicopter from stem to stern with blinking handheld devices and used pliers or knives to pull or snip. Only slowly had it dawned on her they were checking the helicopter for bugs, or GPS tracking devices, or whatever. After their rectangular devices stopped blinking, everyone climbed into the belly of the beast and the black-haired stranger had flown them here.

He'd returned later with Zane's fiancée, Beth, bags of clothes, and boxes of food before disappearing for good.

The clear water of the stream below her feet beckoned, but she didn't move. The bank was too high to dangle her feet in that pristine purity, and it took too much effort to slide down and climb back up.

Frowning, she stared at the water.

When would this numbness wear off?

When would life be worth the effort again?

Although this place did help. There was something soothing about the smoke-laced mountain air, and the sounds . . . the sounds surrounding her were so tranquil: the whisper of wind through the forest canopy, the haunting, mournful whistle of the small brown-and-white birds flitting about in the trees.

She didn't hear Wolf's approach. His feet were too silent for that. One moment she was alone on the bank, and the next he was sitting down beside her.

They sat in silence for a handful of moments.

"Do you regret it, *netee*?" he asked finally, his velvet voice curious.

Without thought, she raised her hands and held them, palms in front of her face. Even now, days later, she expected to see blood.

Which was strange, because there hadn't been much blood.

"No," she said.

And she didn't regret taking that bastard's life. Her babies had deserved that much.

But she'd expected something . . . an easing inside her. Some lift to the pain. Perhaps a lessening of the numbness.

Except, she didn't feel any different.

No difference at all.

Well, maybe a little . . . The numbness, while familiar, was stronger. It blanketed the rage, and doused the vengeance.

"Do you think it will get better once all of those bastards are gone?" she asked without looking at him, because she was afraid she already knew the answer.

"No," he said simply.

And she knew he was right, because even if she rid every last one of them from this earth, it wouldn't bring her babies back.

The arm he wrapped around her shoulders was warm, secure, comforting.

"You're ready to answer their questions now," Wolf said, his black eyes certain.

How did he know?

But she dismissed the question. He seemed to know a lot about her he shouldn't. Like what she was feeling, when she needed to eat even though she wasn't hungry, the way she cried in her sleep.

Or how killing a monster hadn't dulled the grief, or filled the emptiness.

And then there were the things he'd known before her.

Like her brother had been one of the monsters.

The realization had crept in slowly, spurred by flashes of memory. The surplus of cash and weapons she'd seen in his safe. The huge paydays he'd receive after months of being away—enough to pay off her house or buy her a car. The way she could never call him—because he was traveling in a foreign country—so he'd always called her. His razor-sharp reflexes. It had been a standing joke not to startle her brother because he'd react instinctively with a chop to the throat or a punch to the face. But mostly she remembered the icy emptiness that would slip in and out of his eyes.

The iciness she'd tried not to see. Refused to acknowledge.

God, she'd been such a fool.

"He loved us," she said as Russ's smiling, tanned face took root in her mind.

She didn't doubt that for a second, although she wondered about other things. Like his generosity. How much of his support had been generated by guilt?

"I'm sure he did, *nebii'o'oo*." Wolf said. "You wouldn't have been taken if he hadn't."

She frowned, digesting that.

"They took us to use against him?" she asked, a flash of rage streaking through the emptiness as the *why* finally fell into place. "What did they want him to do?"

Wolf frowned, a cold, predatory mask slipping across his face. "We'll ask them, when we find them."

So Russ had been responsible, in a roundabout way, for what had happened to her, to the children. Sorrow mixed with the rage. It must have killed him to know he'd brought such monsters into her life—that he'd put her and the kids in danger.

But it wasn't long before the sorrow died. And the numbness hardened again.

If she was right, he'd brought grief into her life once before, but that slip hadn't stopped him from continuing on the same murderous path and bringing it back into her life again.

"Steve, my husband, was Russ's best friend," she said out loud, giving voice to her fear. "They went through basic training together, joined the same Ranger regiment, and started up a security consulting firm after they bailed on the military." Wolf, she noticed, was sitting very still, his head cocked, listening. She didn't look at him. "He was killed four years ago." She swallowed hard and forced herself to continue. "Russ said it was a car bomb. In Turkey. While they were setting up security for a private corporation."

Wolf's arm tightened around her shoulder. "Did you see any documentation?"

His voice was incredibly gentle.

She shook her head. "Russ handled everything. The paperwork. The insurance . . ." Her voice trailed off. She forced the next words out. "Do you think he started doing, whatever he was doing, after Steve died?"

She prayed, oh God, she prayed she was wrong.

He was quiet for half a dozen beats of her heart, as though he didn't want to answer. But he was a good man. An honest one.

"No," he said on a soft curse. "Your brother was too damn good at what he did. A pro. He had experience. A lot of experience."

She accepted his reasoning with a tight nod, her throat hot and restricted. The numbness settled so deep and thick, it felt like her soul had been dipped in cement.

No wonder Russ had been so determined to support them, why he'd taken over as a father figure for her babies. Whatever he and Steve had been doing had gotten her husband killed.

Steve must have known what Russ was doing, what *they* were doing. He must have been part of it. Which meant her husband had been a monster too. How could she not have seen what lurked below Steve's and Russ's surfaces?

They'd both loved her. She didn't doubt that.

But it didn't soften the realization that the two most important men in her life had lied to her, every day, about almost everything. Or that they'd been capable of horrific, cold-blooded acts all in the name of the all-mighty dollar. Or that their sociopathic ruthlessness had taken the lives of her children.

She concentrated on the warm, sheltering arm around her shoulders, on the strength of the big body burning against her side. Wolf would have recognized the rot they'd kept hidden from her. He would have called them out on it. He would have stopped them before things got out of control.

If only he'd come into her life when he could have made a difference.

Cosky watched Mac pace from one end of the strategy room to the other as Jillian finished talking. And that's what this place was—a strategy room, Wolf's covert ops base.

The remote, defendable location had been the first sign that the place was more than a collection of cabins; the array of antennas on top of the roofs had been the second sign, the giant gas tanks that ran a generator strong enough to power a third world country, the third. But this room had been the biggest giveaway.

The bare log wall across from the dining room table bristled with pinholes. A cluster of desks to the far right housed half a dozen computer monitors, along with a slew of surveillance equipment, white-noise jammers, electronic scramblers, GPS trackers . . . There were so many top-tier electronics, it should have given Rawls a hard-on.

Except, Rawls hadn't noticed.

Frowning, Cosky shot his roommate a hooded glance. His buddy was standing with his back against the wall. Frozen. His body rigid. His face bone white and tense. He looked like a sharp sound could shatter him.

What the hell was going on in his closed-mouthed teammate's head?

He hadn't been the same since Kait had healed him. Physically he was fine, but mentally he was off—jumpy as a rabbit in the shadow of a hawk. He was losing weight too. Christ, he hadn't even touched the chocolate-chip cookies Dr. Ansell had baked. Considering Rawls's sweet tooth, that alone was cause for concern.

But there was a bigger concern, like the fact Cosky had walked in on him shouting savagely into the empty corner of their cabin . . . as though somebody was in there with him.

Cosky pushed the worry aside as he turned back to Mac's restless pacing. Rawls would talk when he was ready.

"You got the list of names?" Mac snapped at Beth, who'd been writing down everything Jillian had told them.

And Jillian had told them a lot. Her brother's given name, the dates and branches of his military service, the names of his friends and business acquaintances. Hell, she'd even given them dates and the countries he may have been in based on the gifts he'd brought back.

The woman had been a fountain of information.

Beth ignored Mac with cool, regal poise and handed the sheets to Zane, who paused long enough to run a hand down the back of her blond head before handing the notes off to Mac.

The byplay had Mac grinding his teeth and a grin edging the corners of Cosky's lips. Mac still wasn't used to Beth being underfoot. Which was too damn bad; their commander would simply have to adjust. Zane was enthralled with his soon-to-be wife, and Cosky—hell, he understood the condition.

He was pretty enthralled himself, only not with Beth.

His gaze drifted to Kait, lingering on her deceptively slender figure with its rope of braided hair. She was an odd mixture of amiability and gritty determination. Most people underestimated Kait, taking her tall, blond beauty at face value without recognizing the intelligence in her eyes, or her determination to stand up for what she believed in—be that her insistence on healing, even knowing it put her life in danger, or the emotional courage that allowed her to calmly let the men she loved disappear into battle.

It was an uncomfortable feeling, how his heart seized when he was around her. How she made him want to be a better man. A more open man. Something he'd never cared about before.

Frowning uneasily, he scrubbed a hand down his face. They needed to get away from this mob and spend some time together. Cement the bonds forming between them. He'd come too damn close to losing her—repeatedly—during the past week and a half. Christ, hearing her say she loved another man had almost brought him to his knees.

He never wanted to hear those words come out of her mouth again.

When Mac swung toward Wolf, Cosky forced himself to listen.

"I need to call these names into Radar," Mac said, his black eyes hard on Wolf's face, the words a demand rather than a request.

They'd been using the satellite phone Wolf had on the premises. Nobody had questioned whether the phone was clean. No way would their host want his base camp locatable.

As Mac rang Radar, Cosky headed for Kait. He snagged a chocolate-chip cookie as he passed the counter. At least Faith Ansell had found a way to combat her tension. The counter was overflowing with cookies and cakes and various sweet breads.

"What the hell are you talking about?" Mac's voice rose.

Cosky turned, finding his commander on the phone.

"No," Mac said tightly. "What channel?" He listened for a second and swore. "I'll call you back."

"What's up?" Zane asked. He'd taken a seat beside Beth on the couch, one of his arms wrapped around her waist, his other hand resting on her belly.

Cosky had an instant of yearning as he watched them. Good God, who would have guessed he'd wind up with white picket fences on his mind.

"Radar says we're on the news." Mac tossed the phone on the table and headed for the bank of computers against the wall.

"Which channel?" Cosky followed him.

"All of them." Mac sounded grim. Everyone clustered around the desks as Wolf started the computer up. It must have cost him a mint, but the building had Internet. It didn't take long to find the breaking news report or the reason for Mac's grimness.

Particularly with the news report titled "From Heroes to Murderers."

A cold tension slicked Cosky's skin.

Video footage rolled, showing a trio of armed men in NVDs cutting a hole in a chain-link fence. One of the men disappeared around the left of the building, the other around the right. The third waited in the shadows of the shrubbery for a few moments and then slipped through the building's gaping door. Cosky recognized the three figures instantly. They were standing beside him.

Zane swore, his voice tight.

The film fast forwarded to the unmistakable sound of gunfire. Minutes later, the three figures rushed out, dragging a fourth man between them.

The scene shifted to a newsroom and a pretty brunette behind a waist-high counter.

"The men involved in the shooting have been identified as Commander Jace Mackenzie, Lieutenant Commander Zane Winters, and Lieutenant Seth Rawlings," she said into the camera. "The victims were unarmed security guards in the process of securing the facility. Local police have issued alerts for the three men involved. If sighted, call nine-one-one. Do not approach. They are considered armed and dangerous with a possible hostage."

"Son of a bitch." The words were forced through Mac's teeth. He gripped the back of his neck with white fingers and glared down at the screen.

"We're obviously getting too close." Zane was the first to break the dead silence as the reporter moved into the attempted hijacking from four months earlier. "They know we're aware of who and what they were after on that plane. They're throwing up damage control."

Mac rounded on his LC, his face livid with rage. "And how does that do us one fucking bit of good? We'll be arrested the moment we show our fucking faces."

Cosky frowned. "We weren't all named. I'm in the clear."

"I'm not on the film," Amy said, her face thoughtful as she stared at the computer screen. "I was there, so was Faith. We should have been on the footage."

"She's right." Mac's voice calmed. "They spliced her and Faith out of the film. Why?"

"So they can't claim they were there, and events didn't happen as reported?" Zane suggested, absently drawing his white-faced fiancée against his side.

"Maybe." But Amy didn't sound like she believed it.

Cosky sighed, suddenly craving Kait's warm weight cuddled against him, like Zane was cradling Beth. "At least we have two avenues open. That's more than we had two weeks ago. Branson's background might point us toward who's behind this. And there's Dynamic Solutions. We need to track down Leonard Embray. The bastard's got to be involved."

Grim nods traveled the room.

As though tracking down the mysterious, intensely private, and obscenely wealthy founder of Dynamic Solutions was going to be a piece of cake.

Assuming the guy wasn't already missing, or dead, as Dr. Ansell suspected.

Her chest tight, Kait listened as the men discussed strategies. Was it too much to ask for a week of calm before everyone launched into battle again? Was it too much to ask for some time to get to know Cosky before he was wrenched away?

After five long years, they were finally tiptoeing into a relationship, damn if she was going to let him take off before they took the next step.

Her feet were moving before she was aware of it. She skirted Wolf's bulky frame, catching the knowing glance he cast her. When she reached Cosky's side, Kait took hold of his hand and held tight.

The touch didn't just turn his head, his whole body shifted and curved toward her. That instant, unequivocal response steadied her, made it easy to put herself out there, something she'd sworn barely a week ago she'd never do again.

"How about we get out of here for a while?" she asked, her hand clinging to his. "Wolf says there's a waterfall up the mountain. We could pack a lunch, have a picnic."

The gray eyes looking down at her warmed. He shot his teammates a contemplative look and turned back to Kait, his gaze glittering with intensity. "We'll need a blanket. Does Wolf have a day pack?"

She tried to smile around the fluttering in her stomach. From the heat shimmering in those silver eyes, there'd be more than lunch consumed on that blanket. "You find the pack and blanket; I'll make some sandwiches." He nodded and started to turn away when she abruptly remembered his knee. "Wait—" Her hand clung to his slipping fingers. "Is your leg up for a hike?"

His face softened. "My knee's fine thanks to you."

Kait frowned. "You'd tell me if you weren't up for this, right?"

The smile that twisted his hard mouth held more arousal than humor. "Trust me. I'm completely *up* for this."

Okay, she'd left herself wide open to that zinger.

Her facing heating, Kait let go of his hand and turned toward the kitchen, ignoring his low laugh. Ten minutes later they were on their way, a backpack strapped to Cosky's shoulders and the rudimentary map Wolf had scribbled for them in hand. Kait tried not to think of the amused, knowing looks that had followed them out the door.

Hell, Cosky's teammates hadn't even asked him why he was leaving in the middle of their strategy session.

The forest was dusky, cool, and slightly damp, the pine needles a thick cushion beneath their feet as they followed the path Wolf had outlined. A mile later, they left the smell of pine pitch and rotting vegetation behind as the forest canopy thinned, and they headed up a rocky slope blanketed by knee-high alpine grass and waist-high shrubs. The last half of the hike was almost straight up the mountain with the sun burning hot above their heads.

Kait kept an eye on Cosky's legs as the hike grew more and more strenuous. At the first sign of a limp, she was sitting him down for another healing. But as the elevation climbed and the path wound up the mountain, his stride never faltered.

By the time they crested the bluff, they were damp with sweat, their lungs laboring. But good God, the beauty below was worth every bit of wobble in her legs.

Sighing in content appreciation, Kait paused to gaze down at the lush little valley below. The meadow was in the shape of a bowl, quilted by a thick pad of emerald grass and rimmed by cliffs, two of which sported healthy waterfalls.

At the base of the cliffs, the waterfalls cascaded into a shimmering pool of blue green.

The spot was absolute perfection.

"It's beautiful, just like Wolf said," Kait murmured, mesmerized by the foaming water as it steamed from the rocks above, colliding with the pool below in a foaming spray that peppered the air and rocks and grassy meadow surrounding it.

"Beautiful," Cosky agreed, his voice husky.

Kait turned a smile in his direction, only to find his gaze locked on her face rather than the idyllic scene below.

A flush warmed her cheeks at the gleam in his platinum eyes. There were equal parts masculine appreciation and arousal stamped across his face. Her face burned even hotter as she turned away; more flustered by the fact he wasn't trying to hide the emotions than by the hunger itself.

As she took a step down the rock-strewn slope that led to the pristine valley below, she skidded. Quick as a dragonfly, his hand flashed out, caught her elbow, and steadied her. Only he didn't let go. Instead, he slipped his arm around her waist, drawing her against him.

Their T-shirts were damp from the hike, but she melted into his embrace anyway. As his arm tightened around her waist, anchoring her against him, she skimmed her palms up his back beneath the clinging cotton of his shirt until his day pack stopped her. He felt so good against her palms, wet sleek skin stretched over a pad of solid muscle.

Without hesitation, she lifted her face to his, watching through the fringe of her lashes as his lips came closer, watching the passion in his eyes burn brighter. It still amazed her how easy he was with his kisses now. How open with his need.

His lips, when they brushed hers, were gentle rather than urgent, soft rather than hard, teasing rather than driven. Her eyes drifted shut and her mouth stretched into a dreamy smile beneath the lazy, sweet pressure.

When those lovely little caresses ceased, she opened her eyes in disappointment and discovered the face staring down at her was anything but lazy. No, sir. It was tight with hunger. Red flags rode his cheekbones.

"A dip in ice-cold water sounds damn good right now," he said tightly, pressing his hips against her belly until she cradled the hard ridge of his penis.

Kait blushed at the evidence of his desire, but didn't pull away. She'd known from the moment she'd suggested this hike that she was suggesting more than an afternoon in his company—that at some point they'd be naked on that blanket, entwined in each other's arms.

Anticipation stirred as he caught her hand, and side-by-side they carefully picked their way down the rocky slope toward the mountain pool below. She'd been ready to accept him back into her heart as well as her body for days now, maybe even since they'd fled Wolf's burning cabin.

He felt something for her, that became more apparent each day.

She wasn't sure what he felt, but it was strong—so strong he'd chosen her safety over his naval career when he'd refused to let her heal the fake Pachico. For a man obsessed with rejoining his team, that instant, furious refusal said a lot.

And then there were the smaller clues. The way he worried that the healings on his leg would drain her. The way he'd reluctantly eased up on his suspicions about Wolf for her sake, the way he instantly found her with his gaze when he entered a room, and the way he'd squeeze in beside her at the table or wrap an arm around her while sitting beside her on the couch.

The way he'd left his team planning their next moves so he could spend the day with her.

But mostly it was in his eyes when he looked at her—the gleam of tenderness and passion.

Oh yeah, he felt something for her—something strong enough to build on.

A mixture of anticipation and nervousness gripped her as they spread the blanket out on the lush grass and emptied his day pack.

"Do you think Rawls is doing any better?" she babbled in an effort to fill the silence as she unpacked sandwiches, oranges, banana bread, and several thick, gooey chocolate-chip cookies.

Cosky frowned, worry dimming the passionate glitter in his eyes. "He's still damn jumpy and closemouthed about it."

Kait's hands slowed as a heavy weight settled over her.

"I think . . . I think he's having hallucinations."

"Yeah." Cosky didn't look surprised. Instead, the worry crept from his eyes across his face.

"What if my healing damaged his brain?" She forced the question out her tight, guilt-stricken throat.

"Hey." Cosky drew her into his arms and ran his palms up and down her back. "He's alive because of you. I don't know what the hell's going on with him. But he's alive. He'll work through this. He just needs time, which you gave him."

His assurance would have been more comforting if he'd looked like he believed it himself. Instead, the worry dug deep creases into his forehead.

She thought she was imagining it when the rhythm of his hands shifted from soothing to caressing until she caught the hungry glitter in his silver eyes. He didn't give her nervousness time to roost. Instead he bent his head, his lips seizing hers, and swept her straight into a storm of sensation.

His mouth wasn't soft this time. Or teasing. Rather it was urgent. Insistent. His lips hard, almost bruising, as they forced her mouth open so his tongue could surge inside. She met the symbolic thrusting of his tongue with flirty little rubs of her own, which sent a current of white-hot electricity through her.

Her breasts swelled. Her scalp tingled. The flesh between her legs throbbed.

"Christ," he said on a groan as he wrenched her T-shirt over her head and flung it aside. "I wanted to go slow. Give you the loving you deserve this time." He unhooked her bra and shoved it down her arms, his face tense, urgent with lust. "But I touch you and I'm fifteen again—no fucking control."

"Slow's overrated," Kait managed on a gasp as his mouth found her right nipple, and he started to suckle.

He abandoned her breast long enough to jerk his shirt over his head, and then dragged her down to the blanket, his mouth returning to her breast and that strong, urgent suckling.

"I didn't think you could taste any better, feel any better than the first time," he whispered, his voice smoky with arousal. "I was wrong."

Liquid fire raced through her. Kait wasn't sure whether the source was his admission or the tug of his lips against her nipple. Wrapping her legs around his hips, she ground the aching cleft between her legs against the bulge of his penis.

He groaned and jackknifed up to unzip her jeans and strip them, along with her panties, down her legs. His own jeans followed. He paused long enough to yank a condom out of his pocket and tossed the pants aside.

Quickly sheathing himself, he bore her down to the blanket, his shoulders blocking the sun, his body hot and heavy and hard on top of her. His mouth found her breast again and drew her nipple into his mouth. As he started back in on that urgent, erotic suckling, he slid a hand up her thigh and into the damp nest between her legs. A quiver raked her as he parted the wet folds and rubbed a finger back and forth along the slit.

Her legs rose and twined around his hips, and her hips lifted in silent entreaty.

"Jesus." His voice was so hoarse it was all but unintelligible.

Her mind went dark and dizzy as he thrust a finger inside her. He pumped her once, twice, and tension drew her muscles tight. He pushed his finger in her a third time and lightning streaked from her throbbing core up her spine. She stiffened, the tension drawing her tight, a choked scream breaking from her tight throat.

"Fuck." His voice was strangled, his breathing hard and fast. "Not yet."

He jerked his hand away, his knees pushing her legs wide, and settled between her thighs, nudging his swollen penis into place. Guiding it forward, he pressed against her throbbing opening.

Kait whimpered, every cell inside her focused on the thick, hot pressure probing at her core. Her legs lifted, wrapping around his waist, and her hips arched.

He pulled back, wrenching a protest from her, and then drove forward, seating himself to the hilt with one long, hard thrust.

The hard, hot pressure of him inside her sizzled through every nerve, every cell, every muscle. She arched beneath him, her legs cinched around his waist, her hips lifting to meet his thrusts.

As he settled into a hard, driving rhythm, her body clenched, drew tight, and hung there for one long, agonizing moment before rupturing beneath an explosion of sensation. She screamed as pleasure splintered through her, her muscles clenching and quivering, clenching and quivering.

The sight of his tight face, the red staining his cheeks as his rigid body arched above her, launched her into another orgasm. She could feel her sheath clamp around the hard length invading her.

His thrusts faltered, lost their rhythmic grace. His body arched almost painfully above her as her muscles clamped down and released, clamped down and released, milking him.

With a hoarse shout, his neck corded with effort, he thrust once more, burying himself to the hilt, and froze, straining as he poured himself into her.

Her heart so full it almost hurt, she wrapped her arms around him and held him tight as his release rocked them both.

His mind a white haze, Cosky's muscles slowly loosened, and he collapsed, his sweaty face pressed against Kait's neck. Her own orgasm still pulsed through her—delicate quivers that caressed his twitching cock, hardening it again.

Christ. He wanted her again. He hadn't even recovered from their first bout and he wanted her again. Even worse than before.

He tensed as a shadow of fear brushed his mind, the realization that he'd never get enough of her. Every touch, every thrust, every second he was with her would fuel the obsession. He faced the fear, the knowledge he'd never be completely whole without her, and let it go.

Because the alternative was much worse, unimaginably worse: to never hold her again, her heart beating against his; to never feel her come apart in his arms, or come apart in hers; to spend the rest of his life wondering who was sharing her bed and building a life with her.

Without question, this loss of control, this constant need was better than losing her.

Suddenly he was aware that the slim, silky body beneath him had tensed. Her breathing was tight. He raised his head, focusing on her cautious, questioning eyes, and his heart clenched. He could almost see her brace herself, waiting for him to pull away.

He caught her hand, his fingers shaking, and lifted it to his chest, pressing it against the heavy beat of his heart.

"I love you." The words were thick and rusty. He pressed her fingers harder against his chest and tried again. "I love you."

This time they flowed a little better. Smoother.

Her solemn brown eyes searched his face and the caution faded. "You're sure?"

"Forever." It was a pledge.

He brushed back a tangle of golden hair, his chest so tight it hurt. She hadn't said the words back.

Hell, who could blame her after his asinine behavior their first time together. He could be patient. Wait for that memory to fade. Wait for the trust to rebuild.

Sighing, he rolled, dragging her with him so she was on top and he wasn't crushing her. Loosening her braid, he combed his fingers through her hair, until the silky golden mass trailed down his shoulders and caressed his chest.

"I dreamed about you for years, about this," he admitted. "Your hands on me, your hair a curtain of gold, your body moving under mine. I'd wake up so damn hard an ice pack couldn't calm me down."

"You must have known I was attracted to you too," she said hesitantly, a frown wrinkling the smooth skin of her forehead.

He smoothed the creases with his fingertips and forced himself to answer the question in her eyes. Trust began with honesty. No matter how much he wanted to avoid the revelations.

"Yeah," he admitted quietly and saw a swift slash of pain cross her face. "But you scared me shitless." He smiled wryly as her eyes widened. "Hell, I hadn't touched you, hadn't tasted you, hadn't even talked to you and I was already obsessed, barely clinging to my control." He paused to stroke her cheek and his cock, still firmly lodged inside her, twitched. "All I could think was how much worse it would be if I did get a taste of you and had to walk away."

Her brow knitted. Huge, serious amber eyes searched his face. "Why would you have to walk away?"

Yeah, he was pretty sure she wasn't going to find his explanation heroic. "Because of my job. The danger involved. The fact I might never make it home."

She rolled her eyes and snorted. "That sounds like a hell of an excuse. You avoided me because of *that*?"

Not exactly . . . He suspected he'd avoided her because of the way she'd made him feel. The rest had been more of an excuse.

The color of her eyes sharpened as she focused on him again. "And now?"

He was quiet for a moment, before shaking his head ruefully. "I'm still scared shitless. The way I feel about you isn't rational. It isn't comfortable. Hell"—his voice deepened in disgust—"it's not normal."

A peal of laughter erupted from her. Her eyes started to shine. "That's got to be the most unromantic declaration of love ever."

From the smile spreading across her face, she didn't seem to mind.

"I'm not very good with the hearts and flowers stuff," he said.

She might as well know exactly what she was getting—or not getting as the case may be.

"I don't know." The words were almost a purr. She locked her arms around his shoulders and pressed herself more firmly against his erection. "I think you've got the important stuff down perfectly."

His breath hissed out of him as she pulled back and then pressed herself against him again. Reining himself in, determined to give her the slow, tender loving she deserved, he began thrusting in a lazy, languid rhythm. But each thrust grew less lazy, less tender, and before long, he was driving them toward that cliff again with urgent, powerful strokes.

This time they came apart together.

"Son of a bitch," he said when he could breathe again, completely disgusted with himself. He'd lasted all of five seconds before he'd started slamming into her like an animal. "Maybe after I've had you a thousand times I'll be able to slow down."

That startled a laugh from her. Her face was rosy as she smiled up at him, and her eyes glowed. A gilded frame of golden hair surrounded her head. She was the most beautiful thing he'd ever seen.

"Jesus," he whispered thickly, his throat tight. "I love you too fucking much."

The smile faded. Solemnly she lifted a hand and touched his cheek. "Never too much. No more than I love you."

It took a second for her words to sink in. When they did, his muscles went limp with relief.

She loved him.

Thank Christ.

Leaning down, he brushed her mouth, then took her bottom lip gently in his teeth and suckled.

This time he managed to keep his pace lazy and gentle and languid, loving her the way she deserved until she shattered in his arms.

An eon later, when the synapses in his brain started firing again, he tightened his arms around her and rolled. She stretched lazily and then settled on top of him with a soft sigh—heart to heart—exactly where she belonged.

SEAL Term Glossary

BUD/s (Basic Underwater Demolition training): A twenty-four-week training course that encompasses physical conditioning, combat diving, and land warfare.

Bullfrog: A nickname given to a highly respected, retired SEAL.

CO: Commanding Officer

CQB (Close Quarter Battle): A battle that takes place in a confined space such as a residence.

Deployment: Active combat or training, deployments last generally between six and ten months.

HQ1 (Naval Special Warfare Group 1 / the West Coast Command): HQ1 has naval bases in Coronado, California; Kodiac, Alaska; Pearl Harbor, Hawaii; and Mare Island, California. Among other naval units, HQ1 houses SEAL Teams 1, 3, 5, and 7.

HQ2 (Naval Special Warfare Group 2 / the East Coast Command): HQ2 has naval bases in Dam Neck, Virginia; Little Creek, Virginia; Machrihanish, UK; Rodman NAS; and Norfolk, Virginia. Among other naval units, HQ2 houses SEAL Teams 2, 4, 8, and 10 and DEVGRU (also known as SEAL Team 6).

Insertion: Heading into enemy territory, whether it's a house or a territory.

JSOC (the Joint Special Operations Command): A joint command that encompasses all branches of special operations. This command ensures the techniques and equipment used by the various branches of the military are standardized. It is also responsible for training and developing tactics/strategy for special operations missions.

LC: Lieutenant Commander

LT: Lieutenant

NAVSPECWARCOM (Naval Special Warfare Command): The naval command for naval special operations. This command is under the umbrella of USSOC and is broken into two headquarters: HQ1 and HQ2.

NVDs: Night vision devices

PST (Physical Screening Test): The physical test a prospective SEAL has to pass. Minimum requirements: 500-yard swim in twelve and a half minutes, rest ten minutes, 50 pushups in two minutes, rest two minutes, 50 sit ups in two minutes, rest two minutes, 10 pull ups in two minutes, rest ten minutes, 1.5-mile run in ten and a half minutes.

SEAL Prep School: A crash course in preparing to take the BUD/s challenge. Prospective BUD/s candidates are put through a physical training program meant to prepare them for BUD/s. This includes timed four-mile runs and one-thousand-meter swims. If the candidates are unable to pass the final qualifications test, they are removed from the SEAL candidates list and placed elsewhere in the navy.

SEAL Teams: Each SEAL team has 128 men, of which 21 are officers and 107 are enlisted. Each team has ten platoons and each platoon has two squads. There are 16 men per platoon and 8 SEALs per squad.

SQT (SEAL Qualification Training): SQT teaches tactics, techniques, and special operations procedures.

USSOC (the United States Special Operations Command): Beneath the umbrella of JSOC, the USSOC is the unified combat command and is charged with overseeing special operations command for the army, air force, navy, and the marines.

Zodiac: A rigid-hull inflatable boat with 470-horsepower jet drives. It can reach speeds of 45-plus knots and has supreme maneuverability. (Also known as the beach boat.)

Arapaho Glossary

3ooxonouubeiht: crabby

betee: heart

bexookeesoo: mountain lion cub

bixoo3etiit: love

hico'ooteehihi: chickadee

ciibehhiiwoohu: don't cry

ciini'i3ecoot: grief

heneeceine3: lion

heneeceine3 betee: lion heart

hiisoh'o: his/her elder brother

hooku bexookee: little mountain lion or cougar

hookecouhu' heeyei: little falcon

hookecouhu hiteseiw: little sister

nebii'o'oo: sweetheart

neehebehe': younger sister

netesei: my sister

netee: my heart

tei'yoonehe: baby

tei'yoonehe: infant

wo'ouusoo: kitten

Don't miss the next Red Hot SEALs novels from Trish McCallan

Forged in Smoke, Fall 2014
Forged in Embers, 2015

Acknowledgments

I credit three people with how well this book turned out.

To Alison Dasho, editor extraordinaire #1—without your eyes and sharp instinct on the early draft of this manuscript, I would still be floundering. You reined me in, straightened me out, and set me back on track. For that I will always be thankful. I hope your authors over at Thomas & Mercer know how blessed they are!

To Charlotte Herscher, editor extraordinaire #2—who took the raw pages of this manuscript, mixed them with her experience, instincts, and excellent editing skills and helped me make those pages shine.

To JoVon Sotak, editor extraordinaire #3—who stepped in to take the book over at the last minute when I was down to the wire on time, and got me the developmental editor I'd requested in less than a day. You are the bomb, and I just know I'm going to love working with you.

About the Author

Photograph by JK Steele, 2013

Trish McCallan was born in Eugene, Oregon, and grew up in Washington State, where she began crafting stories at an early age. Her first books were illustrated in crayon, bound with red yarn, and sold for a nickel at her lemonade stand. Trish grew up to earn a bachelor's degree in English literature with a concentration in creative writing from Western Washington University, taking jobs as a bookkeeper and human-resource specialist before finally quitting her day job to write full time. *Forged in Fire* came about after a marathon reading session and a bottle of Nyquil that sparked a vivid dream. She lives today in eastern Washington. An avid animal lover, she currently shares her home with three golden retrievers, a black lab mix, and a cat.

If you'd like to sign up for Trish McCallan's newsletter to receive new release information, please visit www.trishmccallan.com/contact.html#newsletter.

You can follow Trish McCallan on Facebook at www.facebook.com/trish.mccallan or on Twitter under @TrishMcCallan.

Book updates can be found at www.trishmccallan.com.

A Note from the Author

Thank you for reading *Forged in Ash.*

If you enjoyed this book, I'd appreciate it if you'd help others find it so they can enjoy it too.

- Lend it: This e-book is lending-enabled, so feel free to share it with your friends.
- Recommend it: Please help other readers find this book by recommending it to friends, readers' groups, and discussion boards.
- Review it: Let other potential readers know what you liked or didn't like about *Forged in Ash.*